About the Author

An avid romance reader, **Melanie Milburne** loves writing the books that gave her so much joy as she was busy getting married to her own hero and raising a family. Now a *USA Today* bestselling author, she has won several awards—including The Australian Readers' Association most popular category/series romance in 2008 and the prestigious Romance Writers of Australia R*BY award in 2011.

She loves to hear from readers!

www.melaniemilburne.com.au

www.facebook.com/melanie.milburne

Twitter @MelanieMilburn1

The Rumours

COLLECTION

July 2019

August 2019

September 2019

October 2019

November 2019

December 2019

Rumours: The Ruthless Ravensdales

MELANIE MILBURNE

MILLS & BOON

First Published in Great Britain 2019
By Mills & Boon, an imprint of HarperCollins *Publishers*
1 London Bridge Street, London, SE1 9GF

RUMOURS: THE RUTHLESS RAVENSDALES
© 2019 Harlequin Books S.A.

Ravensdale's Defiant Captive © Melanie Milburne 2015
Awakening the Ravensdale Heiress © Melanie Milburne 2016
Engaged to Her Ravensdale Enemy © Melanie Milburne 2016

ISBN: 978-0-263-27663-3

0719

MIX
Paper from
responsible sources
FSC® C007454

This book is produced from independently certified FSC™ paper
to ensure responsible forest management.

For more information visit: www.harpercollins.co.uk/green

Printed and bound in Spain
by CPI, Barcelona

RAVENSDALE'S
DEFIANT
CAPTIVE

To Ella Carey, a talented writer,
a dear friend and a wonderful person.
I love our writing chats! xxx

CHAPTER ONE

JULIUS RAVENSDALE KNEW his housekeeper was up to something as soon as she brought in his favourite dessert. 'Queen's pudding?' He raised one of his brows. 'I never have dessert at lunch unless it's a special occasion.'

'It *is* a special occasion,' Sophia said as she put the meringue-topped dessert in front of him.

He narrowed his gaze. 'Okay, tell me. What's going on?'

Sophia's expression was sheepish. 'I'm bringing in a girl to help me run the house. It's only for a month until this wretched tendonitis settles. The extra pair of hands will be so helpful and I'll be doing my bit for society. It's a win-win.'

Julius glanced at the wrist brace Sophia had been wearing for the past couple of weeks. He knew she worked far too hard and could do with the extra help but he liked to keep the staff numbers down in the villa. Not because he was mean about paying them. He would pay them triple to stay away and let him get on with his work. 'Who is it?'

'Just a girl who's in need of a bit of direction.'

Julius mentally rolled his eyes. Of all the housekeepers he could have chosen, he had employed the Argentinian reincarnation of Mother Teresa. 'I thought we agreed your lame ducks were restricted to the stables or the gardens?'

'I know, but this girl will go to prison if—'

'Prison?' he said. 'You're bringing a convicted criminal here?'

'She's only been in trouble a couple of times,' Sophia said. 'Anyway, maybe the guy deserved it.'

'What did she do to him?'

'She keyed his brand-new sports car.'

Julius's gut clenched at the thought of his showroom-perfect Aston Martin housed in the garage. 'I suppose she said it was an accident?'

'No, she admitted to it,' Sophia said. 'She was proud of it. That and the message she sprayed on his lawn with weed killer.'

'She sounds delightful.'

'So you'll agree to have her?'

Julius took in his housekeeper's hopeful expression. His sarcasm was lost on her. Sophia was the most charitable person he knew. Always doing things for others. Always looking for a way to make a difference in someone's life. He knew she was lonely since both her adult children had moved abroad for work. What would it hurt to indulge her just this once? He would be busy with fine-tuning his space software. He had less than a month to iron out the kinks in the programming before he presented it to the research team for funding approval.

He let out a long breath. 'I don't suppose you've ever thought of taking up knitting or cross-stitch instead?'

Sophia beamed at him. 'Just wait until you meet her. You're going to love her.'

* * *

Holly considered making a run for it when the van stopped but the size of the villa and its surrounds made her pause. It was big. Way big. Massive. It probably had its own area code. Maybe its own political party. It was four storeys high, built in a neo-classical style with spectacular gardens and lush, rolling fields fringed by thick forest. It didn't look anything like the detention centre she'd envisaged. There was no twelve-foot-high fence with electrified barbed wire at the top. There was no surveillance tower and no uniformed, rifle-toting guards—or, at least, none she could see—casing the joint. It looked like a top-end hotel—a luxurious and very private resort for the rich and famous. Which kind of made her wonder why she'd been sent here. Not that she'd been expecting chains and bread and water or anything, but still. This was seriously over the top.

'It's only for a month,' Natalia Varela, her case-worker, said as the decorative wrought-iron gates opened electronically, allowing them access to the long, sweeping limestone driveway leading to the immaculately maintained villa. 'You got off lightly considering your rap sheet. I know a few people who'd happily swap places with you.'

Holly grunted. Folded her arms across her breasts. Crossed her right leg over her left. Jerked her ankle up and down. Pouted. Why should she look happy? Why should she act *grateful* that she was being sent to live with some man she'd never heard of in his big, old fancy villa?

A month.

Thirty-one days of living with some stranger who

had magnanimously volunteered to 'reform' her. Ha-ha. Like that was going to work. Who was this guy anyway? All she'd been told was he was some hotshot techie nerd from England who had made the big time in Argentina designing software for space telescopes used in the Atacama Desert in neighbouring Chile. Oh, and he was apparently single. Holly rolled her eyes. He'd agreed to take on a troubled young woman for altruistic reasons? And the correctional authorities had actually *fallen* for that?

Yeah, right. She knew all about men and their dodgy motivations.

After being given the all clear from the security intercom device, Natalia drove through the gates before they whispered shut behind the car. 'Julius Ravensdale is doing you a big favour,' she said. 'He's only agreed to this—and very reluctantly at that—because his house-keeper has tendonitis in her wrist. You'll be her right-hand helper. It's an amazing opportunity. This place is like a five-star resort. It'll be great vocational training for you. I hope you'll make the most of it.'

Vocational training for what? Holly thought with a cynical curl of her lip. No one was going to make a housekeeper out of her just because she'd made a few mistakes, which weren't even really mistakes, because her pond-scum stepfather had seriously had it coming to him. It was just a dumb old sports car, for pity's sake. So what if he had to have it re-sprayed and his precious lawn re-sown after the weedkiller incident?

Holly was not going to be some rich man's lowly slave scrubbing floors until her knees grew callouses as big as cabbages. Her days of being pushed around were long over. Julius Ravens-whatever-his-name-was would be in for a big shock if he thought he could exploit her to suit his nefarious needs.

What if it wasn't the kitchen he planned to have her slaving in? What if he had more salacious plans? In her experience, men with money thought they could have anything and anyone they wanted. All that nonsense about him 'reluctantly' agreeing to take her on was just a ruse. Of course he would say that. He wouldn't want to look *too* eager to take in a prison statistic waiting to happen. He would be 'doing his bit for society' by trying to *do her*.

Bring it on, she thought. *Let's see how far you get.*

'Oh, I'll make the most of it, all right,' Holly said as she sent the caseworker a guileless smile. 'You can be sure of that.'

Natalia let out a world-weary sigh as she put her foot back on the accelerator. 'Yeah, that's what I'm afraid of.'

The housekeeper whom she had met a few days before greeted Holly at the door of the villa while Natalia took an urgent call from one of her other charges.

'It's lovely to have you here, Holly,' Sophia said. 'Come in. Señor Ravensdale is busy just now so I'll show you to your suite so you can settle in.'

Holly wasn't expecting a welcoming committee with banners and balloons and a brass band or anything but surely the very least her host could do was make an appearance? If he'd agreed to have her here then he could at least do the polite thing and greet her face to face. 'Where is he?' she asked.

'He's not to be disturbed,' Sofia said. 'I'll show you to the suite I've pre—'

'Disturb him, please,' Holly said. *'Now.'*

Sophia looked a little taken aback. 'He doesn't like to be interrupted while he's working. He doesn't allow anyone into his office unless it's an emergency.'

Holly gently elbowed her way past to the door she took to be the study. It was the only door that was closed along the long, wide corridor. She didn't knock. She turned the handle and barged in.

A man looked up from behind a desk where he was tapping at a computer keyboard. His fingers stalled as she came in, the last click echoing in the silence as his gaze met with hers.

Holly drew in a breath to speak but for some reason her voice wasn't on active duty. It had locked behind her shock at how different he was from her expectations. He was nothing like she had envisaged. He wasn't old or even middle-aged. He was in his early thirties and movie-star handsome, athletically lean and tanned. His hair was a rich dark brown with light waves running through it. It looked as if it had been recently styled with his fingers, for she could see the roughly spaced plough marks that gave him a sexily tousled look, as if he'd just tumbled out of bed after vigorous sex. He had a determined looking jaw, a straight nose and a firm but sensually sculptured mouth that for some reason made the ligaments at the backs of her knees weaken alarmingly.

He pushed back his chair, and the room instantly shrank as he stood. 'Can I help you?' he said with the sort of tone that suggested he was not in the least motivated to do so.

Holly had never been one to beat about the bush. Her tactic was to get in there with a verbal weed-whacker. 'Don't you know it's impolite to ignore your guests when they arrive?'

His eyes held hers with steely focus. 'Strictly speaking, you're not my guest. You're Sophia's.'

Holly hitched up her chin, flashing him an I-know-what-you're-up-to glare. 'I want to let you know straight from the outset I'm not here to be your sex toy.'

His dark brows rose in twin arcs over his impossibly dark blue eyes. With his black hair and olive-skinned complexion, she had been expecting them to be brown. But they were an astonishing sapphire-blue fringed with thick black lashes. He seemed to measure her for a moment; his gaze taking in the tiny diamond nose piercing and the pink streaks in her hair with a tilt of his mouth that was unmistakably mocking.

A knot of bitterness inside Holly tightened. If there was one thing she loathed, it was being made fun of. Belittled. Mocked.

'How do you do, Miss, er…?' He glanced at his housekeeper, who had come in behind Holly, for a prompt.

'Miss Perez,' Sophia said. 'Hollyanne.'

'Holly,' Holly said with a black look.

Julius offered his hand. 'How do you do, Holly?'

She glared at his hand as if he'd just offered her a viper. 'Keep your hands to yourself.'

Natalia entered his office sounding a little flustered. 'I'm terribly sorry, Dr Ravensdale, but I had to take an urgent call about another client—'

Holly swung around and frowned at Natalia. '*Doctor*? You didn't tell me he was a doctor. You said he was a computer geek.'

The caseworker gave Julius a pained smile before addressing Holly. 'Dr Ravensdale has a PhD in astrophysics. It's polite to call him by his correct title, if that's what he prefers.'

Holly swung back to look at Julius. 'What do you want me to call you? Sir? Master? Oh Mighty Learned One? Your Royal Tightness?'

His lips twitched as if he was fighting back a reluctant smile. 'Julius will be fine.'

'As in Caesar?'

'As it turns out, yes.'

'You're into Shakespeare?' Holly said it as if it was a noxious disease from which she had so far managed to escape contamination. No point letting him think she was anything but what he had already judged her as: uneducated and unsophisticated. Trailer trash.

'No, but my parents are.'

'Why'd you agree to have me here?' she said, eyeballing him.

'I didn't want you here,' he said. 'But my current domestic circumstances made it impossible for me to refuse.'

Holly folded her arms across her chest. 'I can't cook,' she said with an obdurate 'so what are you going to do about *that*?' look.

'I'm sure you can learn.'

'And I hate housework,' she said. 'It's sexist expecting women to clean up after you. Just because I've got boobs and ovaries doesn't mean I—'

'Point taken,' he said quickly. So quickly Holly wondered if he was worried she was going to list all of her feminine assets. 'However, you need to do your stint of community service,' he continued. 'I need some help around the house until Sophia gets better. It's win-win.'

Holly made a harrumphing noise and unwound her locked arms, turning her gaze to the caseworker. 'Have you done a police check on him to make sure he's the real deal?'

'I can assure you, Holly, Dr Ravensdale is a totally trustworthy guardian,' the caseworker said.

Holly pushed her bottom lip out like a drawer as she swung back to size Julius up. 'Do you drink?'

'Socially.'

'Smoke?'

'No.'

'Drugs?'

'No.'

Holly upped her brazenness another notch. 'Sex?'

'Holly…' the caseworker began.

'What?' Holly asked with a petulant scowl.

'You're embarrassing Dr Ravensdale.'

'I'm not embarrassed,' Julius said. 'But I'm also not going to answer such an impertinent question.'

Holly coughed out a laugh. 'Which means you're not getting any, right?'

He stared her down with a look that made her insides feel wobbly. He didn't look the type of man to go too long between drinks. He looked the type of man who could take his pick of women. She could feel his sensual allure like a force field. Her mind ran wild with images of him getting down to business. He wouldn't be one for a quick, sleazy grope. He would take his time. He would know his way around a woman's body. He would know how to send female senses spinning into the stratosphere. She could see it in the darkly confident glint of his gaze. 'While we're on the topic,' he said, 'I would appreciate it if you would abstain from bringing men here for the purpose of having intimate relations with them.'

'So…you get to have sex but I don't? That is…' Holly dropped her voice to a deliberately husky purr '…unless we have it with each other?'

'I have to get going,' the caseworker said as her phone buzzed with an incoming message. 'Holly, I hope you'll behave yourself while you're here. This is your last chance, don't forget. If this fails you know where you'll be going.'

'Yeah, yeah, yeah,' Holly said with a bored flicker of her eyelids as she turned to look at the view from one of the windows next to a wall of bookshelves. She didn't want to go to prison but neither did she want to be exploited by yet another man who assumed he had some sort of power over her. If Julius Ravensdale wanted a plaything, why hadn't he cut one from the herd? The herd he belonged to—the 'beautiful people' herd. She wasn't even his type. How could she be, with her cheap chain-store clothes? Not to mention her background. The background she was still trying to escape. It clung to her like thick axle grease. No amount of washing and cleansing and sanitising would remove it.

Julius Ravensdale came from money. She could see it in the way he dressed, in the way he held himself with supreme confidence, with cool and collected authority. She could see it in the furnishings he surrounded himself with: the priceless paintings, the books and the hand-woven floor coverings. He hadn't lived his childhood in sweat-soaked fear. He hadn't had to fight for survival. He'd had everything handed to him on a gilt-edged platter. Why was he agreeing to have her here if not to make use of her? She clenched her back teeth in determination. He would *not* use her.

She would use *him* first.

* * *

'I'll call each day to see how she's getting on,' the case-worker said to Julius as she shook his hand. 'It's very good of you to commit to this programme. It's helped many people turn their lives around.'

'I'm sure everything will be fine,' Julius assured her. 'Sophia will do most of the mentoring.'

'All the same, it's very kind of you to open your home like this.'

'It's a big house,' he said. *Maybe not big enough.*

Julius turned once Sophia had escorted the case-worker out of his office to find Holly looking at him with a flinty gaze. 'How much are they paying you to have me?' she said.

'I've told them to donate the fee to charity.'

'Big of you.'

He leaned against the windowsill behind his desk with his hands balanced either side of his hips to study her. It was a casual pose that belied the havoc her presence caused to his senses. He could feel the blood humming through his veins in a way it hadn't since he'd been a teenager. He looked down at her upturned, defiant face with its flashing caramel-brown gaze and sulky cherry-red mouth. A tiny diamond winked from the side of her right nostril. The bridge of her retroussé nose was dusted with freckles that reminded him of nutmeg sprinkled on top of a dessert. But that was about as far as he could go with the sweetness description. She looked sour and bitter and ready for a fight.

Something about her blatant rudeness made everything that was cultured in Julius stiffen. *Not, perhaps, the best choice of word*, he thought wryly as he scanned her impudent features. But her rudeness wasn't the only thing that was blatant about her. She had an earthy, raw sensuality about her. The way she moved her body. The way she inhabited her body. *His* body recognised it like a stallion scenting a potential mate.

He forced his mind out of the gutter. Clearly he needed to get some work-life balance if this little upstart was attracting his attention.

Her face was not what one would call classically beautiful but there was an arresting quality to it that made him want to study her for longer than was socially polite. He noted the high and haughty cheekbones you could slice a Christmas ham on. Eyelashes that were thick and long without the boost of mascara. Her skin—apart from the freckles and the diamond piercing—was creamy and make-up-free. Her hair was a mass of springy shoulder-length curls and was a mid shade of brown, apart from some rather vivid streaks of pink.

Julius was still waiting for her to make the connection between him and his parents. It didn't usually take this long. He had got used to it over the years. Well, almost: the wide-eyed wonder. The delighted shock that produced a sickening number of gushing comments: *Oh, you're the son of the famous London West End actors Richard Ravensdale and Elisabetta Albertini! Can you get me their autographs? An invitation to opening night? Front-row seats? A back-stage pass? An audition?*

But Miss Holly Perez had either never heard of his parents or was not impressed by his lineage.

Julius had to admit he found her forthrightness strangely appealing. It was such a refreshing change. He'd had his share of sycophants. People who only wanted to be associated with him because of his connection with London theatre royalty. Women who wanted to be squired by him on the red carpet in the hope of catching the eye of a casting agent. It was refreshing to be in the presence of someone who didn't give a toss for the shallowness of his parents' celebrity.

Julius didn't care too much for the word 'guardian' the caseworker had used in reference to him. It made him sound decades older than his thirty-three years. Holly was younger than him certainly but only by about seven or eight years at the most. Twenty-five, but hardened by her experiences. He could see it in her eyes. There was no sheen of innocence in that thickly fringed brown gaze. It was full of cold, hard cynicism. A mess-with-me-at-your-peril gleam. What had led her to a life of petty crime? He'd seen the list of her offences: theft; wilful damage to property; graffiti; vandalism.

Sophia's rescue mission was perhaps going to be a little more challenging than he'd bargained for. He'd agreed to it because he trusted his housekeeper's judgement. But Sophia's judgement was clearly not what it used to be. Holly had come striding in like a denim-and-cheap-cotton-clad whirlwind—asking him about his sex life, for God's sake.

He knew he was acting and sounding like a stern schoolmaster. But he figured it was best to get the ground rules in early. He wasn't going to stand by while Holly conducted drunken parties or all-night orgies under his roof.

Julius didn't care how many impertinent questions she asked, he wasn't going to admit to his current sex drought. He'd been busy. He was working on some new top-secret software. He wasn't like his twin brother, Jake, who had sex as if he were training for the Olympics. Nor was he like his father, who had a reputation as a womaniser that was regrettably well deserved.

Julius enjoyed the company of women. He dated from time to time. He enjoyed the physicality of sex but he didn't care for the politics of it. The agenda women brought to the bedroom irked him. If he wanted to marry and settle down, then he would make the decision when he was good and ready. Although he seriously wondered if he would ever be ready. Having witnessed his parents' turbulent marriage, acrimonious divorce, remarriage and ongoing drama-filled relationship, he wasn't sure he wanted to sign up for the potential for so much disruption and chaos.

'I know why you've agreed to have me here, so don't bother pretending otherwise.' Holly's look had a bad-girl gleam to it that messed with his hormones. He felt a stirring in his groin. A lightning flash of unbidden lust that made his blood throb and pound in his veins. He was surprised—and deeply annoyed—by his reaction to her. She was obviously well aware of her effect on the male gaze, exploiting it for all it was worth. Her unusual beauty, even though it was currently downplayed, was the sort that could stop a bullet train in its tracks. She had a sensual air about her. A way of moving her body that made him ache to see what she looked like naked. He kept his expression masked but he wondered if she sensed the impact she had on him.

How had he got himself into this? Julius thought. He should have called an agency. Employed someone who had credentials. Someone who had training. Manners. Decorum. Why had he allowed Sophia to talk him into taking on someone as cheeky and wilful as Holly Perez? She was going to be living under his roof. For a month!

'You are mistaken, Miss Perez,' he said coolly. 'My taste in women is far more sophisticated.'

She adopted a femme fatale pose, all slinky hips and shoulders, her mouth in a come-and-get-me moue. 'Of course it is,' she said with a devilish little twinkle that matched the diamond in her nose.

Julius felt the swell of his flesh at her brazen sexuality. The pounding and purring of his blood drove every rational thought out of his brain. Sex was suddenly all he could think about. Hot, sweaty, bed-wrecking sex. Mind-blowing caveman sex. Driving himself into her tight, wet warmth and exploding like a bomb. How long had it been? Clearly too long if he was getting jumpy at this outrageous little flirt. Holly Perez was a trouble-maker. It might as well be branded across her forehead. He wasn't going to fall for it. He was not at the mercy of his hormones…or at least he hadn't been before now.

Holly moved around his office with cat-like grace. Slinky, silent, sensuous. Dangerous, if stroked the wrong way. Although when he checked he noticed she didn't have claws. Her fingernails were bitten down to the quick. When she lifted her hand to push her hair back off her face he noticed a long white scar on the fine blue-veined skin of her wrist. 'How did you get that scar?' he asked.

A mask came down over her features as she pushed down her sleeve. 'I broke my arm when I was a kid. I had to have it pinned and plated.'

Julius let a silence slip past. He watched as she fiddled with the hem of her sleeve, her fingertips tugging and twisting the light cotton fabric as if it irritated her skin. Her eyebrows were drawn together, her forehead pleated, her expression broody. It intrigued him how quickly she had switched from impudent vamp to bad-tempered brat.

'Would you like to look around the villa?'

She gave an indifferent shrug. 'Whatever.'

Julius had intended to get Sophia to give Holly a guided tour but he decided he would do it. He told himself it was so he could check she didn't pilfer any of his belongings or carve her initials or a curse word into one of his antiques. Why on earth had he agreed to this? God knew what she would get up to once out of his sight.

He led the way out of his office. 'I detect a trace of an English accent,' he said as they walked along the hall. 'Are you originally from the UK?'

'Yes,' she said. 'We moved out here when I was young. My father was Argentinian.'

'Was?'

'He died when I was three. I don't remember him, so there's no need to get all soppy and sentimental and feel sorry for me.'

Julius glanced down at her walking beside him. She barely came up to his shoulder. 'Is your mother still alive?'

'No.'

'What happened?'

'She died.'

'How?'

Holly threw him a hardened look. 'Didn't Natalia show you my file?'

Julius was a little ashamed he hadn't read it in more detail. But then he hadn't planned on having anything to do with her. Apart from Sophia, he didn't have much to do with his staff on a personal level. They did their job. He did his. He'd focussed on Holly's rap sheet without looking at the story behind the miscreant behaviour. Some people were born bad, others had bad things happen to them and they turned bad as a result. Where did Holly fit on the spectrum? 'I'd like you to tell me.'

'She killed herself when I was seventeen.'

'I'm sorry.'

She gave another careless shrug. 'So what about your parents?'

'They're both alive and well.' And driving him nuts as usual.

Holly stopped in front of a painting. It was a landscape he'd bought at an auction his sister, Miranda, had given him the heads-up on. Miranda was an art restorer, yet another Ravensdale sibling who had disappointed their parents by not treading the boards.

Holly resumed walking, idly picking up objects he had on display, turning them over in her hands and putting them down again. Julius hoped she wasn't sizing them up for later theft.

'You got any brothers or sisters?' she asked after a long silence.

Julius was finding it a novel experience, meeting someone who knew nothing about his family. Didn't the girl have a smartphone? Internet access? Read newspapers or gossip magazines? 'I have a twin brother and a sister ten years younger.'

She stopped walking to look up at him. 'Are you identical?'

'Yes.'

Her eyes suddenly danced with impish mischief, dimples appearing either side of her mouth, completely transforming her features. 'Ever swapped places with him?'

He put on what his kid sister called his 'I'm too old for all that nonsense' face. 'Not for a very long time.'

'Can your parents tell you apart?'

'They can now but not when we were younger,' he said. Mostly because they hadn't been around enough. Their fame was far more important to them than their family. Not that he was bitter. Much. 'What about you? Do you have any siblings?'

'No.' Her dimpled smile faded and the frown reinstated itself on her forehead as she resumed walking along the corridor. 'There's just me…'

Julius heard something in her tone that suggested a resigned sense of profound aloneness. He hadn't expected to feel sorry for her. He had strong values on what constituted good and bad behaviour. The law was the law. Breaking it just because you'd had a difficult childhood wasn't a good enough excuse, in his opinion. But something about her intrigued him. She was light and dark. Moon shadows and bright sunlight. She reminded him of a complicated puzzle that would need more than one attempt to solve it.

Maybe his housekeeper's mission would prove far more interesting than he'd first thought.

Holly stopped in front of the windows overlooking the formal gardens. 'Do you live here alone?' she asked.

'Apart from my staff, yes, but they have separate quarters. Sophia is the exception. She has a suite on the top floor.'

Holly turned and looked at him with a direct gaze. 'Seems a pretty big place for a single guy.'

'I like my own space.'

'Must cost a ton to keep this place ticking over.'

'I manage.'

'Yeah, well, money and possessions don't impress me,' she said, turning to look at the gardens again.

'What does?'

She swivelled to face him and tilted one of her hips, lowering one shoulder lower than the other so her thin chain-store sweater slipped to reveal the creamy cap of her shoulder. She looked at him through eyes half-shielded by the thick dark fans of her lashes. 'Let's see...' She pursed her full lips in thought before releasing them on a breath of air. 'I'm impressed by a man who knows his way around a woman's body.'

Julius was doing his darnedest not even to think about her luscious little body. Or that full-lipped mouth and the mayhem it could cause if it came too close to his. He had a feeling she was testing him. Testing his motives. Seeing if he was going to exploit her. Had she been exploited before? Was that how she viewed all men? As manipulators and bullies who forced their will on her?

He might be a man who liked his own way but there was no way he would ever describe himself as a bully. He could be arrogant at times—stubborn, even—but he was a firm believer in treating women with respect. Having a shy and reserved much younger sister had instilled in him the importance of men taking a stand against all forms of violence against women and girls.

'That's it?' he said. 'Just whether he can perform?'

'Sure,' she said, eyes gleaming with pertness. 'How a man has sex tells you a lot about them as a person. Whether they're selfish or not. Whether they're uptight or casual.' She tapped two of her fingertips against her mouth in a musing manner. 'Let's take you, for instance.'

Let's not, he thought. 'This theory of yours is imminently fascinating but I think—'

'You're a man who likes to be in control,' she said. 'You like order and predictability. You don't do things on impulse. Your life is planned, timetabled, scheduled to the nth degree. Am I right?'

Julius didn't feel too comfortable at being so rapidly written off as a boring stereotype, as nothing more than a cliché. He liked to think he wasn't *that* predictable. He had nuances; sure he did. Layers to his personality that were there if you took the time to find them. He might spend a lot of time in the land of logic and reason but it didn't mean he couldn't use the right side of his brain. Well…occasionally.

He stepped towards the nearest door. 'This is the library,' he said. 'You're welcome to help yourself to books as long as you don't dog-ear them or leave them outside.'

'See?' She gave a bell-like laugh. 'I was spot-on.'

He gave her a look before he moved to the next door farther down the corridor. 'This is the music room.'

'Let me guess,' she said with another one of her impish smiles. 'You don't mind if I play the piano as long as my fingers aren't sticky or I don't drop crumbs between the keys. Correct?'

Julius found the picture she was painting of him increasingly annoying. What gave her the right to sum him up in such disparaging terms? She made him sound like some sort of house-proud obsessive. 'Do you play an instrument?' he asked.

'No.'

'Would you like to learn?' Music was supposed to tame wild things, wasn't it? He could engage a tutor for her. What was that saying about the devil and idle hands? Piano lessons would at least keep her out of his way.

'What?' she said, the cynical glint back in her gaze. 'You think you can teach me the piano in a month?'

'I have other instruments.'

'I just bet you do.'

He gave her a droll look. 'Flute. Tenor recorder. Saxophone.'

She looked at him, one side of her plump mouth curved in a mocking arc. 'Impressive. Gotta love a man who's good with his mouth *and* his hands.'

Julius put his hands deep in his trouser pockets in case he was tempted to show her just how good he was. Why was she being so damn brazen? Winding him up for what reason? To prove he was as predictable as all the other men she'd dealt with? What did she hope to gain? Would he be just another male trophy for her to gloat over? Another man she had slayed with her sensual allure? He wasn't going to fall for it. He had no time for vacuous game playing. She might think him predictable and a walking, talking cliché but he was not when it came to this. She could flirt and tease and taunt him as much as she wanted but he wasn't going to fall into her honey trap. He might be his father's son by blood, name and looks but he wasn't like him by nature.

'I'll leave Sophia to show you around the rest of the house,' he said, his tone formal, clipped. Dismissive.

Her mischievous gaze danced. 'Aren't you going to show me where I'll be sleeping?'

'I'm not sure where Sophia has put you.'

But I hope to God it's nowhere near me, Julius thought as he turned and strode briskly away.

CHAPTER TWO

HOLLY WATCHED AS Julius Ravensdale made his way down the lengthy and wide corridor with long, purposeful strides. She felt strangely breathless after their encounter. Her pulse was thrumming too hard and too fast. It felt as if something small and scared was scrabbling inside the valves of her heart.

Her reaction to him confounded her. Confused her.

Men didn't usually have that effect on her. Even good-looking ones. And they didn't come much better looking than Julius Ravensdale. She'd been expecting some long-haired, bushy-bearded, shoulder-hunched computer geek and instead had found a man who looked as if he could fill in for a European male model in an aftershave or designer watch advertisement. His tall, broad-shouldered athletic build gave him an air of authority that was compelling. There was something about his looks that rang a faint bell of recognition in her head. Had she seen a picture of him somewhere? Or was his twin famous? Even his name struck a chord of familiarity but she couldn't remember where she'd heard it before.

His thick, wavy dark brown hair was tousled in a mad professor sort of way she found intensely attractive.

He was clean-shaven but with just enough regrowth to confirm he hadn't been holding the door for everyone else while the testosterone was being handed out. She had felt the impact of his male hormones as soon as she'd entered his office. It was like a collision against her flesh. Potent. Powerful. Primal. Making her aware of her body in a way she hadn't been in years. Maybe had never been.

He triggered something in her, something deeply instinctive. Something rebellious. She felt an irresistible desire to dismantle his façade of cool civility. To unpick the lock on the brooding passion she could sense was under lockdown. She wanted to tease out the primitive man behind the aristocratic manners. He was so rigidly controlled with an aloof and haughty air. There was an invisible wall around him warning her not to come close. But what if she did? What if she dared to come so close he wouldn't be able to keep that iron control in place? She gave a secret smile. *Tempting thought.*

Holly couldn't get over his incredible eyes. Dark as navy fringed with thick lashes and strong eyebrows. Intelligent eyes. Observant. Intuitive. He had a straight nose and a jaw that hinted at a streak of stubbornness. He looked like he lived in his head a lot. Thoughts and logic were his currency. Action would come later after due consideration.

If nothing else it would make a change from the men she'd been forced to share quarters with—her low-life stepfather being a perfect case in point.

Maybe this month wouldn't be such a hardship after all. It was exhilarating, winding Julius up. It amused her to see him act all schoolmasterish and stern in the face of her brazen behaviour. She was picky when it came to whom she shared her body with but that didn't mean she couldn't have a bit of fun rattling his chain. He was starchy and formal in that 'stiff upper lip' way the well-born English male was known for. Maybe it would fill in the time to try and loosen him up a bit. Show him a top-notch university degree didn't make him any different from any other man she'd met. Men driven by hormones. Greedy to have their lust slaked with whomever was available. She'd prove to him he had no right to look down his nose at her.

Holly gave a little smile. Yep, this period of house arrest could prove to be the best fun she'd had in years.

The housekeeper appeared at the end of the corridor and came towards Holly with her wrist supported in a brace. It brought back memories of the time her step-father had snapped her wrist when she'd been eleven and then told her he would kill her or her mother if she told anyone how she'd got injured. She'd had to pretend she'd fallen off her bike. A bike she hadn't even pos-sessed. The plates and screws in her wrist weren't the only scars her stepfather had left her with.

Her issues with authority, her rebellious streak, her distrust of men and her cold sweat nightmares were the hoofmarks of a childhood and adolescence spent at the mercy of a madman. She wouldn't have had to be here doing this ridiculous programme if it hadn't been for the way her stepfather and his bullying lawyer had made it seem as if *she* was the criminal.

'Come this way, Holly,' Sophia said as she led the way to the next floor. 'So, what do you think of the place so far?'

'It's okay, I guess.' Holly didn't see the point in get-ting too friendly with the natives. Sophia seemed nice enough but it would be a waste of energy striking up a friendship when in a matter of weeks—if not before— she'd be gone.

'I had to twist Señor Ravensdale's arm to agree to having you here,' Sophia said as they came to the first-floor landing. 'It's not that he doesn't want to do his bit for charity. He's incredibly generous and supports lots of causes. He just likes to be left alone to get on with his work.'

'Has he got any lady friends?' Holly asked.

Sophia's expression closed down. 'Señor Ravensdale's privacy is of paramount importance to him.'

'Come on, there must be someone in his life,' Holly said.

Sophia's mouth tightened as if she were physically restraining herself from being indiscreet about her employer. 'I value my job too much to reveal such personal information.'

Holly gave a lip shrug. 'He sounds pretty boring, if you ask me. All work and no play.'

'He's a wonderful employer,' Sophia said. 'And a decent man with honour and sound principles. You're very lucky I was able to talk him into having you stay here. It's not something he would normally do.'

'Lucky me.'

Sophia gave her a warning look. 'I hope you're not going to cause trouble for him.'

Who, me? Holly thought with another private smile. Julius Ravensdale's loyal housekeeper thought he had sound principles, did she? How long before his honourable motives were exposed for what they were? She'd seen the way he'd run his gaze over her. He might be clever and sophisticated but he had the same needs as any man his age. He was healthy and fit and in the prime of his life. Why wouldn't he take advantage of the situation? She wasn't vain but she knew the power she had at her disposal. It was the only power she had. She didn't have money or prestige or a pedigree. She had her body and she knew how to use it.

'How'd you injure your wrist?' Holly asked to fill the silence.

'It's just a bit of tendonitis,' Sophia said. 'I get it now and again. It will settle if I rest up. All part of getting old, I'm afraid.'

Holly followed the housekeeper to the third floor of the villa. The Persian carpet was as thick as velvet, the luxurious décor showing French and Italian influences. Gorgeous artworks decorated the walls, portraits and landscapes of various sizes, and marble busts and statues were positioned along the gallery-wide corridor. Chandeliers hung like crystal fountains above and the wall lights sparkled with the same top-quality glitter.

Holly had never been in such an opulent place. It was like a palace. A showcase of every fine thing a sophisticated and wealthy person could acquire. But there were no personal items scattered about. No family photographs or memorabilia. Not a thing out of place and everything in its place. It looked more like a museum than a home.

'This is your room,' Sophia said, opening a door to a suite a third of the way along the corridor. 'It has its own bathroom and balcony.'

Balcony?

Holly stopped dead. Her heart tripped. Fear sent a shiver through the hairs of her scalp. The silk curtains at the French doors leading onto the balcony billowed with the afternoon breeze like the ball gown of a ghost.

How many times had she been dragged to the rickety balcony of her childhood? Locked out there in all types of weather. Forced to watch helplessly as her mother had been knocked around on the other side of the glass. Holly had learned not to react because when she had it had made her mother suffer all the more. Holly's distress revved up her stepfather so she taught herself not to show it.

But she felt it.

Oh, dear God, she felt it now.

Her chest was tight, heavy. Every breath she took felt like she was trying to lift a bookcase. She couldn't speak. Her throat was closed with a stranglehold of panic.

'It's breath-taking, isn't it?' Sophia said. 'It's only been recently renovated. You can probably still smell the fresh paint.'

A shudder passed through Holly's body like an earthquake. Her legs went cold and then weak as if the ligaments had been severed with the swing of a sword. Beads of perspiration trickled down between her shoulder blades, as warm and as sticky as blood. Her stomach was a crowded fishbowl of nausea. Churning. Rising in a bloated tide to her blocked throat.

'I—I don't need such a big room,' she said. 'Just put me in one of the downstairs rooms. We passed a nice one on the second floor. That blue one back there. That'll do me. I don't need my own balcony.'

'But there are nice views all over the estate and you'll have much more privacy. It's one of the nicest rooms in the—'

'I don't care about the view,' Holly said, stepping back from the door to stand near a marble statue that felt as cold as her body. 'It's not as if I'm an honoured guest, is it? I'm here under sufferance. Your employer's and mine. I just need a bed and a blanket.' Which was far more than she'd had in the not-so-distant past.

'But Señor Ravensdale insisted you—'

'Yeah, yeah, I know—be put as far away from his room as possible,' Holly said, hugging her arms across her body. 'Why? Doesn't he trust himself?'

The housekeeper's mouth pulled tight like the strings of an old-fashioned evening purse. 'Señor Ravensdale is a gentleman.'

'Yeah, well, even gentlemen have hormones.'

Sophia let out a frustrated breath. 'Will you at least look at the suite? You might change your mind once you see how—'

'No.' Holly swung away and went back down the stairs, one flight after another, her feet barely landing long enough on each step before it clipped the next one. She didn't draw breath until she got to the nearest exit. She stopped once out in the sunshine, bending forward, hands on her knees, her lungs all but exploding as she gasped in the warm summer air.

There was no way she was going to sleep in a room with a balcony.

No way.

Julius was standing at his office window when he saw Holly striding off towards the lake past the formal part of the gardens. Was she running away already? Absconding as soon as she saw an opportunity? He was supposed to call her caseworker if there was an issue.

He glanced at his phone and then back at Holly's slight figure as she stopped in front of the lake. If she'd wanted to escape she surely would have gone in the other direction. The wide, deep lake and the thick forest fringing it behind were as good a barrier as any. He watched as she bent down and picked up a pebble and skimmed it across the surface of the water. It skipped several times before sinking, leaving a ring of concentric circles in its wake. There was something poignant and sad about her slim figure standing there alone.

There was a tap on his door. 'Señor? Can I have a word?'

Julius opened the door to Sophia. 'Is everything all right?'

'Holly won't have the room I prepared for her,' Sophia said.

He tilted his mouth in a sardonic arc. 'Not good enough for her?'

'Too big for her.'

He frowned. 'Is that what she said?'

Sophia nodded. 'I made it all nice for her and she won't have it. She stalked off as if I'd told her she'd be sleeping in the stables.'

'Whose idea was it to bring her here again?' he said with mock rancour.

'I'm sure she'll grow on you,' Sophia said. 'She's a spirited little thing, isn't she?'

'Indeed.'

'Will you talk to her?'

'I just spent the last half hour with her.'

'*Please?*' Sophia, for all that she was close to retirement, had a tendency to look like a pleading three-year-old child when she wanted him to do things her way.

'What do you want me to say to her?'

'Insist she take the room I prepared for her,' Sophia said. 'Otherwise where will I put her? You told me you didn't want her on your floor.'

'All right.' Julius let out a long breath of resignation. 'I'll talk to her. But you'd better get the first aid kit out.'

'Come, now. You wouldn't hurt a fly.'

He gave her a wry look as he shouldered open the door. 'No, but our little guest looks as if she could stick a knife in you and laugh while she's doing it.'

Julius found her still skimming rocks across the surface of the lake. She was damn good at it, too. The most he could get was thirteen skips. Her last one had been fourteen. She must have heard him approach as his feet made plenty of noise on the pebbles at the edge of the lake but she didn't turn around. She kept skimming pebble after pebble with a focussed, almost fierce concentration.

'I believe you have an issue with the accommodation I've provided,' he said.

She threw another pebble but not as a skimmer. It went sailing overhead and landed with a loud *plop* in the centre of the lake. 'I don't need a suite in first class. I belong in steerage,' she said.

'Surely that's up to me to decide?'

She turned and faced him. It unnerved him a little to see she had a stone rather than a pebble clutched in her fist. Her eyes flashed at him. 'What are you trying to do? Conduct your own Pygmalion experiment? Well, guess what, Mr Higgins? I'm no fair lady.'

'No; you're a bad tempered little miss who seems intent on biting the hand that's generously offered to feed you.'

She glowered at him with her chest rising and falling as if she was only just managing to control her fury. 'You didn't offer me anything,' she shot back. 'You don't want me here any more than I want to be here.'

'True, but you're here now and it seems mature and sensible to make the best of the situation.'

Holly turned and flung the stone at the lake but it hit a tree on the left-hand side with a loud thwack. 'How are you going to explain me to your fancy friends or family?' she said.

'I don't feel the necessity to explain myself to anyone.'

'Lucky you.'

Where was the cheeky little flirt now? he wondered. In her place was a woman brooding with anger. Anger so thick he could feel it in the air like the humidity before a violent storm.

Julius picked up a pebble and sent it skimming across the surface of the lake. 'That's a personal best,' he said as he counted fifteen skips. 'Think you can match it?'

She turned and looked at him with a watchful gaze. 'What about your girlfriend? What's she going to say when she hears you've got me living with you?'

He bent down and picked up another pebble, rolling it over to check its suitability. 'I don't have a current girlfriend.'

'When was your last one?'

He glanced at her before he skimmed the pebble. 'You ask a lot of questions, don't you?'

'I know you're not gay because no gay man would look at me the way you did back in your office,' she said. 'You fancy me, don't you?'

Julius tightened his mouth as he reached down for another pebble. 'Your ego is as appalling as your manners.'

She gave a cynical laugh as she threw another pebble, even farther this time, as if all her pent up energy went into the throw. 'I suppose no one without a university degree with honours need apply. So what do you talk about in bed? Quantum physics? Einstein's theory of relativity?'

He looked down at her upturned face with its mocking smile and impossibly cute dimples. What was it about her that made him feel this was all a front? He was all too familiar with theatrical talent. His parents were some of the best in the theatre. Even he had to acknowledge that. But this defiant tearaway was putting on an award-winning performance. 'Why don't you want the room Sophia prepared for you?' he asked.

Her eyes lost their cheeky sparkle and her expression became sulky again. 'I don't want to be shoved at the top of your grand old house like some freak you want to hide in case she does the wrong thing in front of your fancy guests. I suppose you'll insist on me taking my meals in there or with the servants in the kitchen.'

'I don't have servants,' Julius said. 'I have staff. And, yes, they make their own arrangements over dining but that's more out of convenience than convention.' He paused for a beat before adding. 'I expect you to dine with me each evening.' *Are you out of your mind? The less time you spend with her the better.*

'Why?' she said with a surly look. 'So you can criticise me when I use the wrong fork or knife?'

'Why do you think everyone you meet is automatically against you?'

She turned and looked at the lake rather than meet his gaze. He could see the flicker of a tiny muscle in her cheek as if she was grinding down on her molars.

It was a while before she spoke and when she did it was with a voice that was pitched slightly lower than normal with a distinctly husky edge. 'I don't want *that* room.'

'Why not?'

'It's…too posh.'

'Fine,' Julius said, mentally rolling his eyes. 'You can choose your own room. God knows there are plenty to choose from.'

'Thank you.' It was not much more than a whisper of sound and she still wasn't looking at him but there was something in her posture that suggested enormous relief. Her shoulders had lost their tense, bunched-up-to-her-ears look. Her spine was no longer ramrod straight. Her hands were not curled into tight fists or clutching pebbles but hanging loosely by her sides.

He had a strong urge to reach out, take one of her hands and give it a reassuring squeeze but somehow refrained from doing so. Just. 'Do you want to walk back with me or hang around down here for a little bit?' he said.

She turned her head to look at him. 'Aren't you worried I might run away when your back is turned?'

He studied her for a moment, taking in her shuttered gaze and the pouty set to her mouth. 'You'd be running towards prison if you do. Hardly something to look forward to, is it?'

She bit down on her lower lip and turned to look at a water bird that had flown in to land in the centre of the lake, its paddling feet sending out concentric circles of disturbance. He watched as a slight breeze played with some loose tendrils of her hair and she absently brushed them back with one of her hands. His chest gave a sharp little squeeze when he saw her hand was shaking. There was no sign of the tough, angry girl. No sign of the brash guttersnipe. Right then she looked like your average girl next door who had suddenly found herself at an anxiety-inducing crossroads.

Julius bent down, picked up a pebble and handed it to her. 'My brother Jake holds the record down here. Seventeen skips.'

She took the pebble from him but as her fingers touched his he felt an electric shock run up along his arm. She slowly raised her gaze to mesh with his. A pulsing moment passed when he lost all sense of time and place. It could have been seconds or minutes or even days.

His eyes kept tracking to her mouth, the shape of it, the fullness of it that suggested passion and heat, and yet a strange sense of untouched innocence. He felt like a magnet was pulling his head down towards it. He had to fight every muscle and sinew and throbbing cell in his body to counter its force.

He watched as the tip of her tongue slipped out between her lips and moistened the top lip, then the bottom one, leaving each one glistening with a tempting sheen. Blood rushed to his groin, thickening him with a rocket blast of lust.

He had a sudden feeling he had been asleep all of his life until this moment. It was like coming out of cold storage. A slow melt was moving through his body; he could feel it all the way to his fingertips, the urge, the compulsion to touch, to feel her soft skin, sliding, stroking, moving against his own.

His mind was not following its usual logical pathways. It was short-circuiting with erotic images, hot fantasies of him burying himself inside her body, bringing them both to completion in a matter of seconds.

Could she sense the turmoil in him? Had she any idea of the effect she was having on him? He tried to read her expression but her eyelids were lowered over her eyes as she focussed on his mouth.

He lifted his hand to her cheek, barely aware he was doing it until he felt the creamy softness of her skin against his palm, tilting her face so she had to meet his gaze. Those bewitching eyes made his pulse pound all the harder. Every beat of his heart felt like a hammer blow, each one sending a deep, resounding echo to his pelvis. Her skin felt like silk against his palm and fingers. Warm. Smooth. Sensuous. Her eyes contained a glint of anticipation, of expectation. Of triumph.

He moved the pad of his thumb over the small, neat circle of her chin, watching as her pupils flared like pools of ink. Her lips were slightly apart, just enough for him to feel the soft waft of her vanilla-scented breath. How easy would it be to close the distance and touch his lips to hers? The urge to do so was strong, perhaps stronger than at any other time in his life, but he knew if he did it he would be crossing a line. Breaking a boundary. Inviting trouble.

'I'm not going to do it,' he said, dropping his hand from her face.

Her look was all innocence. 'What?'

'You know what.'

She met his eyes with a hard gleam in her own. 'I could make you disregard those principles you're clinging to. I could do it in a heartbeat.'

Julius frowned until his eyebrows met. 'Why are

you trying to ruin your one chance of getting your life in order?'

She glared at him. 'I don't need you to get my life in order. I don't need anyone.'

'How's that been working out for you so far?'

Her eyes were twin flashpoints of heat. 'You know what I hate about men like you? You think just because you have it all, you can have it all.'

'Look,' Julius said. 'I get this is a tough gig for you. You don't want to be here. But what's your alternative?'

She pressed her lips together and looked at him mulishly. 'I'm not the one who should be threatened with going to prison.'

'Yes, well, apparently most prisons are full of innocent people,' he said. 'But according to our current laws you can't steal or damage property or whatever else you did and not be punished for it.'

She swung away. 'I don't have to listen to this.'

'Holly.' Julius caught her by the arm and turned her to face him. 'I want to help you. Can't you see that?'

She gave him a disdainful look as she tested his hold. 'How? By making me get used to all this luxury, only to be tossed back out on the streets as soon as the month is up?'

Julius's frown deepened. 'Don't you have a home to go to?'

Her eyes skittered away from his. 'Let go of my arm.'

He loosened his hold but kept her tethered to him with the bracelet of his fingers. 'No one is going to toss you anywhere,' he said. *What are you going to do with her once the month is up?* The thoughts were like pop-up signs in his head. If she didn't have a home to go to, then where would she go? Where did his responsibility towards her begin and end?

Did he have a responsibility towards her?

'Is that where you've been living?' he asked. 'Out on the streets?'

She slipped her wrist out of his hold and folded her arms across her body, shooting him a fiery glare. 'What would *you* care? People like you don't even notice people like me.'

Julius noticed her all right. A little too much. His hand was tingling where he'd been holding her wrist. It was as if his blood was bubbling through his veins like boiling soda. He noticed the way her brown eyes sparked with venom one minute, glittering with an erotic come-on the next. He noticed the way she moved her body like a sleek pedigree cat, only to turn around, spit and hiss at him like a cornered feral one.

He had no idea how to handle her. He wasn't supposed to *be* the one handling her. This was his housekeeper's mission, not his. He was supposed to be getting on with his work while Sophia did her bit for society by taking in a stray and reforming her.

But Holly Perez was no ordinary stray.

She was a feisty little firebrand who seemed determined to cause trouble with everyone who dared to come too close.

'While you're under my roof I'm responsible for you,' Julius said. 'But that means you have responsibilities, too.'

Her chin came up. 'Like what? Servicing you in the bedroom?'

He set his mouth. 'No. Definitely not.'

Her look said it all. Cynicism on steroids. 'Sure and I believe you.'

'I mean it, Holly,' Julius said. 'I'm not in the habit of bedding young women who have no manners, no respect and no sense of propriety.'

She gave a musical sounding laugh. 'I am *so* going to make you eat your words.'

He stoically ignored the throb of lust that charged through his pelvis. 'I'll see you at dinner,' he said. 'I expect you to dress for the occasion. That means no jeans, no flip-flops and no plunging necklines or bare midriff. Sophia will organise suitable attire if you have none with you.'

Holly gave him a mock salute and a deep, obsequious bow. 'Aye-aye, Captain.'

Julius strode about thirty or so paces before he swung back to look at her but she had already turned back to face the lake. He watched as she hurled a rock as far as she could. It landed in the middle of the water and sank with a loud *plop*, but not before it created tsunami-like ripples over the surface.

CHAPTER THREE

HOLLY WAITED UNTIL Julius was out of sight before she left the lakeside. What right did he have to tell her how to dress? No man was going to tell her what she could and couldn't do. If she wanted to wear jeans, she would wear them. She'd wear high-cut denim shorts and trashy high heels to his stuck-up dinner table if she wanted to. He couldn't force her to dress up like one of his posh girlfriends. He might deny having a current lady friend but no man with his sort of looks went long between hook-ups.

He had *so* been going to kiss her. She had been waiting for him to do it. Silently egging him on. Waiting for him to break. What a triumph it was going to be when he finally did. She would get the biggest kick out of seeing him topple from his high horse. He had no right to lecture her as if she were ten years old. She would show him just how grown up she was. He wasn't dealing with a wilful child. He was dealing with a woman who knew how to make a man weaken at the knees. She would *do* him before he could do her. Although, the thought of having him do her was strangely appealing. He wasn't her type, with his control freak ways, but he was so darn attractive it almost hurt her eyeballs to look at him.

What was it about him that seemed vaguely familiar? His surname kept ringing a faint bell of recognition in her head. Where had she heard the name Ravensdale before?

And then it finally dawned on her.

He was the son—one of the twin sons—of the famous Shakespearean actors Richard Ravensdale and Elisabetta Albertini. They were London theatre royalty; Holly had seen articles about them in gossip magazines. Not that she ever had the money to buy such magazines but occasionally one of the shelters she had stayed in had them lying about.

Julius's parents had married thirty-four years ago after an affair during a London season of *Much Ado About Nothing* and celebrated their first wedding anniversary with the birth of identical twin boys. Seven turbulent years later, they had had a very public and acrimonious divorce. Then, three years later, they'd reunited in a whirlwind of publicity, remarried in a big celebrity-attended wedding service, and exactly nine months later Elisabetta had given birth to a daughter called Miranda.

Holly wondered if Julius had chosen to work and live in Argentina as a way of putting some distance between himself and his famous parents. The attention they attracted would be difficult to deal with, especially since what she had read indicated neither he nor his siblings had any aspirations to be on the stage. He hadn't once mentioned his parents' fame, although he'd had plenty of opportunity to do so.

Was that why he had initially been so reluctant to

have her here? Would her presence draw press attention his way he would rather avoid? If the press got a whiff of her chequered background it might cause all sorts of speculation. Holly could imagine the headlines: *Celebrities' Son Living with Trailer Trash with Criminal Record.* How would that go down with Julius's sense of propriety?

Holly pursed her lips as she thought about her next move. If she called the press it would draw too much attention to herself just now. She didn't want her creepaholic stepfather to know where she currently was, although, given the friends in high places he had, she wouldn't put it past him to know already or to make it his business to find out.

Franco Morales had influence that had already stretched further and wider than she had planned and prepared for. No sooner would she get herself back on her feet in a new job and a new place than something would go wrong. Her last employer had accused her of stealing from the till. Holly might have a rebellious streak that got her into trouble now and again but she was no thief. But the money had been found in her purse and she'd had no way of explaining how it had got there. Even the shop's security cameras had 'mysteriously' been switched off at the alleged time of the theft.

Holly had been evicted from her last three flats due to property damage that had been wrongfully levelled at her. But she knew her stepfather had staged it, along with the shop theft. He had set her up by sending in a mole to do his dirty work. That was why she had keyed his brand-new sports car and sprayed that message in weed killer on his perfectly manicured front lawn right where his neighbours would see it: *wife beater.*

Holly believed her mother would never have killed herself if it hadn't been for the long years of physical, emotional and financial abuse dished out to her by a man who had insisted on total obedience. Slavish obedience. Demeaning obedience that had left her mother a shadow of her former self. Franco had kept Holly and her mother oscillating between grinding poverty and occasional, large cash hand-outs that he'd never explained where they were sourced from. It was feast or famine. One minute the fridge was full of food. The next it was empty. Or sold. Furniture and appliances would be bought and then they would be sold to solve a 'cash-flow problem'. Things Holly had saved up for and bought with her meagre and hard-earned pocket money would be tossed out in the garbage or disappear without any explanation.

Holly vowed she would *never* break under Franco's tyranny. Even as a young child she had suffered his slaps and back-handers and put-downs without shedding a tear. Not even a whimper had escaped her lips. Not even her 'time-outs' on the balcony had made her give in. Even if her mother hadn't been abused on the other side, Holly would have locked off her feelings; cemented them deep inside. Hardened herself so she could withstand the abuse without giving him the satisfaction of breaking her spirit.

But unfortunately her mother had not been as strong, or maybe it had just become too hard for her to try to protect Holly as well as herself. Holly had never doubted her mother's love for her. Her mother had done everything she could to protect Holly from her stepfather but eventually it had become too much for her. She had become drug- and alcohol-dependent as a way to anaesthetise herself against the prison of her marriage to a beast of a man who had exploited her from the moment he'd met her.

Even though she had only been four at the time, Holly remembered the way Franco Morales had charmed her poor, grieving mother a few months after Holly's father had been killed in a work-place accident. He had taken control of her mother as soon as he'd married her.

At first he had been supportive, taking care of everything so she no longer had to worry about keeping a roof over their heads. He'd even been kind to Holly, buying her toys and sweets. But then things had started to change. He'd begun subjecting her mother to physical and verbal punishment. It had started with the occasional blow-out at first. One-off losses of temper that he would profusely apologise for and then everything would return to normal. Then a week or two would pass and it would happen again. Then it was every week. Then it was every day—twice a day, even.

And then he'd started in on Holly. Insisting she be brought up according to his rules. His regulations. The slaps had begun for supposed disobedience. The backhanders for insolence or often for no reason at all. Holly had got so stressed and wound up by the anticipation of his abuse she would often trigger it so it was out of the way for that day.

Although he'd no longer smacked her once she got a little older, his verbal sprays had worsened as she'd got to her teens. He'd called her filthy names, taunting her with how unattractive she was, how unintelligent she was, how no one would ever want her. All of which had been confirmed when her mother had died. Holly hadn't known what to do, where to go, how to manage her life.

During that awful, anchorless time she had done things she wished she hadn't and not done things she wished she had. She had mixed with the wrong people for the right reasons and mixed with the right people for the wrong reasons.

But things were going to be different now.

Holly was determined to get her life heading in the right direction. Once this community service was over, she was going to go to England, as far away as possible from her stepfather, back to the country of her mother's birth.

Then, and only then, would she be free.

Holly walked back towards the villa via the gardens. There were hectares of them, both formal and informal. There was even a swimming pool set on a sundrenched terrace that overlooked the fields where some glossy-backed horses were grazing. The summer sun was fiercer now than earlier. The clouds had shifted and the bright light sparkled off the swimming pool like thousands of brilliant diamonds scattered over the surface. She bent down and trailed her fingers in the water to test the temperature. It was deliciously, temptingly cool. Not that she was much of a swimmer, but the thought of cooling off was irresistible.

She glanced at the villa to see if anyone was watching. Not that she cared. If she wanted to have a dip in her underwear who was going to stop her? She kicked off her sandals and shimmied out of her jeans, dropping them in a heap by the pool. She hauled her cotton sweater and the vest top she was wearing under it over her head and sent it in the same direction as her jeans.

Holly stood for a moment as the sun's rays soaked

into her all but naked flesh. She pushed all her thoughts about her bleak childhood out of her head. They were like toxic poison if she allowed them to stay with her too long. Instead, she pretended she was on holiday at an exclusive resort where she had total freedom to do what she wanted.

And then, taking a deep breath, she slipped into the water and let it swallow her into its refreshingly cool and cleansing embrace.

Julius heard a splash and pushed his chair back from the computer to check who was using the pool. He should've guessed and he *definitely* shouldn't have looked. Holly was swimming, wearing nothing but what looked like a transparent bikini. Or was it a bikini or just her bra and knickers? He knew he should get away from the window. He even heard the left side of his brain issue the order. But the right side wilfully drank in the sight of her. Lustfully feasted on the vision of her playing like a water sprite. Her lithe limbs and pert breasts with their pink-tipped nipples showing through the thin cotton of her bra tantalised his senses and drove his blood at breakneck speed to his groin. Her wet hair was slicked back and looked as dark as the pelt of a seal. She did a duck dive, and he caught a delicious glimpse of her neat bottom, long legs and thoroughbred-slim ankles. She kicked herself to the bottom of the pool before re-surfacing like a dolphin at play. He heard the sound of her tinkling laughter just as she went back down for another dive.

When she came up she had her back to him. He saw the neat play of the muscles of her back and shoulders as she lifted her hair off her neck, using its length to tie it in a makeshift knot on top of her head. She went back under the surface with a splash of her legs and ballerina-like feet.

The agility of her firm young body drove his stunned senses into overdrive. She could have been a model showcasing a new line of swimwear. She was athletically slim but with just the right amount of curves to make his blood pound with heightened awareness.

He couldn't take his eyes off her. He was mesmerised by the vision of her. The way she moved as if she had no care for whoever might be watching. The way she played like a fun-loving child and yet her body was all sensual woman.

When she came up the next time she turned her body so she was facing his window. As if she had some internal tracking device, her gaze honed in on his office window. She raised one of her brows before her mouth slanted in a knowing smile as she gave him a cheeky little fingertip wave.

Julius let out a stiff curse and turned away. He raked a hand through his hair, hating himself for the way his body reacted to her of its own volition. He had no control over it.

He saw. He ached. He throbbed. He *lusted*.

It shocked him how easily she reduced him to the level of an animal looking for a chance to mate. Surely he had more taste than to have his tongue hanging out for an outrageous tease? How was he going to survive a month of this? With her flaunting herself at every available opportunity? What was she doing, playing in the pool? This wasn't a holiday resort, for God's sake. She was here to work.

And, God damn it, he would make sure she did.

* * *

Holly heard the tread of firm footsteps coming along the flagstones as she sat on the top step of the pool idly kicking her feet just under the water. She stopped kicking and looked over her shoulder to see Julius striding towards her with a brooding expression on his face.

'Having fun, are we?' he said.

'Sure.' She gave him a breezy smile. 'Why don't you join me? You look like you could do with a little cooling off.'

Something dark and glittering flashed in his navy-blue gaze as it collided with hers. 'You're not here on holiday.' His tone was terse. Curt.

Holly felt a little thrill course through her body at the way he was trying not to look at her wet breasts. Her well-worn cheap bra was practically as sheer as cling film. His jaw had a tight clench to it as if his teeth were being ground together like chalk. She could see the tiny in-out movement of a muscle near the side of his flattened mouth. *Go on*, she silently dared him. *Have a good old look*. She arched back against the pool steps so that her breasts were above the water line. She watched as his eyes dipped to her curves, where the water was lapping her erect nipples, before he dragged his gaze back to hers, his mouth a flat line of disapproval.

'I don't see why I shouldn't be allowed to make use of what's on offer,' she said with a sultry smile.

'Get out,' he said with a jerk of his head.

Holly arched one brow at him. 'I would've thought those posh celebrity parents of yours would've taught you better manners than that. Say the magic word.'

He said a word but it had nothing to do with magic. It was a colourful swear word with distinctly sexual connotations that made the atmosphere between them even more electric.

Holly felt an unexpected frisson deep in her core, a flicker of arousal that licked along her flesh like the tail of a soft leather whip. Julius's nostrils were wide, flaring like a stallion about to rear up to take charge of its selected mate. She had never seen a man look so magnificently stirred by her. The sense of power it gave her was tempered only by the fact he stirred her in equal measure. He *aroused* her. He turned her on to the point where she could feel her body contracting with want. It was a new experience for her. She was usually the object of desire while feeling nothing herself. But this was different. She felt urges and cravings that were overpowering to say the least.

'You either get out on your own or I'll get you out,' he said through clenched teeth.

Holly gave a mock shudder. 'Ooh! Do you promise? I love it when a man gets all macho with me.'

His jaw clamped down so hard she heard his back teeth connect. 'Firstly, you're not dressed appropriately,' he said. 'I have staff members about the property— both young and old—who would be offended by your lack of modesty.'

Holly laughed at his priggishness. He wasn't worried about his staff. He was worried about himself. How she made him feel—out of control and unsettled by it. *What fun this was turning out to be.* 'Are you in some sort of time warp?' she said. 'This is the twenty-first century. Women can dress how they want, especially on private property.'

'Secondly, you're not here to party,' he said as if she hadn't spoken. 'You're here to work. W-O-R-K. Maybe you haven't heard that word before. But by the time you leave I swear you'll know it intimately or I'll die trying. Sophia is waiting for you in the kitchen. There's a meal to prepare.'

'Go help her yourself,' she said with playful splash of her toes that sent a spray of water over his crisply ironed trousers. 'You've got two arms.'

Those two strongly muscled arms suddenly reached down into the water and hauled her to her feet to stand dripping in front of him. Close to him. So close she could feel his body heat radiating towards her. Any second now she thought she would hear the hissing of steam.

'I gave you an order,' he said, breathing hard, eyes glittering darkly.

Holly stood her ground even though his hands gripping the tops of her arms were searing through her flesh like scorching-hot brands. The proximity of his hard body was doing strange things to hers. She could feel a pulse of excitement roaring through her flesh, a zinging awareness of all that was different between them: his maleness, her femaleness, his determination to keep control and her determination to dismantle it.

It crackled in the air they shared like a current set on too high a voltage.

She looked at his grimly set mouth and the dark shadow of sexy stubble that surrounded it. The clench of his jaw that suggested he was only just holding on to his temper. Her heart began to thump, but not out of fear. It wasn't him she was afraid of but her reaction to him. She had never felt her body react in this way. His touch triggered something raw and primal in her. She had never felt her body *ache*. Pulse and contract with a longing she couldn't describe because she had never felt it quite like this before. She wasn't a virgin but none of her few sexual encounters had made her flesh sing like this. He hadn't even kissed her and yet she felt as if she was on a knife-edge. Every nerve in her body was standing up and waiting. Anticipating. Wanting. *Hungering.*

But then he suddenly dropped his hands from her arms. The movement was so unexpected she nearly toppled backwards into the pool but somehow managed to regain her balance. She maintained her composure—*just*—with a cool look cast his way. 'One thing you should note,' she said. 'I *don't* take orders. Not from you or from anyone.'

His jaw worked for a moment. She saw the way his eyes went to her heaving chest as if he couldn't stop himself. When his gaze re-engaged with hers it burned with heat as hot as a blacksmith's fire. 'Then you will learn how to do so,' he said with a thread of steel in his voice. 'If I achieve nothing else out of this month, I *will* achieve that. You will do as I say and not question my authority. Not for a moment.'

Holly inched up her chin. 'Game on.'

Julius paced the floor of his office a short time later. How could he have let Holly get under his skin like that? He had gone down there to draw a line with her but she had flipped things so swiftly he had ended up acting like a caveman. He had never felt more like slaking his lust just for the heck of it and to hell with the consequences. His body was still thrumming with the thunderous need she had stirred in him.

Holly was doing her best to break him, to reduce

him to the level of a wild animal. She was taunting him with every trick she had in her repertoire. She was in his house, in his private sanctuary, for the next four weeks. *Four weeks!* How was he going to withstand the assault on his senses?

She was so determined, so devious, so...*distracting.* His flesh still tingled with the aftershocks of touching her. Her skin against his had felt hot. Scorching hot. Blistering. He could still feel the sensation firing through his body. Touching her had unleashed something frighteningly primal in him. It roared through his blood like a wild fire. He had been knocked sideways by the sensation of holding her so close to the throbbing need of his body. It had been all he could do to keep himself from ripping that ridiculous see-through underwear away, driving himself into her and thrusting madly until he exploded.

Was he so sex-deprived that her teasing come-on had reduced him to the behaviour of a wild beast? The temptation of her, the thrill of touching her, of smelling that intoxicating scent of jasmine, musk and something else he couldn't pin down had wiped out the motherboard of his morality like a lightning strike.

What was it about her that caused him to react this way? She was wilful, wild, unpredictable and wanton. Being anywhere near her was like fighting an addiction he hadn't even known he possessed. He wanted her. He ached to have her. He pulsed with the need to feel her surround him with her hot little body. He could feel it rippling through him: lust let loose taking charge of him, demanding, dictating, directing. Dismantling all of his efforts to resist it.

He *would* resist it.

He would resist her.

He was not a hedonist. He wasn't a knuckle-dragging Neanderthal who could only respond to primal urges. He had intellect, discipline and self-control. A moral compass. A conscience.

Julius sat down heavily on his Chesterfield office chair, rotating it from side to side as he gathered his fevered thoughts. What was that crack Holly had made about his celebrity parents? So she knew exactly who he was, did she? Had she known all along or had someone told her? Sophia wouldn't have said anything. He trusted his housekeeper to take a bullet for the sake of his privacy. Had Holly somehow stumbled on his identity? No doubt that was why she was playing her seduction game. She wanted a celebrity trophy to hang on her belt. A show business shag to boast about to her friends. Could there be anything more nauseatingly vacuous?

He was lucky the press left him alone here in Argentina. He was able to walk around without the paparazzi documenting his every move. In England it was different. As a child he had found the intrusion terrifying. As an adult it was nothing less than sickening. Being chased down the street, cameras shoved in his face, when he was coming and going to lectures at university. Hounded while he was trying to go on a date with someone. It had got to the point where he had stopped dating. It wasn't worth the effort.

He was often mistaken for his brother, Jake, and that caused heaps of trouble, the sort of trouble for which he had no time or patience. Jake had no issues with the press. Jake accepted it as part of being related to famous people, but then, he had always been the more outgoing twin. Although Jake had no aspirations to be on the stage, he loved being the centre of attention and used their parents' fame to get what he wanted—a constant stream of beautiful women in and out of his bedroom. Jake didn't mind being compared to their father. He wore it like a badge of honour.

Julius would rather poke a skewer in his eye.

He would *not* have people compare him to his father. It wasn't that he didn't love his father. He loved both of his parents in a hands-off sort of way. He had never been one to wear his emotions on the outside. Even as a child he had never been the sort of person who was comfortable with over-the-top displays of emotion. His parents' loud arguments, their torrid displays of temper and their passionate and very public reunions had always made Julius cringe with embarrassment. He was glad he'd spent most of his childhood and adolescence at boarding school. He had found study an escape from the unpredictability of his home life. He had found the structure, order and strictly timetabled life a natural fit for his personality.

Jake, on the other hand, loved spontaneity. Jake hadn't enjoyed the discipline of school and had always found ways to buck the system. He was like their father in that he lapped up the attention and if it wasn't shining his way he found a way to make it do so.

Julius hated the limelight. He liked to work quietly in the background without the world's eye honed on him. His success as an astrophysicist had drawn far more attention to him than he would have liked but he comforted himself with the fact that he was successful in his own right, that he hadn't used his parents' fame as a way of opening any doors. He took a great deal of satisfaction in his work and, although the hours and the responsibility of heading a software company, along with his regular work came with its own set of problems, he enjoyed the flexibility of working from home, flying in and out as necessary.

The fact that the sanctuary of his home was now occupied by a mischievous hoyden was a state of affairs he would have to address, and soon. How was he supposed to concentrate with her flouncing around his villa?

The way she had challenged him as if fighting a duel. *Game on.* What exactly was she trying to prove? Hadn't she done enough by that little strip show in the pool? She was supposed to be making a new start. Reforming her bad ways. But from the moment she'd arrived she'd been playing him like a puppet master. Tugging on his strings until he was so churned up with lust he couldn't think straight. That was no doubt why she wouldn't accept the room Sophia had prepared for her on the third floor. Of course that room wouldn't suit Miss Bedroom Eyes. It was too far away from his. What did she have in mind? A midnight foray into his suite?

He would *not* allow her to win this. She would *not* get the better of him. She might think he was just like any other man she had lured into her sensual web in the past. She might think he was weak and spineless and driven by hormones—but she would soon find she had underestimated him. Big time.

He was putting an end to this before it got started.

Holly Perez was going straight to jail and he was making damn certain she wasn't collecting two hundred pounds—or anything else of his—on the way past.

CHAPTER FOUR

HOLLY WAS HELPING Sophia by preparing the vegetables for dinner while the housekeeper had a lie-down. Not because Julius had *commanded* her to get to work but because Sophia clearly couldn't do much with her wrist in a restrictive brace. Holly remembered all too well how painful a damaged limb could be. The simplest tasks were a nightmare and if you did too much it could compromise the healing process.

Besides, she quite liked cooking, for all that she'd told Julius she couldn't boil an egg, or words to that effect. She even liked cleaning. The repetitious nature of it was somehow soothing. It had helped her many a time as a child and teenager to put some order into the chaos of her home life. Her mother had got to the point of not being able to cope with the running of the home so Holly had taken it over. From a young age she knew how to cook, clean, tidy cupboards, fold washing and iron. It had also been a way to keep her stepfather from criticising her mother for not doing things properly around the house. If the house was as perfect as Holly could make it then a day or two might pass without a showdown.

What Holly didn't like was being ordered about. *Con-*

trolled. No one was going to command her like a serf.
If she chose to do something, then she would do it because it was the decent thing to do, or she wanted to do
it, not because someone was trying to lord it over her.

As if Holly had summoned him with her thoughts,
Julius came striding into the kitchen. 'I want a word,'
he said. 'In my office. Now.'

She blithely continued peeling the potato she was
holding. 'I'll be there in ten minutes. I've still got the
tomatoes and the courgettes to do.'

He came to the opposite side of the island bench to
where she was standing and slammed his hands down
on the surface, nailing her with his gaze. 'When I issue
you an order, I expect you to obey it immediately.'

Holly held his intensely sapphire gaze with an arch
look. 'Why can't you talk to me here?' She lowered her
voice to a husky drawl. 'Or are you worried your housekeeper will come in and catch us at it on the kitchen
bench?'

His eyes went to her mouth for the briefest moment
before flashing back to hers, twin flags of dull red riding high on his cheekbones. 'I want you out of here by
morning,' he said. 'I'm withdrawing my support for the
scheme. You can find some other fool to take you on or
you can go straight to jail where you belong. I don't care.'

'Fine.' Holly put down the peeler, untied the apron
Sophia had given her and tossed it on the bench. 'I'll
go and pack my things. Sophia can take over here. I'll
just go and wake her from her nap and tell her. Her
wrist was giving her a lot of discomfort earlier so she
took a stronger painkiller. I reckon she's been doing too
much because she doesn't want to let you down. But,
hey, that's what she's paid for, right?'

He glanced at the half-prepared meal before reconnecting with Holly's gaze. 'You—' he bit out. 'This is one big game to you, isn't it?'

Holly leaned over the bench so her cleavage was on show. He reared back as if the backdraft of a fire had hit him in the face. 'You know what your trouble is, Julius? You don't mind if I call you that, do you? It makes things a little less formal between us since we're living together and all, don't you think?' She heard his teeth audibly grind together as she fluttered her eyelashes at him but she carried on regardless. 'Your problem is you're sexually frustrated. All that pent-up energy's gotta have an outlet. You're tearing strips off me when what you really want to do is tear my clothes off.'

His expression was thunderous. 'I have *never* met a more audaciously wanton woman than you. You have zero shame.'

Holly gave him an impish smile. 'Aw, how sweet of you to say so. Such flattery is music to my ears.'

He muttered a savage swear word and pushed his hair back from his forehead. It looked as if it wasn't the first time he'd done it that evening. The thick, glossy strands were in a rumpled state of disorder. His whole body was taut, rippling with tension. He reminded her of a tightly coiled spring about to snap.

'Here's what you've got wrong about me,' he said, facing her again with a hardened glare. 'I *can* resist you. You might think all those come-on looks will make me fall on you like some hormone-driven teenager, but you're wrong.'

Holly held out her hand, palm up. 'Want to lay a bet on it?'

He eyed her hand as if it were something poisonous. 'I don't gamble.'

She laughed. 'You're even more boring than I thought. What are you afraid of, Julius? Losing money or compromising one of your starchy old principles?'

He gave her a black look. 'At least I have some, unlike some other people I could mention.'

'Like your father?' Holly wasn't sure why she thought immediately of his father. But she'd heard enough about Richard Ravensdale's reputation to wonder how Julius could possibly be his son. Julius was an apple that had rolled so far away from the tree it was in another orchard. He was so uptight and conservative. His brother, Jake, was another story, however. Jake's exploits were plastered over the internet. It made for very entertaining reading.

Julius's brows snapped together in a single black bar. 'What do you know about my father?'

'He's a ladies' man,' Holly said. 'He's what I'd call a triple-D kind of guy: dine them, do them, dump them is his credo, isn't it? A bit like your twin brother's.'

'You didn't let on that you knew who my family was earlier,' he said. 'Why not?'

Holly gave him a cheeky smile. 'Fame doesn't impress me, remember?'

His mouth tightened until his lips almost disappeared. 'This is a bloody nightmare.'

'Hey, I'm not judging you because of your parents,' Holly said as she resumed preparing the vegetables. 'I reckon it would totally suck to have famous parents. You'd never know who your friends were. They might only be hanging out with you because of your connection with celebrity.' She looked up to find Julius staring at her with a frown between his brows. 'What's wrong?'

He gave his head a little shake, walked over to the fridge and opened it to take out a bottle of wine. 'Do you want one?' He held up the bottle and a glass.

'I don't drink.'

His gaze narrowed a fraction. 'Why not?'

Holly shrugged. 'I figure I've got enough vices without adding any more.'

He leaned back against the counter at the back of the kitchen as he poured a glass and took a deep draught of his wine. And another. And another.

Holly shifted her lips from side to side. 'You keep going like that and Sophia won't be the only one around here needing strong painkillers.'

'Tell me about your background,' Julius said suddenly.

Holly washed her hands at the sink. 'I expect it's pretty boring compared to yours.'

'I'd still like to know.'

'Why?'

'Humour me,' he said. 'I'm feeling sorry for myself for having a triple-D dad.'

'Aww. All those silver spoons stuffed in your mouth giving you toothache, are they? My heart bleeds. It really does.'

He screwed up his mouth but it wasn't a smile. More of a musing gesture, as if he were trying to figure her out. 'I know I come from a privileged background,' he said. 'I'm grateful for the opportunities it's afforded me.'

'Are you?' Holly asked with an elevated eyebrow.

His frown carved a V into his forehead. 'Of course I am.'

'So that's why your housekeeper had to twist your arm to do your bit for charity?' she said. 'To convince you to help someone a little less fortunate than yourself? Yeah, I can totally see how grateful you are.'

He had the grace to look a little uncomfortable. 'Okay, so you weren't my first choice as a charity, but I give to other causes. Generously, too.'

'Anyone can sign a cheque,' Holly said. 'It takes guts to get your hands dirty. To actually physically help someone out of the gutter.'

'Is that where you were?'

She challenged him with her gaze. 'What do you think?'

He held her look for another pulsing moment. 'Look, I'm sorry we got off to a bad start. Maybe we could start over.'

'I don't think so,' Holly said. 'You've already made your mind up about me. It's what people like you do. You make snap judgements. You judge people on appearances without taking the time to get to know them.'

'I'm taking the time now,' Julius said. 'Tell me about you.'

'Why should I?'

'Because I'm interested.'

'You're not interested in me as a person,' Holly said as she checked the oven where she had put the galantine of chicken earlier. 'You just want me out of here because I make you feel uncomfortable.'

'That was your intention, wasn't it?'

Holly closed the oven door and faced him. 'You want to know about me? I'm twenty-five years old. I had my first kiss at thirteen and my first sex partner at sixteen. I left school at seventeen without finishing my education. I have no qualifications. I speak two languages, English and Spanish—three, if you count sarcasm. I don't drink. I don't do drugs. I hate controlling men and I have issues with authority. That's about it.'

He glanced at the vegetable dish she had prepared. 'You told me you couldn't cook.'

'So I lied.'

'Why?'

Holly gave a lip-shrug. 'Felt like it.'

He came over to where she was standing. He stopped within touching distance but kept his hands by his sides. Even so, she could feel the magnetic pull of his body against hers. It was like a force field of energy. Strong. Powerful. Irresistible.

She glanced at his mouth, wondering if he was going to lean in to kiss her. She suddenly realised how much she wanted him to. Not to prove her point; somehow that agenda had taken a back seat, so far back it was now in the boot. No, she wanted him to kiss her because she really wanted to know what his mouth felt like. How it would feel as it moved over hers. How it would taste. How his tongue would feel as it stroked along hers. *Mated* with hers.

Then he did touch her. It was a fleeting stroke of two of his fingers down the slope of her cheek in a movement as soft as an artist's sable brush. It sent a shockwave through her senses. Every nerve in her face began tingling, spiralling in dizzy delight. She moistened her lips, barely aware she was doing it until she saw the way his sexily hooded gaze followed the pathway of her tongue.

Holly slowly brought her gaze back up to the midnight-sky-dark intensity of his. His expression was unfathomable. She didn't know what he was thinking. What he was feeling. She was scarcely able to think clearly herself. And as to her feelings… She didn't allow her feelings to get involved when she got physical with a man. *Never*.

'Who are you, Holly Perez, and what do you want?'

'I really should've made you lay down some money,' she said.

'You think I'm going to kiss you?'

'You're thinking about it—that much I *do* know.' *Why am I speaking in such a husky whisper?* Holly thought. Anyone would think she was falling under some sort of crazy spell. Sure, he was handsome and he smelled good. Way too good, compared to some of the men she'd been up close and personal with. But he was a man who wanted to tame her and that she could never allow. Not in a million years.

His mouth tilted in a half smile. 'You think you can read my mind?'

'I don't know about your mind but your body's giving off one heck of a signal,' she said.

'So is yours.'

Tell me something I don't already know, Holly thought, sneaking in a hitching breath. Somehow the power base between them had shifted. She was no longer in charge of her body. It was reacting according to its own schedule, a schedule she had no control over. Her senses were scrambled. Caught up in a maelstrom of feelings she had never encountered before. Desire was running like a hot fever in her blood. She could feel her own wetness between her legs. She wondered if he could smell the musk of her arousal. She could feel the tingling of her breasts in anticipation of him reaching for them. As it was, his chest was barely half an inch away from hers.

In the past her breasts had felt nothing when a man stood close to her. They were just there—part of her anatomy. Now they were deeply sensitive erogenous zones that craved contact. They pushed against the fabric of her bra, swelling in need, her nipples peaking in response to his presence.

She could even sense the swell of his erection close to where her pelvis pulsed with need. The hot, hard, swollen heat of him was sending out a signal like sonar to her body, making her ache and throb with want.

'I would only sleep with you to prove a point,' Holly said in a way she hoped sounded offhand. 'Sorry if that offends your ego.'

He picked up one of her curls and wound it around his index finger. The gentle tug on her scalp sent a shot of lust between her legs, turning her core to molten fire. His eyes were so dark they reminded her of deep outer space. Limitless. Fathomless. 'It doesn't, because we're not going to sleep together.' His voice was only slightly less husky than hers.

'Could've fooled me.'

He pressed the pad of his thumb against her lower lip, holding it there for a moment before lifting it away. But still he didn't move away from her. His body was toe to toe with hers. If she leaned forward a fraction, their thighs would touch. The temptation to do so was like an invisible hand pushing her from behind. She brushed against the unmistakable hardness of him. Felt the shock through her flesh like a powerful current. It shot through her body in an arc of erotic energy that left no part of her unaffected. She saw the way his pupils flared, his eyes darkening, pulsing and glinting with want.

'You want me so bad I bet all it would take is one lit-tle kitten-lick of my tongue to send you over the edge,' Holly said, shocking herself at her wanton goading of him. Why was she being so utterly brazen? He had the edge on her here. He had already told her he would evict her from the programme. That had been his intention when he'd come down to speak to her. She would be sent to prison. She had no second chances. If she pushed him too far, he would get rid of her. Wasn't that what *every-one* did to her? She knew what was at risk but even so she couldn't stop herself. She was driven by the urges of her body—her traitorous body—which seemed to have developed an agenda of its own.

Julius sent a fingertip from the top of her cleavage, down the length of her sternum, over her quivering belly and then down to the zip of her jeans. He outlined the seam of her body through the denim and metal teeth of her zip, all the while holding her gaze with the smoul-dering blaze of his own. 'I bet I could make you come first,' he said in a two-parts gravel, one-part honey tone.

Holly almost came on the spot. She felt the flicker-ing of her nerve endings, the swelling of her body as it ached and throbbed for more stimulation. She had to get away from him before he won this. He had far more self-control than she had bargained for and certainly far more than she had. What was he…made of steel?

'I could be faking it and how would you know?' she said.

His mouth slanted again in a cynical smile. 'I would know.'

Holly let out a breath that caught at her throat like a tiny fishhook. 'In my book, sexual confidence in men is arrogance in disguise.'

He outlined her mouth with that same lazy, tantalising glide of his finger. Tracing, touching, teasing her lips until she wanted to suck his fingertip into her mouth and draw on it as if she was drawing on him intimately. Not that she ever did that. Not for anyone. She hated it. It was gross and so were the men who insisted on it. But something about Julius made her want to step outside her boundaries. He triggered all sorts of forbidden urges in her. Was it because he was so conservative? Or was it because he was the first man she had ever felt this raging, red-hot passion for?

'You think I'm arrogant because I can pleasure you like you've never been pleasured before?' he asked.

'Promises, promises,' Holly said in a singsong voice.

He upped her chin between his finger and thumb so her gaze had nowhere to go but to mesh with his. The burn of his touch moved through her body like a trail of fire. The scorching circle of his thumb beneath her chin sent her pulse into overload.

His eyes moved between hers, back and forth, like the beam of a searchlight. She felt the magnetism of him, the sheer power he had over her with his laserlike touch. The touch she craved in every pore of her body. Her flesh ached to feel his hands move all over her. To shape and caress her breasts, her thighs and what pulsed and fizzed with longing between them. The need was thrumming inside her like the twang of a cello string plucked too hard. It reverberated through her racing blood, tripled her heartbeat and sent her already scudding pulse haywire.

'You're beautiful, but you know that, don't you?' Julius said in a deep, rough baritone that sent another tremor of want through her core. 'You know the power you have over men and you use it every chance you get.'

'A girl's gotta do what a girl's gotta do,' Holly said, trying to keep her gaze from skittering away from his probing one, trying to keep the fragile hold on her equilibrium disguised. Never had she felt such a compulsion to indulge her senses, to lose herself in a feast of the flesh, to allow herself to be consumed by the power and force of attraction and lust.

He threaded his fingers through her hair, lifting it away from her scalp, only to let it fall in a bouncing cascade against her neck and shoulders. 'That's why you were cavorting out in the pool,' he said. 'You wanted my attention. How better to get it than to strip off and parade that beautiful, tempting body beneath my office window?'

'You didn't have to look,' Holly said. 'You could have drawn the curtains or pulled the blind.'

He gave a little sound of sardonic amusement. 'You're not going to pull my strings like I'm some spineless puppet. I'm made of much sterner stuff.'

That goading little devil was back on Holly's shoulder, urging her to push Julius as far as she could. 'So that's why you came stomping out to the pool and manhandled me out of the water, was it? Just to show how stern and disciplined you are? Don't make me laugh.'

His eyes flashed with a flicker of anger. The same beat of anger she could see in a muscle beside his mouth, flicking on and off like a faulty switch.

The tug of war between his gaze and hers went on for endless seconds.

The air bristled with static.

But then he suddenly stepped back from her with

a muttered expletive. Holly hadn't realised she'd been holding her breath until he walked out of the kitchen without a backward glance.

She expelled the banked-up air in a long, jagged stream.

Round one a draw, she thought. *You'll win the next*.

But a nagging doubt tapped her lightly on the shoulder… *Maybe you won't*.

CHAPTER FIVE

JULIUS STRODE OUT of the villa in search of fresh air. Of common sense. *Control*. Where the hell was his control? He was furious with himself for allowing that toffee-eyed little temptress to trigger his hormones. Why hadn't he kept to his plan? He owed her nothing. What did he care if she went to prison? It was where she belonged. Why had he allowed her to manipulate his conscience?

Or maybe it wasn't his conscience she'd manipulated…

He was disgusted with himself for wanting her like he had wanted no other woman. He was annoyed he had allowed her to needle him to the point where he was as close to breaking as never before. How could he have allowed that to happen? He wasn't the sort of man who put sex before sense. This was nothing but a game to her.

She could tease and taunt him all she liked. She could walk around his villa scantily clad. She could flash her delectable cleavage at him. She could wiggle her hips and pert bottom. She could pout her sexy little mouth at him all day long. She could swim in his pool stark naked for all he cared.

He would *not* let her win this.

He had been tricked by her chameleon-like behaviour. The way she'd fooled him by her charitable act of taking over the cooking while Sophia had rested, after she'd been so adamant she wasn't going to take orders from him or anyone.

What was true about her and what were lies?

She was a smart-mouthed, streetwise siren. Flirting with him, teasing him, daring him, goading him until his blood ran so hot and fast through his veins it scorched him. He was burning for her. Throbbing with the ache to have her. He had never felt desire like it. It was like a storm in his body. A powerful combustion of energy that built each time he was near her. It was brooding inside him even now. The pressure of high arousal. The ache of unreleased desire was a burning ache he couldn't tame or dismiss. It consumed his thoughts as well as his flesh. Wicked, damning thoughts of what he would like to do to her—*craved* to do to her.

His brain was racing with a constant loop of hot images of them having sex like jungle animals. No 'finesse' sex. Hard and fast sex. 'Any position' sex.

Holly Perez was the most dangerous woman he had ever met. With her bedroom eyes and wily ways, she threatened everything he stood for. She made him feel things he had trained himself not to feel. Emotions were things he controlled. Desires were something he properly channelled. He did not rush into mad flings and one-nighters with strangers, especially ones with a criminal past.

He had standards. Principles. He was a good citizen who paid his taxes on time. He never coloured outside the lines. Damn it, he didn't even park outside of them.

Call him conservative, or even obsessive, but rules were things he respected because for most of his life his parents had disregarded them. Rules provided structure in a disordered world. He liked order. He liked predictability. Planning was his forte. He didn't do things on the fly. He wasn't spontaneous. He wasn't a risk taker. He left that sort of thing to his brother, Jake, who loved to live life in the fast lane. Julius was only happy in the fast lane if he knew exactly how fast it was, how long, how wide and how long he would have to be in it.

He did the calculations and *then* he acted.

And right now his calculations told him in big neon flashing letters: Holly Perez was danger personified.

But for all that something about her got to him…not just physically, but on an entirely different level. He felt something for her. Something he hadn't expected to feel. He was drawn to her. He couldn't get her out of his mind. He couldn't forget her touch. The way she moved. Even the sound of her laughter—the tinkling-bell sound that made his spine shiver. She was blatant, brazen and in-your-face, yet beguiling. He'd seen a glimpse of vulnerability down at the lake. And when he'd asked her about the scar on her arm. For just a moment he had seen a flicker of something behind the mask she wore. He couldn't help feeling there was more to her than met the eye. Yes, she made him uncomfortable. Yes, she was a flirt. But he had some sort of responsibility towards her, didn't he?

It was only for a month. He would be away for part of that with work. He would hardly have to have contact with her if he chose not to.

And right now the less contact he had with her the better.

Julius was back in his office trying to work when his phone rang. He was in two minds to ignore it when he saw it was his brother calling. 'Jake,' he said heavily.

'Whoa, bro, you sound a little tense there, man,' Jake said. 'So I take it you've already heard the news?'

Julius sat upright in his chair. 'Heard *what* news?'

A list of possibilities went through his head in the nanosecond that followed. His father had had another heart scare. His parents were splitting up. Again. His sister was finally going on a date after losing her child-hood sweetheart to cancer when she was sixteen. *No*, he thought; Miranda was too intent on martyrdom. Jake was getting married… *No*. That would *never* happen.

'A skeleton has come out of Dad's closet,' Jake said.

'Another one?' Julius asked, thinking of the veri-table cast of mistresses and hook-ups his father had dallied with over the years in spite of 'working at his marriage'. Not that his mother, Elisabetta, could stand in judgement. She'd had a fling or two herself. 'How old is she this time?'

'Twenty-three.'

'God, the same age as Miranda,' Julius said.

'It gets worse,' Jake said.

'Go on, ruin my day,' Julius said.

'She's not his mistress.'

Julius's heart stopped as if a horse had kicked him in the chest. 'He's not a bigamist? Tell me he's not got a secret wife?' *Please, God, spare us all that shame.*

'She's his daughter.'

'His *daughter*?'

'Yep,' Jake said in a grim tone. 'He's sired himself a love child. Katherine Winwood.'

'Dear God, what does Elisabetta think of this?' Julius said. 'How's she taking it?'

'How do you think?' Jake said wryly. 'Hysterically.'

Julius groaned at the thought of the temper tantrums, door slamming and object throwing that would be going on in his parents' hotel suite in New York. He couldn't face another divorce. The last one had been bad enough. The press. The publicity. All of their private lives exposed. 'Is it in the papers?'

'Papers, internet, every social media platform you can poke a finger at,' Jake said. 'It's gone viral. And that's not all.'

Julius's stomach pitched. 'It gets worse?'

'Way worse,' Jake said. 'Kat Winwood was born two months after Miranda.'

Julius did the maths. 'So that means Dad was still seeing this woman's mother when he reconciled with Mum?'

'Got it in one.'

Julius let out a colourful curse. 'What's Dad got to say for himself? Or is he denying it?'

'You can't deny the results of a paternity test.'

'How did this Kat girl get one done?' Julius said. 'Who is she? Where did she come from? Why's she revealed herself now? Why didn't her mother tell Dad she was pregnant, or has he always known?'

'He knew all right,' Jake said. 'He paid the woman to have an abortion. Handsomely, too.'

Julius swallowed a mouthful of bile. Just when he thought his father couldn't shock him any more, he raised it to a whole new level of indecency. 'But she didn't go through with it,' he said unnecessarily.

'Nope,' Jake said. 'She had the kid and kept the father's identity a secret. Even the birth certificate says "father unknown".'

'So why come forward now?' Julius asked.

'She died recently of a terminal illness,' Jake said. 'She told Kat on her death bed who her father was.'

'So this girl Kat is after money.'

'What else?'

Julius scored a hand through his hair. 'How many more like her could there be out there? Why can't Dad keep it in his trousers? He's nudging seventy, for God's sake.'

'I just thought I'd give you the heads up on it in case the press come sniffing around you for an exclusive,' Jake said. 'They've been parked outside my place since the first Tweet went out.'

His brother's words sent an army of invisible ants across Julius's scalp. A drumbeat of panic started up in his chest. His blood ran hot and cold. He felt beads of sweat break out across his brow. If the press came here they would find Holly—*living with him*. A girl not much older than his father's love child. In fact, Holly looked younger than twenty-five. What would the press make of her holed up here with him? Especially if they caught a glimpse of her flaunting her flesh at every available opportunity. They wouldn't wait for the truth. They would jump to sensational conclusions to razz up a storm of scandal.

He had to keep her away from the press. God knew what she would say to them to stir up trouble for him. One look at her and they would assume he was indulging in a lust fest and was no different from his Lothario father. With her sexy little body and her cheeky personality, why wouldn't they assume he was making the most of the situation? Why, oh, why, had he agreed to have her here? It was a disaster of monumental proportions.

'You okay, bro?' Jake cut through Julius's racing thoughts. 'I know it's a shock but think how Miranda's taking it.'

That was enough to snap Julius back into protective big-brother mode. 'How *is* she taking it?'

'I haven't spoken to her yet,' Jake said. 'She wasn't answering her phone. Probably switched it off to keep the press off her back. But think about it. She's always been the baby of the family. How's it going to feel to know there's a new half-sister who's now the youngest?'

'I'll call her as soon as I finish with you,' Julius said, expelling a long ragged breath. 'Poor kid. You know how embarrassed she gets by Mum and Dad's behaviour. This will be hardest on her. We've already been through one divorce with them so we know what we're in for. She has no idea of how ugly this could get.'

'Yeah, tell me about it,' Jake said. 'But it might not come to that.'

'You seriously think Mum won't want a divorce after Dad produces a secret love child out of the woodwork?' Julius said. 'Come on, Jake. This is our mother we're talking about. Any chance for a scene and she's right there in full costume and make-up.'

'I know, but Flynn's trying to smooth things over,' Jake said. 'Another divorce will be costly to both of them, and not just financially. Their popularity could rise or fall according to how they handle this scandal. You know how fickle the fans are. Flynn's hoping he can silence the girl with a one-off payment. Something big enough to keep her mouth shut and go away. Preferably both.'

Julius was relieved to hear it was all in good hands. Flynn Carlyon was the family lawyer; he'd been a year ahead of them at school. He handled Julius's parents' legal affairs as well as run offices in London. Flynn wasn't just a solicitor to the stars. He had won several high-profile property settlement cases that had given him the tagline around the courts: *Flynn equals win.* He had a sharp mind, an even sharper tongue and a cutting wit.

'Have you met this girl?' Julius asked.

'Not yet,' Jake said. 'You might want to drop by next time you're in town and say hello. After all, she's your new baby sister.'

How could I possibly forget? Julius thought with a despairing groan.

Holly put the finishing touches to dinner before she went up to her room on the second floor to have a shower. The room she had chosen was four doors down from Julius's suite but on the opposite side of the wide corridor. It didn't have a balcony—*thank God*—but it did have a nice view over the front gardens and the tree-lined driveway. It had its own en suite, which was decorated in a Parisian style with lovely ceramic-and-brass tap handles and a claw-footed bath that was centred in the middle of the floor, with a telephone-handle fitting as well as taps. There was a separate shower stall big enough for a football team and lots of gorgeous, fluffy white towels, fragrant French soaps and expensive hair products. A gilt-framed oval mirror hung over the pedestal washbasin and there was another full-length one in the bedroom.

The only issue Holly had was with her clothes. They didn't feel right for her surroundings. All this high-end luxury made the clothes she'd brought with her look even dowdier than usual. She had never been financially stable enough to follow fashion. Fashion was something other people followed. Shopping was a pastime other people indulged in. Rich people, people who had money, security and the safety net of family. Holly had taught herself not to want things she could never afford. She had deadened her desire for nice feminine things. It was pointless to wish she could dress like the women she saw about town. Smart women; educated, sophisticated, polished and poised, with hair, make-up and nails done like models and movie stars. She could never compete with that. It was so far out of her reach, she didn't bother trying.

But right now she would have loved a nice dress to put on and some high heels to go with it. Some classy underwear—not cheap, faded cotton but some slinky, cobwebby lace. She would have liked some make-up—not much, just enough to highlight her features, to put some colour on her eyelids and some tinted gloss on her lips. She would have liked to get a decent haircut, perhaps get some professional foils done to cover the pink streaks she'd done with a home kit that hadn't turned out quite the way she'd planned. Maybe a bit of jewellery—pearls, perhaps—to give her a touch of elegance.

But what was the point of wishing she could dress like a glamour girl when all her life she had been the girl with the charity shop clothes? The girl with the bad haircut, the bitten nails and the cheap shoes with the soles worn through? She had always felt like a donkey showing up at a posh dressage event.

Why should now be any different?

After her shower Holly slipped off her towel in front of the mirror. At least she had a good figure. It was her only asset. Good bones; long, slim limbs; a neat waist; nicely shaped breasts; mostly clear skin, apart from that ridiculously childish patch of freckles over the bridge of her nose.

Her gaze went to a pattern of damson-coloured marks around the tops of her arms. She reached up and touched them, her stomach doing a funny little dip and dive when she realised what they were. Julius's fingerprints had branded her flesh with light but unmistakable bruises.

She bit her lip, looking at the grey cotton tank top she had been planning to wear with another pair of jeans—her only pair without holes in them, although they did have a frayed hem. She put on the tank top and picked up a green cardigan, even though the evening was warm, and slipped it on. It wasn't the nicest weave—the acrylic in it always made her skin feel itchy. But it was either that or a denim jacket or a pilled woollen sweater that would have her sweating within seconds. Finally, she bunched up her hair and secured it with an elastic tie in a makeshift knot at the back of her head.

Holly drew in a breath and let it out in a long, slow sigh. Why she was trying to look half-decent for Julius Ravensdale wasn't something she wanted to examine too closely. It wouldn't matter if she'd been dressed in the finest designer wear; he would still look down his imperious nose at her.

Just like everyone else.

CHAPTER SIX

JULIUS HADN'T BEEN able to track down Miranda or his father. But he had fielded several calls from his mother, who was beyond hysterical. He did what he always did. He listened, he stayed calm, he bit his tongue. His mother vented, raged and fumed so much that he began to wonder if she was actually enjoying herself. It was an opportunity to play the victim, one of her favourite roles. His parents' relationship was toxic. He hated the way they were madly in love one minute then hated each other the next. When one did something out of line, the other went into payback mode. It was childish and puerile.

The press was having a ball with this latest bombshell. He'd clicked on a couple of links Jake had sent him. The girl in question was stunning. If her mother had looked anything like Katherine Winwood, Julius could see why his father's head had been turned. Julius only hoped no one would track him down for a comment. His life here in Argentina was his way of flying under the radar. Over here hardly anyone knew who he was and he wanted it to stay that way. But what was he going to do if the press came sniffing around? Holly was a loose cannon. There was a possibility she would deliberately mislead the press if given half a chance. Should he send her away? He looked at his phone. He had the number of her caseworker on speed dial. His finger hovered over it…but then he pushed his phone away.

For all her feistiness and brazen behaviour, there was something about Holly that mystified him. She seemed so determined to challenge him, yet he had seen that glimpse of touching vulnerability down at the lake. He had never met anyone quite like her before. He found her…interesting. Stimulating, and not just because of his overactive hormones. There was a hint of the lost waif about her. Or was he completely hoodwinked by her? Was it his rescue complex in overdrive? He wasn't the sort of person to walk away from a person in need. Holly was difficult and disruptive but if he sent her away now she would have no choice but to go into detention. He knew enough about the penal system to know it was not the place he would want anyone under his care and protection to go. Sophia had been so keen to take Holly on. He would be letting her down if he quit now. The least he could do was talk to Sophia about it. Get her perspective on things.

It was Julius's routine to go to the sitting room before dinner each evening to have a quiet drink with Sophia before she served the meal. It was a pattern they had fallen into over the past few months. He enjoyed hearing about Sophia's extended family and her interesting childhood as the daughter of Italian immigrants. They often spoke in Italian, as he was fluent, given his mother was from Florence.

He wanted to use this time to inform her of his father's latest peccadillo so she could put steps in place to maintain Julius's privacy.

His parents—most particularly his mother—would be appalled at Julius for being so familiar with his housekeeper or, indeed, any of his staff. When he'd been growing up, his parents' housekeeping staff had not been considered part of the family. There'd been strict codes of behaviour forbidding anything but the strictest formality from the staff towards family members. One did not discuss one's private affairs with the staff. One did not fraternise with or consider them as friends. They were employees. They were kept at arm's length. They were taught to know their place and never stray from the boundaries of it.

The only exception had been Jasmine Connolly, the daughter of Hugh Connolly, the gardener at the family property in Buckinghamshire called Ravensdene. Jasmine had come to live with her father after her mother had dropped her at Ravensdene on a visit and was never seen or heard from again. Julius's parents had taken pity on Hugh Connolly—unusual for them, considering their almost pathological self-centredness—and had offered to pay for Jasmine's education. Jasmine was like a surrogate sister to Julius, and certainly to Miranda, as they were much the same age.

Jake, however, had a tricky relationship with Jasmine after an incident when she'd been sixteen. Both blamed the other and as a result they were sworn enemies, which made for some rather interesting dynamics at family gatherings.

But this time it wasn't Sophia who joined Julius for a drink. In walked Holly, carrying a tray with savouries on it, which she put down on the table in front of him, but not before he got a tantalising glimpse of her cleavage as she leaned over.

'Sophia sends her apologies,' Holly said. 'She's having an early night.'

Julius frowned. 'Is she all right? I haven't seen her all day.'

'She's fine. Just needs a rest, is all.'

He watched as Holly poured him a glass of white wine. Clearly Sophia had filled her in on his preferences. She handed it to him with a tight-lipped smile. 'Two standard drinks is all I'll serve. Just so you know.'

He took the glass, only just restraining himself from draining it dry. Mixing one glass of wine with Holly Perez was like drinking five tequilas and expecting to remain sober. It was impossible to remain sober and sensible in her company. He could already feel the tightening of his groin; the stirring of lust her presence triggered was like someone flicking a switch inside him.

For all that he'd wanted to get rid of her, she had turned things around with her concern for Sophia. But was it concern...or conniving behaviour to serve her own ends? He wanted to know more about her. He wanted to know why she was so determined to make trouble for him. It didn't add up. If she made too much trouble, she would be sent to jail. Why then sabotage her last chance at making something of her life? She seemed intent on destroying any hope of a positive future. If he sent in a bad report to her caseworker, it would be disastrous for her. She knew that. He knew that. Why then was she so determined to ruin everything for herself? It didn't make sense. It wasn't logical.

If there was one thing in life Julius demanded, it was sense and logic.

'I thought I told you not to wear jeans to dinner,' he said.

A flash of defiance—or was it pride?—sparked in her caramel-brown gaze. 'I don't have any dresses. I could've come in shorts or my underwear. I can go upstairs and change or I could strip off here. You choose. I'm easy.'

'Undoubtedly.'

She gave him a withering look. 'Not as easy as your old man, according to the news I heard just now.' She sat on the edge of the sofa opposite him. 'He's quite a cad, isn't he? Nothing like you, or so you say.'

Julius forcibly had to relax his hold on the stem of his glass in case he snapped it. 'I would appreciate it if you would refrain from discussing my father's affairs with anyone. If you say one word to the press, I'll send you packing so fast you won't know what hit you.'

'Are you going to fly home to England to meet your new sister?'

He tightened his jaw. 'I'm not planning to.'

'It's not her fault your old man's her father,' Holly said. 'You shouldn't judge her for something she had no control over.'

Julius took another mouthful of wine. She was right and he wanted to hate her for pointing it out to him. But he needed time to get used to the idea of having a half-sibling. He thought he was used to his father's scandals but this one took the prize. The press had been still banging on about it last time he'd looked. Katherine Winwood might be gorgeous to look at but who knew what her motives were in coming forward? Money, most probably. That she might be entitled to some compensation for how his father had treated her mother was not something he wanted to comment on. He was sick to the stomach over his family's dramas. What or who would turn up next?

Julius decided a change of subject was called for. 'I'll order some clothes for you. Let me know your size and I'll make sure you have what you need.'

Holly's eyes danced. 'So you're going to be like a sugar daddy to me or something?'

He ground his teeth until his jaw ached. 'No.'

She picked up a canapé and bit into it. 'Pity.'

'It's rude to speak with your mouth full.'

'I'll make sure I remember that when we're in the bedroom,' she said with a naughty smile.

Julius kept his gaze locked on hers but he wondered if she could sense the fireball of lust that hit him. He was suddenly so erect he could feel it pressing against his trouser zip. The thought of her hot little mouth on him made his blood pound in excitement.

He distracted himself by leaning forward to take one of the canapés off the platter. 'Where did you learn to cook?'

'Picked it up along the way.'

He sat back and crossed his right ankle over his left thigh in the most casual and relaxed pose he could manage while his erection still throbbed. Painfully. 'Along the way where?'

'Here and there and everywhere.'

It seemed he wasn't the only one keen to avoid discussing family issues, Julius thought. 'What are your plans once you leave here?'

She gave a loose little shrug before taking another appetiser. 'I want to get a job and save up enough money to go to England.'

'To holiday?'

'To live.' She took a noisy bite and munched away, like a bunny rabbit chewing a crunchy carrot.

Julius knew she was doing it to annoy him. Her rebellious streak was kind of cute, when he thought about it. It reminded him a bit of Jasmine Connolly, the gardener's daughter, who liked to have a bit of fun at times—mostly with Jake, who for some reason didn't see the funny side.

Cute?

What was he thinking? Holly wasn't cute. She was as cunning as a vixen. She was out to prove he was unable to resist her. He was out to prove he could. He had the edge on her. She might be doing all she could to get thrown out of his house but without him as her guardian she would find herself doing time. Why then was she pushing him to evict her? Was it deliberate or a knee-jerk thing? Was her behaviour a pattern she had developed in order to survive? From the scant details she'd given him, her childhood clearly hadn't been a picnic. Did she push people away before they pushed her?

And why did *he* give a damn?

'Do you have relatives in England?' Julius asked.

'My mum was an orphan. My dad was, too. An English couple adopted him, which is how he met my mum over there. It's why they hit it off so well. They were two lonely people who found true love.' Her mouth took a sudden downturn and she looked at the remaining piece of her canapé as if it had personally offended her. 'Pity they didn't get the happy ending they deserved.'

'How did your father die?'

'He was killed in an accident at work.'

'What sort of accident?' Julius pressed a little further.

'A fatal one.'

He gave her a look. 'I realise it's probably painful to talk about but I—'

'It happened a long time ago,' Holly said, interrupting. 'Anyway, I only remember what I've been told.'

'What were you told?'

'That he died in a work-place accident.'

She was a stubborn little thing, Julius thought. She would only reveal what she wanted to reveal. 'Did your mother ever remarry?'

Holly got up abruptly from the corner of the sofa and dusted her fingers on the front of her jeans. 'You want to make your way to the dining room? I'll only be a minute or two. I promised I'd take Sophia's meal up to her.'

Julius sat back and sipped his wine, a thoughtful frown pulling at his brow. So it wasn't his imagination after all. There was definitely something about Holly's background that made her reluctant to speak of it. Could he get her to trust him enough to reveal it?

He pulled himself up short. Why on earth was he even *trying* to understand her?

He was supposed to be keeping his distance. He wasn't the type of guy to let his emotions get the better of him. It was fine to care about her welfare—perfectly fine. Any decent person would do that. But if he thought *too* much about her cute dimples, and pert manner and that far away look she sometimes got in her eyes when she didn't know he was looking, he would be feeling stuff he had no right to be feeling. It was bad enough being attracted to her physically. God forbid he should start liking her as a person. Feeling affection. Holly was a temporary inconvenience and he couldn't wait to get rid of her so he could get his life back into its neat, ordered groove.

Even if at times—he reluctantly conceded—it was a little boring.

* * *

Holly made sure Sophia was settled in her suite with her meal, a drink and the television remote handy. She had cut up the chicken and the vegetables so Sophia could eat with her left hand using a fork. 'I'll be back in half an hour to bring up dessert and to clear your dishes,' she said.

'Muchas gracias,' Sophia said with a soft smile. 'You're a good girl.'

Holly gave a little grunt of a laugh. 'Try telling your boss that.'

Sophia looked at her thoughtfully for a moment. 'You don't need to be bad to be noticed. There are other ways to get his attention.'

Holly frowned. 'I'm not trying to get anyone's attention.'

Sophia gave her a sage look. 'Earning someone's respect takes time. It also takes honesty.'

Holly fiddled with a loose button on her cardigan. 'Why should I bother trying to earn someone's respect when I'm not going to be here long enough to reap the benefits?'

'Señor Ravensdale could help you get on your feet,' Sophia said. 'He could give you a good reference. Find employment for you. Recommend you to someone.'

Holly snorted. 'Recommend me for what? Scrubbing someone's dirty floors? No thanks.'

Sophia released a sigh. 'Do you think someone who's in charge of maintaining the upkeep of a house is not worthy of respect? If so, then you're not the person I thought you were. People are people. Jobs are jobs. Some people get the good ones, others the bad ones—sometimes because of luck, other times because of opportunity. But as long as each person is doing the best job they can where they can, then what's the difference between being a CEO and a cleaner?'

'Money. Status. Power.'

'Money will buy you nice things but it won't make you happy.'

'I'd at least like the chance to test that theory,' Holly said.

Sophia shook her head at her. 'You're young and angry at the world. You want to hit out at anyone who dares to come close in case they let you down. Not everyone will do that, *querida*. There are some people you can trust with your love.'

Holly swallowed a golf ball-sized lump of sudden emotion. Her father had called her *querida*. She still remembered his smiling face as he'd reached for her and held her high up in his arms, swinging her around until she got dizzy. His eyes had been full of love for her and for her mother. They had been a happy family, not wealthy by any means, but secure and happy.

But then he had died and everything had changed.

It was as though that life had happened to another person. Holly *felt* like a different person. She was no longer that sweet, contented child who embraced love and gave it unquestioningly in return. She was a hardened cynic who knew how to live on her wits and by the use of her sharp tongue. She didn't feel love for anyone.

And she was darn certain no one felt it for her.

'I'd better go serve His High and Mightiness his dinner,' Holly said. 'I'll see you later.'

'Holly?'

She stopped at the door to look back at the housekeeper. 'What?'

'Don't make things worse for him by speaking to the press if they come here. He doesn't deserve that. He's trying to help you, in his way. Don't bite the hand that's reached out to help you.'

'Okay, okay, already. I won't speak to the press,' Holly said. 'Why would I want to? They'll only twist things and make me look bad.'

'Can I trust you?'

'Yes.'

'He won't let you win, you know.'

Holly kept her expression innocent. 'Win what?'

Sophia gave her a knowing look. 'I know what you're trying to do but it won't work. Not with him. If he wants to get involved with you then it will be on his terms, not yours. He won't be manipulated or tricked into it.'

'That's quite some pedestal you've got him on,' Holly said. 'But then, he pays you good money. You'd say anything to keep your job.'

'He's a good man,' Sophia said. 'And deep down I know you're a good woman.'

You don't know me, Holly thought as she closed the door. *No one does.*

I won't let them.

CHAPTER SEVEN

JULIUS WAS STANDING at the windows of the dining room when Holly came in with the food. She unloaded the tray on the table and then turned briskly to leave.

'Aren't you joining me?' he asked.

Her chin came up. 'Apparently I'm not dressed for the occasion.'

There was a bite to her tone that made him wonder if he had upset her. Embarrassed her. Hurt her, even. She always acted so defiant and in-your-face feisty that to hear that slightly wounded note to her voice faintly disturbed him. There was so much about her that intrigued him. The more time he spent with her, the more he wanted to uncover her secrets. The secrets he caught a glimpse of in her eyes. The shifting shadows on her face he witnessed when she didn't think he was looking at her.

She was an enigma. A mystery he wanted to solve. She played the bad girl so well, yet he saw elements to her that showed her vulnerability, her kindness. Like the way she had taken over the kitchen so Sophia could rest. That showed sensitivity and kindness, didn't it? Or was he being the biggest sucker out to fall for it? Was it all an act? A charade? How could she be as bad as she made out? What was her motive to make him think she was out to seduce him? Was it because he wasn't taking her up on it? Did his refusal to succumb to the temptation she offered make her see him as even more of a challenge?

'It's not a formal dinner,' Julius said. 'If I had guests, then, yes, I would insist on you dressing appropriately. I'm sorry I didn't realise you haven't the suitable attire in which to do so but that will be rectified as soon as possible tomorrow.'

Her small, neat chin came up. 'Once you've coughed up that dictionary you've swallowed, maybe you'll have room for the dinner I've prepared. *Bon appetit.*'

He let out an exasperated breath. 'Look, if I've upset you I'm sorry. But things are a little crazy for me just now.'

Her eyes flashed with unbridled disdain. 'Why would I be upset by someone like you? I don't care about your opinion of me or my clothes. It means nothing to me. *You* mean nothing to me.'

Julius pulled out the chair to the left of his. 'Please join me for dinner.'

Her mouth took on a mutinous pout. 'Why? So you can train me like a pet monkey?' She put her hands on her hips, deepened her voice and did a surprisingly credible imitation of his British accent. 'Don't hold your knife like a dagger. That's the wrong fork. Don't cut your bread. Break it. No, don't call it a serviette, call it a napkin.'

Julius couldn't stop his mouth from twitching. She had definitely missed her calling. She could tread the boards as well as anyone. 'I promise not to criticise you.'

She narrowed her gaze in scepticism. 'Promise?'

He didn't know which Holly he preferred—the snarky challenger or the hot little seductress. Both, he realised with a jolt of surprise, were vastly entertaining. 'Promise.'

She made a little huffing noise. 'Fine.'

He seated her then came around to his own chair and took his place. He spread his napkin out across his lap and watched as Holly expertly served the vegetable dish with silver-service expertise. Then she served the herbed chicken galantine with the same level of competence. She sent him a look from beneath half-mast lashes that made him realise how much he had underestimated her. How much he had misjudged her. She might come across as a bad girl from the wrong side of the tracks but underneath that don't-mess-with-me attitude was a young woman with surprising dignity and class. And pride.

During the course of their meal he made desultory conversation: stuff about the weather, movies and the state of the economy but she didn't seem inclined to talk. The questions he asked her were greeted with monosyllabic responses. He tried using open-ended questions but she just shrugged in a bored manner and mumbled something noncommittal in reply. She didn't eat much, either. She just moved the food around her plate, only taking the occasional mouthful. Was she doing it to punish him? To make him regret his all-too-quick summation of her character and seeming lack of abilities? She was more than capable of holding her own in sophisticated company. Why had she let him believe otherwise? Or was she just contrary for the heck of it? Thumbing her nose up at anyone who judged her without getting to know her?

'Are you not feeling well?' Julius asked.

'I'm fine.'

He studied her for a beat or two. 'You're sweating.'

She gave him a haughty look. 'Ladies don't sweat. They perspire.'

He felt another smile tug at his mouth at the way she so expertly parodied his accent. 'Take off your cardigan if you're hot.'

Her eyes skittered away from his. 'I'm not hot.'

He watched as she made another attempt at her meal but every now and again she would shift in her seat or wriggle her neck and shoulders as if her clothing was making her itchy.

'Holly.'

'What?'

'Take it off. You're clearly uncomfortable.'

'I'm not.'

'Would you like me to adjust the air-conditioning?'

'I told you, I'm fine.'

He shook his head at her in disbelief. 'This afternoon you were parading around half-naked and now you're acting like a nun. What is it with you? Take it off, for God's sake, or I'll take it off for you.'

Her eyes were narrowed as thin as twin hairpins. 'You wouldn't dare.'

'Wouldn't I?'

She shot up from the table and spun around to leave but Julius was too quick and intercepted her. He caught her by the back of her cardigan but when she pulled away from him it peeled off her like sloughed skin.

His heart came to a scudding stop when he saw what was on her upper arms before her hands tried to cover it. The cardigan he was holding slipped out of his hand

and fell to the floor. His mouth went completely dry. His stomach dropped as if it had been booted from the top of a skyscraper.

'Did *I* do that?' His voice came out rusty, shocked. He was ashamed. Mortified.

'It's nothing. I can't even feel it.'

His stomach churned in disgust. 'I hurt you.'

'I bruise easily, that's all.'

Julius scraped a distracted hand through his hair. Dragged the same hand over his face. How could he have *done* this? How could he have been so...so *brutish* to mark her flesh? For what? To prove a point? What point was worth proving if a woman was hurt in the process? It was against everything he believed in. It was against everything that defined him as a man—as a civilised human being. Real men did not use violence. It was the lowest of the low to inflict physical hurt on another person, particularly a woman or a child. How could he have lost control of his emotions to such a point that he would do something like that? He had grabbed her on impulse. He had been so het up about her goading behaviour it had overridden all that was decent and respectful in him.

'Don't make excuses for me,' he said. 'I'm appalled I did that to you. I can only say I'm deeply, unreservedly sorry and assure you it will never, *ever* happen again.'

'Apology accepted.' Her chin came up again, her gaze as hard and brittle as shellac. 'Now, may I get on with serving the rest of the meal?'

Julius had never felt less like eating. His stomach was a roiling pit of anguish. Shame and self-loathing were curdling the contents like acid. He'd thought his father's scandal was bad. This was even worse. *He* was worse.

His behaviour was reprehensible. He had hurt Holly like a thug. 'I think I'll give dessert a miss. Thanks all the same.'

'Fine.' She made a move towards the table. 'I'll just clear these plates.'

'No. Let me,' he said, but stopped short of putting a hand on her arm to stop her. He curled his fingers into his palms. Put his hands stiffly by his sides. 'You see to Sophia. I'll clear away.'

Her eyebrows rose ever so slightly as if she found the thought of him doing anything remotely domestic in nature totally incongruous to her opinion of his personality and station. 'As you wish.'

Julius bent down, picked up her cardigan from the floor and handed it to her. 'I'm sorry.'

'So you said.'

'Do you believe me?' It was so terribly important she believed him. He could think of nothing more important. He couldn't bear it if she didn't believe him—if she didn't trust him. If she didn't feel safe with him. Sure, they could flirt and banter with each other, try to outwit each other with smart come-backs, but there was no way he could bear it if she didn't feel physically safe under his roof—under his protection.

She held his gaze for a long beat, searching his features as if peeling back the skin to the heart of the man he was inside.

'Yes,' she said at last. 'I do. You don't strike me as the sort of man to take his frustration out on a woman.'

'You have experience of those who do?'

Her eyes fell away from his to focus on his top shirt button. 'None I care to recall in any detail.'

Julius wanted to push her chin up so she had to meet

his gaze but he was wary of touching her. He *longed* to touch her. To *hold* her. To reassure her. To remove the stain of his careless fingerprints with a caress as soft as a feather. To press his mouth to her and kiss away those horrible marks; to make her feel secure and safe under his protection.

But instead he stood silently, woodenly, feeling strangely, achingly hollow as she turned and walked out of the room.

Holly had finished seeing to Sophia and tidying up the kitchen. Not that she'd had to do much, as Julius had loaded the dishwasher and washed up by hand the baking dish she'd cooked the chicken in. It surprised her he knew how to do such mundane stuff. He was from such a wealthy, privileged background. He'd had servants waiting on him all of his life. He wouldn't have had to lift a finger before some servant would have come running and seen to his needs and that of his siblings. And yet he had left the kitchen and the dining room absolutely spotless. The uneaten food was packaged away with cling film in the fridge. The benches had been wiped. The lights were turned down. The blinds were drawn.

Holly was too restless to go to bed. She thought about going for another swim but didn't want to encounter Julius. Well, that was only partly true. She could face him when he was stern and headmaster-ish but, when he got all caring and concerned and…*protective*, it did strange things to her insides. She had never had anyone to protect her. Not since her father had died. No one had ever stood up for her. Everyone was so quick to judge her. They never waited to get to know her, to try and understand the dynamics of her personality and what had formed it. Tragedy, abuse, maltreatment and neglect did not a happy person make. She knew she should try harder to be nicer to people. She knew she should learn to trust people because not everyone was an exploitative creep.

The news of his father's love child was clearly a terrible shock to Julius. Finding out he had a half-sister would have rocked him to the core. He hadn't wanted to discuss it, which she could understand, given his personality. He didn't like surprises. He liked time to think things over. She suspected he would eventually come round to wanting to meet his half-sister. He was too principled simply to pretend she didn't exist.

But the news of the existence of a love child certainly did raise the chance of the press hounding him. He was obviously worried Holly would exploit the situation—dish the dirt on him or make things look salacious between him and her. She might like to rattle his chain for a bit of fun but there was no way she would take her games into the public sphere. She didn't want her stepfather to know where she was. If she drew attention to herself by speaking to the press, who knew what would happen.

Holly wandered along the corridor past the library on her way to her room. The door was slightly ajar and the room was in darkness except for the moonlight shining through the waist-high window. One of the windows must have been mistakenly left open for she could see one of the sheer curtains fluttering on the light breeze coming from outside. She considered leaving it but then remembered Sophia was tucked up in bed upstairs. It would be a shame if it rained overnight and some of those precious books nearest the window were damaged.

Holly moved over to the window without bothering to turn on the light, as the moonlight was like a silver beam across the floor. She closed the window and straightened the breeze-ruffled curtain. She stood there for a long moment looking out at the moonlit gardens and fields beyond. It was such a beautiful property. So peaceful and isolated. There wasn't a neighbour for miles. No wonder Julius loved working and living here. She had spent most of her life in cramped flats in multi-storey buildings with the roar of traffic below and the sound of neighbours packed in on every side. But here it was so serene and peaceful she could hear frogs croaking and owls hooting. It was like listening to a night orchestra. The moonlight cast everything in an opalescent glow that gave the gardens a magical, storybook quality.

It was only when Holly turned around to leave that she saw the silent, seated figure behind the large mahogany leather-topped desk. 'Oh, sorry,' she said, somehow managing to smother her startled gasp. 'I didn't see you there. The light wasn't on so I thought someone must've left the window open. It looks like we could get a storm so I thought I'd better shut it since Sophia's gone to bed.' *Shut up. You're gabbling.*

Julius's leather chair creaked in protest as he rose from behind the desk. 'I'm sorry for giving you a fright.'

'You didn't,' Holly said then, seeing the wry lift of one of his eyebrows added, 'well, maybe a little. Why didn't you say something? Why are you sitting here in the dark?'

'I was thinking.'

'About your family…um…situation?'

'I was thinking about you, actually.'

Her heart gave a stumble. 'Me?' His eyes went to her arms. 'Oh. Well, you said sorry, so it's all good.'

His frowning gaze meshed with hers. 'How can you be so casual about something so serious? I hurt you, Holly. I physically hurt you.'

'You didn't mean to,' Holly said. 'Anyway, it was probably my fault for stirring you up.'

'That's no excuse,' he said. 'It shouldn't matter how much provocation a man receives. No man should ever use physical force. I can never forgive myself for that. I'm disgusted with myself. Truly disgusted.'

Holly rolled her lips together for a moment. 'I've not been the easiest house guest.'

A host of emotions flickered over his face. Emotions she suspected he wasn't used to feeling. It was there in the dark blue of his eyes. It was in the thinned-out line of his sculptured mouth. 'You don't have to be anything but yourself,' he said in a husky tone. 'You're fine just the way you are.'

No one had ever accepted her for who she was. Why would they? She wasn't the sort of person people found acceptable. If it wasn't her background, then it was her behaviour. She rubbed people up the wrong way. How could he say she was fine the way she was? *She* wasn't fine with the way she was.

'So, how are things with your family?' Holly said to fill the heavy silence.

He turned away as he pushed a hand through his hair. 'I haven't been able to contact my sister. The legitimate one, I mean.'

'You're worried about her?'

'A little.'

Holly couldn't help feeling a little envious of Miranda Ravensdale. How wonderful to have a big brother to watch out for you. Two, in fact. Not that she knew if Julius's twin brother, Jake, had the same protective qualities as Julius. She got the impression Jake was a bit of a lad about town.

'Maybe her phone is flat, or she's turned it off or something,' she said.

'Maybe.'

Another silence ticked past.

'Oh, well, then,' Holly said, making a step towards the door. 'I'd better let you get on with it.'

'Holly.'

She turned and looked at him. 'Would you like me to get you a coffee? A night cap or something? Since Sophia's off-duty you'll have to put up with me doing the housekeeper stuff.'

His dark eyes moved over her face, centred on her mouth and then came back to her gaze. 'Only if you'll have one with me.'

Holly chewed the inside of her mouth. She didn't trust herself around him. He was dangerous in this gentle and reflective mood. Keeping her game face on was easy when he was being sarcastic and cynical towards her. But this was different. 'It's a bit late at night for me to drink coffee, and since I don't drink alcohol I'd be pretty boring company...'

His mouth twisted ruefully. 'I suppose I deserve that brush off, don't I?'

'I'm not brushing you off. If I were brushing you off then you'd know about it, let me tell you,' she said.

'I'm not the sort of person to hand out a parachute for anyone's ego.'

He gave a soft laugh, the low, deep sound doing something odd and ticklish to the base of Holly's spine. 'That I can believe.'

There was another beat of silence.

'What would you do if you found out you had a half-sibling?' he asked.

Holly shifted her lips from side to side as she thought about it. 'I would definitely want to meet him or her. I've always wanted a sister or brother. It would've come in handy to have someone to stick up for me.'

He studied her for a long moment. The low light didn't take anything away from his handsome features. If anything, it highlighted them. The aristocratic landscape of his face reminded her of a hero out of a nineteenth-century novel. Dark and brooding; aloof and unknowable.

'Things were pretty tough for you as a kid, weren't they?'

Holly moved her gaze out of reach of his. 'I don't like talking about it.'

'Talking sometimes helps people to understand you a little better.'

'Yeah, well, if people don't like me at "hello" then how is telling them all about my messed-up childhood going to change their opinion?'

'Perhaps if you worked on your first impressions you might win a few friends on your side.'

Holly thought of how she'd stomped into his office that morning—had it really only been a day?—with her verbal artillery blazing. She'd put him on the back foot at the outset. But she'd been angry and churned up over everything. Her forthrightness had been automatic. She liked to get in first before people took advantage. 'I could've come in and been polite as anything but you'd already made up your mind about me. You'd heard about my criminal behaviour. Nothing I could've said or done would've changed your opinion.'

Julius took a step that brought him close to where she was standing. Holly held her breath as he sent a fingertip down the length of her arm, from the top of her shoulder to her wrist. The nerves fluttered like moths beneath her skin. Her heart skipped a beat. Her stomach tilted. 'Are you sure I didn't hurt you?' His voice was low, a deep burr of sound that made the base of her spine fizz.

'I'm sure.'

He sent the same fingertip down the curve of her cheek, outlining her face from just behind her ear to the base of her chin. 'I think underneath that brash exterior is a very frightened little girl.'

Holly quickly disguised a knotty swallow. 'Keep your day job, Julius. You'd make a rubbish therapist.'

His eyes held hers for another long moment. 'I'll see to the rest of the windows,' he said. 'You go on up to bed. Sleep well.'

Like that's going to happen, Holly thought as she turned and slipped out of the room.

Holly didn't see Julius for over a week. He hadn't informed her he was leaving at all. She heard it from Sophia, who told her he was working on some important software and had to attend meetings in Buenos Aires, as well as flying to Santiago in Chile. It annoyed Holly he hadn't bothered to tell her what his schedule was. He could have done so that night in the library, especially as she'd heard him leave the very next morning. But then, she reminded herself, she was just a temporary hindrance for him. The more time away from the villa—*away from her*—the better. The bruises on her arms had faded but the bruise to her ego had not. Why couldn't he have talked to her in person? Told her his plans?

The fact was, it was dead boring without him. Sophia was kind and sweet and did her best to make sure Holly had plenty to do without exploiting her. But spending hours with a middle-aged woman who reminded her too much of the mother she no longer had was not Holly's idea of fun. The more time she spent with the gentle and kind housekeeper, the more she ached for what she had lost. Sophia had a tendency to mother her, to treat her like a surrogate daughter. Holly appreciated the gesture on one level but on another it made her feel unutterably sad.

Which was all the more reason she missed the verbal sparring she'd done with Julius. She missed his tall figure striding down the corridors with a dark frown on his handsome face. She missed the sound of his cultured accent in that mellifluous baritone that did such strange things to her spine. She missed the excitement in her body, the buzzing, thrilling sensation of female desire he triggered every time he looked at her. Her body felt flat and listless without him around to charge it up with energy.

The days dragged with an interminable slowness that made Holly's restlessness close to unbearable. Although she enjoyed the tasks Sophia set her, as the villa was beautiful and full of exquisite works of art and priceless collector's pieces, it just wasn't the same without

Julius there. The nights were even worse. Sophia usually went to bed early, which meant there was no one to talk to. The rest of the villa staff—the gardener and the man who looked after the horses on the property—lived in accommodation separate from the villa. There was only so much television Holly could watch and, even though she enjoyed reading, the evenings were particularly tiresome.

The one thing Julius had done for her since he'd gone away, however, was have some clothes delivered to the villa for her. They were mostly smart-casual separates, as well as a couple of dresses, including a long, slinky formal one made of navy blue silk. There were shoes and underwear the likes of which she had never seen before: cobweb-fine lace, some with fancy little bows and embroidered rosebuds or daisies. There were bathing suits as well, a one-piece black one and a fuchsia-pink bikini.

Make-up and perfume arrived in neat little packages. A hairdresser arrived at the villa and worked on Holly's hair until she barely recognised herself in the mirror. Gone were the pink streaks and split ends. Her wild curls were toned, tamed and cut in a shoulder-length style that could be worn up or down, depending on her mood or the occasion.

But for all the finery Holly felt dissatisfied. What was the point of all these gorgeous clothes if she had no one to see her in them? She didn't even have anywhere to go because she wasn't allowed to leave the premises unless Julius accompanied her as her official guardian. It was part of the diversionary programme's fine print.

Late on Sunday, well after Sophia had retired for the night, Holly turned off the show she had been only half-watching on television and made her way to her room. But on the way past Julius's suite she stopped. She had been in a couple of days ago with Sophia to do a light clean. His suite had a balcony but the doors had been closed and Holly had kept her back to it. She had worked briskly and efficiently with the minimum of talk, desperate to stave off a panic attack if Sophia asked her to dust or sweep out there. If Sophia had sensed anything was amiss, she hadn't said, although Holly suspected there was not much that would escape the housekeeper's attention.

Before Holly could change her mind she turned the handle on the door of the suite and stepped inside. The balcony doors were closed and locked, the gauzy curtains pulled across the windows. Even though the room had been empty for days, Holly could still smell the lemon and lime notes of Julius's aftershave. She turned on one of the bedside lamps rather than the top light in case Sophia saw the spill of light from her room on the top floor.

The forbidden nature of what Holly was doing made a frisson of excitement shiver over her flesh. This was where Julius slept. This was where Julius made love with his occasional lovers. The lovers Sophia stalwartly, stubbornly, refused to comment on or reveal any information about. Holly had looked on the internet on the library's computer for any press items on him but there was virtually nothing about his private life. There was stuff about Julius's work in astrophysics and about his software company that had come about after he had designed a special computer programme used on the space telescopes in the Atacama Desert and which had turned him into a multi-millionaire overnight.

There was plenty of stuff about his father's love-child scandal. Every newsfeed was running with it. There was also plenty of information on Julius's twin, Jake. Jake was the epitome of the 'love them and leave them' playboy: the 'Prince of Pickups' as one article described him. It was uncanny seeing the likeness to Julius. They were mirror images of each other. She wondered if she met them together if she would be able to tell them apart. The only slight difference she could see was in every photo Jake was smiling as if that was his default position. Julius, on the other hand, was not one to smile so readily. He was serious in demeanour and nature. He was conservative where, from what some of the photos suggested, his twin was a boundary-pusher—a born risk-taker.

Holly wandered about Julius's suite, stopping to check out a photo of his younger sister on his dressing table. Miranda was pretty in a pixyish, girl-next-door sort of way. She was petite with porcelain-white skin and auburn hair. Nothing like her extraordinarily beautiful mother, Elisabetta Albertini, Holly duly noted. She put the photo down and stepped over to the walk-in wardrobe, hesitating for a nanosecond before she slid the door back and walked inside.

All of his shirts, suits and jackets were in neat rows. His sweaters were folded in symmetrical colour-coordinated stacks. His shoes were all polished and paired and perfectly aligned on the tiered shoe rack.

She picked a pair of cufflinks up from the waist-high shelf above a bank of drawers. The cufflinks were a designer brand with diamonds in the shape of a J. She wondered if he had bought them for himself or whether they had been a gift from a member of his family. Miranda, perhaps? The photo of her in his room suggested he adored her. It was the only photo she had seen of any of his family in the villa.

The sound of a footfall in the bedroom startled Holly so much she felt her flesh shrink away from her skeleton. She slipped into the shadows of Julius's suits, using them as a shield to hide behind. Her heart hammered. Her breath halted. She couldn't allow Julius to find her in here. But how on earth was she going to get out? Why hadn't he told her and Sophia he was coming home tonight? Why turn up unannounced? What if he went to bed while she was stuck here, hiding in his wardrobe? She would have to hope and pray he'd go to the en suite and have a shower or something so she could sneak out without being detected. Hopefully the fact his bedside lamp was on wouldn't make him suspicious. He might think Sophia had left it on in anticipation of him coming home…or something.

The thoughts were a tumbling mess inside her head. Round and round they went until she felt dizzy. Her skin was breaking out in a sweat. She could feel beads of it rolling down between her breasts, under her arms, across her top lip.

'Holly?' Sophia's voice called out. 'Is that you?'

The relief Holly felt was so great it was as if her legs were going to fold beneath her as the tension washed out of her. Even her arms felt boneless, her shoulders dropping as if had just been relieved of carrying a tremendous weight. She took a steadying breath and walked out of the wardrobe with what she hoped was a calm, collected and innocent look on her face. 'Sorry,' she said. 'Did I give you a scare?'

Sophia was frowning. 'What were you doing in Señor Ravensdale's wardrobe?'

'I was just…checking to see if I'd put his shirts I ironed the other day in the right place,' Holly said, mentally marvelling at her ability to construct a credible excuse at such short notice. 'You know how fussy he is. I didn't want him to come home and get antsy about the blue shirts mixed up with the white ones. Oh, and I straightened his ties. One was hanging half a millimetre lower than the others.'

Sophia's frown lessened slightly but didn't completely disappear. 'You don't have to work at this time of night. You're entitled to time off.'

'I know, but I was bored, so I thought I'd double-check stuff.'

'You've worked hard this week,' Sophia said. 'Much harder than I thought you would.'

'Yeah, well, I'm not afraid of hard work,' Holly said. 'So, why are you up? I thought you were in bed.'

'My wrist is giving me a bit of pain,' Sophia said, wincing as she cradled her arm against her body. 'I was coming past to go downstairs to make a hot drink when I heard a sound.'

'Weren't you worried it might be a burglar?'

'No, I knew it was you.'

'How?'

'I could smell your perfume,' Sophia said. 'The one Señor Ravensdale bought for you. It was a good choice. It suits you.'

Holly gave the housekeeper a quick stretch of her lips as a smile. 'That man has serious class. Does he always buy women such expensive gifts?'

Sophia gave her the sort of reproachful look a parent would give to a persistently naughty child. 'Come and make me a hot chocolate,' she said. 'Then it's time, young lady, for bed.'

'When is Julius coming home?' Holly asked as they walked down to the kitchen together. 'Have you heard from him?'

'He sent a text a couple of hours ago,' Sophia said. 'His plane was delayed in Santiago.'

'Maybe he's catching up with a lady friend.'

Sophia pursed her lips without responding.

'Why do you call him "Señor" instead of Julius?' Holly asked.

'He's my employer.'

'I know but you and he seem to be pretty chummy,' Holly said. 'How long have you worked for him?'

'Since he moved to Argentina eight years ago.'

'So you would've seen quite a few girlfriends come and go in his life, huh?'

Sophia cast her a glance. 'Why are you so interested in his private life? Do you have designs on him?'

Holly coughed out a laugh. 'Me? Interested in him? Are you joking? He's the last person I would fall for. The very last.'

Sophia released a soft sigh. 'That's probably a good thing.'

'Because I'm too far below his station?'

Sophia shook her head. 'No. He wouldn't let something like that be an issue. I think he wouldn't fall in love too easily, that's all.'

'Like we have a choice in these things,' Holly said, then quickly added, 'not that I'm speaking from experience or anything.'

'So you haven't lost your heart to anyone yet?' Sophia asked with another sideways glance.

The word *yet* seemed to hang in the air. It was like a gauntlet being thrown down. Fate issuing a challenge. A dare.

Holly laughed again. 'Not yet.' *Not ever. Not going to happen.*

Not in a million years.

CHAPTER EIGHT

JULIUS HADN'T PLANNED to drive home so late but his flight back to Buenos Aires from Santiago had been delayed several hours due to a storm. A solid week of work, long hours of meetings and field research had done little to quell the errant feelings he had for Holly. Feelings he hadn't expected to feel. Didn't want to feel. She occupied his thoughts whenever his mind drifted away from work. She filled his brain. She filled his body with forbidden desires and wicked urges. She filled his every waking moment—and even his dreams—with visions of her lithe body, her pert breasts, her cheeky smile and the way she upped her chin in a challenge or twinkled her brown eyes in a dare.

He could not remember a time when he had been more obsessed with a woman. She was as far from an ideal partner as any he could imagine. Her wilfulness, her defiance and her rebellious nature made everything that was rational, logical and intellectual inside him shrink away in abject horror. But everything that was male and primal in him wanted to possess her. He ached and pulsed to feel her body, to be surrounded by her. Every hormone in his body twanged with longing. Every nerve-ending craved the stroke or glide of her touch. He had X-rated dreams about her pouty little mouth on him, drawing on him, pleasuring…

Julius was disgusted with himself. Not just because of his uncontrollable desire for her but because he still couldn't forgive himself for the way he had hurt her. What had he been thinking, hauling her bodily from the pool like that? There was *no* excuse. So what if she had goaded him? So what if she had defied him? Disobeyed him? He was an adult. He was a civilised, educated man. What had he hoped his action would achieve?

Or had he secretly—*unconsciously*—wanted to touch her? To hold her sexy, wet body against the throbbing heat of his…

He had wanted to kiss her so badly it had tortured him not to. Her mouth had been so close he'd felt the breeze of her sweet breath. It had taken every ounce of self-control he possessed and then some to drop his hold on her and step back. He could still feel the silk of her skin against his fingers. He could still feel the magnetic force of her body drawing his closer. It was stronger, way more powerful than anything he had ever felt before. How he had not slammed his mouth down on hers and thrust his tongue through her lush lips still surprised him.

He had been so close.

So terrifyingly, shamefully close.

Work had legitimately called him away, thankfully. He hadn't trusted himself to be around her. He still didn't trust himself, which was even more worrying.

But it wasn't just the physical attraction that was so troubling to him. There were other feelings he was experiencing that were far more dangerous. Tiny sprouts of affection were popping up inside him. He actually *liked* her. He admired her spirit. Her edginess. Her blatant disregard for the rules. For propriety. He found himself missing her teasing playfulness. He missed her dimpled smile and the way her eyes danced with mischief.

He had no business missing her. He wasn't supposed to get attached to her. She wasn't his type. And he clearly wasn't hers. She only wanted to sleep with him to prove a point. It was nothing but a game to her.

He was nothing but a game to her.

Another bonus of being called away to work was that the press had stayed away from his villa. He had been intercepted at the airport and issued his usual 'no comment' response to the media. The last thing he wanted was the press sniffing around his home and finding a young woman in residence, especially as he didn't trust Holly to behave herself. He'd left strict instructions with Sophia on monitoring Holly's movements and making sure she didn't speak to anyone if they should turn up at the villa. No one had, which gave him some measure of comfort, but how long before someone did?

Julius parked in the garage and walked into the villa as quietly as he could so as not to disturb anyone. It was two in the morning so he hoped his little house guest was tucked away safely in bed.

She wasn't.

Holly came out of the kitchen as he came in the back door. She was wearing one of the outfits he'd bought her. The cashmere separates looked far slinkier on her than it had in the online catalogue. But then she would make a bin liner look like a designer gown, he thought. The fabric draped her slim curves like the skin of an evening glove.

'How was your trip?' she asked.

Julius wasn't in the mood for trite conversation. Not with her looking good enough to eat and swallow whole. How did she manage to stir him up so easily? 'Tiring.'

She moved towards him with catlike grace. 'Fancy a snack?'

'What's on the menu?' *Bad choice of words.*

Her eyes glinted. 'What do you fancy?'

He tried not to look at her mouth but a force far more powerful than his resolve pulled his gaze to its lush ripeness. 'What's on offer?' What was it with him and the double entendres? He was acting like Jake, for God's sake.

'Whatever you want,' she said. 'Your wish is my command.'

'I thought you didn't take too kindly to commands?'

She tiptoed her fingers along the corded muscles of his arm. 'Maybe I'll make an exception tonight.'

He suppressed a shiver as her fingers lit every nerve under his skin with red-hot fire. Need pulsed in his groin. Lust growled, roared. 'Why?'

'Because I've missed you.'

Julius barked out a laugh and gently pushed her arm away as he moved past. 'Go to bed.'

'Why didn't you tell me you were going away?'

He turned back to look at her. 'You're answerable to me. Not me to you. Or has that somehow slipped your attention?'

Her caramel-brown eyes ran over him like a lick of flame. 'Were you with a lover?'

He gritted his teeth until his jaw ground together like two tectonic plates. 'No. I was working. Remember that word you seem to have so much difficulty with?'

She leaned one shoulder against the door jamb. 'I've been working. Go ask Sophia.'

'I will, but not at this time in the morning.'

Her eyes did another scan of his body, her chin coming to rest at a haughty height. 'I even cleaned your room.'

Julius didn't like the thought of her in his room. Actually, he liked the thought way too much. His mind filled with images of her laid out on his bed, her gorgeous, luscious body as hungry for him as he was for her. His flesh crawled with lust. It was like a fever in his blood. Raging. Taking him. Taking over his control like a shot of a powerful drug. 'I'd prefer it if you'd stay out of there.'

'Why?' she said. 'You let Sophia change your bed. Why shouldn't I?'

Because I want you in it, not changing it, he thought with a savage wave of self-disgust. 'I trust you left everything as you found it?' he said.

Her brows drew together. 'What's that supposed to mean?'

'I seem to recall your rap sheet includes theft.'

'So?'

'So I want you to keep your hands clean.'

Her top lip curved up on one side. 'Don't worry,' she said. 'You have nothing I want.'

'Only my body.'

A dark, triumphant glint shone in her gaze. 'Not as much as you want mine.'

'You think?'

'I know.'

Julius wanted to prove he could resist her. He *needed* to prove it, if not to her then to himself. He reached for her, encircling her wrists with his fingers. Holding her. Securing her. Her eyes widened but not in fear. He could read her signals as easily as she read his. Mutual desire ran between them like the shock of an electric current. He could feel it through her flesh where it was in contact with his. He looked at her mouth and watched as she ran the tip of her tongue over her lips, leaving a glistening sheen.

Her eyelashes came down over her eyes, her breath dancing over his lips as she rose on tiptoe. He felt the brush of her body against his just before her mouth touched his. He didn't move. Didn't respond. Willed himself not to respond. Her tongue licked his top lip and then his lower one. The tantalising friction set his nerves screaming for more but still he stayed statue-still.

She came at him again, her tongue sweeping over his lower lip in a drugging caress that made his groin tighten to the point of pain. The need to taste her, to take control of the kiss, was like an unstoppable tide. He let out a muttered swear word as he splayed his hands through her hair and covered her mouth with his.

Her lips were soft and full, her mouth tasting of chocolate, milk and temptation. He drove his tongue through her parted lips, plundering her mouth, seeking her tongue to tangle with it in a duel that made the blood pump all the harder in his veins. She made a sexy little sound of approval as he pulled her closer to his body, letting her feel his hardness, the need he couldn't hide even if he'd wanted to.

Julius succoured on her mouth as if it was his only source of sustenance. She was a drug he hadn't known he had a taste for until now. He was lethally addicted to her. His body craved hers. Ached for hers. He pulled at her lower lip with his teeth, taking little nips and bites before using his tongue to salve where he had been. She responded with her own little series of playful bites, not just on his mouth, but also on his neck, and his earlobes, sucking on them until he thought he was going to disgrace himself. He shivered as her tongue came back to play with his, in and outside of their mouths in little flicks and thrusts of lust.

He took charge again by backing her up against the wall, his hands shaping her curves as his mouth crushed hers. She made a little whimpering sound as one of his hands cupped her breast. She moved against him, a gesture of encouragement he was in no state to resist. He shoved aside her top and bra to access her naked flesh. He brought his mouth down to suckle on her erect nipple before he swirled his tongue around her areole. He kissed his way over her breast, lingering on the underside when he heard her gasp as if he had found a particularly sensitive erogenous zone.

The skin there was as soft and smooth as silk. He trailed his tongue like a rasp along that scented curve, his senses in overload as he thought of how much he wanted to possess her. It was a driving force in his body. A primal urge he had no hope of controlling. His desire was a wild, primitive beast that had broken free of its chains and was now on the rampage.

Julius uncovered her other breast and subjected it to the same sensual assault, breathing in the fragrance of her body—a mixture of the flowery perfume he had bought her and her own bewitching female scent. The scent that was filling his nostrils, making him crazy, making him want her more than he had wanted anyone.

He left her breasts to come back to her mouth, driving his tongue through the seam of her lips, as he wanted to drive through the seam of her body. She gave a breathless whimper and reached between their hard-pressed bodies to uncover him. Her hands were on his belt buckle and then his zip, but he didn't do anything to stop her. It was too intoxicating to feel those wicked little hands moving over him, releasing him, stroking him, pleasuring him.

He smothered a rough curse as her thumb caressed the sensitive head of his erection while her mouth played with his. He had never had a more exciting encounter. He wanted to feel her mouth on him, to have her submit to his wildest fantasies.

And, as if she was acting a role scripted right from his imagination, she sank to her knees in front of him, cupping him, breathing over him with her dancing breath, her moist tongue poised.

He put a hand on the top of her head and pulled back. 'No,' he said. 'You don't have to do that.'

She looked up at him questioningly. 'But I thought all guys…?'

'It's not safe without a condom,' Julius said.

She got to her feet, pushing a strand of her hair back behind one of her ears as she did so. 'That's a first.'

He frowned as he thought of all the men who had been with her. How many? Did it matter? Who was he to judge? He'd had his share of sexual encounters. Not as many as his brother, but enough to forget times, places and, yes, even some names.

But there would be no forgetting Holly Perez, he thought. The taste of her was still fizzing on his tongue.

The feel of her was still tingling in his fingertips. His need of her was still firing in his blood.

'Holly.'

She rounded on him with a combative look. 'So who won that round, do you think? I kissed you but you took it to another level.'

Julius blew out a jagged breath. 'That should never have happened.'

Her chin inched up, her eyes flashing at him. 'You want me but you hate yourself for it, don't you?'

'I don't want to complicate my life, or indeed yours.'

'That wasn't the message I was getting a few minutes ago when you had your mouth on my breast—'

'Will you stop it, for God's sake?' Julius said. 'This is not going to happen, okay?'

Her brown eyes shone with a victorious gleam. 'It already did,' she said, moving up so close he could feel her breasts against his chest. 'You're not going to get that wild animal back in its cage any time soon, are you, Julius?'

He looked down at the tempting curve of her sinful mouth. The mouth he had savaged, pillaged and supped on like a starving man. The luscious and deliciously ripe mouth that had offered to pleasure him. *God strike him down for wanting her to.* He put his hands on her hips to gently push her back from him but then his right hand felt a cube-shaped ridge against her hip. 'What's that in your pocket?'

Her expression faltered for a moment before she tried to move away. 'What? Oh…nothing.'

Julius held her steady, his hands anchoring her so she had to face him. 'Empty your pockets.'

Her eyes flickered with something that looked suspiciously like panic. 'Why?'

'Because I asked you to.'

'Just because you asked me doesn't mean I'll—'

Julius held her left hip with one hand while he dug in her right pocket with the other. He pulled out the cufflinks Miranda had bought him for his last birthday, holding them right in front of Holly's defiant face. 'Want to tell me how they got in there?'

Her teeth sank into her bottom lip. Her eyes skittered away from his. 'I—I can explain…'

He dropped his hands from her as if she was burning him. Which she was. Burning him. Exploiting him. *Stealing* from him while his back was turned. How could he have thought she might not be as bad as she acted? How could he have been so stupid as to feel *affection* for her? What an idiot he was. How could he have let her fool him into believing she was worthy of a second chance? She wasn't just deceitful—she was dangerous. He was nuts to have let her get under his guard. She was a liar and a thief and he'd been too damn close to getting caught in her sugar-coated web.

'I want you out of here by morning,' he said. 'I don't want to hear your explanation. There isn't an explanation you could give that would satisfy me.'

'I was in your walk-in wardrobe earlier tonight.'

'Doing what?'

'Straightening your ties.'

Julius laughed. 'What? You can't do better than that?'

Her chin came up to a pugnacious height. 'I got caught off-guard when Sophia came in unexpectedly. I panicked. I hid in your wardrobe as I thought it was you. I didn't realise I'd put the cufflinks into my pocket until just now. I honestly don't remember doing it. It must've been an impulse or…or something…'

He rolled his eyes. 'Do you really think I'm *that* stupid?'

She bit her lower lip again. 'I know it looks bad…'

'Why were you in my room?'

She shrugged one of her shoulders. 'I was having a look around.'

'For what?' he said. 'Loose change?'

She gave him a gimlet glare. 'I know you think I'm nothing but a petty thief but I didn't take them on purpose. It was an…an accident.'

Julius gave another cynical laugh. 'Yes, Officer,' he said in a parody of her voice. 'I was just walking past Mr Ravensdale's wardrobe and the diamond cufflinks fell into my pocket *by accident*.'

Holly set her mouth. 'I don't care what you think. I know I didn't steal them and that's all that matters.'

'Actually,' Julius said. 'It's not all that matters. Your caseworker will ask me when she calls in the morning and I'll have to tell her you've been stealing.'

Her eyes blazed as they met his. 'Tell her. See if I care.'

She did care. Julius was sure of it. He came to stand in front of her, close enough to feel the heat of her body emanating towards his. He picked up a handful of her hair close to her scalp, making her feel each strand pulling as he brought her mouth close to his. He let his breath mingle with hers, teasing her with the promise of what was to come. 'Here's where your little game backfires, *querida*,' he said. 'You want me just as much as I want you. You weren't expecting that, were you? You thought this would be a one-sided game but it's not.'

Her body brushed against his, by intention or chance he couldn't quite tell. But he saw the reaction on her face—the flicker of want that flashed across her features. The way her pupils dilated, the way her tongue sneaked out to moisten her lips. 'Get your hands off me,' she said.

'When I'm good and ready.' He brought his mouth even closer, breathing in the scent of her, bumping noses with her, nudging her with his chin, rasping his tongue along the seam of her mouth. Teasing her the way she had teased him. He heard her sharp intake of breath as his tongue stroked harder, more insistently. He could feel the struggle in her. The will she had to resist him was faltering just as his had faltered in him. She leaned towards him, her mouth open, her hands on his chest, not flat in the effort of pushing him away, but her fingers curling into the front of his shirt as if she never wanted to let him go.

He allowed himself one touchdown on her mouth. But one wasn't enough. How could he have thought it would ever be enough? Her mouth flowered open even further beneath the light pressure of his until he was suddenly swept up in a passionate exchange that had his blood thundering all over again.

Her tongue entwined with his, her arms looped around his neck, drawing him closer. His hands went to her neat behind, holding her against his throbbing heat. Her breasts were pushed against his chest so hard he could feel her pert nipples through the layers of their clothes.

Her hand reached between their bodies and stroked the hardened length of him, inciting his lust to fever pitch. He did the same to her, outlining her feminine form with the stroke of his fingers until she was breathing as hard as him. He took it one step further, driven by an urge he couldn't control. He tugged her trousers down past her hips so he could access her naked skin. He slipped one finger inside her, his control almost blowing when he felt how hot and wet and tight she was. She gasped and moved against his hand in a plea that needed no language other than the one their bodies were speaking. He stroked the bud of her core with the pad of his thumb, feeling it swell and peak under the pressure of his touch.

She suddenly gripped his shoulders and arched up as she convulsed. Violently. Repeatedly. He felt every contraction of her orgasm. Watched as the pleasure rose in a tidal glow over her face.

He kissed her mouth. Hard. Passionately. Swallowing the last of her breathless gasps as the aftermath of release flowed through her.

But then she slipped out of his hold, not quite able to hold his gaze. Her hands pulled up her trousers and fixed her gaping shirt before going across her body in a defensive, keep-away-from-me pose.

'Holly…'

She gave him a tight smile that didn't reach her eyes. 'What's the protocol here? Should I say thanks? Or offer to do you in return?'

He let out a long breath. 'That won't be necessary.'

'Well, thanks anyway,' she said. 'I didn't know I had it in me to get off like that. That's quite some technique you've got there.'

Julius scraped a hand through his hair. 'I shouldn't have taken things that far.'

'*No problemo,*' she said. 'I enjoyed it, as you could probably tell. Which is another first.'

He frowned. 'What do you mean?'

'I've never had an orgasm with a guy before.'

'Never?'

'No, but don't tell any of my ex-partners that,' she said. 'You know how fragile the male ego is.'

'How many partners have you had?'

'Four. Five, if you count yourself,' she said. 'But does that count, since you didn't actually put your...?'

'No,' Julius said. 'It doesn't.'

She shifted her lips from side to side. 'So, are we done here?'

He moved far enough away from her so he wouldn't be tempted to touch her. 'I'll see you in the morning. Goodnight.'

'You mean you're not sending me on my way to prison after all?'

Julius clenched his jaw. 'I'm giving you one more chance.' He hoped he wouldn't regret it.

She walked to the door to leave but at the last moment turned and looked at him. 'If I'd wanted to pinch your cufflinks, do you think I'd be carrying them around in my pocket?'

'Maybe you haven't had time to hide them in your room.'

Her eyes held his without shame. Without flinching. 'I had time to do lots of things. I could've called the press, for instance. I could've given them an exclusive.'

'Why didn't you?'

She gave one of her cute little lip-shrugs. 'I don't like it when people say stuff about me that isn't true, so why would I do that to someone else?'

Julius had measured the risks when he'd left to go away for work. But he'd figured Sophia would keep things in check. His housekeeper guarded his privacy almost more zealously than he did himself. But it was true Holly could have made things difficult for him. She could have made herself a small fortune. All it would have taken was a phone call. Why hadn't she? It wouldn't even have broken her probation conditions. Had he misjudged her? Or was this a clever ploy of hers, to get him to trust her before she went for broke? 'Thank you for acting so…honourably,' he said.

Her features took on a cynical cast. 'Haven't you heard there's honour amongst thieves?'

'But you keep insisting you're not a thief.'

'I'm not.'

Julius wanted to believe her. He wasn't sure why. Maybe to reassure himself he wasn't harbouring a criminal under his roof. Maybe so he could justify his growing affection for her. Something about the way she held herself, the stubborn pride he could see glittering in her gaze as it held his, made him wonder if he wasn't the only one to have misjudged her. He knew enough about the legal system to know the courts did not always serve justice. Attack-dog lawyers could swing a case. Evidence could be planted. Reputations ruined by innuendo. Holly had no money, no way of defending herself against a powerful lawyer. She had already hinted about the bleakness of her background. What chance would someone like her have against a system that favoured those with unlimited money and power at their disposal?

'It's late,' he said. 'You should've been in bed hours ago.'

'By the way, thanks for the clothes and make-up and stuff.'

'You're welcome,' he said. 'Your hair looks nice, by the way.'

'Much more acceptable, huh?'

'It was fine the way it was, but I thought—'

'It's fine, Julius,' she said with another stiff smile. 'Do you airbrush all of your girlfriends?'

'You are not my girlfriend. And, no, I do not.'

There was an odd little silence.

Julius watched as she sank her teeth into her lower lip as if she had suddenly found herself out of her depth. Had he offended her by organising a hairdresser? Sophia had suggested it, but now that he thought about it, maybe it had sent the wrong message. Had the clothes also been too much? Had he made her feel she wasn't acceptable without fine feathers? He thought he'd been helping her. She'd been bathing in her underwear. Surely it was the decent thing to do, to buy her appropriate clothing? The make-up and perfume... Well, didn't all girls enjoy that sort of stuff? She had come with so little luggage. Just a beaten-up backpack that hardly looked big enough to carry anything. Surely it hadn't been wrong to give her a few things to make her feel better about herself...or was he trying to make himself feel better about those fingerprints on her arms?

His gut clenched sickeningly as he thought of how easily she could have exploited him. All it would have taken was a photo of those bruises and a call to a nosy journalist and his reputation would have been shot. She'd had the perfect opportunity to get back at him, yet she hadn't. The week had passed without incident. Sophia had informed him Holly had been a perfect house guest, going out of her way to be helpful.

A good girl...

Not a moment's trouble...

'If you say you didn't intend to steal the cufflinks, then I believe you.' It was only once Julius said the words that he believed they were true. Her explanation was perfectly reasonable. She could have been startled and slipped them into her pocket without realising. How many times had he done the same with his keys when something or someone distracted him?

Or was he looking for a way to keep her with him?

It was a shock to think his motives were perhaps not as altruistic as they ought to be. The energy he felt with Holly, the electric buzz of sensation and thrill of her, overrode everything that was logical and responsible in him.

Her eyes widened momentarily before narrowing. 'Why?'

'I just do.'

She dropped her gaze from his. 'Thank you.' Her voice was just a thread of sound. Then she seemed to gather herself and brought her eyes back to his for a brief moment. 'Well, goodnight, then,' she said and left him with just the lingering scent of her fragrance to haunt his senses.

CHAPTER NINE

HOLLY CLOSED THE door to her bedroom and leaned back against it as she let out a long, shuddering breath. Julius *believed* her. He actually believed she hadn't tried to steal those wretched cufflinks. She hadn't registered she'd put them there, or at least not consciously. It had been a knee-jerk reaction to being discovered in his room. She must have slipped them into her pocket when she'd first heard Sophia and forgotten about them.

But Julius said he believed her.

How could he? She would never have believed him if the tables had been turned. But then, she was cynical. She didn't trust anyone. She was always on guard, always watching out for someone to take advantage, to rip her off or exploit her.

Was Julius different? Was he the sort of person to suspend judgement until reliable evidence came in?

Holly wondered if she had done herself a disservice by antagonising him so much. He might turn out to be the best ally she had ever had. But from the moment she had met him she had put him off-side. Winding him up, needling him, making him believe things about her that weren't true.

Was it too late to turn things around? Could she even

bother? She would only be here another couple of weeks and then she'd be gone. It had never worked for her to get too attached to anyone or any place. They always changed. People changed. Circumstances changed. One minute she would feel marginally secure and then the rug would be ripped out from beneath her and she would hit the hard, cold floor. This time with Julius in his flash villa was a temporary thing. There would be no point in getting too comfortable. He hadn't even wanted her here in the first place. She was a burden he had to bear.

Why was she always a burden?

Why couldn't someone want her in spite of all her faults? In spite of all her failings? In spite of all her stupid impulses that caused her more trouble than she wanted?

Her body was still firing with the sensations Julius had made her feel. Cataclysmic sensations she had never felt before. He had barely touched her and she had gone off like a firecracker. But he had remained in control. She had even offered to pleasure him and he'd held back. She still couldn't understand why she had done that. Why she had felt such an urgent desire to take him in her mouth bewildered her. She loathed oral sex. The musky, stale scent of a man usually nauseated her.

But with him it was different.

He wasn't musky and stale. He was fresh and intoxicating in his maleness. She had wanted to explore him, to pleasure him, to make him buckle at the knees in the same way he had done to her. But he hadn't insisted on her doing it. He hadn't pressured her.

He'd *protected* her by his restraint.

He'd pleasured her without wanting or insisting on anything in return. Even now she could feel the aftershock tremors moving through her body, awakening more news: new needs, needs that wanted—craved and hungered—to be assuaged. Maybe that was his power trip. Maybe that was his way of keeping a step in front of her. Maybe his self-control was superior after all. Far more superior than she'd thought.

Something had changed in their relationship…something she couldn't quite put her finger on. No one had given her the benefit of the doubt before. No one.

No one had made her feel the things Julius made her feel. No one.

No one had seen behind the mask she wore to the person she wanted to be.

No one.

When Holly came downstairs to organise breakfast the following morning, Sophia was already up and about. 'I'm going to spend a few days with my sister,' Sophia said. 'You're doing so well managing things here I thought I'd make the most of it by having some time off. Maria's picking me up in a few minutes.'

Holly frowned. 'Is Julius okay with that? I mean, leaving me in charge?'

'He's the one who suggested it.'

Holly's frown deepened. 'Really?'

Sophia nodded. 'He's also worried I might be tempted to do too much. I think he's right. I have been overdoing it. But this little break will help.'

'But what will Natalia have to say?' Holly said. 'Aren't you supposed to be the one mentoring me?'

Sophia's expression turned to one of concern. 'Would you rather I didn't go? I can cancel if you like. I'm sure my sister won't mind.'

'No, don't do that. I'm just wondering about the pro-gramme.' *And being left alone in the villa with Julius without a chaperone.*

'Señor Ravensdale is the one who is ultimately re-sponsible for you,' Sophia said. 'I'm here as a guide but you don't need me. In many ways you're more compe-tent than me. Your cooking is restaurant standard. I'm the one who should be taking lessons off you.'

'Yeah, well, it's easy to cook nice things when you have access to top quality ingredients,' Holly said.

Sophia smiled. 'Would you mind taking Señor Ra-vensdale's breakfast to him? He's in the morning room upstairs.'

'Sure.'

'Ah, that's Maria's car now.' Sofia gave her one last smile and left.

Holly waited for the coffee to percolate before she put it on the tray to take upstairs. The morning room was on the second level of the villa, which wasn't con-venient to the kitchen in terms of serving breakfast, but it had a lovely easterly aspect overlooking the gar-dens and the lake. She had been in a couple of times to dust and vacuum. It was decorated in soft yellows and cream with a touch of blue, giving it a fresh energetic look perfect for the start of the day.

When Holly shouldered open the door, a quake of dread moved through her. The French doors leading to the balcony were wide open. Julius was sitting in a patch of sunlight at the wrought-iron table with some papers set in front of him. The slight breeze was ruf-fling the pages, and she watched as one of his hands reached out to anchor them.

He must have sensed her presence, or maybe he heard

the slight rattle of the cup in the saucer on the tray she was carrying, for he looked up. 'Good morning.'

Holly swallowed a bird's nest of panic. Fear crawled over her scalp. Her blood chilled, freezing in her veins until she was certain her heart would stop. Her feet were nailed to the floor. She couldn't move. She was frozen.

Julius frowned. 'What's wrong?'

'Nothing.' Holly took a step forward but couldn't go any farther. 'Um, would you come and get this? I've left something on the hob downstairs.'

'Why don't you come back and join me?' he said as he took the tray from her and placed it on the table on the balcony.

'No thanks.'

'Got out of the wrong side of the bed, did we?'

'Wasn't in it long enough,' she said with a little scowl.

He surveyed her features for a beat or two. 'Come on and join me once you've turned off the hob. It's a lovely morning. There's enough food and coffee here for both of us. Just get another cup and saucer.'

'I said no.'

Julius shrugged as if he didn't care either way. 'Suit yourself.'

'Could you bring the tray back down when you're done?' Holly said as she got to the door.

He turned around to look at her. 'Isn't that your job?'

She held his penetrating look. 'Is that why you've sent Sophia away? What is it about having someone wait on you that gives you such a thrill? Is it the power? The authority? The ego trip?'

A frown tugged at his brow. 'Doesn't the fact I asked

you to join me for breakfast demonstrate I'm not on any power trip?'

She crossed her arms and sent him a hard glare. 'So what was last night all about, then?'

He let out a rough-sounding breath. 'Last night was… I was wrong to let things get to that point,' he said. 'I'm sorry.'

Holly wasn't ready to be mollified. She was still feeling annoyed he'd been able to prove his point so easily. He had won that round. She had responded to him like a sex-starved fool. Which was basically what she was, but still…

He came to where she was standing. He didn't touch her but was close enough for her to feel the tempting warmth of his body. His dark-blue eyes held hers in a gentle lock that made her wonder if he was seeing much more than she wanted him to see. She tried to keep her expression blank but she wasn't quite able to stop her tongue from quickly moistening her lips. She watched as his gaze dipped to follow the movement before coming back to reconnect with hers.

'This thing we have…' he began.

'What thing?'

'I've never met someone who's got my attention quite the way you have,' he said.

'Well, they wouldn't have a chance with you locked away in your mansion with no social life to speak of, now, would they?'

He gave her a wry hint of a smile. 'I get out when I need to.'

'When was the last time you—' Holly put her fingers up in air-quotation-marks '—got out?'

'I had a brief relationship a few months back.'

'Who was she? What was she like?'

'Someone I met at a conference in Santiago,' he said. 'She was beautiful, well educated, came from a good family. She had a nice personality...'

'I'm hearing a big "but".'

'No chemistry.'

'Not good.'

'Definitely not good.' He brushed a stray strand of hair back from her forehead. It was the lightest touch but it made every nerve in her body shudder in delight. Had anyone ever touched her as gently? Had anyone ever looked at her so intently? As if they wanted to see right into the very heart of her?

'So who broke it off?' Holly said. 'You or her?'

'Me.'

'Was she disappointed?'

'If she was, it can't have lasted long as she got engaged a few weeks later to a guy she'd been dating before me.'

'You win some, you lose some.'

His eyes did that back-and-forth searching thing with each of hers. 'It would be highly inappropriate for me to get involved with you,' he said. 'You do understand that, don't you?'

'We're both consenting adults.'

His finger traced the underside of her jaw in a feather-light touch. 'It's not a matter of consent. It's a matter of convention.'

Holly twisted her mouth in a cynical manner. 'Oh, right—the upstairs, downstairs thing.'

He frowned. 'That's not what I meant at all. It wouldn't reflect well on me if I were to engage in a relationship with you. It would look like I'm exploiting you.'

'But making me fetch and carry and ordering me about doesn't?'

He dropped his hand from her face. 'You really suit your name. I don't think I've ever met anyone more prickly.'

'Your breakfast is getting cold,' Holly said, nodding towards his abandoned tray out on the balcony.

Julius narrowed his gaze in thoughtful contemplation. His forehead was lined like tidemarks on the seashore. She could almost hear the cogs of his brain going around. 'You don't have anything on the hob, do you?'

Holly tried to disguise a swallow. His dark blue gaze was probing. Like a strong light shining into the outer limits of her soul. 'No…'

'So unless it's my company there's some other reason you don't want to have breakfast with me on the balcony,' he said in a tone that sounded as if he was thinking out loud.

A loaded silence passed.

Holly let out a shaky sigh. 'I have a…a thing about balconies.'

'You're scared of heights?' He didn't say it in a mocking way. He simply stated it as if it was perfectly reasonable for her to be scared and he wouldn't judge her for it.

Holly felt something hard and tight slip away from her heart. As if a rigid band had come undone. 'Not heights, specifically. Just balconies.'

He took one of her hands and held it in the shelter of his. His thumb stroked the back of her hand in a slow, soothing motion. 'That's why you didn't want the room Sophia prepared for you, isn't it?'

Holly pressed her lips together. Hard. She never spoke to anyone about this stuff. It was stuff she had locked away. But for some reason Julius's gentle tone picked the lock of her determination. He had unravelled the tightly bound knot of her stubborn pride. She released another sigh. 'I got locked out on the balcony when I was a kid,' she said. 'It was something my stepfather thought was entertaining. Seeing me out there in all sorts of weather. He wouldn't let me come in until I said sorry for whatever I'd supposedly done. Not that I ever did much; I only had to look at him a certain way and he'd shove me out there.'

Julius's frown was so deep it was like a trench between his eyes. 'You poor little kid. What about your mother? Didn't she stand up for you?'

'My mum was unable to stand up for herself, let alone me,' Holly said. 'He'd done such a good job of eroding her self-esteem, she chose death instead of life. He drove her to it. He hates me because I didn't cave in to him. That's why he keeps making trouble for me. He follows me wherever I go. He has ways and means of reminding me I can't escape. But I *will* escape. I'm determined to get away and make a new life for myself.'

Julius took both of her hands in his, holding them gently but securely. 'He can't touch you while you're with me. I'll make sure of it.'

Holly's chest swelled with hope at his implacable tone. How long had it been since she'd felt safe? Truly safe? 'Thank you…'

He touched her face with a barely there brush stroke of his bent knuckles. His eyes had a tender look that made the base of her spine hum. 'I can't imagine how difficult your life must've been compared to mine,' he said. 'No wonder you came in that first day with your fists up.'

'Yeah, well, sorry about that, but I like to get in first in case things turn out nasty, which they invariably do,' she said. 'Maybe it's my fault. I attract trouble. I can't seem to help myself. It's automatic.'

'No.' His hands took hers again in a firm but gentle hold. 'You shouldn't blame yourself. Your stepfather sounds like a creep. He belongs in jail, not you.'

Holly looked at their joined hands. Hers were so small compared to his. She slowly brought her gaze up to his. His eyes meshed with hers in a look that made her legs feel fizzy. 'Why are you looking at me like that?' she said.

'How am I looking at you?' His voice was a deep, resonant rumble.

'Like you're going to kiss me.'

He brushed an imaginary strand of hair away from her face. 'What gives you the idea I'm going to kiss you?' His mouth was half an inch from hers, his breath a warm, minty breeze against her lips.

'Just a feeling.'

His lips nudged hers in a playful manner. 'Do you always trust your feelings?'

Holly slipped her arms around his neck and pressed herself closer. 'Mostly.'

His mouth brushed hers, once, twice, three times. 'This is crazy. I shouldn't be doing this.'

'*This* being…?'

He rested his forehead against hers. 'Tell me to stop.'

'No.'

'Tell me, Holly. I *need* you to tell me.'

'I want you to kiss me,' Holly said. 'I want you to make love to me.' As soon as she said the words, she realised how much she meant them. How from the moment she'd met him she'd been drawn to him like a moth to a bright streetlight on a hot summer's night. The desire he triggered in her was unlike anything she'd ever felt before. She wanted him. She ached for him. She burned for him.

He looked at her with darkened eyes, the pupils wide with desire. 'Why?'

'Because we're attracted to each other and we might as well make the most of it.'

One of his hands cupped her face, the other rested in the small of her back. 'Why me?'

'Why not you?' she said. 'You're single. I'm single. What's the problem?'

He was still frowning. 'Is once going to be enough?'

Holly stroked the side of his jaw. 'Do you have to think about everything before you act? Don't you ever just go with the flow?'

He turned her palm towards his mouth and kissed it, all the while holding her gaze. 'Do you ever stop and think before you act?'

She shivered as his kiss travelled all the way to her core. 'I'm thinking we should make the most of the fact that Sophia's away with her sister.' Is that why he'd sent his housekeeper away? Perhaps it was unconscious on his part but he had cleared the way for them to indulge in an affair without an audience.

He framed her face with his hands, his expression darkly serious. 'I want you like I've never wanted anyone else.'

'Same.'

His head came down, and his mouth sealed hers in a kiss as hot as a flashpoint. Heat pooled between her legs as his tongue drove through the seam of her mouth to find hers. Lust raced through her blood as he stroked and thrust and cajoled her tongue into play. His body crushed hers to his, every hard contour of his enticing every softer one of hers. Her breasts peaked against his chest, her pelvis thrumming with want as she felt the thickened ridge of him.

His hands moved over her lightly, touching, exploring, discovering. He came to her breasts, lifting her top out of the way so he could access them. He swirled his tongue over and around her nipple, making her ache with longing as his teeth gently nipped and tugged at her flesh.

His hands skimmed down the sides of her body to grasp her hips, holding her tightly against the throb of his need. He made a deep sound at the back of his throat as she moved against him. A sound of approval, of want, of raw, primal lust.

'Not here,' he said as he swept her up in his arms and carried her towards his suite.

Holly noticed the balcony doors were open as she pulled him down with her on the mattress, but she pushed her fear away, not willing to be separated for a second in case he changed his mind. Her whole body was on fire. Pulsating with a longing so intense it was mind-blowing. Every part of her body was alive and sensitive. Every inch of her skin ached for his touch.

Julius must have read her mind for he began working on her clothes while she did her best to get him out of his. Her hands weren't cooperating in her haste to feel his naked skin. They were fumbling in excitement, and he had to take over. Holly watched as he unbuttoned his shirt before shrugging it off and tossing it to the floor. She put her hands on his chest, spreading her fingers over his pectoral muscles, her palms tickled by the light covering of masculine hair sprinkled over his chest.

He came down to her to caress her breasts with his lips and tongue, making her squirm and shiver with delight with every movement he made. He kissed his way from her breasts down over her stomach, dipping his tongue into the shallow cave of her belly button before going lower.

Holly sucked in a breath when he came to the heart of her. The feel of his lips separating her and the sexy rasp of his tongue against her sensitive flesh made her arch her spine like a well-pleasured cat. The ripples of an orgasm took her by surprise, taking over her body, shaking it, tossing it into a maelstrom of ecstasy that made her gasp out loud.

But even as the pleasure faded he was stirring her to new feelings, new sensations, new anticipations, as he sourced a condom and positioned himself between her thighs.

His mouth came back to hers as he entered her in a slick, deep thrust that made her whole body quake in response. His thrusts were slow and measured at first, allowing her time to get used to him. But then as she breathlessly urged him on he upped the pace, deeper, harder, faster, until she was rocking against him for that final push into paradise. He reached between their bodies to give her that extra bit of friction that pitched her over the edge. She cried out as the sensations tore through her in a rush, delicious wave upon delicious wave, roll upon roll. He waited until she was coming down from the spike before he let go. Holly felt him tense and then spill, his whole body shuddering until he finally went still.

It was a new thing for Holly to lie in a man's arms without wanting to push him off or rush off to the shower. It was a new thing for her to not feel uncomfortable with the silence. Not to have regrets over what her body had done or had had done to it by a partner. Her body was in a delicious state of lassitude, every limb feeling boneless, her mind drifting like flotsam.

After a moment Julius propped himself up on his arms to look at her. 'Am I too heavy for you?'

Holly stroked her hands down to the dip in his spine. 'No.'

He brushed a fingertip over her lower lip, his expression thoughtful. 'I might've rushed you. It's been a while.'

'You didn't,' she said. 'It was…perfect. You were perfect.'

He kissed her on the mouth softly. Lightly. 'This is usually when I say I have work to do or head to the shower.'

'Classy.'

He gave a wry smile. 'If you give me a couple of minutes, I'll be ready for round two.'

Holly arched her brows. 'So this isn't a one-off then?'

His eyes darkened as they held hers. 'Is that all you want?'

She shrugged noncommittally and looked away. 'The itch has been scratched, hasn't it?'

He took her chin between his finger and thumb and made her look at him. 'This isn't the sort of itch that can be cured with one scratch.'

Holly kept her expression screened. 'What're you suggesting? A fling? A relationship? Not sure what your family would have to say about you and me hanging out as a couple. Or the press, for that matter.'

His frown pulled at his forehead like stitches beneath the skin. 'What I do in my private life is my business, no one else's, including my family.'

'What about Sophia?'

'What about her?'

Holly tiptoed her fingers up his spine to the back of his neck where his hair was curling. 'What's she going to say when she finds out we're sleeping together?'

'We won't tell her.'

Holly laughed. 'Like that's going to work. She'll know as soon as she comes back.'

He rolled away and got off the bed to dispense with the condom, a deep frown still dividing his forehead. He picked up his trousers and stepped into them, zipping them up with unnecessary force. 'What's your caseworker going to say when you tell her about us?'

'I'm not going to tell her,' Holly said. 'Why would I? It's none of her business.'

Julius scooped his shirt and thrust his arms into the sleeves. 'We can't continue this. It's wrong. I shouldn't have allowed it to happen. I'm sorry; I take full responsibility.'

Holly swung her legs over the edge of the bed and reached for her nearest article of clothing. 'Yeah, well, I guess it was just a pity thing on your part, huh?'

'What?' His tone was sharp, shocked…annoyed.

'You only slept with me because you felt sorry for me after I told you about my crappy childhood.'

His frown was so deep his eyebrows met over the bridge of his nose. 'That's not true.'

She gave him a direct look. 'Isn't it?'

He scraped a hand through his hair. 'No. Yes. Maybe. I don't know.'

Holly finished pulling on her clothes before she came over to him. 'It's fine, Julius. Stop stressing. I'm okay with a one-off. Doesn't make sense to get too cosy, since I'll be on my way in a couple of weeks.'

He looked at her for a long, pulsing moment. 'I suppose you got what you wanted.'

She arched a brow. 'That being?'

'From the moment you stepped into this place, you had your mind set on getting me to break, didn't you?' he said. 'It was your goal. Your mission. You did everything you could to prove I couldn't resist you. Well, you were right. I couldn't.'

Holly was a little ashamed of how close to the mark he was. But what was even more concerning was how she had ended up wanting him more than she had wanted anyone. She didn't know how to handle such want. Such longing. The need was still there. It was a sated beast that would all too soon wake again and be growling, prowling for sustenance. Even now she could feel her body stirring the longer she looked into Julius's dark navy eyes with their glittering cynicism.

'What will you do now you've achieved your goal?' he said. 'Give a tell-all interview to the press?'

Holly shifted her gaze from his in case he saw how hurt she felt. 'You have serious trust issues.'

He laughed. '*I* have trust issues?'

She swung back to glare at him. 'Do you really think I would share my body with you and then tell everyone about it? I'd be hurting myself more than you.'

'They pay big money for scandalous stories. Big money. You could set yourself up on this.'

Holly pressed her lips together as she went in hunt of her shoes but she could only find one. Frustration and hurt tangled in a tight knot in her chest, making it hard for her to breathe. She had given him every reason to think she would sell out to score points against him. The shaming truth was a few days ago she might well have done it. But something had changed. *She* had changed. His touch, his concern, his promise of protection had made something inside her shift. She couldn't find a way to reassemble herself. It was as if the puzzle pieces of her personality had been scattered and she didn't know how to get them back into order. The things she had wanted before were not what she wanted now.

It was disturbing—terrifying—to allow her nascent hopes and dreams to get a foothold. For the first time in her life, she'd caught a glimpse of what it would be like to be secure in a relationship. To be with a man who looked out for her, who wanted the best for her, who would help her reach her potential instead of sabotaging it. To be honoured and cherished. To be celebrated instead of ridiculed. To be accepted.

To be trusted.

To be loved.

Holly took a scalding breath and forced herself to look at him. 'I guess you'd better call Natalia and get her to take me away, then.'

Something passed over his features. 'No.'

'Why not?' Holly said, trying to squash the bubble of hope that bloomed in her chest. 'I'm nothing but trouble. I belong in jail, or so you said the other day.'

He let out a long breath and came back to where she was standing. He put his hands on her hunched shoul-

CHAPTER TEN

A FEW DAYS later Holly watched as Julius slept. He was a quiet sleeper, not restless and fidgety like her. She could have watched him for hours, memorising his features, storing them in her mind for the time when she would be gone from his life. She had been playing a game of pretend with herself over the past few days, a silly little game where she wouldn't have to leave at the end of the time she had left.

She had even been so foolish as to picture her and Julius building a life together. Having a family together. Building a future together. Things she had never allowed herself to dream of before. She hadn't even realised she wanted those things until now. Every day she spent in his company she found herself wanting him more. Not just physically, although that had only got better and better. It was more of an intellectual connection, one she had never felt with anyone else. He inspired her, excited her, and challenged her.

Holly traced one of his eyebrows with her fingertip. 'Are you awake?'

'No.'

She smiled and traced the other eyebrow. That was the other thing she liked about him—he had a sense of humour underneath all that gruff starchiness. 'Are you dreaming?' she said.

'Yes, of this hot girl who's in my bed touching me with her clever little hands.'

Holly reached down and stroked his swollen length. 'Like this?'

'Mmm, just like that.'

'And in this dream did that same girl slide down your body like this?' She moved down his body, letting her breasts touch him from chest to groin.

'That's it,' he said in a low growl. 'I never want to wake up.'

She sent her tongue down the length of his shaft, then swirled it over the head and around the sensitive glans.

'Condom, *querida*.'

'I want to taste you.'

He muttered an expletive as she opened her mouth over him, drawing on him until he was breathing heavily. 'You don't have to…'

'I want to,' Holly said. 'You do it to me. Why shouldn't I do it to you?'

'I've never had someone do it in the raw before.'

'Lucky me to be the first.'

He frowned for a moment but it soon disappeared as Holly got to business. She watched him as she drew on him, her own excitement building as she saw the effect she was having on him. He pulled out just as he spilled, the erotic pumping of his essence thrilling her in a way she hadn't expected.

He threaded his fingers through her hair in long, soothing strokes that made her scalp tingle in delight. 'Holly…'

She looked up from where she had been resting her cheek against his stomach. 'What?'

He had one of his deep-in-thought frowns on his forehead. After a moment the frown relaxed as he smiled faintly. 'Just… Holly.'

She stroked his stubbly jaw. 'Not getting all sentimental on me, are you?'

The frown was back. 'What do you mean?'

Holly propped herself on one elbow as she trailed her fingers up and down his chest. 'This is just for now. Us, I mean. I'm going to England once I'm done here.'

He pushed her hand away and got off the bed. 'I know you are. I'm glad you are. It's the right thing to do.' He pulled on a bathrobe and tied the belt, his expression shuttered.

'You don't sound very happy about it.'

He threw her an irritated look. 'Why wouldn't I be happy about it?'

She gave a shrug. 'Thought you might miss me.'

'I will but that doesn't mean I want you to stay.'

Holly sat up and pulled her knees into her chest. 'I wouldn't stay if you asked me.'

'I'm not going to ask you.'

'Fine. Glad we got that settled.'

He went to the balcony doors and unlocked them. Holly stiffened. 'What are you doing?'

'I want some fresh air.'

Bitterness burned in her gullet. 'You're only doing that to get rid of me. It's cruel, Julius. You know how much it freaks me out. I thought you understood. I'll only come in here if those doors are closed.'

'It's just a balcony, for God's sake.'

Tears sprouted but Holly tried to blink them back.

'It's not just a bloody balcony!' She got off the bed, pulling the sheet with her to cover herself. 'I spent hours and hours—years—of my life frightened out of my wits, and now you're using that fear, *exploiting* that fear, to push me away because you're scared of how you feel about me leaving.'

He flung the doors wide open and stepped out on to the balcony, standing with his back to her as he looked out over the estate.

Holly felt a gnarled knot of emotion clog her throat. Her heart was beating too fast, too erratically. Her skin was icy-cold and then clammy-hot. Her vision blurred with tears. She tried to get away but the sheet wrapped around her halted her progress. She tripped, stumbled and then fell in an ungainly heap on the floor.

'Are you all right?' Julius was by her side in seconds.

Holly batted his hand away. 'No, of course I'm not all right. Close the freaking doors, will you?'

He gripped her chin between his finger and thumb. 'You're fine, Holly. Look at me. You're fine. No one's going to hurt you.'

She glared at him. 'You hurt me. You did. You shouldn't have done that.' Tears leaked out of her eyes in spite of all she did to try and stop them. She landed a punch on his arm but it glanced off as if she had hit stone. 'You sh-shouldn't have done that.'

'Hey…hey…hey…' He drew her against him, resting his chin on top of her head as he gently stroked her back in soothing circles. 'It's all right, *querida*. I'm sorry. I shouldn't have done it. I'm sorry. Shh, don't cry.'

'I'm not c-crying.'

'Of course you're not.' He kept stroking her, holding her.

'I'm angry, that's all.'

'Of course you are. You have every right to be. I was being a jerk.'

'If you want me to leave the room or get out of your life just say so, okay?' she said against his chest. 'I can take a hint. I'm not stupid.'

There was a deep silence.

Holly listened to the sound of his breathing. Felt the steady rise and fall of his chest against her cheek and the slow beat of his heart. Felt his hand gently stroking her hair, his chin resting on top of her head. Felt her heart squeeze at the thought of how soon this was going to end.

Before she knew it, she would be on her way to a new life in England. The only contact she would have with him would be seeing articles about his family in the press. She wasn't falling in love with him. She wasn't. It was just that he was so...so different from all the men she had met in the past. He was impossibly strong, yet tender when he needed to be. He was a control freak but that showed he had discipline and self-control. He was a man with honour and standards. No one had ever taken the time to get to know her like he had done. He was interested in what made her the person she was and he inspired her to become who she was meant to be.

How could she not feel a little regret over her imminent departure? It was normal. It didn't mean she was falling in love with him. She had never been in love before and didn't intend to be now. She had seen first-hand the damage loving someone could do. You lost your power, your autonomy, your self-respect and your freedom. Love was a trap. A cage that, once you were in, you couldn't get out of. That wasn't what she had planned for her life.

Julius eased back to look down at her. 'I want you to do something for me.'

'What?'

He took her by the hands in a gentle hold. 'I want you to come out on the balcony with me.'

Holly tried to pull away but his grip tightened. 'No. *No.* Don't ask me to do that. I won't. I can't.'

He kept her imprisoned hands close to his chest. 'I'll be with you the whole time. I won't let go of you. Trust me, Holly.'

She felt the panic rise in her chest. Felt the bookcase flatten her lungs until she could barely inflate them enough to breathe. Could she do it? Could she trust him to stand by her and hold her, to help her confront her worst nightmare? Her skin crawled with dread. Her heart raced. Her stomach churned. 'I—I'm not sure I can do it… My stepfather used to drag me out there by the hair. He would lock me out there and then beat up my mum while I watched. Don't make me do it. I c-can't.'

Julius's expression flinched as she spoke but he kept hold of her hands, holding her gaze as he kissed her clenched knuckles one by one. 'Don't let him win any longer, *querida*. All this time he's had it over you by controlling you with fear. Give your fear to me. Trust me. I won't let you fall.'

I think I'm already falling, Holly thought. Feelings she had never expected to feel for anyone were slipping past the barriers she had erected around her heart. Her defences were no match for his tenderness, his concern, his steadiness and support. She couldn't allow herself to fall for him. This was a temporary arrangement that would end once her community service was over. She was a fool to imagine any other outcome. He was from a completely different world. He would have no place for her in it. She didn't belong. She was an outcast. A misfit. A nobody that nobody wanted.

'Okay…' Her voice came out scratchy as it squeezed past the strangulation of her fear.

He led her to the balcony doors. 'Okay so far?'

She nodded, swallowing another wave of panic. He opened the doors, and the fresh air wafted over her face. She gripped his hand so tightly she wondered why he didn't wince in pain.

'Good girl,' he said. 'Now, take one step at a time. We'll stop if it gets too much. It's your call.'

Holly took one step onto the balcony on legs as unsteady as a new-born foal's. The smell of freshly mown grass drifted past her nostrils. She tried to concentrate on the view, hoping it would distract her from thinking about the fear that chilled her to the bone.

'You're doing so well,' he said. 'Want to try a couple more steps?'

She took another thorny breath and moved one step forward. His hands squeezed hers in encouragement. She looked up at him and gave him a wobbly smile. 'Nice view from up here.'

'Yes,' he said but she noticed he wasn't looking at the view.

Holly looked at their joined hands. He wasn't letting her go. He wasn't pushing her beyond her limits. He had held true to his promise. The weight of fear began to lift off her chest. She could breathe. She could feel her heart rate gradually slowing. She wasn't cured by any means but she had made progress. She hadn't been anywhere near a balcony since she'd been a teenager. Years of terror had stalked her. Controlled her. She had taken two steps forward into a future without fear. Two steps. It wasn't much but it was enough to give her a glimmer of hope.

Holly looked up into his deep-blue gaze. 'Thank you...'

'I haven't done anything,' he said. 'I was just holding your hand. Next time will be easier. Soon you'll be doing it all by yourself.'

'I'm not so sure about that,' she said with a little shudder.

'You underestimate yourself,' he said. 'You can do anything if you try. You have so much potential. Don't let anyone take it away from you.'

Holly pulled away to go back inside. She hugged her elbows with her hands crossed over. It was all very well for him to talk about potential. He'd had a good education. Family money and opportunities she could only dream about. He might find his parents difficult but at least he had them.

She had no one.

Julius came up behind her and put his hands on her shoulders. 'Would you like to go out to dinner?'

Holly turned to look at him with a frown. 'In public?'

'That's where the restaurants tend to be.'

'Yes, and so are people with camera phones.'

'I know a quiet little place where we won't be disturbed,' he said. 'I know the guy who runs it. He'll let us have a private room.'

Holly hadn't quite let her frown go. 'Why are you doing this?'

'Doing what?'

'Acting like this is a normal relationship.'

A muscle moved near his mouth. 'You deserve a break from cooking, surely?'

'Then order takeaway.'

'It's just dinner,' he said. 'I sometimes take Sophia out for a meal.'

'I'd rather not.'

'Why not? You have the clothes to wear.'

Holly unwrapped her body from the sheet she was wearing and reached for a bathrobe. 'I'm happy to sleep with you, okay? But don't ask me to act like we're a proper couple. Date nights are out of the question.'

'Fine,' he said casually but it didn't fool her for a second. 'Forget I asked.'

Holly bit down on her lip as he strode into the en suite. He was upset with her for refusing but what else could she do? Dinner would have been nice but how could she control her emotions if he pressed her to do couple stuff? A romantic dinner for two was just plain wrong. She was not his romantic partner.

She never would be.

Julius knew he had no right to feel annoyed Holly had refused to go out in public with him. He knew they weren't in a relationship. It was just a fling. A convenient interlude that was going to end once her community service was up. He should, in principle, be in agreement about keeping their affair out of the public eye but he had wanted to spend time with her away from the villa where she felt like a member of his staff rather than his equal. He wanted them to be just two ordinary people who had an attraction for each other. He wanted to spoil her in a way she had never been spoilt before.

The very fact she didn't want to go public about their

involvement was a confirmation of the sort of person she was underneath all that 'junkyard dog' bluster. She was sensitive and easily hurt. She hid that vulnerability behind her don't-mess-with-me façade. The horror of her past sickened him. He wanted to make it up to her. To make her feel safe in a way she had never felt before. He needed time to do that. But how much time did he have? Not much. Not enough.

For some reason every time he thought of her leaving he got a pain below his ribs. A tight, cramping pain as if someone was jabbing him. What would happen to her when she went to England? She had no one. No family to watch out for her. She would be totally alone. His family annoyed the hell out of him most of the time but at least he knew they were there when he needed them. Who would Holly turn to if things went sour?

The way she had trusted him to take her out on the balcony had moved him deeply. He had seen the years of terror in her face. Felt it in her hands as they gripped his so tightly. And yet she had stood out there in his arms and given him a shaky smile, *trusting* him to keep her safe. Who would keep her safe once she left him?

Why the heck was he ruminating so much about her leaving? Of course she had to leave. It was what she wanted. A new start in her mother's homeland. A chance to get her life back on track, to pursue her dreams and put her past behind her. A past Julius would be part of. Would she ever think of him? Miss him?

He gave himself a mental shake and tried to refocus on the programme code in front of him. He wasn't supposed to be developing feelings for her. It was fine to care about someone, sure. It was fine to want to see her get on her feet and reach her potential. But caring so much he couldn't bear to think of letting her go was ridiculous. He hadn't wanted her to come here in the first place. How could he possibly want her to stay indefinitely?

He didn't do indefinitely.

Julius's mobile rang, and he was about to ignore it but changed his mind when he saw it was his sister, Miranda. Finally. 'Nice of you to get back to me.'

'I'm sorry but I didn't feel like talking to anyone,' Miranda said.

It was what his baby sister did when things got difficult. She went to ground. He knew she would call him eventually but it worried him she had left it so long. 'You okay?'

'God, it's just so embarrassing,' she said. 'Mum is beside herself and for once I can't blame her.'

'Have you met the girl yet?'

'No,' Miranda said. 'Dad's pushing for it. He wants a big family reunion. Can you believe it? Talk about lack of sensitivity. I just want to run away and hide some place until it all blows over.'

'Have the press hassled you for a comment?'

'Like, every day,' she said. 'The worse thing is they keep making comparisons. I'm now officially known as the ugly sister.'

'That's rubbish and you know it,' Julius said.

'Have you seen her, Julius?' Miranda asked. 'She's stunning. Like one of those lingerie supermodels. And guess what? She's an aspiring actor. Dad is so proud he finally produced a child with theatrical ambition. He keeps going on and on about it. It's nauseating.'

'What's she been in? I haven't heard of her before now.'

'She's only been in amateur things but now all she'll

have to do is name drop and the red carpet will be rolled out for her. You wait and see.'

'Connections will only get her so far,' Julius said. 'She'll need talent.'

Miranda gave a gusty sigh. 'I don't want to talk about it any more. So, how are you?'

'Fine. Been busy working.'

'Same old.'

He gave a rueful smile. 'Same old.'

'When are you coming over?' she said. 'Have you got any plans to visit?'

'Not right now.'

There was a short silence.

'Are you dating someone?' Miranda asked.

Julius tossed the question back even though he already knew the answer. 'Are you?'

'I know you think I'm wasting my life but I loved Mark,' Miranda said in her stock-standard defensive tone she used whenever the topic of her moving on with her life was brought up.

'I know you did, sweetheart,' Julius said gently. 'And he loved you. But if things were the other way around I reckon he would've moved on by now.'

'You obviously haven't been in love,' Miranda said. 'You don't know what it's like to lose the only person in the world you want to be with.'

Julius felt that sudden pang beneath his ribs again. He was going to lose Holly. In a matter of days, she would be gone. He would never see her again.

Which was how it should be, as she had a right to move on with her new life without him interfering.

Julius put his phone down after he'd finished listening to his little sister tell him a thousand reasons why she would never date another man. He let out a long sigh. There were times when he wondered if love was worth all the heartache. So far he had avoided it.

So far…

CHAPTER ELEVEN

A COUPLE OF days later Julius finished a tele-conference that had taken longer than he'd expected and went in search of Holly. She was out by the pool scooping out leaves with the net. 'One of the groundsmen can do that,' he said.

She turned around and smiled one of her cheeky smiles. 'Have you got something you'd rather me do indoors?'

He put his arms around her, bringing her bikini-clad body against his fully clothed one. 'Why are you always wandering around the place half-dressed?' he growled at her playfully.

'All the better to tempt you, my dear,' she said.

Julius brought his mouth down to hers. The heat of their mouths meeting always surprised him. Delighted him. She didn't kiss in half-measures. She kissed with her whole body. He drew her closer, his body responding to the slim, sun-kissed contours of hers. He kept on kissing her as he unhooked her bikini top so he could access her breasts. Her hands went to the buttons of his shirt, undoing each one with spine-tingling purpose.

He put his mouth to her breast, sucking, licking and teasing the engorged flesh until she was making breathless little sounds of need. He untied the strings of her bikini bottoms and cupped the pert curves of her bottom in his hands.

She tilted her head back to look at him. 'This is a little unfair. I'm completely naked and you're fully dressed.'

Julius swept his tongue over her pouting bottom lip. 'Let's take this indoors.'

She rubbed against him sensuously. 'Why not have a swim with me first?'

He couldn't resist her in this mood. She was so damn sexy he could barely hold himself in check. Within seconds he, too, had stripped off—apart from a quickly sheathed condom—and was in the pool with her, holding her against his aroused body as she smiled up at him with those dancing, caramel-brown eyes. He lowered his mouth to hers, his senses reeling as her tongue came into play with his. Her hands were around his waist, then caressing his chest, then going even lower to hold him until he was ready to explode. The water only heightened the sensations. The silky cool of it against their heated bodies made him all the more frantic for release.

He walked her backwards until she was up against the edge of the pool but, rather than have her back marked by the pool's edge, he turned her so her back was against the front of his body. He kissed his way from her earlobe to her neck and back again, trailing his tongue over her scented flesh, wondering how he was going to stop himself coming ahead of schedule with her bottom pressed up against his erection. She made a sound of encouragement, part whimper, part gasp, as he moved between legs.

He entered her deeply, barely able to control himself as her hot, wet body gripped him like a clamp. He kept thrusting, building a pace that had her hands gripping the edge of the pool for balance. He felt every delicious ripple of her inner flesh, the contraction of her around him as she came, triggering his own mind-blowing release.

He didn't want to move. He wanted to stand there on his still shaking legs and hold her against him.

She turned in his arms, looking up at him with a face glowing with the aftermath of pleasure. 'Ever done it in the pool before?'

'No.'

'Lucky me to be your first pool—'

Julius put his fingertip over her mouth to stop her saying the crude word he suspected she was going to say. 'Don't.'

She pushed his hand away. 'Don't be so squeamish, Julius. It's just sex.'

Just sex.

Was it? Was it just sex for him? Maybe for her it was but for him it didn't feel anything like the sex he'd had in the past. His whole body felt different with her. *He* felt different. Not just in his flesh but in his mind. Sex had gone from being a purely physical experience to a more cerebral—dared he admit it?—emotional one. He liked having Holly around. She was funny and playful, exciting and daring in a way that made him shift out of his comfort zone. But he had helped her out of her comfort zone, too. She had even allowed the balcony doors to be open in his suite when they made love the past few nights.

Made love.

The words jolted him. Maybe it wasn't 'just sex' after all. He made love to her. His body worshipped hers, pleasured hers and delighted in giving as well as receiving it. He had never wanted a woman more than her. She made him feel aroused by just looking at him. The scent of her was enough to make him hard. He only had to walk into a room she had been in earlier and his blood would be pumping. Her touch made his flesh tingle all over. The dancing tiptoe movements of her fingers made his pulse thunder and his heart race. Everything about her turned him on. He couldn't imagine another woman being as thrilling and satisfying as her.

But she was leaving in four days...

Which was fine. Just fine. She had her plans. He had his. He wasn't after anything serious. They'd had their fun. And it had been fun, much more fun than he'd realised a fling could be. She had taught him to loosen up. He had helped her confront her fears. She had revealed her past to him, which he hoped meant she was ready to move on from it. He wanted her to succeed. She had so much going for her. Her energy, passion and drive were wonderful qualities if channelled in the right direction.

Holly linked her arms around his neck. 'What's that big, old sober frown for?'

Julius forced a smile. 'Was I frowning?'

She put her fingertip between his brows. 'You get this deep ridge right here when you're thinking.'

He captured her finger and trailed his tongue the length of it. 'I'm thinking it might be good to go inside before we both get burned to a crisp.'

'Good point,' she said and walked up the steps of the pool.

Julius stood spellbound as she emerged from the

water like a nymph. She draped her wet hair over one shoulder as she squeezed the water out, reminding him of a mermaid. Her creamy skin was lightly tanned in spite of the sunscreen he'd seen her using. Her body was fit and toned yet utterly, irresistibly feminine.

She stepped into her bikini bottoms and tied the strings before she went in search of her top. Her smooth brow suddenly creased. 'Is that a car?' she asked, hurriedly covering herself.

Julius had been too focussed on her delectable body even to register anything but how gorgeous she looked. But now he could hear the scrabble of tyres over the gravel of the driveway.

'Are you expecting anyone?' Holly asked.

He vaulted out of the pool and reached for his trousers, not even stopping to dry himself. 'No,' he said. 'No one can get through the gates without the security code, unless it's one of the gardeners coming back in after mowing out front.'

'That doesn't sound like a ride-on mower,' she said, speaking Julius's thoughts out loud.

He shrugged on his shirt and quickly buttoned it. Under normal circumstances he would have got Sophia to answer the door. But with his housekeeper still away with her sister he could hardly send Holly dressed in nothing but a bikini. 'I'll see who it is,' he said. 'You stay here.'

Julius's heart sank when he saw the chauffeur-driven black limousine pull up in front of the villa. His mother. Dressed to the nines. There was no press entourage that he could see but he knew it wouldn't be long. His mother didn't go anywhere without the press documenting her every move.

'I'm coming to stay, Julius,' she said as her driver helped her alight from the car as if she were stepping out on the red carpet. 'I had to get away. The press haven't left me alone for a minute.'

'Have they followed you here?' he said.

'Not that I know of,' Elisabetta said. 'Why are you frowning? Aren't you pleased to see me? I cancelled the rest of my season on Broadway to spend time with you. This is the only place I'll be left alone. I was going to stay with Jake but he's always got some girl coming and going. And Miranda refuses to get involved. Not that I'd want to stay in her poky little flat.'

'Look, now's not a good time,' Julius said.

Elisabetta pouted. 'Don't give me your stupid work excuse. Your work can wait for your mother, surely? Don't you realise how desperate I am? Your father's ruined everything.' She paused long enough to narrow her gaze at him. 'Why are you all wet? And your shirt is buttoned up the wrong way.'

Julius gave himself a mental kick. 'I was having… er…a quick dip. You caught me by surprise.'

Elisabetta continued her tirade. 'I'm *so* furious. Do you know the girl's mother was a housemaid at the hotel he was staying in? A housemaid! How could he be so pathetic?'

Julius pushed back his wet hair with his hand. 'I really don't have time for this right now.'

'You never have time,' Elisabetta said, flouncing up the steps. 'All you have time for is work.'

'Mother, you can't stay,' Julius said. 'It's not…convenient. My housekeeper's away for a few days and I'm not prepared for visitors.'

Elisabetta turned with a theatrical swish of her designer skirt. 'Why do you always push me away? Can't you see I need you to support me right now?'

'I understand things are awful for you just now but you can't just dump yourself here without giving me notice,' Julius said. 'You could've at least called or texted first.'

Elisabetta's gaze narrowed again. 'Have you got someone with you? A lover? Who is it? You're such a dark horse. You never tell me anything. Even the press never knows what you're up to—unlike your brother.'

How could he explain his relationship with Holly to his mother? How could he explain it to himself? Was it even a relationship? Wasn't it just a fling? A temporary thing they both knew would come to an end at the end of the week? 'I like to keep my private life out of the news,' Julius said. 'Which is why you coming here is such a problem for me. You're a press magnet.'

'I hope you're not going to suddenly take your father's side in this,' Elisabetta said as if she hadn't heard a word he'd said.

'Why would I do that?' Julius said. 'What he did was unconscionable.'

'I blame that tramp who seduced him,' his mother said as she entered the front door of the villa. 'She betrayed him by not having the abortion he paid for. At least he offered to sort things out for her but what did she do? Went ahead and had the brat. The decent thing would've been to get rid of the mistake. Pretend it never happened. But no. Those ghastly little gold-diggers are all the same.'

His mother's logic—if he could call it that—had always been hard to follow. He was pretty certain Katherine Winwood would not like to be referred to as a 'mistake' or hear her deceased mother referred to as a 'ghastly little gold-digger'.

'If Kat's mother was such a gold-digger why did she wait until she was on her death bed to reveal her daughter's paternity?' he asked. 'Why not come forward years ago and line her pockets with silence money?'

Elisabetta threw him a fulminating look. 'How can you *defend* her? She was a housemaid, for God's sake.'

Just then Holly appeared dressed neatly in a skirt and blouse with her still-damp hair scraped back in a neat chignon. 'Welcome, Ms Albertini,' she said. 'Would you like me to take your things upstairs to your room?'

Elisabetta gave Holly an assessing look before turning to Julius. 'I thought you said your housekeeper was away?'

'She is,' he said. 'Holly's filling in for her.'

Elisabetta looked at Holly and then back at Julius, her expression tightening. 'So that's how it is, is it? You're sleeping with the hired help. Just like your father.'

Julius clenched his jaw. 'I won't have you insult Holly.'

His mother glared at Holly. 'I suppose you think you've got yourself a meal ticket by seducing my son.'

Holly hitched up her chin, her stance one of cool dignity. 'Would you like a drink brought up to your room? A bite to eat? Some fresh fruit?'

Elisabetta flattened her mouth. 'Did you hear what I said?'

'Yes, Ms Albertini, but I chose to ignore it on account of you being travel weary and upset over recent events,' Holly said. 'Now, if you'd like a drink or some other refreshment, I'll see to it, otherwise I'll leave Julius to show you to your room.'

His mother's brown eyes flashed as she turned to

Julius. 'Did you hear how she spoke to me? Get rid of her. Get her out of my sight. I won't be patronised as if I'm a child!'

'Then don't act like one,' Julius said. 'Holly might be acting as my housekeeper but that doesn't mean she isn't entitled to respect.'

'It's fine, Julius,' Holly chipped in. 'I can handle snobs like your mother.'

Elisabetta bristled. Her lips were pursed, her eyes blazing, her hands clenched. 'You disgusting little sow,' she threw at Holly. 'He can have anyone he wants. Why would he want *you*?'

'I'm great in bed,' Holly said. 'Plus, I cook an awesome meal. Oh, and did I mention I give great—?'

'That's enough,' Julius cut in quickly. 'Mother, you need to leave. Find a hotel somewhere. This is not the place for you right now.'

Elisabetta narrowed her eyes to slits. 'You'd choose *her* over your own mother? What sort of son are you? Anyone with eyes could see she's nothing but trailer trash.'

'Takes one to know one,' Holly said, calmly inspecting her cuticles.

Elisabetta's eyes bulged in outrage. 'What did you say?'

'Right. Time to go.' Julius took his mother's arm and led her back to the waiting car. His mother didn't like being reminded of her poverty-stricken background. It was mostly a well-kept secret, how she had grown up on the back streets of Florence, child of a single mother who had turned tricks to put food on the table. Elisabetta had reinvented herself when she'd moved to London to find a modelling job, which had then led to acting. Julius had never met his grandmother even though she had died three years after he and Jake were born. Not because he had been told of his grandmother's death. He had by chance come across the death certificate when he'd been a teenager sorting out things in the library down at Ravensdene. It was as if Elisabetta's past hadn't existed. It was erased from her memory.

But now, having got to know a little about Holly's desolate background, he wondered if his mother had had good reason to distance herself from it. Perhaps the memories, like Holly's, were too painful. Perhaps it wasn't a matter of pride and arrogance on his mother's part but shame. Was that why Elisabetta found it hard to be a mother herself? She hadn't been nurtured in the way most loving mothers nurtured their children. Elisabetta had pushed her children away unless she'd needed them to do something for her.

Like now, for instance. His mother would never come to visit him unless she'd wanted the visit to be all about her. She had never shown any interest in his work. He suspected she barely knew anything about his career. She had certainly never asked. He had always felt resentful towards her for her lack of interest but he wondered now if that was just the way life had shaped her.

Elisabetta got back in the car with a haughty flick of her Hermes scarf. 'I wouldn't demean myself by staying under the same roof as someone as common as that little tart. She'll bring you nothing but trouble. You mark my words.'

Julius closed the door and stepped back. 'I'll call you in a couple of days. Take care of yourself.'

His mother tightened her mouth as she looked straight

ahead. 'Drive me back to the airport,' she told the driver. 'It seems I'm not welcome here.'

Holly came down the steps to join him as he watched his mother's car disappear down the driveway. 'I might've overstepped the mark…just a little,' she said.

Julius put an arm around her shoulders and brought her close to him, kissing the top of her head. 'Only a little.'

She clasped his hand around her shoulder as she watched the dust stirred up by the car finally settle. 'Why did you defend me like that, anyway?'

He turned her in his arms to look at her. 'Why wouldn't I defend you? She was being rude and disrespectful.'

Holly's mouth twisted. 'No one's ever done that for me, or at least, not for a long time.'

Julius squeezed the tops of her shoulders. 'Then it's about time somebody did.'

Her eyes flicked away from his. 'It's nice of you and all that, but I'd hate for you to be estranged from your mother just because of me. It's not like I'm even going to be here much longer.'

Julius hated being reminded of the timeline. It was getting closer and closer to the end, and he knew he had to face it, but it was like facing a yawning chasm. Once Holly left, his life would go back to normal. Normal and ordered and…empty. 'What if you stayed a little longer?'

Her gaze was suddenly wary. Guarded. 'Why would I want to do that?'

Why indeed? he thought with a stab of disappointment. Clearly he was the one with the larger emotional investment in their relationship. *Emotional investment?* What the hell did that even mean? He wasn't in love with her. Was he? No. Of course he wasn't. He just had feelings for her. Feelings that were about care and concern for her welfare. Affection. She was a sweet girl underneath that façade. He'd come to respect her. To admire her. He'd come to enjoy their relationship.

Why was he persisting in calling it a relationship? It was a fling…wasn't it? Why had he been so convinced she was developing feelings for him? He'd fooled himself their love-making had made her fall in love with him. But sex was just sex for her. Hadn't she told him that repeatedly? The ironic thing was he'd said the same thing to women he'd dated in the past.

Julius shrugged. 'Just thought you might like to come out to the desert with me.'

Her brow wrinkled like crushed silk. 'The…*desert*?'

'I'm going on a trip to check on the software in the Atacama Desert,' he said. 'It's the highest and driest desert on the planet—that's why we do the infrared astronomy there, because of the absence of water vapour. I thought you might like to come with me.'

She pulled half of her bottom lip inside her mouth before releasing it. 'Look, it's a really nice offer, but I've already booked my air fare and I don't want to be charged a rebooking fee.'

'Don't worry about the money. I can help you with that.'

Her eyes met his with the kind of implacability and pride he had come to associate with her. And admire. 'It's not about the money. I've made up my mind, Julius. I'm leaving at the end of the week. I've waited years for this. You can't ask me to change my plans just because you want to have another week or two of sex.'

'It's not about the sex, damn it,' Julius said.

Her chin came up. 'Then what is it about?'

He framed her face in his hands. He felt as if he was stepping into mid-air off a vertiginous cliff. His stomach was pitching. Her eyes were giving nothing away but he could see a tiny muscle near her mouth moving like a pulse. 'It's about you. About wanting to be with you. Not because of the sex, although that's great. The best, in fact. But because I like you.'

Her eyes took on a cynical sheen. 'You *like* me.' She didn't frame it as a surprised question or a delighted statement. It sounded like she was mocking him for using such a trite word.

Julius brushed his thumbs over her creamy cheeks. 'I like how you make me feel.'

'How do I make you feel?' Her voice was toneless. As if she didn't really care how he answered.

'You make me feel alive.'

'Just…alive?' Was that a hint of delight he was hearing in her voice? Was that a sparkle of hope shining in her toffee-brown eyes?

Julius stepped off the cliff. He could no longer deny what he felt. 'I think I'm falling in love with you. No, strike that—I *am* in love with you. There's no thinking required. I know.'

Her eyes widened to the size of billiard balls. 'You're joking.'

'I'm not joking.'

'You're mad.'

'Mad? No. Madly in love? Yes.'

She opened and closed her mouth. Swallowed. 'But… but *why*?'

'Why?' Julius asked on the tail end of a laugh. 'Because you're the most fascinating, adorable, complicated and yet sweetest person I've ever met.'

Her forehead was lined again with worry. 'But your mother hates me.'

He smoothed away her frown. 'Only because she doesn't know you yet. She'll fall for you like I did once she gets to know how wonderful you are.'

She kept pulling at her lower lip with her teeth. 'Look, I really like you, Julius, but love? I'm not sure I even know what that word means.'

Julius tried not to be put off by her lack of enthusiasm. He understood her caution. She was used to people letting her down, exploiting her. She would be the last person to speak her feelings first. She would have to feel totally secure, trust that her heart was not going to be destroyed by someone who wasn't genuine. He could live with that. He loved her enough to be patient. He didn't need the words. He needed the action. The evidence. 'Love means wanting the best for someone,' he said. 'I want the best for you, *querida*. I want you to be happy. To feel safe and secure and loved.'

Her frown was back. 'I can't feel safe. Not here. Not in Argentina.'

'Because of your stepfather?'

She held her arms against her body, visibly shrinking her frame, as if trying to contain every bit of herself into the smallest package possible. 'You don't know the power he has. The reach he has. If he knew we were involved it could get ugly. Really ugly.'

'I can handle bullies like your stepfather,' Julius said. 'I survived English boarding school, after all!'

Her eyes showed her doubts in long, dark shadows

that went all the way back to her childhood. Julius could see the fear. He could sense it. It was like a presence.

She suddenly unpeeled her arm from around her body and held it wrist-up. 'This is what my stepfather did,' she said. 'He broke my arm in four places. He told me to lie to the doctors at the hospital or he would kill my mother or me or both.'

Julius looked at the white scar on her wrist, his gut boiling with rage at what she had suffered. 'The man is a criminal,' he said. 'He needs to be charged. He needs to be locked up and the key thrown away.'

Holly laughed but it wasn't with humour. It bordered on hysteria. 'He has friends in such high places he could wriggle his way out of any charge. He's done it numerous times. I know he's out there waiting for a chance to hurt me. I'm surprised he hasn't tracked me down yet. It's unusually slow for him.'

He took her in his arms and held her close. 'I won't let him hurt you,' he said. 'I won't let anyone hurt you.'

She pressed her cheek against his chest. 'You're the nicest man I've ever met.' Her voice was so soft he had to strain his ears to hear her. 'If I was going to fall in love it would be with someone like you.'

Julius rested his chin on top of her head, holding her in the circle of his arms. He swore he would do everything he could to make her feel safe. He would not settle until he had achieved that for her. Whatever it took, he would do.

Whatever it took.

CHAPTER TWELVE

HOLLY WOKE WELL before Julius the next morning. But then, she hadn't really been asleep. Even though Julius had made love to her with exquisite tenderness and had made her feel treasured and cherished, she had lain awake most of the night with a gnawing sense of unease. Sophia was returning today after extending her break with her sister. But it wasn't just about the housekeeper finding out about Holly's relationship with Julius. It was a sense the world outside—the world she had been pretending didn't exist—was coming for her. To seek her out. To make her pay the price for the bubble of happiness she had been in.

The fact that Julius had told her he loved her should have made her feel the most blessed person in the world but instead it made her feel the opposite. It was like tempting fate. Whenever things were going well for her, something always happened to ruin it. It was the script of her life. She had no control over it. She didn't dare to be happy. Happiness was for other people—for lucky people who didn't have horrible backgrounds they couldn't escape from.

Holly slipped out of bed and padded across the room, quietly opening the balcony doors and stepping outside.

It still amazed her how Julius had helped her overcome her crippling fear. But he was right. She had allowed her stepfather to control her through fear. She stood on the balcony and breathed in the fresh morning air. The sun was just peeping over the horizon, the red and gold and crimson streaks heralding a warm day ahead.

Julius's phone beeped on the bedside table, and Holly heard him grunt as he reached out to pick it up. She turned to look at him, all sexily tousled from a deep sleep after satisfying sex. He pushed his hair back off his forehead as he read the message. She saw his face blanch. Watched as his throat moved up and down in a convulsive swallow.

She stepped back into the room, pushing away the gauzy curtain that clung to her on the way past. 'What's wrong?'

He clicked off the phone but she noticed he didn't put it back on the bedside table. He was gripping it in his hand so tightly, she was sure the screen would crack. Every knuckle on his hand was white with tension. 'Nothing.'

Holly came over to him and sat on the edge of the bed beside him. 'It can't be nothing. You look like you just received horrible news. Is it your father? Your mother? One of your siblings?'

He pressed his mouth together so flatly his lips turned white. He swung his legs over the bed and stood, still gripping his phone. 'There's been a press leak.' He let out a hissing breath. 'About us.'

This time it was Holly's turn to swallow. 'What does it say?'

His expression was so rigid with anger, she could see

every muscle outlined as if carved in stone. 'It's not so much what it says as what it shows.'

Her stomach dropped. 'There are pictures? Of us?'

He scraped a hand through his hair. 'Yes.'

'Show me.'

'No.'

Holly got off the bed and held out her hand for his phone. 'Show me.'

He held the phone out of her reach, his face so tortured with anguish her heart squeezed. 'No, Holly. Please. It's best if you don't. I'll make it go away. I'll get my lawyer onto it.'

Her eyes widened. '*Your lawyer*? Surely they can't be that bad. How did anyone get photos of us? We haven't been out together in public.'

Julius was looking so ashen Holly felt sick to her stomach. She took the phone from him. This time he didn't fight her for it. It was like he was stunned. Shocked into inertia. She clicked on his most recent message. It was from his twin brother with a short message— WTF?—with a link to a press article with two pictures. They were erotic, almost pornographic shots of her and Julius making love in the pool.

Her mouth went dry. Dry as sandpaper. She couldn't get her voice to work. All she could think was how horrible this was for Julius. How shaming. How mortifying. Someone had captured them in their most intimate moments and splashed it all over the world's media. The media Julius did everything in his power to avoid. *This* was what she had brought to his life. *She* had done this to him. She knew exactly who was behind that long-range camera lens. This was how it was always going to be. She could never have a normal life. Not while her stepfather was alive. He would hunt her down. He would destroy her and anyone she dared to care about.

'I can make it go away,' Julius said into the canyon of silence.

Holly began collecting her things and stuffing them haphazardly into the backpack she had stored in his wardrobe.

'What are you doing?'

'I'm leaving.'

'You can't leave.'

She slung the straps of her backpack over one shoulder. 'I have to leave, Julius. I reckon I've caused enough trouble for you. I admit I wanted to when I first arrived, but even by my standards this is going too far.'

He frowned so hard his brows met over his eyes. 'You don't think I'm blaming *you* for this?'

'It's my fault,' Holly said. 'I've done this to you because I do this kind of stuff to the people I care about. I wreck their lives. I stuff up everything for them just by breathing.'

'You care about me?'

Holly mentally bit her tongue. 'I'm not in love with you, if that's what you're asking.'

'I don't believe you,' he said. 'You *do* love me. That's why you're running away like a spooked rabbit. You're too frightened to let me handle this. You want to trust me to keep you safe when no one's ever been able to do it before. But I *can* keep you safe, Holly. You have to trust me. I will *not* allow anyone to hurt you.'

Holly wanted to believe him. She ached to believe he cared enough to sacrifice his privacy, his reputation and even his family for her. But she wasn't worth it. She knew he would come to resent her for it. The press would never leave them alone. Her stepfather would see to it. Her stepfather would taint their relationship. He would sully it. Cheapen it.

And ultimately destroy it.

'I don't think you're listening to me, Julius,' Holly said. 'I don't *want* to stay. I wouldn't stay if you paid me to. I've got plans. I'm not changing them. My future is in England; it's not here with you.'

His mouth tightened. His hands clenched and unclenched by his sides. Holly got the feeling he was at war with himself. Fighting back the impulse to reach for her. 'Fine,' he said at last. 'Leave. I'll call Natalia and get her to pick you up. You won't be able to leave the country until your community service time is up.'

Holly knew it would be the longest three days of her life.

Julius stood in a stony silence as Holly was driven away by her caseworker. It felt as if his heart was tied to the rear of the car. The tugging, straining, gutting sensation took his breath away. He was sure she was lying and yet…and yet what if he was wrong? What if she had set him up from the start? She was a troublemaker. A rebel. She had openly admitted to wanting to make his life difficult. He thought back to the pool. Both times she had lured him out there…hadn't she? It had been her idea to make love out there. It wasn't something he would normally do. She was always poking fun at his conservative nature. Was that why? So she could set him up and shame him the in the most shocking way possible?

But then he thought of how she had trusted him enough to tell him about the horrible stuff that had happened to her as a child. That wasn't an act. She had the scars to prove it. Her stepfather was behind this photo scandal. He had to be. Julius just had to prove it.

If he could make Holly feel safe by seeing justice served then maybe, just maybe, she would trust him enough to admit to her feelings.

He reached for his phone and called a close friend, Leandro Allegretti. Leandro was a forensic accountant who occasionally did some work for Jake's business analysis company. They had gone to school together and Leandro had spent many a weekend or holiday at Ravensdene while they'd been growing up. If anyone could uncover secrets and lies, it was Leandro. He made it his business to uncover fraud, money laundering and other white-collar crime.

'Leandro?' Julius said. 'Yeah, it's me. Listen, I have a little project for you...'

Holly had finally made it to England. She had found a tiny flat in central London and even landed a job in a deli, which should have made her feel as if all her boxes were ticked, but she felt miserable. The weather was freezing, for one thing. And it never seemed to stop raining. She had spent years dreaming of the time when she would be here, doing normal stuff like normal people, and yet she felt lost. Empty. Hollow. As if something was missing. Even the shops didn't interest her. She hadn't heard from Julius, but then she didn't expect to, not really. She had cut him from her life in the only way she knew how. Bluntly. Permanently.

But she missed him. She missed everything about him. The security she felt when she was with him was only apparent to her now it had been taken away. She had felt *safe* with him. Now she was anchorless. Like a paper boat bobbing about in the middle of the ocean.

Holly was on a tea break in a nearby café when she

flicked through the day's newspaper and her eyes honed in on an article that was only a couple of paragraphs long about a recent criminal charge in Argentina. Her eyes widened in shock when she saw her stepfather's name cited as the man at the centre of the investigation that had uncovered a money-laundering and drug-running scheme that had gone on for over twenty years.

Holly sat back in her seat with a gasp of wonder. It had finally happened. Franco Morales's lawyer said his client had pleaded guilty and bail was denied. How had that come about? Who was behind it? Who had shone the light of suspicion on her stepfather?

A cramped space inside Holly's chest suddenly opened. *Julius.* Of course he would have gone after her stepfather. Hadn't he promised he would not allow anyone to hurt her? He had been true to his word. He had taken on one of Argentina's most notoriously elusive criminals and brought about justice. *For her.*

Holly shot out of her seat. She had to see him. She had to see him to thank him in person. To tell him… what? She sat back down in her seat. Huddled back into her coat. She didn't belong in his world. How could she? She worked in a deli. She had no qualifications. He was the son of London theatre royalty.

And his mother hated her.

'Is this seat taken?'

Holly looked up to see a woman standing next to the empty chair on the opposite side of the table. She looked vaguely familiar but Holly couldn't quite place her. Maybe she had served her in the shop in the past week or so. 'No; I'm leaving soon, in any case.'

The woman sat down. 'You don't recognise me, do you?'

Holly blinked as the woman took off her sunglasses. Why anyone would be wearing sunglasses on such a miserably wet day in London had occurred to her but then she figured it took all types. Now she realised it was all part of a disguise. A very clever one, too. No one would ever guess Elisabetta Albertini would frequent a humble little café in Soho dressed like a bag lady. 'No,' Holly said. 'Even your accent is different. But then, I guess you can do just about any accent.'

Elisabetta gave her a sly smile. 'So, how's London working out for you?'

'Great. Fine. Brilliant.'

'You'd better stick to your day job,' Elisabetta said. 'You're a terrible actor.'

Holly grimaced. 'Yeah, I know. But I hate my day job. I don't want to do this for the rest of my life. Nor do I want to be cleaning up after people.'

'What did you want to be when you were a little girl?'

'I wanted to be a kindergarten teacher—but why are you even asking me this after the way you spoke to me at Julius's? And how did you find me?'

'Julius told me.'

Holly frowned. 'But how does he know where I am?'

'He made it his business to find out,' Elisabetta said. 'Look, I was wrong to speak to you the way I did. Richard's parents did the same thing to me all those years ago when he brought me home to introduce me to them. They made me feel so worthless. I swore I would never treat any daughter-in-law of mine like that, but then I went and did it to you.'

'Daughter-in-law?' Holly said, frowning harder. 'No one said anything about marriage. We had a fling, that's all, and now it's over.'

'He loves you, Holly,' Elisabetta said. 'He'll want to marry you because that's his way. Jake would be another thing entirely. But with Julius you can be assured he'll always do the right thing.'

Holly narrowed her eyes. 'Did he *make* you come here to apologise to me?'

Elisabetta gave her a coy look. 'Does it matter? If he's going to marry you, then I'm going to have to accept it or lose him.'

Holly's frown deepened another notch. 'He shouldn't have done that. You're his mother. He's lucky to have you. I wish I had a mother. I have no one. No one at all.'

Elisabetta put her hand over Holly's and gave it a light squeeze. 'I'm not the best mother in the world. I know that, and it upsets me if I allow myself to think about it, so I don't think about it.' She pulled her hand away as if she had a time limit on touch and sat back in her seat. 'But who knows? Maybe I'll do a better job as a mother-in-law.'

'You mean you wouldn't…*mind*?'

Elisabetta gave a short but not very pleasant-sounding laugh. 'Of course I mind. But I'm an actor; I'll pretend I don't. But don't tell Julius. It can be our little secret.'

Holly gave her a telling look. 'You won't be able to fool him no matter how brilliant an actor you are.'

The older woman's gaze was suddenly very direct. 'Do you love my son?'

Holly gave a heartfelt sigh. 'So much it hurts to think I might never see him again.'

Elisabetta smiled a mercurial smile and popped her sunglasses back on as she got up to leave. 'I have a feeling you'll be seeing him very soon. *Ciao.*'

Holly gathered her things and made to get up but a tall

shadow fell over her. She looked up to see Julius standing there, beads of rain clinging to his cashmere coat, his hair and even to the ends of his eyelashes. 'I know my mother's a hard act to follow, but here I am. Did she apologise?'

'Yes…' Holly licked her suddenly dry lips. Maybe now wasn't the right time to talk about his mother's 'apology'. 'I can't believe what you did for me. It was… amazing. Unbelievable. I can never thank you enough.'

'There is one way,' he said. 'Will you do me the honour of becoming my wife?'

Holly thought her heart was going to burst out of her chest cavity with sheer joy. Could this really be happening? 'Why me? You could have anyone. I'm no one.'

He took her by the hands and gripped them tightly. 'You're everything to me. Everything. I love you, Holly. More than I can ever tell you. I know this isn't a dream proposal. In fact, I can't believe I'm proposing to you in a public place—but I can't bear another moment without knowing you'll agree to spend the rest of your life with me. You don't have to come back to Argentina if you don't want to. I can move back to England.'

Holly looked at him in stunned surprise. 'You'd do that for me?'

'Of course.'

She wrinkled her nose. 'But the weather's foul.'

'I know, but at least we could cuddle up in bed,' he said with a glint in his eyes.

Holly grinned back. 'I guess we could split the time between here and there. Summer here, winter there.'

'Sounds like a good plan to me,' he said, drawing her close. 'I missed you so much. I never realised what a boring life I've been living until you came into it.'

Holly felt the sting of happy tears at the back of her eyes. 'I was miserable from the moment I got on that plane. I'd planned that moment for years. I'd looked forward to it. Counted the days, the hours, even the minutes. But as soon as we took off I felt empty. As if I was leaving a part of myself behind.'

Julius blotted a tear that had escaped from her left eye. 'Do you love me or have I been deluding myself?'

Holly held his hand against her cheek. 'I love you. I'm not sure when I started. Maybe when you took me out on the balcony. You were so kind and patient. I didn't stand a chance after that.'

He smiled a tender smile. 'So will you marry me, my darling?'

Holly wanted to pinch herself to check she wasn't dreaming. 'No one's ever proposed to me before.'

'Lucky me to be the first.'

Holly put her arms around his waist and smiled as his mouth came down towards hers. 'Lucky us.'

* * * * *

AWAKENING
THE RAVENSDALE
HEIRESS

To Holly Marks. Thank you for being such a wonderful fan. Your lovely comments on Facebook have lifted me so many times. This one is for you with much love and appreciation. xxxx

CHAPTER ONE

MIRANDA WOULDN'T HAVE seen him if she hadn't been hiding from the paparazzi. Not that a fake potted plant was a great hiding place or anything, she thought. She peeped through the branches of the ornamental ficus to see Leandro Allegretti crossing the busy street outside the coffee shop she was sheltering in. He didn't seem aware of the fact it was spitting with rain or that the intersection was clotted with traffic and bustling with pedestrians. It was as if a transparent cube was around him. He was impervious to the chatter and clatter outside.

She would have recognised him anywhere. He had a regal, untouchable air about him that made him stand out in a crowd. Even the way he was dressed set him apart—not that there weren't other suited men in the crowd, but the way he wore the sharply tailored charcoal-grey suit teamed with a snowy white shirt and a black-and-silver striped tie somehow made him look different. More civilised. More dignified.

Or maybe it was because of his signature frown.

Had she ever seen him without that frown? Miranda wondered. Her older twin brothers, Julius and Jake, had been boarding school buddies with Leandro. He had spent occasional weekends or school holidays and even university breaks at the Ravensdale family home, Ravensdene, in Buckinghamshire. Being a decade younger, she'd spent most of her childhood being a little intimidated by Leandro's taciturn presence. He was the epitome of the strong, silent type—a man of few words and even fewer facial expressions. She couldn't read his expression at the best of times. It was hard to tell if he was frowning in disapproval or simply in deep concentration.

He came into the coffee shop and Miranda watched as every female head turned his way. His French-Italian heritage had served him well in the looks department. Imposingly tall with jet-black hair, olive skin and brown eyes three or four shades darker than hers.

But if Leandro was aware of his impact on the female gaze he gave no sign of it. It was one of the things she secretly most liked about him. He didn't trade on his appearance. He seemed largely unaware of how knee-wobblingly gorgeous he looked. It was as if it was irrelevant to him. Unlike her brother Jake, who knew he was considered arm candy and exploited it for all he could.

Leandro stood at the counter and ordered a long black coffee to take away from the young, blushing attendant, and then politely stood back to wait for it, taking out his phone to check his messages or emails.

Miranda covertly studied his tall, athletic figure with its strongly corded muscles honed from long hours of endurance exercise. The broad shoulders, the strong back, the lean hips, taut buttocks and the long legs. She had seen him many a time down at Ravensdene, a solitary figure running across the fields of the estate in all sorts of weather, or swimming endless laps of the pool in summer.

Leandro took to exercise with an intense, single-minded concentration that made her wonder if he was doing it for the health benefits or for some other reason known only to himself. But, whatever reason it was that motivated him, it clearly worked to his benefit. He had the sort of body to stop female hearts. She couldn't stop looking at him, drinking in the male perfection of his frame, her mind traitorously wondering how delicious he would look in a tangle of sheets after marathon sex. Did he have a current lover? Miranda hadn't heard much about his love life lately, but she'd heard his father had died a couple of months ago. She assumed he'd been keeping a low profile since.

The young attendant handed Leandro his coffee and as he turned to leave his eyes met Miranda's through the craggy branches of the pot plant. She saw the flash of recognition go through his gaze but he didn't smile in welcome. His lips didn't even twitch upwards. But then, she couldn't remember ever seeing him smile. Or, at least, not at her. The closest he came to it was a sort of twist of his lips that could easily be mistaken for cynicism rather than amusement.

'Miranda?' he said.

She lifted her hand in a little fingertip wave, trying

not to draw too much attention to herself in case anyone lurking nearby with a smart phone recognised her. 'Hi.'

He came over to her table screened behind the pot plant. She had to crane her neck to meet his frowning gaze. She always felt like a pixie standing in front of a giant when she was around him. He was an inch shorter than her six-foot-four brothers but for some reason he'd always seemed taller.

'Are the press still hassling you?' he asked, still frowning.

Of course, Leandro had heard about her father's scandal, Miranda thought. It was the topic on everyone's lips. It was splashed over every newsfeed or online blog. Could it get any more embarrassing? Was there anyone in London—*the entire world*—who didn't know her father had sired a love child twenty-three years ago? As London theatre royalty, her parents were known for drawing attention to themselves. But this scandal of her father's was the biggest and most mortifying so far. Miranda's mother, Elisabetta Albertini, had cancelled her season on Broadway and was threatening divorce. Her father, Richard Ravensdale, was trying to get his love child into the bosom of the family but so far with zero success. Apparently Katherine Winwood had failed to be charmed by her long-lost biological father and was doing everything she could to avoid him and her half-siblings.

Which was fine by Miranda. Just fine, especially since Kat was so beautiful that everyone was calling Miranda 'the ugly sister'. *Argh!*

'Just a little,' Miranda said with a pained smile. 'But

enough about all that. I'm so sorry about your father. I didn't know about him passing otherwise I would've come to the funeral.'

'Thank you,' he said. 'But it was a private affair.'

'So, how are things with you?' she said. 'I heard you did some work for Julius in Argentina. Great news about his engagement, isn't it? I met his fiancée Holly last night. She's lovely.' Miranda always found it difficult to make conversation with Leandro. He wasn't the small talk type. When she was around him she had a tendency to babble or ramble to fill any silence with the first thing that came into her head. She knew it made her seem a little vacuous, but he was so tight-lipped, what else was she to do? She felt like a tennis-ball machine loping balls at him but without him returning any.

Fortunately this time he did.

'Yes,' he said. 'Great news.'

'It was a big surprise, wasn't it?' Miranda said. 'I didn't even know he was dating anyone. I can't believe my big brother is getting married. Seriously, Julius is such a dark horse, he's practically invisible. But Holly is absolutely perfect for him. I'm so happy for them. Jasmine Connolly is going to design the wedding dress. We're both going to be bridesmaids, as Holly doesn't have any sisters or close friends. I don't know why she doesn't have loads of friends because she's such a sweetheart. Jaz thinks so too. You remember Jaz, don't you? The gardener's daughter who grew up with me at Ravensdene? We went to school together. She's got her own bridal shop now and—'

'Can I ask a favour?'

Miranda blinked. A favour? What sort of favour? What was he going to say? *Shut up? Stop gabbling like a fool? Stop blushing like a gauche twelve-year-old schoolgirl?* 'Sure.'

His deep brown gaze was centred on hers, his dark brows still knitted together. 'Will you do a job for me?'

Her heart gave a funny little skip. 'Wh-what sort of job?' Stuttering was another thing she did when she was around him. What was it about this man that turned her into a gibbering idiot? It was ridiculous. She had known him *all* her life. He was like a brother to her...well, sort of. Leandro had always been on the fringe of her consciousness as the Ideal Man. Not that she ever allowed herself to indulge in such thoughts. Not fully. But they were there, like uninvited guests at a cocktail party, every now and again moving forward to sneak a canapé or a drink before melting back against the back wall of her mind.

'My father left me his art collection in his will,' Leandro said. 'I need someone to catalogue it before I can sell it; plus there are a couple of paintings that might need restoring. I'll pay you, of course.'

Miranda found it odd he hadn't told anyone his father had died until after the funeral was over. She wondered why he hadn't told her brothers, particularly Julius, who was the more serious and steady twin. Julius would have supported Leandro, gone to the funeral with him and stood by him if he'd needed back up.

She pictured Leandro standing alone at that funeral. Why had he gone solo? Funerals were horrible enough.

The final goodbye was always horrifically painful but to face it alone would be unimaginable. Even if he hadn't been close to his father there would still be grief for what he had missed out on, not to mention the heart-wrenching realisation it was now too late to fix it.

When her childhood sweetheart Mark Redbank had died of leukaemia, her family and his had surrounded her. Supported her. Comforted her. Even Leandro had turned up at the funeral—she remembered seeing his tall, silent dark-haired figure at the back of the church. It had touched her that he'd made the time when he'd hardly known Mark. He had only met him a handful of times.

Miranda had heard via her brothers that Leandro had a complicated back story. They hadn't told her much, only that his parents had divorced when he was eight years old and his mother had taken him to England, where he'd been promptly put into boarding school with Miranda's twin brothers after his mother had remarried and begun a new family. He had been a studious child, excelling both academically and on the sporting field. He had taken that hard work ethic into his career as a forensic accountant. 'I'm so sorry for your loss,' she said.

'Thank you.'

'Did your mother go to the funeral?' Miranda asked.

'No,' he said. 'They hadn't spoken since the divorce.'

Miranda wondered if his father's funeral would have brought back painful memories of his estranged relationship with him. No son wanted to be rejected by his father. But apparently Vittorio Allegretti hadn't wanted custody after the divorce. He had handed over Leandro as a small boy and only saw him on the rare occasion he'd been in London on business. She had heard via her brothers that eventually Leandro had stopped meeting his father because Vittorio had a tendency to drink to the point of abusing others and/or passing out. There had even been one occasion where the police had had to be called due to a bar-room scuffle Leandro's father had started. It didn't surprise her Leandro had kept his distance. With his quiet and reserved nature he wasn't the sort of man to draw unnecessary attention to himself.

But there was so much more she didn't know about him. She knew he was a forensic accountant—a brilliant one. He had his own consultancy in London and travelled all over the globe uncovering major fraud in the corporate and private sectors. He often worked with Jake with his business analysis company and he had recently helped Julius in exposing Holly's ghastly stepfather's underworld drug and money-laundering operations.

Leandro Allegretti was the go-to man for uncovering secrets and yet Miranda had always sensed he had one or two of his own.

'So this job…' she began. 'Where's the collection?'

'In Nice,' he said. 'My father ran an art and antiques business in the French Riviera. This is his private collection. He sold off everything else when he was first diagnosed with terminal cancer.'

'And you want to…to get rid of it?' Miranda asked,

frowning at the thought of him selling everything of his father's. In spite of their tricky relationship, didn't he want a memento? '*All* of it?'

The line of his mouth was flat. Hardened. Whitened. 'Yes,' he said. 'I have to pack up the villa and sell that too.'

'Why not use someone locally?' Miranda knew she was well regarded in her job as an art restorer even though she was at the early stages of her career. But she wouldn't be able to do much on site. Art restoration was more science now than art. Sophisticated techniques using x-rays, infrared technology and Raman spectroscopy meant most restoration work was done in the protective environment of an established gallery. Leandro could afford the best in the world. Why ask her?

'I thought you might like a chance to escape the hoo-hah here,' Leandro said. 'Can you take a couple of weeks' leave from the gallery?'

Miranda had already been thinking about getting out of London for some breathing space. It had been hell on wheels with her father's dirty linen being flapped in her face. She couldn't go anywhere without being assailed by press. Everyone wanted to know what she thought of her father's scandal. *Had she met her half-sister? Was she planning to? Were her parents divorcing for the second time?* It was relentless. Along with the press attention, she had also been subjected to her mother's bitter tirades about her father, and her father's insistence she make contact with her half-sister and play happy families.

Like that was going to happen.

This would be a perfect opportunity to escape. Besides, October on the Côte d'Azur would be preferable to the capricious weather London was currently dishing up. 'How soon do you want me?' she said, blushing when she realised her unintentional double entendre. 'I mean, I can probably get away from work by the end of next week. Is that okay?'

'Fine,' he said. 'I don't collect the keys to the villa until then anyway. I'll book your flight and email you the details. Do you have a preference for a hotel?'

'Where will you be staying?'

'At my father's villa.'

Miranda thought about the expense of staying at a hotel, not that Leandro couldn't afford it. He would put her in five-star accommodation if she asked for it. But staying in a hotel put her at risk of being found by the press. If she stayed with Leandro at his father's villa she could work on the collection without that looming threat.

Besides, it would be an opportunity to see a little of the man behind the perpetual frown.

'Is there room for me at your father's place?'

Leandro's frown deepened until two vertical lines formed between his bottomless brown eyes. 'You don't want to stay in a hotel?'

Miranda snagged her lip with her teeth, warm colour crawling further over her cheeks until her whole face felt on fire. 'I wouldn't want to intrude if you've got someone else staying…'

Who was his someone else?

Who was his latest lover? She knew he had them

from time to time. She had seen pictures of him at charity events. She had even met one or two over the years when he had brought a partner to one of the legendary parties her parents had put on at Ravensdene for New Year's Eve. Tall, impossibly beautiful, elegant, eloquent types who didn't blush and stumble over their words and make silly fools of themselves. He wasn't as out there as her playboy brother Jake. Leandro was more like Julius in that he liked to keep his private life out of the public domain.

'I haven't got anyone staying,' he said.

He hadn't got anyone staying? Or he hadn't got *anyone*?

And why was she even thinking about his love life? It wasn't as if she was interested in him. She was interested in no one. Not since Mark had died. She ignored attractive men. She quickly brushed off any men who flirted with her or tried to charm her. Not that Leandro was super-charming or anything. He was polite but distant. Aloof. And as for flirting...well, if he could learn to smile now and again it might help.

Miranda wasn't sure why she was pushing so hard for an invitation. Maybe it was because she had never spent any time with him without other people around. Maybe it was because he had recently lost his father and she wanted to know why he hadn't told anyone before the funeral. Maybe it was because she wanted to see where he had spent the first eight years of his life before he had moved to England. What had he been like as a child? Had he been playful and fun-loving, like most kids, or had he been as serious and inexpressive as he was now? 'So would it be okay to stay with you?' she said. 'I won't get in your way.'

He looked at her in that frowning manner he had. Deep thought or disapproval? She could never quite tell. 'There isn't a housekeeper there.'

'I can cook,' she said. 'And I can help you tidy things up before you sell the place. It'll be fun.'

A small silence ticked past.

Miranda got the feeling he was mulling it over. Weighing it up in his mind. Doing a risk assessment.

He finally drew in a breath and then slowly released it. 'Fine. I'll email you those flights.'

She rose from the table and began to shrug on her coat, tugging her hair free from the collar. 'Do you mind if I walk out with you? There was a pap crew tailing me earlier. I ducked in here to escape them. It'd be nice to get back to work without being jostled.'

'No problem,' he said. 'I'm heading that way anyway.'

Leandro walked beside Miranda on the way back to the gallery. He was always struck by how tiny she was. Built like a ballerina with fine limbs and an elfin face, with big tawny-brown eyes and auburn hair, yet her skin was without a single freckle—it was as white and pure as Devon cream. She had an ethereal beauty about her. She reminded him of a fairy-tale character—an innocent waif lost in the middle of a crazy out-of-control world.

Seeing her hiding in that café had tripped a switch inside his head. It was like he'd had a brain snap. He hadn't thought it through but it seemed...*right* some-how. She needed a bolthole and he needed someone to help him sort out the mess his father had left behind. Maybe it would've been better to commission some-one local. Maybe he could have sold the lot without proper valuation. Hell, he didn't really know why he had asked her, except he knew she was having a tough time of it with her father's love-child scandal still doing the rounds.

That and the fact he couldn't bear the thought of being in that villa on his own with only the ghosts of the past to haunt him. He hadn't been back since the day he'd left when he was eight years old.

It wasn't like him to act so impulsively but seeing Miranda hiding behind that pot plant had made him re-alise how stressed she was about her father's latest pec-cadillo. He had heard from her brothers the press had camped outside her flat for the last month. She hadn't been able to take a step without a camera or a micro-phone being shoved in her face. Being the daughter of famous celebrities came with a heavy price tag. Or, at least, it did for her.

Leandro had always felt a little sorry for Miranda. She was constantly compared to her flamboyant and glamorous mother and found lacking. Now she was being compared to her half-sister. Kat Winwood *was* stunning. No two ways about that. Kat was the bill-board-beautiful type. Kat would stop traffic. Air traf-fic. Miranda's beauty was quiet, the sort of beauty that grew on you. And she was shy in an endearingly old-fashioned way. He didn't know too many women who blushed as easily as her. She never flirted. And she never dated. Not since she had lost her first and only boyfriend to leukaemia when she was sixteen. Leandro couldn't help admiring her loyalty, even if he privately thought she was throwing her life away.

But who was he to judge?

He hadn't got any plans for happy-ever-after either.

Miranda was the best person to advise him on his father's collection. Of course she was. She was reliable and sensible. She was competent and efficient and she had an excellent eye. She had helped her brother Julius buy some great pieces at various auctions. She could spot a fraud at twenty paces. It would only take a week or two to sort out the collection and he would be doing her a favour in the process.

But there was one thing she didn't know about him.

He hadn't even told Julius or Jake about Rosie.

It was why he had gone to his father's funeral alone. Going back to Nice had been like ripping open a wound.

There'd been numerous times when he could have mentioned it. He could have told his two closest friends the tragic secret he carried like a shackle around his heart. But instead he had let everyone think he was an only child. Every time he thought of his baby sister his chest would seize. The thought of her little chubby face with its dimpled, sunny smile would bring his guilt crashing down on him like a guillotine.

For all these years he had said nothing. To anyone. He had left that part of his life—his former life, his childhood—back in France. His life was divided into two sections: France and England. Before and After. Sometimes that 'before' life felt like a bad dream—a horrible, blood-chilling nightmare. But then he would wake up and realise with a sickening twist of his gut that it was true. Inescapably, heartbreakingly true. It didn't matter where he lived. How far he travelled. How hard he worked to block the memories. The guilt came with him. It sat on his shoulder during the day. It poked him awake at night. It drove vicious needles through his skull until he was blind with pain.

Speaking about his family was torture for him. Pure, unadulterated torture. He hated even thinking about it. He didn't have a family.

His family had been blown apart twenty-seven years ago and *he* had been the one to do it.

CHAPTER TWO

'YOU'RE GOING TO FRANCE?' Jasmine Connelly said, eyes wide with sparkling intrigue. 'With Leandro Allegretti?'

Miranda had dropped into Jasmine's bridal boutique in Mayfair for a quick catch-up before she flew out the following day. Jaz was sewing Swarovski crystals onto a gorgeous wedding dress, the sort of dress for every girl who dreamed of being a princess. Miranda had pictured a dress just like it back in the day when her life had been going according to plan. Now every time she saw a wedding dress she felt sad.

'Not going *with* him as such,' she said, absently fingering the fabric of the wedding gown on the mannequin. 'I'm meeting him over there to help him sort out his father's art collection.'

'When do you go?'

'Tomorrow… For a couple of weeks.'

'Should be interesting,' Jaz said with a smile in her voice.

Miranda looked at her with a frown. 'Why do you say that?'

Jaz gave her a worldly look. 'Come, now. Don't you ever notice the way he looks at you?'

Miranda felt something unhitch in her chest. 'He never looks at me. He barely even says a word to me. This is the first time we've exchanged more than a couple of sentences.'

'Clues, my dear Watson,' Jaz said with a cheeky smile. 'I've seen the way he looks at you when he thinks no one's watching. I reckon if it weren't for his relationship with your family he would act on it. You'd better pack some decent underwear just in case he changes his mind.'

Miranda pointedly ignored her friend's teasing comment as she trailed her hand through the voluminous veil hanging beside the dress. 'Do you know much about his private life?'

Jaz stopped sewing to look at her with twinkling grey-blue eyes. 'So you are interested. Yay! I thought the day would never come.'

Miranda frowned. 'I know what you're thinking but you couldn't be more wrong. I'm not the least bit interested in him or anyone. I just wondered if he had a current girlfriend, that's all.'

'Not that I've heard of, but you know how close he keeps his cards,' Jaz said. 'He could have a string of women on the go. He is, after all, one of Jake's mates.'

Every time Jaz said Jake's name her mouth got a snarly, contemptuous look. The enmity between them was ongoing. It had started when Jaz was sixteen at one of Miranda's parents' legendary New Year's Eve parties. Jaz refused to be drawn on what had actually happened in Jake's bedroom that night. Jake too kept tight-lipped. But it was common knowledge he despised Jaz and made every effort to avoid her if he could.

Miranda glanced at the glittering diamond on her friend's ring finger. It was Jaz's third engagement and, while Miranda didn't exactly dislike Jaz's latest fiancé, Myles, she didn't think he was 'The One' for her. Not that she could ever say that to Jaz. Jaz didn't take too kindly to being told what she didn't want to hear. Miranda had had the same misgivings over Fiancés One and Two. She just had to hope and trust her headstrong and stubborn friend would realise how she was short-changing herself before the wedding actually took place.

Jaz stood back and cast a critical eye over her handiwork. 'What do you think?'

'It's beautiful,' Miranda said with a sigh.

'Yeah, well, I'm going cross-eyed with all these crystals,' Jaz said. 'I've got to get it done so I can start on Holly's. She's awfully nice, isn't she?'

'Gorgeous,' Miranda said. 'It's amazing, seeing Julius so happy. To tell you the truth, I wasn't sure he was ever going to fall in love. They're total opposites and yet they're so perfect for each other.'

Jaz looked at her with her head on one side, that teasing glint back in her gaze. 'Is that a note of wistfulness I can hear?'

Miranda rearranged her features. 'I'd better get going.' She grabbed her tote bag, slung it over her shoulder and leaned in to kiss Jaz on the cheek. 'See you when I get back.'

* * *

When Miranda landed in Nice she saw Leandro waiting for her in the terminal. He was dressed more casually this time but if anything it made him look even more heart-stoppingly attractive. The dark blue denim jeans clung to his leanly muscled legs. The rolled back sleeves of his light blue shirt highlighted his deep tan and emphasised the masculinity of the dark hair liberally sprinkled over his strong forearms. He was cleanly shaven but she could see where he had nicked himself on the left side of his jaw. For some reason, it humanised him. He was always so well put together, so in control. Was being back in his childhood home unsettling for him? Upsetting? What emotions were going on behind the dark screen of his eyes?

As he caught her eye a flutter of awareness rippled deep and low in her belly. Would he kiss her in greeting? She couldn't remember him ever touching her. Not even by accident. Even when he'd walked her back to the gallery last week he had kept his distance. There had been no shoulder brushing. Not that she even reached his shoulders. She was five-foot-five to his six-foot-three.

Miranda smiled shyly as he came towards her. 'Hi.'

'Hello.' Was it her imagination or was his voice deeper and huskier than normal? The sound of it moved over her skin as if he had reached out and stroked her. But he kept a polite distance, although she couldn't help noticing his gaze slipped to her mouth for the briefest moment. 'How was your flight?' he said.

'Lovely,' she said. 'But you didn't have to put me in first class. I was happy to fly coach.'

He took her carry-on bag from her, somehow without touching her fingers as he did so. 'I didn't want anyone bothering you,' he said. 'There's nothing worse than being a captive audience to someone's life story.'

Miranda gave a light laugh. 'True.'

She followed him out to the car park where he opened the door of the hire car for her. She couldn't fault his manners, but then, he had always been a gentleman. She had never known him to be anything but polite and considerate. She wondered if this was difficult for him, coming back to France to his early childhood home. What memories did it stir for him? Did it make him wish he had been closer to his father? Did it stir up regrets that now it was too late?

She glanced at him as they left the car park and joined the traffic on the Promenade des Anglais that followed the brilliant blue of the coastline of the Mediterranean Sea. He was frowning as usual; even his hands on the steering wheel were clenched. She could see the tanned flesh straining over his knuckles. The line of his jaw was grim. Everything about him was tense, wound up like a spring. It looked like he was in physical pain.

'Are you okay?' she asked.

He looked at her briefly, moving his lips in a grimace-like smile that didn't reveal his teeth. 'I'm fine.'

Miranda didn't buy it for a second. 'Have you got one of your headaches?' She had seen him once at Ravensdene when he had come down with a migraine.

He was always so strong and fit that to see him rendered helpless with such pain and sickness had been an awful shock. The doctor had had to be called to give him a strong painkiller injection. Jake had driven him back to London the next day, as he had still been too ill to drive himself.

'Just a tension headache,' he said. 'Nothing I can't handle.'

'When did you arrive?'

'Yesterday,' he said. 'I had a job to finish in Stockholm.'

'I expect it must be difficult coming back,' Miranda said, still watching him. 'Emotional for you, I mean. Did you ever come back after your parents divorced?'

'No.'

She frowned. 'Not even to visit your father?'

His hands tightened another notch on the steering wheel. 'We didn't have that sort of relationship.'

Miranda wondered how his father could have been so cold and distant. How could a man turn his back on his son—his only child—just because his marriage had broken up? Surely the bond of parenthood was much stronger than that? Her parents had gone through a bitter divorce before she'd been born and, while they hadn't been around much due to their theatre commitments, as far as she could tell Julius and Jake had never doubted they were loved.

'Your father doesn't sound like a very nice person,' she said. 'Was he always a drinker? I'm sorry. Maybe you don't want to talk about it. It's just, Julius told me you didn't like it when your father came to London to see you. He said your dad embarrassed you by getting horribly drunk.'

Leandro's gaze was focussed on the clogging traffic ahead but she could see the way his jaw was locked down, as if tightened by a clamp. 'He didn't always drink that heavily.'

'What made him start? The divorce?'

He didn't answer for a moment. 'It certainly didn't help.'

Miranda wondered about the dynamics of his parents' relationship and how each of them had handled the breakdown of their marriage. Some men found the loss of a relationship far more devastating than others. Some sank into depression, others quickly re-partnered to avoid being alone. The news was regularly full of horrid stories of men getting back at their ex-wives after a broken relationship—cruel and vindictive attempts to get revenge, sometimes involving the children, with tragic results. 'Did he ever remarry?' she asked.

'No.'

'Did he have other partners?'

'Occasionally, but not for long,' Leandro said. 'He was difficult to live with. There were few women who would put up with him.'

'So it was his fault your mother left him?' Miranda asked. 'Because he was so difficult to live with?'

He didn't answer for so long she thought he hadn't heard her over the noise of the traffic outside. 'No,' he said heavily. 'That was my fault.'

Miranda looked at him in shock. '*You?* Why would

you think that? That's ridiculous. You were only eight years old. Why on earth would you blame yourself?'

He gave her an unreadable glance before he took a left turn. 'My father's place is a few blocks up here. Have you ever been to Nice before?'

'A couple of years ago—but don't try and change the subject,' she said. 'Why do you blame yourself for your parents' divorce?'

'Don't all kids blame themselves?'

Miranda thought about it for a moment. Her mother had said a number of times how having twins had put pressure on her relationship with her father. But then, Elisabetta wasn't a naturally maternal type. She was happiest when the attention was on her, not on her children. Miranda had felt that keenly as she'd been growing up. All of her friends—apart from Jaz—were envious of her having a glamorous showbiz mother. And Elisabetta could *act* like a wonderful mother when it suited her.

It was the times when she didn't that hurt Miranda the most.

But why did Leandro think *he* was responsible for his parents' break-up? Had *they* told him that? Had they made him feel guilty? What sort of parents had they been to do something so reprehensible? How could they make a young child feel responsible for the breakdown of a marriage? That was the adults' responsibility, not a child's, and certainly not a young child's.

But she didn't pursue the conversation for at that point Leandro pulled into the driveway of a rundown-looking villa in the Belle Epoqué style. At first she thought he must have made a mistake, pulled into the wrong driveway or something. The place was like something out of a gothic noir film. The outside of the three-storey-high building was charcoal-grey with the stain of years of carbon monoxide pollution. The windows with the ragged curtains drawn were like closed eyes.

The villa was like a faded Hollywood star. Miranda could see the golden era of glamour in its lead-roofed cupolas on the corners and the ornamental ironwork and flamboyance of the stucco decorations that resembled a wedding cake.

But it had been sadly neglected. She knew many of the grand villas of the Belle Époque era along the Promenade des Anglais had not survived urban redevelopment. But the extravagance of the period was still apparent in this old beauty.

It made Miranda's blood tick in her veins. What a gorgeous old place for Leandro to inherit. It was a piece of history. A relic from an enchanted time when the aristocracy had flaunted their wealth by hiring architects to design opulent villas with every imaginable embellishment: faux stonework, figureheads, frescos, friezes, decorative ironwork, ornamental stucco work, cupolas, painted effects, garlands and grotesques. The aristocracy had indulged their taste for the exotic, with Italian and Classic influences as well as Gothic, Eastern and Moorish.

And he was packing it up and *selling* it?

Miranda looked up at him as he opened her car door for her. 'Leandro, it's amazing! What a glorious building. It's like a time capsule from the Art Nouveau period. This was your childhood home? *Really?*'

He clearly didn't share her excitement for the building. His expression had that closed-off look about it, as shuttered as the windows of the villa they were about to enter. 'It's very run-down,' he said.

'Yes, but it can be brought back to life.' Miranda beamed at him, clasping her hands in excitement. 'I'm so glad you asked me to come. I can't wait to see what's inside.'

He stepped forward to unlock the door with the set of keys he was holding in his hand. 'Dust and cobwebs mostly.'

Miranda's gaze went to his tanned hand, that funny fluttery feeling passing over the floor of her belly as she watched the way his long, strong fingers turned the key in the lock. Who was the last woman he'd touched with those arrantly masculine but beautiful hands? Were his hands smooth or rough or something deliciously in between? She couldn't stop herself from imagining those strong, capable hands exploring female flesh. Caressing a breast. Gliding down a smooth thigh. Touching the silken skin between her legs.

Her legs?

Miranda jerked back from her wayward thoughts as if a hand had grabbed and pulled on the back of her clothing. What was she doing thinking of him that way? She didn't think of *any* man that way.

That way was over for her.

It had died with Mark. She owed it to his memory, to all he had meant to her and she to him.

Miranda could not allow herself to think of moving on with her life. Of having a life. A normal life. Her dreams of normal were gone.

Dead and buried.

Leandro glanced at her. 'What's wrong?'

Miranda felt her face flame. Why did she always act like a flustered schoolgirl when she was around him? She was an adult, for God's sake. She had to act mature and sensible. Cool and in charge of her emotions and her traitorous needs. She could do that. *Of course she could.* 'Erm…nothing.'

His frown created a deep crevasse between his brows. 'Would you rather go to a hotel? There's one a couple of blocks down. I could—'

'No, of course not.' She painted on a bright smile. 'Don't spoil it for me by insisting I stay at some plush hotel. This is right up my alley. I want to be in amongst the dust and cobwebs. Who knows what priceless treasures are hidden inside?'

Something moved at the back of his gaze, as quick as the twitch of a curtain. But then his expression went back to its default position. 'Come this way,' he said.

Miranda followed him into the villa, her heels echoing on the marbled floor of the grand foyer. It made her feel she was stepping into a vacuum, moving back in time. Thousands of dust motes rose in the air, the sunlight catching them where it was slanting in from the windows either side of the opulently carved and sweeping staircase.

As Leandro closed the door, the central chandelier

tinkled above them as the draught of the outside air breathed against its glittering crystals.

Miranda felt a rush of goose bumps scamper over every inch of her flesh. She turned a full circle, taking in the bronze, marble and onyx statues positioned about the foyer. There were paintings on every wall, portraits and landscapes from the seventeenth and eighteenth centuries; some looked even older. It was like stepping into a neglected museum. A thick layer of dust was over everything like a ghostly shroud.

'Wow…' she breathed in wonder.

Leandro merely looked bored. 'I'll show you to your room first. Then I'll give you the guided tour.'

Miranda followed him upstairs, having to restrain herself from stopping in front of every painting or *objet d'art* on the way past. She caught tantalising glimpses of the second floor rooms through the open doors; most of the furniture was draped with dust sheets but even so she could see in times gone past the villa had been a showcase for grandeur and wealth. There were a couple of rooms with the doors closed. One she assumed was Leandro's bedroom but she knew it wasn't the master suite as they had passed it three doors back. Did he not want to occupy the room his father had slept in all those years?

Miranda felt another prickle of goose bumps.

Had his father perhaps *died* in there?

Thankfully the room Leandro had assigned her had been aired. The faded formal curtains had been pulled back and secured by the brass fittings and the window opened so fresh air could circulate. The breeze was playing with the gossamer-sheer fabric of the curtain in little billowy puffs and sighs.

'I hope the bed's comfortable,' Leandro said as he placed her bag on a velvet-topped chest at the foot of the bed. 'The linen is fresh. I bought some new stuff when I got here yesterday.'

Miranda glanced at him. 'Did your father die at home?'

His brows came together. 'Why do you ask?'

She gave a little shrug, absently rubbing her upper arms with her crossed-over hands. 'Just wondering.'

He held her look for a beat before turning away, one of his hands scoring a pathway through the thickness of his hair. 'He was found unconscious by a neighbour and died a few hours later in hospital.'

'So you didn't get to say goodbye to him?'

He made a sound of derision. 'We said our good-byes a long time ago.'

Miranda looked at the landscape of his face—the strong jaw, the tight mouth with its lines of tension running down each side and the shadowed eyes. 'What happened between the two of you?' she said.

His eyes moved away from hers. 'I'll leave you to unpack. The bathroom is through there. I'll be down-stairs in the study.'

'Leandro?'

He stopped at the door and she heard him release a 'what now?' breath before he turned to look at her with dark eyes that flashed with unmistakable irritation. 'You're not here to give me grief counselling, okay?'

Miranda opened her eyes a little wider at his acerbic tone. She had never seen him even mildly angry before. He was always so emotionless, so neutral and blank...apart from that frown, of course. 'I'm sorry. I didn't mean to upset you.'

He scrubbed his hand over his face as he let out another whoosh of air. 'I'm sorry,' he said in a weighted tone. 'That was uncalled for.'

'It's fine,' she said. 'I realise this is a difficult time for you.'

His mouth twisted but it was nowhere near a smile, not even a quarter of one. 'Let me know if you need anything. I'm not used to catering for guests. I might've overlooked something.'

'Don't you have visitors come and stay with you at your place in London?' Miranda said.

His eyes were as unfathomable as ever as they held hers. 'Women, you mean?'

Miranda felt another blush storm into her cheeks. Why on earth was she was discussing his sex life with him? It was crossing a boundary she had never crossed before. She'd thought about him with other women. Many times. How could she not? She'd seen the way other women looked at him. The way their eyes flared in interest. The way they licked their lips and fluttered their eyelashes, or moved or preened their bodies so he would take notice. She had been witnessing his effect on women for as long as she could remember. He wasn't just eye candy. He was an eye banquet. He was intelligent, sophisticated, cultured and wealthy to boot. Alpha, but without the arrogance. He was everything a woman would want in a sexual partner. He was the stuff of fantasies. Hot, erotic fantasies she never allowed herself to have. What did it matter to her what he did or who he did it with?

She didn't want to know.

Well, maybe just a little.

'You do have them occasionally, don't you?' Miranda said.

One of his dark brows rose in a quizzical arc. '*Have* them?'

She held his look but it took an enormous effort. Her cheeks were on fire. Hot enough to sear a steak. He was teasing her. She could see a tiny glint in the dark chocolate of his eyes. Even one corner of his mouth had lifted a fraction. He was making her out to be a prude who couldn't talk about sex openly. Why did everyone automatically assume because she was celibate she was uptight about all things sexual? That she was some old-world throwback who couldn't handle modernity? 'You know exactly what I'm talking about so stop trying to embarrass me.'

His eyes didn't waver from hers. 'I'm not a monk.'

Miranda couldn't stop her mind running off with *that* information. Picturing him with women. Being very un-monk-like with them. Touching them, kissing them, making love to them. She imagined his body naked—the toned, tanned and taut perfection of him in the throes of animal passion.

She could feel her own body stirring in excitement, her pulse kicking up its pace, her blood pulsing with the primitive drumbeat of lust, her inner core contracting with a delicious clench of desire. She quickly moistened her lips with the point of her tongue, an electric jolt of awareness zapping her as she saw his dark-as-night gaze follow every micro-millimetre of its pathway across her mouth.

The subtle change in atmosphere made the air suddenly super-charged. She could feel the voltage crackling in the silence like a singing wire.

He was standing at least two metres away and yet she felt as if he had touched her. Her lips buzzed and fizzed. Throbbed. *Ached.* Would he kiss soft and slow or hard and fast? Would his stubble scrape or graze her? What would he taste of? Salty or sweet? Good quality coffee or top-shelf wine? Testosterone-rich man in his prime?

Miranda became aware of her body shifting. Stirring. Sensing. It felt like every cell was unfurling from a tightly wound ball. Her body stretched its cramped limbs like a long-confined creature. Her frozen blood thawed, warmed, heated. Sizzled.

Needs she had long ignored pulsed. Each little ripple of want in her inner core reminded her: she was a woman. He was a man. They were alone in a big, rundown old house with no one as buffer. No older brothers. No servants. No distractions.

No chaperone.

'I hope it won't cramp your style, having me here,' Miranda said with what she hoped was suitably cool poise.

There was little to read on Leandro's face except for the kindling heat in his gaze as it continued to

hold hers. 'So you wouldn't mind if I brought someone home with me?'

Oh, dear God, *would* he? Would he bring someone
back here? Would she have to watch some gorgeous
woman drape herself all over him? Would she have to
watch as they simpered up at him? Flirted and fussed
over him? Would she have to go to bed knowing that,
only a few thin walls and doors away, he was doing all
sorts of wickedly sensual, un-monk-like things with
someone else?

Miranda lifted her chin. 'Just because I've sworn
a vow of celibacy doesn't mean I expect those around
me to follow my example.'

He studied her for an infinitesimal moment, his eyes
going back and forth between each of hers in an assessing manner that was distinctly unnerving. Why
was he looking at her like that? What was he seeing?
Did he sense her body's reaction to his? She was doing
her level best to conceal the effect he had on her but
she knew most body language was unconscious. She
had already licked her lips three times. *Three times!*

'Do you think Mark would've sacrificed his life like
you're doing if the tables were turned?' he said at last.

Miranda pursed her lips. *At least it would stop her
licking them*, she thought. She knew exactly where
this was going. Her brothers were always banging on
about it. Jaz, too, would offer her opinion on how she
was missing out on the best years of her life, yadda-
yadda-yadda.

'I'll make a deal with you, Leandro,' she said, eyeballing him. 'I won't tell you how to live your life if you don't tell me how to live mine.'

His mouth took on a rueful slant. 'Put those kitten claws away, *cara*,' he said. 'I don't need any more enemies.'

He had never used a term of endearment when addressing her before. The way he said it, with that hint of an Italian accent all those years living in England hadn't quite removed, made her spine tingle. But why was he addressing her like that other than to tease her? To mock her?

Miranda threw him a reproachful look. 'Don't patronise me. I'm an adult. I know my own mind.'

'But you were just a kid back then,' he said. 'If he'd lived you would've broken up within a couple of months, if not weeks. It's what teenagers do.'

'That's not true,' Miranda said. 'We'd been friends since we were little kids. We were in love. We were soul mates. We planned to spend the rest of our lives together.'

He shook his head at her as if she was talking utter nonsense. 'Do you really believe that? Come on. *Really?*'

Miranda aligned her spine. Straightened her shoulders. Steeled her resolve to deflect any criticism of her decision to remain committed to the promises she had made to Mark. She and Mark had become close friends during early childhood when they had gone to the same small village school before she'd been sent to boarding school with Jaz. They'd officially started dating at fourteen. Her friendship with Mark had been longer than that with Jaz who had come to Ravensdene when she was eight.

Along with Mark's steady friendship, his stable home life had been a huge draw and comfort for Miranda. His parents were so normal compared to hers. There'd been no high-flying parties with Hollywood superstars and theatre royalty coming and going all hours of the day and night. In the Redbank household there'd been no tempestuous outbursts with door-slamming and insults hurled, and no passionate making up that would only last a week or two before the cycle would begin again.

Mark's parents, James and Susanne, were supportive and nurturing of each other and Mark and had always made Miranda feel like a part of the family. They actually took the time to listen to any problems she had. They were never too busy. They didn't judge or dismiss her or even tell her what to do. They listened.

Leandro had no right to doubt her convictions. No right to criticise her choices. She had made up her mind and nothing he or anyone could say or do would make her veer from the course her conscience had taken. 'Of course I do,' she said. 'I believe it with all my heart.'

The humming silence tiptoed from each corner of the room.

Leandro kept looking at her in that measuring way. Unsettling her. Making her think of things she had no right to be thinking. Erotic things. Forbidden things. Like how his mouth would feel against hers. How his hands would feel against her flesh. How their bodies would fit together—her slight curves against his toned male hardness. How it would feel to glide her mouth along his stubbly jaw, to press her lips to his and open her mouth to the searching thrust of his tongue.

She had never had such a rush of wicked thoughts before. They were running amok, making a mockery of her convictions. Making her aware of the needs she had for so long pretended weren't there. Needs that were moving within that dark, secret place in her body. The way he was looking at her made her ache with unspent passion. She tried to control every micro-expression on her face. Stood as still as one of his father's cold, lifeless statues downstairs.

But, as if he had seen enough to satisfy him, he finally broke the silence. 'I'll be in the study downstairs. We'll eat out once you've unpacked. Give me a shout once you're done.'

Miranda blinked. Dining out? With him? In public? People would assume they were dating. What if someone took a photo and it got back to Mark's parents? Even though they had said—along with everyone else—she should get on with her life, she knew they would find it heartbreakingly difficult to watch her do so. How could they not? Everything she did with someone else would make their loss all the more painful. Mark had been their only son. Their only child. The dreams and hopes they'd had for him had died with him. The milestones of life: dating, engagement, marriage and children would be salt ground into an open wound.

She couldn't do it to them.

'You don't want me to fix something for us here?' Miranda said.

Leandro gave a soft sound that could have been his version of a laugh. 'You're getting your fairy tales mixed up,' he said. 'You're Sleeping Beauty, not Cinderella.'

Miranda felt a wick of anger light up inside her. What right did he have to mock her choice to remain loyal to Mark's memory? 'Is this why you've asked me here? So you can make fun of me?'

'I'm not making fun of you.'

'Then what *are* you doing?'

His gaze dipped to her mouth for a nanosecond before meshing with hers once more. 'I have absolutely no idea.'

Miranda frowned. 'What do you mean?'

He came over to where she was standing. He stopped within a foot of her but even so she could feel the magnetic pull of his body as she lifted her gaze to his. She had never been this close to him. Not front to front. Almost toe to toe.

Her breathing halted as he placed a gentle but firm fingertip to the underside of her chin, lifting her face so her eyes had no possible way of escaping the mesmerising power of his. She could feel the slow burn of his touch, each individual whorl of his blunt fingertip like an electrode against her skin. She could smell the woodsy and citrus fragrance of his aftershave—not heady or overpowering, but subtle, with tantalising grace notes of lemon and lime.

She could see the dark pinpricks of his regrowth

along his jaw, a heady reminder of the potency of his male hormones charging through his body. She could feel her own hormones doing cartwheels.

Her tongue sneaked out before she could stop it, leaving a layer of much-needed moisture over her lips. His gaze honed in on her mouth, his eyelashes at half-mast over his dark-as-pitch eyes.

Something fell off a high shelf in her stomach as his thumb brushed over her lower lip. The grazing movement of his thumb against the sensitive skin of her mouth made every nerve sit up and take notice. She could feel them twirling, pirouetting, in a frenzy of traitorous excitement.

His large, warm hand gently slid along the curve of her cheek, cupping one side of her face, some of her hair falling against the back of his hand like a silk curtain.

Had *anyone* ever held her like this? Tenderly cradled her face as if it were something delicate and priceless? The warmth of his palm seared her flesh, making her ache for him to cup not just her face but her breasts, to feel his firm male skin against her softer one.

'I shouldn't have brought you here,' he said in a deep, gravelly tone that sent another shockwave across the base of her belly.

A hummingbird was trapped inside the cavity of Miranda's chest, fluttering frantically inside each of the four chambers of her heart. 'Why?' Her voice was barely much more than a squeak.

He moved his thumb in a back-and-forth motion

over her cheek, his inscrutable eyes holding her prisoner. 'There are things you don't know about me.'

Miranda swallowed. What didn't she know? Did he have bodies buried in the cellar? Leather whips and chains and handcuffs? A red room? 'Wh-what things?'

'Not the things you're thinking.'

'I'm not thinking those things.'

He smiled a crooked half-smile that had mockery at its core. 'Sweet, innocent, Miranda,' he said. 'The little girl in a woman's body who refuses to grow up.'

Miranda stepped out of his hold, rubbing at her cheek in a pointed manner. 'I thought I was here to look at your father's art collection. I'm sorry if that seems terribly naïve of me but I've never had any reason not to trust you before now.'

'You can trust me.'

She chanced a look at him again. His expression had lost its mocking edge. If anything he looked…sad. She could see the pained lines across his forehead, the shadows in his eyes, the grim set to his mouth. 'Why am I here, Leandro?' Somehow her voice had come out whispery instead of strident and firm.

He let out a long breath. 'Because when I saw you in London I… I don't know what I thought. I saw you cowering behind that pot plant and—'

'I wasn't cowering,' Miranda put in indignantly. 'I was hiding.'

'I felt sorry for you.'

The silence echoed for a moment with his bald statement.

Miranda drew in a tight breath. 'So you rescued me

by pretending to need me to sort out your father's collection. Is there even a collection?'

'Yes.'

'Then maybe you'd better show it to me.'

'Come this way.'

Miranda followed him out of the suite and back downstairs to a room next door to the larger of the two sitting rooms. Leandro opened the door and gestured for her to go in. She stepped past him in the doorway, acutely conscious of the way his shirt sleeve brushed against her arm. Every nerve stood up and took notice. Every fine hair tingled at the roots. It was like his body was emitting waves of electricity and she had only to step over an invisible boundary to feel the full force of it.

The atmosphere inside the room was airless and musty, as if it had been closed up a long time. It was packed with canvasses, on the walls, and others wrapped and stacked in leaning piles against the shrouded furniture.

Miranda sent her gaze over the paintings on the walls, examining each one with her trained apprentice's eye. Even without her qualifications and experience she'd have been able to see this was a collection of enormous value. One of the landscapes was certainly a Gainsborough, or if not a very credible imitation. What other treasures were hidden underneath those wrapped canvasses?

Miranda turned to look at Leandro. 'This is amazing. But I'm not sure I'm experienced enough to handle such a large collection. We'd need to ship the pieces back to London for proper valuation. It's too much for one person to deal with. Some of these pieces could be worth hundreds of thousands of pounds, maybe even millions. You might want to keep some as an investment. Sell them in a few years so you can—'

'I don't want them.'

She frowned at his implacable tone. 'But that's crazy, Leandro. You could have your own collection. You could have it on show at a private museum. It would be—'

'I have no interest in making money out of my father's collection,' he said. 'Just do what you have to do. I'll pay for any shipment costs but that's as far as I'm prepared to go.'

Miranda watched open-mouthed as he strode out of the room, the dust motes he'd disturbed hovering in the ringing silence.

CHAPTER THREE

LEANDRO WORKED THE floor of his father's study like a lion trapped in a cat carrier. It had been a mistake to bring Miranda here. Here to the epicentre of his pain and anguish. He should have sold the collection without consulting anyone. What did it matter if those wretched paintings were valuable? They weren't valuable to him. Making money out of his father's legacy seemed immoral somehow to him. He didn't understand why his father had left everything to him.

Over the last few years their relationship had deteriorated to perfunctory calls at Christmas or birthdays. Most of the time his father would be heavily inebriated, his words slurred, his memory skewed. It had been all Leandro could do to listen to his father's drunken ramblings knowing *he* had been the one to cause the destruction of his father's life. Surely his father had known how difficult this trip back here would be? Had he done it to twist the knife? To force him to face what he had spent the last two decades avoiding? Everything in this run-down villa represented the misery of his father's life—a life spent drinking himself to oblivion so he could forget the tragedy of the past.

The tragedy Leandro had caused.

He looked out of the window that overlooked the garden at the back of the villa. He hadn't been able to bring himself to go out there yet. It had once been a spectacular affair with neatly trimmed hedges, flowering shrubs and borders filled with old-world roses whose heady scent would fill the air. It had been a magical place for he and his sister to scamper about and play hide and seek in amongst the cool, green shaded laneways of the hedges.

But now it was an overgrown mess of weeds, misshapen hedges and skeletal rose bushes with one or two half-hearted blooms. Parts of the garden were so overrun they couldn't be seen properly from the house.

It reminded Leandro of his father's life—sad, neglected, abused and abandoned. Wasted.

How could he have thought to bring Miranda here? How long before she discovered Rosie's room? He couldn't keep it locked up for ever. Stepping in there was like stepping back in time. It was painfully surreal. Everything was exactly the same as the day Rosie had disappeared from the beach. Every toy. Every doll. Every childish scribble she had ever done. Every messy and colourful finger-painting. Every article of clothing left in the wardrobe as if she were going to come back and use it. Even her hairbrush was on the dressing table with some of her silky dark-brown hairs still trapped in the bristles—a haunting reminder of the last time it had been used.

Even the striped towel they had been sitting on at the beach was there on the foot of the child-sized princess bed. The bed Rosie had been so proud of after moving out of her cot. Her 'big-girl bed', she'd called it. He still remembered her excited little face as she'd told him how she had chosen it with their mother while he'd been at school.

It was a lifetime ago.

Why had his father left the room intact for so long? Had he wanted Leandro to see it? Was that why he'd left him the villa and its contents? Knowing Leandro would have to come in and pack up every single item of Rosie's? Why hadn't his father seen to it himself or got someone impartial to do it? It had been twenty-seven years, for pity's sake. There was no possibility of Rosie ever coming home. The police had been blunt with his parents once the first few months had passed with no leads, no evidence, no clues and no tip-offs.

Leandro had seen the statistics. Rosie had joined the thousands of people who went missing without trace. Every single day families across the globe were shattered by the disappearance of a loved one. They were left with the stomach-churning dread of wondering what had happened to their beloved family member. Praying they were still alive but deep down knowing such miracles were rare. Wondering if they had suffered or were still suffering. It was cruel torture not to know and yet just as bad speculating.

Leandro had spent every year of his life since wondering. Praying. Begging. Pleading with a God he no longer believed in—if he ever had. Rosie wasn't coming back. She was gone and he was responsible.

The guilt he felt over Rosie's disappearance was a band around his chest that would tighten every time he saw a toddler. Rosie had been with him on the pebbly beach when he was six and she was three. He could recall her cute little chubby-cheeked face and starfish dimpled hands with such clarity he felt like it was yesterday. For years he'd kept thinking the life he was living since was just a bad dream. That he would wake up and there would be Rosie with her sunny smile sitting on the striped towel next to him. But every time he would wake and he would feel that crushing hammer blow of guilt.

His mother had stepped a few feet away to an ice-cream vendor, leaving Leandro in charge. When she'd come back, Rosie had gone. Vanished. Snatched from where she had been sitting. The beach had been scoured. The water searched. The police had interviewed hundreds of beach-goers but there was no sign of Rosie. No one had seen anything suspicious. Leandro had only turned his back for a moment or two to look at a speedboat that was going past. When he'd turned around he'd seen his mother coming towards him with two ice-cream cones; her face had contorted in horror when she'd seen the empty space on the towel beside him.

He had never forgotten that look on his mother's face. Every time he saw his mother he remembered it. It haunted him. Tortured him.

His parents' marriage hadn't been strong in the first

place. Losing Rosie had gouged open cracks that were already there. The divorce had been bitter and painful two years after Rosie's disappearance. His father hadn't wanted custody of Leandro. He hadn't even asked for visitation rights. His mother hadn't wanted him either. But she must have known people would judge her harshly if she didn't take him with her when she went back to her homeland, England. Mothers were meant to love their children.

But how could his mother love him when he was responsible for the loss of her adored baby girl?

Not that his mother ever blamed him. Not openly. Not in words. It was the looks that told him what she thought. His father's too. Those looks said, *why weren't you watching her?* As the years went on his father had begun to verbalise it. The blame would come pouring out after he'd been on one of his binges. But it was nothing Leandro hadn't already heard echoing in his head. Day after day, week after week…for years now the same accusing voice would keep him awake at night. It would give him nightmares. He would wake with a jolt and remember the awful truth.

There wasn't a day that went past that he didn't think of his sister. Ever since that gut-wrenching day he would look for her in the crowd, hoping to catch a glimpse of her. Hoping that whoever had taken her had not done so for nefarious reasons, but had taken her to fulfil a wish to have a child and had loved and cared for her since. He couldn't bear to think of her coming to harm. He couldn't bear to think of her lying cold in some grisly shallow grave, her little body bruised and broken. As the years had gone on he imagined her growing up. He looked for an older version of her. She would be thirty now.

In his good dreams she would be married with children of her own by now.

In his nightmares…

He closed the door on his torturous imaginings. For twenty-seven years he had lived with this incessant agony. The agony of not knowing. The agony of being responsible for losing her. The agony of knowing he had ruined his parents' lives.

He could never forgive himself.

He didn't even bother trying.

Miranda spent an hour looking over the collection, carefully uncovering the canvasses to get an idea of what she was dealing with. Apart from some of the obvious fakes, most of the collection would have to be shipped back to England for proper evaluation. The paintings needed to be x-rayed in order to establish how they were composed. Infrared imaging would then be used to see the original drawings and painting losses, and Raman spectroscopy would determine the identity of the varnish. It would take a team of experts far more qualified and experienced than her to bring all of these works to their former glory. But she couldn't help feeling touched Leandro had asked her to be the first to run her eyes over the collection.

Why *had* he done that?

Had it simply been an impulsive thing, as he had intimated, or had he truly thought she was the best one to do it? Whatever his reasons, it was like being let in on a secret. He had opened a part of his life that no one else had had access to before.

It was sad to think of Leandro's father living here on his own for years. It looked like no maintenance had been done for a decade, if not longer. Cobwebs hung from every corner. The dust was so thick she could feel it irritating her nostrils. Every time she moved across the floor to look at one of the paintings the floorboards would creak in protest, as if in pain. The atmosphere was one of neglect and deep loneliness. As she lifted each dustsheet off the furniture she got a sense she was uncovering history. What stories could each piece tell? There was a George IV mahogany writing table, a Queen Anne burr-elm chest of drawers, a seventeenth-century Italian walnut side cabinet, a Regency spoon-back chair, as well as a set of four Regency mahogany and brass inlaid chairs, and an Italian gilt wood girandole mirror with embellished surround. How many lives had they watched go by? How many conversations had they overheard?

Along with the furniture, inside some of the cabinets there were Chinese glass snuff bottles, bronze Buddhas, jade Ming dynasty vases and countless ceramics and glassware. So many beautiful treasures locked away where no one could see and enjoy them.

Why was Leandro so intent on getting rid of them? Didn't he have a single sentimental bone in his body? His father had painstakingly collected all of these valuable items. It would have taken him years and years and oodles of money. Why then get rid of them as if they were nothing more than charity shop donations? Surely there was something he would want to keep as a memento?

It didn't make sense.

Miranda went outside for a breath of fresh air after breathing in so much dust. The afternoon was surprisingly warm, but then, this was the French Riviera, she thought. No wonder the English came here in droves for their holidays. Even the light against the old buildings had a certain quality to it—a muted, pastel glow that enhanced the gorgeous architecture.

She took a walk about the garden where weeds ran rampant amongst the spindly arms of roses and underneath the untrimmed hedges. A Virginia creeper was in full autumnal splendour against a stone wall, some of the rich russet and gold leaves crunching and crackling underneath her feet as she walked past.

Miranda caught sight of a small marble statue of an angel through a gap in the unkempt hedge towards the centre of the garden. The hedge had grown so tall it had created a secret hideaway like a maze hiding the Minotaur at the centre of it. The pathway leading to it was littered with leaves and weeds as if no one had been along here for a long time. There was a cobweb-covered wooden bench in the little alcove in front of the statue, providing a secluded spot for quiet reflection. But when she got close she realised it wasn't a statue of an angel after all; it was of a small child of two or three years old.

Miranda bent down to look at the brass plaque that

was all but covered by strangling weeds. She pushed them aside to read:

Rosamund Clemente Allegretti.
Lost but never forgotten.

There was a birth date of thirty years ago but the space where the date of passing should be was blank with just an open-ended dash.

Who was she? Who was this little girl who had been immortalised in white marble?

The sound of a footfall crunching on the leaves behind her made Miranda's heart miss a beat. She scrambled to her feet to see the tall figure of Leandro coming towards her but then, when he saw what was behind her, he stopped dead. It was like he had been struck with something. Blind-sided. Stunned. His features were bleached of colour, going chalk-white beneath his tan. The column of his throat moved up and down: once. Twice. Three times. His eyes twitched, and then flickered, as if in pain.

'You startled me, creeping up on me like that,' Miranda said to fill the eerie silence. 'I thought you were—'

'A ghost?'

Something about his tone made the hair on the back of her neck stand on end. But it was as if he were talking to himself, not her. He seemed hardly even aware she was there. His gaze was focussed on the statue, his brow heavily puckered—even more than usual.

Miranda leaned back against the cool pine-scented

green of the hedge as he moved past her to stand in front of the statue. When he touched the little child's head with one of his hands, she noticed it was visibly shaking.

'Who is she?' she said.

His hand fell away from the child's head to hang by his side. 'My sister.'

She gaped at him in surprise. 'Your *sister*?'

He wasn't looking at her but at the statue, his brows still drawn together in a deep crevasse. 'Rosie. She disappeared when I was six years old. She was three.'

Disappeared? Miranda swallowed so convulsively she felt the walls of her throat close in on each other. *He had a sister who had disappeared?* The shock was like a slap. A punch. A wrecking ball banging against her heart. Why hadn't he said something? For all these years he'd given the impression he was an only child. What a heart-breaking tragedy to keep hidden for all this time. Why hadn't he told his closest friends? 'You never said anything about having a sister. Not once. To anyone.'

'I know,' he said on an expelled breath. 'It was easier than explaining.'

Why hadn't she put two and two together before now? Of course that was why he was so standoffish. Grief did that. It kept you isolated in an invisible bubble of pain. No one could reach you and you couldn't reach out. She knew the process all too well. 'Because it was too…painful?' she said.

He looked at her then, his dark eyes full of silent

suffering. 'It was my way of coping,' he said. 'Talking about her made it worse. It still does.'

'I'm sorry.'

He gave her a sombre movement of his lips before he turned back to look at the statue. He stood there for a long moment, barely a muscle moving on his face apart from an in-and-out movement on his lean cheek, as if he were using every ounce of self-control to keep his emotions in check.

'My father must've had this made,' he said after a long moment. 'I didn't know it existed until now. I just glanced at the garden when I came yesterday—I couldn't see this from the house.'

Miranda bit her lip as she watched him looking at the statue. He had his hands in his pockets and his shoulders were hunched forward slightly. Bone-deep sadness was etched in the landscape of his face.

She silently put a hand on his forearm and gave it a comforting squeeze. He turned his head to look down at her, his eyes meshing with hers as one of his hands came down on top, anchoring hers beneath his. She felt the imprint of his long, strong fingers, the warmth of his palm—the skin-on-skin touch that made something inside her belly shift sideways.

His gaze held hers steady.

Her breathing stalled. Her pulse quickened. Her heartbeat tripped and then raced.

Time froze.

The sounds of the garden—the twittering birds, the breeze ruffling the leaves, the drip of a leaky tap near one of the unkempt beds—faded into the background.

'My father wouldn't allow my mother to pack anything away,' Leandro said. 'He couldn't accept Rosie was gone. It was one of the reasons they split up. My mother wanted to move on. He couldn't.'

'And you got caught in the crossfire,' Miranda said.

He dropped his hand from where it was covering hers, stepping away from her as if he needed space to breathe. To think. To regroup. 'I was supposed to be looking after her,' he said after another beat or two of silence. 'The day she disappeared.'

Miranda frowned. 'But you were only what—six? That's not old enough to babysit.'

He gave her one of his hollow looks. 'We were on the beach. I can take you to the exact spot. My mother only walked ten or so metres away to get us an ice-cream. When she came back, Rosie was gone. I didn't hear or see anything. I turned my head to look at a boat that was going past and when I turned back she wasn't there. No one saw anything. It was crowded that hot summer day so no one would've noticed if a child was carried crying from the beach. Not back then.'

Miranda felt a choking lump come to her throat at the agony of what he had been through—the heartache, the distress of not knowing—*never* knowing what had happened to his baby sister. Wondering if she was alive or dead. Wondering if she had suffered. Wondering if there was something—*anything*—he could have done to stop it. How had he endured it?

By blaming himself.

'It wasn't your fault,' she said. 'How can you feel it was your fault? You were only a baby yourself. You shouldn't have been blamed. Your parents were wrong to put that on you.'

'They didn't,' he said. 'Not openly, although my father couldn't help himself in later years.'

So many pennies were beginning to drop. This was why Leandro's father had drunk to senselessness. This was why his mother had moved abroad, remarried, had three children in quick succession and had been always too busy to make time to see him. This was why Leandro had spent so many weekends and school holidays at Ravensdene, because he'd no longer had a home and family to go to. It was unbearably sad to think that all the times Leandro had joined her brothers he had carried this terrible burden. Alone. He hadn't told anyone of the tragedy. Not even his closest friends knew of the gut-wrenching heartache he had been through. And was *still* going through.

'I don't know what to say...' She brushed at her moist eyes with the sleeve of her top. 'It's just so terribly sad. I can't bear the thought of how you've suffered this all alone.'

Leandro reached out and grazed her cheek with a lazy fingertip, his expression rueful. 'I didn't mean to make you cry.'

'I can't help it.' Miranda sniffed and went searching for a tissue but before she could find one up her sleeve he produced the neatly ironed square of a clean white handkerchief. She took it from him with a grateful glance. 'Thanks.'

'My father stubbornly clung to hope,' Leandro said. 'He kept Rosie's room exactly as it was the day she went missing because he'd convinced himself that one day she'd come back. My mother couldn't bear it. She thought it was pathological.'

Miranda scrunched the handkerchief into a ball inside her hand, thinking of the football sweater of Mark's she kept in her wardrobe. Every year on his birthday she would put it on, breathing in the ever-fading scent of him. She kept telling herself it was time to give it back to his parents but she could never quite bring herself to do it. 'Everyone has their own way of grieving,' she said.

'Maybe.'

'Can I see it?'

'Rosie's room?'

'Would you mind?' she said.

He let out a ragged-sounding breath. 'It will have to be packed up sooner or later.'

Miranda walked back to the villa with him. She was deeply conscious of how terribly painful this would be for him. Didn't she feel it every time she visited Mark's parents? They had left his room intact too. Unable to let go of his things because by removing them they would finally have to accept he was gone for ever. But at least Mark's parents were in agreement.

How difficult it must have been for Leandro's mother, trying to move on while his father had been holding back. The loss of a child tested the strongest marriage. Leandro's parents had divorced within two years of Rosie's disappearance. How much had Leandro suffered during that time and since? Estranged from his alcoholic father, shunned by his mother, too busy with her new family.

After the bright light of outdoors the shadows inside the villa seemed all the more ghostly. A chill shimmied down her spine as she climbed the groaning stairs with Leandro.

The room was the third along the corridor—the door she had noticed was locked earlier. Leandro selected a key from a bunch of keys he had in his pocket. The sound of the lock turning over was as sharp and clear as a rifle shot.

Miranda stepped inside, her breath catching in her throat as she took in the little fairy-tale princess bed with its faded pink-and-white cover and the fluffy toys and dolls arranged on the pillow. There was a doll's pram and a beautifully crafted doll's house with gorgeous miniature furniture under the window. There was a child's dressing table with a toy make-up set and a hairbrush lying beside it.

There was a framed photograph hanging on the wall above the bed of a little girl with a mop of dark brown curls, apple-chubby cheeks and a cheeky smile.

Miranda turned to look at Leandro. He was stony faced but she could sense what he was feeling. His grief was palpable. 'Thank you for showing me,' she said. 'It's a beautiful room.'

His throat moved up and down over a swallow. 'She was a great little kid.' He picked up one of the fluffy toys that had fallen forward on the bed—a floppy-eared rabbit—and turned it over in his hands. 'I bought this for her third birthday with my pocket money. She called him Flopsy.'

Miranda blinked a couple of times, surprised her voice worked at all when she finally spoke. 'What will you do with her things once you sell the villa?'

His frown flickered on his forehead. 'I haven't thought that far ahead.'

'You might want to keep some things for when you have your own children,' Miranda said.

She got a sudden vision of him holding a newborn baby, his features softened in tenderness, his large, capable hands cradling the little bundle with care and gentleness. Her heart contracted. He would make a wonderful father. He would be kind and patient. He wouldn't shout and swear and throw tantrums, like her father had done when things hadn't gone his way. Leandro would make a child feel safe and loved and protected. He would be the strong, dependable rock his children would rely on no matter what life dished up.

He put the rabbit back down on the bed as if it had bitten him. 'I'll donate it all to charity.'

'But don't you—?'

'No.'

The implacability of his tone made her stomach feel strangely hollow. 'Don't you want to get married and have a family one day?'

His eyes collided with hers. 'Do you?'

Miranda shifted her gaze and rolled her lips together for a moment. 'We're not talking about me.'

The line of his mouth was tight. White. 'Maybe we should.'

She pulled back her shoulders. Lifted her chin. Held his steely look even though it made the backs of her knees feel fizzy. 'It's different for me.'

A glimmer of cynicism lit his dark gaze. 'Why's that?'

'I made a promise.'

Leandro gave a short mocking laugh. 'To a dying man—*a boy*?'

Miranda gritted her teeth. How many times did she have to have this conversation? 'We *loved* each other.'

'You loved the idea of love,' he said. 'He was your first boyfriend—the first person to show an interest in you. It's my bet if he hadn't got sick he would've moved on within a month or two. He used your sweet, compliant nature to—'

'That's not true!'

'He didn't want to die alone and lonely,' he went on with a callous disregard for her feelings. 'He tied you to him, making you promise stuff no one in their right mind would promise. Not at that age.'

Miranda put her hand up to her ears in a childish attempt to block the sound of his taunting voice. 'No! *No!*'

'You were a kid,' he said. 'A romantically dazed kid who couldn't see how she was being used towards the end. He had cancer—the big, disgusting C-word. In an instant he had gone from being one of the top jocks to one of the untouchables. But he knew *you* wouldn't let him down. Not the sweet, loyal little Miranda Ravensdale who was looking for a Shakespearean tragedy to pin her name on.'

'You're wrong,' she said. 'Wrong. Wrong. *Wrong.* You have no right to say such things to me. You don't understand what we had. *You* don't commit to a relationship longer than a few weeks. What would you know of loyalty and commitment? Mark and I were friends for years—*years*—before we became…more intimate.'

He tugged her hands down and loosely gripped her wrists in his hands so she could feel every one of his fingers burning against her flesh. 'Am I wrong?' he asked. 'Am I really?'

Miranda pulled out of his hold with an almighty wrench that made her stumble backwards. How dared he mock her? How dared he make fun of her? How *dared* he question her love and commitment for Mark and his for her? 'You have no right to question my relationship with Mark. No right at all. I loved him. I loved him and I *still* love him. Nothing you can say or do will ever change that.'

His mouth slanted in a cynical half-smile. 'I could change that. I know I could. All it would take is one little kiss.'

Miranda coughed out a laugh but even to her ears it sounded unconvincing. 'Like *that's* ever going to happen.'

He was suddenly close. Way too close. His broad fingertip was suddenly on the underside of her chin without her knowing how it got there. All she registered was the warm, branding feeling of it resting there, holding her captive with the mesmerising force of his bottomless dark gaze.

'Is that a dare, Sleeping Beauty?' he said in a silky tone.

Miranda felt his words slither down her spine like an unfurling satin ribbon running away from its spool. Her knees threatened to give way. Her belly quivered with a host of needs she couldn't even name. She couldn't tear her eyes away from his coal-black gaze. It was drawing her in like a magnet does a tiny iron filing.

She became aware of her breasts inside the lacy cups of her bra. They prickled and swelled as if stimulated to attention by the deep, burry sound of his voice. The below-the-ocean-floor, rumbly bass of his voice—the voice that did strange things to her feminine body.

Her inner core clenched in a contraction of raw, primal need. Her blood ticked, raced, through the network of her veins at breakneck frenzied speed. Every pore of her body ached for his touch, for the sensuous glide of his fingers, for the hot sweep of his tongue, for the stabbing thrust of his body.

But finally a vestige of pride came to her rescue.

Miranda dipped out from under his fingertip and rubbed at her chin as she sent him a warning glare. 'Don't play games with me, Leandro.'

A sardonic gleam shone in his dark eyes. 'You think I was joking?'

She didn't know what to think. Not when he looked at her like that—with smouldering black-as-pitch eyes that seemed to see right through her defences. That sensually contoured mouth shouldn't tempt her. She shouldn't be wondering what it would feel like against her own. She shouldn't be looking at his mouth as if she had no control over her gaze.

He was her brothers' friend. He was practically one

of the family. He had seen her with pimples and braces. He had seen her lying on the sofa with a hot-water bottle pressed to her cramping belly. He could have any girl he wanted. Why would he want to kiss her unless it was to score points? He thought her loyalty to Mark was ridiculous. How better to prove it by having her go weak-kneed when he kissed her?

Not. Going. To. Happen.

She bent her head and made to go past him. 'I'm going to do something about dinner.'

He caught her left arm on the way past, his fingers forming a loose bracelet around her wrist. His gaze drew hers to his with an unspoken command. She couldn't have looked away if she tried. Her breath caught as his thumb found her pulse. The warmth of his fingers made her spine fizz and her knees tremble. 'There's no food in the house,' he said. 'I haven't had time to shop. Let's go out.'

Miranda chewed the inside of her lip. 'I'm not sure that's such a good idea…'

His thumb stroked the underside of her wrist in slow motion. 'Just dinner,' he said. 'Don't worry. I won't try any moves on you. Your brothers would skin me alive if I did.'

The thought of him making a move on her made the hot spill in her belly spread through her pelvis and down between her thighs like warmed treacle. It was hard enough controlling her reaction to him as he stroked her wrist in that tantalising manner. Her senses went into a tailspin with every mesmerising movement of his fingers against her skin. What would it do to her to feel his mouth on hers? To feel his molten touch on her breasts and her other aching intimate places?

But then, she thought: *what had her brothers to do with anything?* If she wanted to get involved with Leandro—if things had been different, that was—then that would be up to her, not to Julius and Jake to give the go ahead. 'I'm hardly your type in any case,' Miranda said, carefully extricating her wrist from his fingers.

His expression was now inscrutable. 'Does that bother you?'

Did it?

Of course it did. Men like Leandro didn't notice girls like her. She was the type of girl who was invisible to most men. She was too girl-next-door. Shy and reserved, not vivacious and outgoing. Pretty but not stunning. Petite, not voluptuous. If it hadn't been for his friendship with her brothers he probably wouldn't have given her the time of day. She wasn't just a wallflower. She was wallpaper. Bland, boring, beige wallpaper.

'Not at all,' Miranda said, rubbing at her still-tingling wrist. 'You've a perfect right to date whomever you chose.'

But please don't do it while I'm under the same roof.

CHAPTER FOUR

LEANDRO WAITED AT the foot of the stairs for Miranda. He had showered and changed and tried not to think about how close he had been to kissing her earlier. He had always kept his distance in the past. It wasn't that he hadn't noticed her. He had. He was always viscerally aware of how close she was to him. It was like picking up a radar frequency inside his body. If she was within touching distance, his body was acutely aware of her every movement. Even if it was as insignificant as her lifting one of her hands to her face to tuck back a stray strand of hair. He felt it in his body.

If she so much as walked past him every cell in his body stood to attention. If she sent her tongue out over her beautiful mouth he felt as if she had stroked it over him intimately. When she smiled that hesitant, shy, nervous smile every pore of his skin contracted with primal need as he imagined her losing that shyness with him. As soon as he caught a trace of her scent he would feel a rush through his flesh. His blood would bloom with such heat he could feel it charging through his pelvis and down his legs.

But he kept his distance.

Always.

She was the kid sister of his two closest friends. It was an unspoken code between mates: no poaching of sisters. If things didn't work out, it would strain everyone's relationship. He had seen enough with the angst between Jake and Jasmine. The air could be cut with a knife when those two were in the same room. The fallout from their fiery spat still made everyone uncomfortable even seven years after the event. You couldn't mention Jaz's name around Jake without his expression turning to thunder. And Jaz turned into a hissing and spitting wildcat if Jake so much as glanced her way.

Leandro wasn't going to add to the mix with a dalliance with Miranda, even if she did somehow manage to move on from the loss of her teenage boyfriend. She wasn't the type to settle for a casual fling. She was way too old-fashioned and conservative for that. She would want the fairy tale: the house with the picket fence and cottage flowers, the kids and the dog.

He wondered if she had even had proper sex with her boyfriend. They had started officially dating when she'd been fourteen, which in his opinion was a little young. He knew teenagers had sex younger than ever but had she been ready emotionally? Why was she so determined to cling to a promise that essentially locked her up for life? He didn't understand why she would do such a thing. How could she possibly think she'd loved Mark enough to make that sort of sacrifice?

He had always had the feeling Mark Redbank had clung to Miranda for all the wrong reasons. She be-

lieved it to have been true love but Leandro wasn't
so sure. Call him cynical, but he'd always suspected
Mark had used Miranda, especially towards the end.
He thought Mark had played up his feelings for her
to keep her tied to him. The decent thing would have
been to set her free but apparently Mark had extracted
a death-bed promise with her that she was stubbornly
determined to stick to.

But touching her had awakened something in Leandro. He had never touched her before. Not even when
he came to visit the family at Ravensdene. He had always avoided the kiss on the cheek to say hello, mostly
because she was too shy to offer it and he would never
make the first move. He had never even shaken her
hand. He had made every effort to avoid physical contact. He knew she saw him as a cold fish, aloof, distant.
He had been happy to keep it that way.

But being in that room with all those memories and
all that crushing grief had pushed him off-balance.
Something had been unleashed inside him. Something
he wasn't sure he could control. Now he had touched
Miranda he wanted to touch her again. It was an urge
that pulsed through him. The feel of her creamy skin
beneath his palm, against his fingers, her silky hair
tickling the back of his hand, had stirred his blood
until it roared through his body like an out of control
freight train. It made him think forbidden thoughts.
Thoughts he had never allowed himself to think before now. Thoughts of her lying pinned by his body, his
need pumping into her as her cries of pleasure filled
the air.

The brief flare of temper she had shown confirmed everything he had suspected about her. Underneath her ice-maiden façade was a passionate young woman just crying out for physical expression. He could see it in the way she held herself together so primly, as if she was frightened of breaking free from the tight moral restraints she had placed around herself. Kissing her would have proven it. He wanted to taste that soft, innocent bow of a mouth and feel her shudder all over with longing. To thrust his tongue between those beautiful lips and taste the sweet, moist heat of her mouth. To have her tongue tangle with his in a sexy coupling that was a prelude to smoking-hot sex.

He clenched his hands into tight fists as he wrestled with his conscience. He wasn't in a good place right now. He was acting totally out of character. It would be wrong to try it on with her. He could slake his lust the way he usually did—with someone who knew the game and was happy with his rules. He didn't do long term. The longest he did was a month or two—any longer than that and women got ideas of bended knees, rings and promises he couldn't deliver on.

It wasn't that he was against marriage. He believed in it as an institution and admired people who made it work. He even believed it *could* work. He believed it was a good framework in which to bring up children and travel through the cycles and seasons of life with someone who had the same vision and values. He was quietly envious of Julius's relationship with Holly Perez. But he didn't allow himself to think too long about how it would be to have a life partner to build a future with—to have someone to hope and dream with.

He was used to living on his own.

He preferred it. He didn't have to make idle conversation. He didn't have to meet someone else's emotional needs. He could get on with his work any hour of the day—particularly when he couldn't sleep—and no one would question him.

Leandro heard a soft footfall at the top of the stairs and looked up to see Miranda gliding down like a graceful swan. She was wearing a knee-length milky-coffee-coloured dress with a cashmere pashmina around her slim shoulders. It would have been a nondescript colour on someone else but with her porcelain skin and auburn hair it was perfect. She had scooped her hair up into a makeshift but stylish knot at the back of her head, which highlighted the elegant length of her slim neck. She was wearing a string of pearls and pearl studs in her earlobes that showcased the creamy, smooth perfection of her skin and, as she got closer, he could pick up the fresh, flowery scent of her perfume. Her brown eyes were made up with subtle shades of eye shadow and her fan-like lashes had been lengthened and thickened with mascara.

Her mouth—*dear God in heaven, why couldn't he stop looking at her mouth?*—was shiny with a strawberry-coloured lip gloss.

A light blush rode along her cheekbones as she came to stand before him. 'I'm sorry for keeping you waiting...'

Leandro felt her perfume ambush his senses; the

freesia notes were fresh and light but there was a hint of something a little more complex under the surface. It teased his nostrils, toyed with his imagination, tormented him with its veiled sensual promise. He glanced at her shoes. 'Can you walk in those?'

'Yes.'

'The restaurant is only a few blocks from here,' he said. 'But I can drive if you'd prefer.'

'No, a walk would be lovely,' she said.

They walked to a French restaurant Leandro informed Miranda he had found the day before. Every step of the walk, she was aware of the distance between them. It never varied. It was as if he had calculated what would be appropriate and rigorously stuck to it. He walked on the road side of the footpath just like the well-bred gentleman she knew him to be. He took care at the intersections they came to making sure it was safe to cross against the traffic and other pedestrians.

Miranda was aware of him there beside her. Even though he didn't touch her, not even accidently to brush against her, she could feel his male presence. It made her skin lift, tighten and tingle. It made her body feel strangely excited, as if something caged inside her belly was holding its breath, eagerly anticipating the brush of his flesh against hers.

Miranda realised then she had never been on a proper dinner date with an adult man. When she and Mark went out they had done teenage things—walks and café chats, trips to the cinema and fast-food outlets and the occasional friend's party. But then he had been diagnosed and their dates had been in the hospital or, on rare occasions when he'd been feeling well enough, in the hospital cafeteria. They had never gone out to dinner in a proper restaurant. They had never gone clubbing. They had never even gone out for a drink as they had been under age.

How weird to be doing it first with Leandro, she thought. It made her feel as if something had shifted in their relationship. A subtle change that put them on a different platform. He was no longer her brothers' close friend but her first proper adult dinner-date. But of course they weren't actually dating, no matter what Jaz thought about the way he looked at her. Jaz was probably imagining it. Why would Leandro be interested in her? She was too shy. Too ordinary. Too beige.

The small intimate restaurant was tucked in one of the cobbled side streets and it had both inside and outside dining. When Leandro asked her for her preference, Miranda chose to sit outside, as the October evening was beautifully mild, but also because after the dusty, brooding, shadowy interior of his father's villa she thought it would be nice to have some fresh air. For Leandro, as well as her.

The weight of grief in that sad old villa had been hard enough for her to deal with, let alone him. It pained her to think he carried the burden of guilt— guilt that should never have been laid on his young child's shoulders. She couldn't stop thinking of him as a six-year-old boy—quiet, sensitive, intelligent, caring. How could his parents have put that awful yoke upon his young shoulders?

It was a terrible tragedy that his sister Rosie had gone missing. A heart-breaking, gut-wrenching tragedy that could not be resolved in any way now that would be healing. But his parents had been the adults. They'd been the ones with the responsibility to keep their children safe. It hadn't been Leandro's responsibility. Children could not be held accountable for doing what only an adult should do. Children as young as six were not reliable babysitters. Not even for two or three minutes. They were at the mercy of their immature impulses. It wasn't fair to blame them for what was typical of that stage of childhood development. It wasn't right to punish a child for simply being a child.

How much had Leandro suffered with that terrible burden? He had shouldered it on his own for all this time—twenty-seven years. He had stored it away deep inside him—unable to connect properly with people because of it. He always stood at the perimeter of social gatherings. He was set apart by the tragic secret he carried. He hadn't even told her brothers about Rosie and yet he had asked Miranda to come here and help him with his father's collection. What did *that* mean? Had it been an impulsive thing on his part? She had never thought of him as an impulsive man. He measured everything before he acted. He thought before he spoke. He considered things from every angle.

Why *had* he asked her?

Was it a subconscious desire on his part to connect? What sort of connection was he after? Could Jaz be right? Could he be after a more intimate connection? Was that why he was challenging her over her commitment to Mark? Making her face her convictions in the face of temptation—a temptation she had never felt quite like this before?

He thought her silly for staying true to her commitment to Mark. But then Leandro wasn't known for longevity in relationships. He wasn't quite the one-night-stand man her brother Jake was but she hadn't heard of any relationship of Leandro's lasting longer than a month or two. He moved around with work a lot which would make it difficult for him to settle. But even so she didn't see him as the guy with a girl in every port.

Would Miranda's time here with him help him to move past the tragedy of Rosie? Would he feel freer once his father's things were packed up and sold? Once all this sadness was put away for good?

Once they were seated at their table with drinks in front of them Miranda took a covert look at him while he perused the menu. The sad memories from being in his little sister's room were etched on his face. His dark-chocolate eyes looked tired and drawn, the two lines running either side of his mouth seemed deeper and his ever-present frown more firmly entrenched.

He looked up and his eyes meshed with hers, making something in her stomach trip like a foot missing a step. 'Have you decided?' he said.

Miranda had to work hard not to stare at his mouth. He had showered and shaved, yet the persistent stubble was evident along his jaw and around his well-shaped mouth. She had to curl her fingers into her palms to stop herself from reaching across the table to touch the peppered lean and tanned skin, to trace the sculptured line of his beautiful mouth. His thick hair was cut in a short no-nonsense style, although she could see a light sheen amongst the deep grooves where he had used some sort of hair product. Even with the distance of the table between them she could smell the hint of citrus and wood in his aftershave.

'Um…' She looked back at the menu, chewing on her lower lip. 'I think I'll have the *coq au vin*. You?'

He closed the menu with a definitive movement. 'Same.'

Miranda took a tentative sip of her white wine. He had ordered one as well but he had so far not touched it. Did he avoid alcohol because of his father's problems with it? Or was it just a part of his careful, keeping-control-at-all-times personality?

Self-discipline was something she admired in a man. Her father had always lacked it, which was more than obvious, given this latest debacle over his love child. But Leandro wasn't the sort of man to be driven by impulse. He was responsible, mature and sensible. He was the sort of man people came to for help and advice. He was reliable and principled. Which made what had happened to him all the more tragic. How hard it must be for him to come back here to the place where it all began. His life had changed for ever. He carried that burden of guilt. It had defined him. Shaped him. And yet he had kept it to himself for all those years.

'If I hadn't found Rosie's statue in the garden would you have told me about her?' Miranda said into the little silence.

His fingers toyed with the stem of his glass. 'I was planning to. Eventually.'

She watched as his frown pulled heavily at his brow. 'Leandro… I really want to say how much I feel for you. For what you're going through. For what you've been through. I feel I'm only just coming to understand you after knowing you for all these years.'

He gave her a ghost of a smile. It was not much more than a flicker across his lips but it warmed her heart, as if someone had shone a beam of light through a dark crack. 'I was a little hard on you earlier,' he said.

'It's okay,' Miranda said. 'I get it from my brothers and Jaz too. And my parents.'

'It's only because they love you,' he said. 'They want you to be happy.'

Miranda put her glass down, her fingers tracing the gentle slope on the circular base. 'I know…but it wasn't just Mark I loved. His family—his parents—are the loveliest people. They always made me feel so special. So included.'

'Do you still see them?'

'Yes.'

'Is that wise?'

Miranda frowned as she met his unwavering gaze. 'Why wouldn't I visit them? They're the family I wish I'd had.'

'It might not be helping them to move on.'

'What about your mother?' she said, deftly changing the subject. 'Does she want you to be happy?'

He gave a nonchalant shrug but his mouth had taken

on that grim look she always associated with him. 'On some level, maybe.'

'Do you ever see her?'

'Occasionally.'

'When was the last time?' Miranda asked.

He turned the base of his glass around with an exacting, precise movement like he was turning a combination lock on a safe. 'I went down for one of my half-brother's birthdays a couple of months ago.'

'And?'

He looked at her again. 'It was okay.'

Miranda cocked her head at him. 'Just okay?'

He gave her a rueful grimace. 'It was Cameron who invited me. I wouldn't have gone if he hadn't wanted me to be there. I didn't stay long.'

Miranda wondered what sort of reception he'd got from his mother. Had she greeted him warmly or coldly? Had she tolerated him being there or embraced his presence? How did his mother's husband treat him? Did he accept him as one of the family or make him feel like an outsider who could never belong? There were so many questions she wanted to ask. Things she wanted to know about him, but she didn't want to bombard him. It would take time to peel back the layers to his personality. He was so deeply private and going too hard too soon would very likely cause him to clam up. 'How old are your half-brothers?'

'Cam is twenty-eight, Alistair twenty-seven and Hugh is twenty-six.' He turned his glass another notch. 'My mother would have had more children but it wasn't to be.'

'Three boys in quick succession…' she murmured, thinking out loud.

'But no girl, which was what she really wanted.'

Miranda saw the flash of pain pass over his features. 'I'm not sure having any amount of children would make up for the one she lost. But in a way she lost two children, didn't she?'

Leandro's mouth tilted cynically. 'Don't feel sorry for me, *ma petite*,' he said. 'I'm a big boy.'

Hearing him switch to French from Italian endearments was enough to set her pulse racing all over again. His voice was so deep and mellifluous she could have listened to him read a boring financial report and still her heart would race. 'It seems to me you've always had to be a big boy,' Miranda said. 'You've spent so much of your childhood and adolescence alone.'

'I had your family to go to.'

'Yes, but it wasn't *your* family,' she said. 'You must have felt that keenly at times.'

He picked up his wine glass and examined the contents, as if it were a vintage wine he wanted to savour. But then he put it back down again. 'I owe a lot to your family,' he said. 'In particular to your brothers. We had some good times down at Ravensdene. Some really great times.'

'And yet you never once mentioned Rosie to them.'

'I thought about it a couple of times… Many times, actually.' He fingered the base of his glass again. 'But in the end it was easier keeping that part of my life separate. Except, of course, when my father came to town.'

'You were worried he would blurt something in his drunken state?' Miranda said.

He gave her a world-weary look. 'Anyone being drunk is not a pretty sight but my father took it to a whole new level. He always liked a drink but I don't ever remember seeing him flat-out drunk as a child. Losing Rosie tipped him over. He numbed himself with alcohol in order to cope.'

'Did he ever try and get help for his drinking?'

'I offered to pay for rehab numerous times but he wouldn't hear of it,' Leandro said. 'He said he didn't have a problem. He was able to control it. Mostly he did. But not when he was with me, especially in latter years.'

Miranda's heart clenched. How painful it must have been for him to witness the devastation of his father's life while being cognisant that *he* was deemed responsible for it. It was too cruel. Too sad. Too unbearable to think of someone as decent, sensitive and wonderful as Leandro being tortured so. 'It must have been awful to watch him slide into such self-destruction and not be able to do anything to help,' she said. 'But you mustn't blame yourself, Leandro. Not now. Not after all this time. Your father made choices. He could've got help at any point. You did what you could. You can't force someone to get help. They have to be willing to accept there's a problem in the first place.'

He looked back at the glass of untouched wine in front of him, his brows drawn together in a tightly knitted frown. Miranda put her hand out and covered his where it was resting on the snowy-white tablecloth.

He looked up and met her gaze with the dark intensity of his. 'You're a nice kid, Miranda,' he said in a gruff burr that made the base of her spine shiver.

A nice kid.

Didn't he see her as anything other than the kid sister of his best mates? And why did it bother her if he didn't see she was a fully grown woman? It shouldn't bother her at all. She wasn't going to break her promise to Mark. She couldn't. For the last seven years she had stayed true to her commitment. She took pride in being so steadfast, so strong and so loyal, especially in this day and age when people slept with virtual strangers.

Her words were the last words Mark had heard before he'd left this world. How could she retract them?

A promise was a promise.

Miranda lowered her gaze and pulled back her hand but even when it was back in her lap she could feel the warmth of Leandro's skin against her palm.

The rest of the meal continued with the conversation on much lighter ground. He asked her about her work at the gallery and, an hour and two courses later, she realised he had cleverly drawn her out without revealing anything of his own work and the stresses and demands it placed on him.

'Enough about me,' she said, pushing her wine glass away. 'Tell me about your work. What made you go into forensic accounting?'

'I was always good at maths,' he said. 'But straight accounting wasn't enough for me. I was drawn to the challenge of uncovering complicated financial systems. It's a bit like breaking a code. I find it satisfying.'

'And clearly financially rewarding,' Miranda said.

He gave a slight movement of his lips that might have been considered a smile. 'I do okay.'

He was being overly modest, Miranda thought. He didn't brandish his wealth as some people did. There were no private jets, Italian sports cars and luxurious holidays all over the globe; he had invested his money wisely in property and shares and gave a considerable amount to charity. Not that he made that public. She had only heard about it via her brother Julius, who was also known for his philanthropy.

Just as they were leaving the restaurant, once Leandro had paid the bill, a party of people came towards them from down the lane. Miranda wouldn't have taken much notice except a woman of about thirty or so peeled away from the group to approach Leandro.

'Leandro?' she said. 'Fancy running into you here! I haven't heard from you for a while. I've come over for a wedding of a friend. Are you here on business?'

'How are you?'

Leandro gave the young woman a kiss on both cheeks. 'Fine. You?'

The woman eyed Miranda. 'Aren't you going to introduce us?' she asked Leandro with a glinting look.

'Miranda, this is Nicole Holmes,' he said. 'We worked for the same accounting firm before I left to go out on my own. Nicole, this is Miranda Ravensdale.'

Nicole's perfectly shaped brows lifted. 'As in *the* infamous Ravensdales?' she said.

Miranda gave a tight smile. 'Pleased to meet you, Nicole.'

Nicole's gaze travelled over Miranda in an assessing, sizing-up manner common to some women when they encountered someone they presumed was competition. 'I've been reading all about your father's secret love-child in the papers and gossip mags,' she said. 'Have you met your new sister yet?'

Miranda felt the muscles in her spine tighten like concrete. 'Not yet.'

Nicole glanced at Leandro. 'So are you two…?' She left the sentence hanging suggestively.

'No,' Leandro said. 'We're old friends.'

Miranda knew it was silly of her to be feeling piqued that he hadn't made their relationship sound a little more exciting. But the woman was clearly an old flame of his, by the way she kept giving him the eye. Why couldn't he have pretended they were seeing each other? Or was he hoping for a little for-old-times'-sake tryst with Nicole? The thought of Leandro bringing someone like Nicole back to the villa made Miranda's stomach churn. Nothing against Nicole, but surely he could do better than that? Nicole seemed… hard—too streetwise to be sensitive. But maybe that was all he wanted, Miranda thought. Sex without sensitivity. Without strings. Without attachment.

'So what are you doing in Nice?' Nicole said.

'I'm seeing to some family business,' Leandro said.

Nicole's green eyes met Miranda's. 'And you're helping him?'

'Erm…yes,' Miranda said.

Nicole turned her cat's gaze back on to Leandro. 'How about we meet for a drink while you're here?'

she said. 'I'm here another couple of days. Name the time and the place. I'm pretty flexible.'

I just bet you are, Miranda thought with a savage twist of jealousy deep in her gut.

'I'll give you a call tomorrow,' Leandro said. 'Where are you staying?'

'At Le Negresco.' Nicole lifted her hand in a girlish fingertip wave as she backed away to join her friends who were waiting for her at the end of the lane. 'I'll be seeing you.'

Miranda waited until Nicole and her cronies had disappeared before she turned to Leandro with a look of undiluted disgust. '*Really?*' she said.

He looked down at her with his customary frown. 'What's wrong?'

She blew out a breath. 'I swear to God I will *never* understand men. What do you see in her? No, don't answer that. I saw the size of her breasts. Are they real? And is she really blonde or did it come out of a bottle?'

Leandro's frown softened. 'You're jealous.'

Miranda cast him a haughty glare. 'Jealous? Seriously? Is that what you think?'

'She's just someone I hang out with occasionally.'

'Oh, I understand,' she said with icy disdain. 'A friend with benefits.'

'You disapprove?'

Miranda didn't want to sound like a Sunday school teacher from the last century but the thought of him hooking up with Nicole made her insides twist into painful knots. 'It's none of my business what you do. I'd just appreciate it if you'd spare me the indignity of having to hear your seduction routine while I'm under the same roof.'

His expression didn't change. He could have been sitting at a poker tournament but she still got the feeling he was amused by her reaction. 'Don't worry,' he said. 'I never bring women like Nicole home. That's what hotels are for.'

Miranda swung away. 'I don't want to hear about it.'

He walked alongside her. 'Do you lecture Jake like this?' he said after they had gone a few paces.

'No, because Jake isn't like you,' she said. 'You're different. You have class—or so I thought.'

'I'm sorry for being such a bitter disappointment.'

Miranda flashed him a glare. 'Will you *stop* it?'

His look was guileless. 'Stop what?'

'You're laughing at me. I know you are.'

He reached out and gently tucked an escaping tendril of her hair back behind her ear. 'It's just sex, *ma petite*. No one is hurting anyone.'

Miranda's breath caught in her throat. His fingers had left the skin at the back of her ear tingling. Was he as tender with a casual lover? Did he touch that woman Nicole as if she were a precious piece of porcelain? Or was it wham, bam, thank you, mam? 'How long have you been—' she put her fingers up in air quotes '—seeing her?'

'A year or two.'

A year or two? Did that mean he was serious about her? Miranda had always got the impression he was a casual dater. But if he'd been seeing Nicole for that long surely it must mean he was serious about her? Was he in love with her? He hadn't looked like a man in love. He had kissed Nicole in a perfunctory way, and on the cheeks, not on the lips. He hadn't even hugged her. 'That seems a long time to be seeing someone,' she said. 'Does that mean you're thinking of—?'

'No,' he said. 'It's not that sort of relationship.'

'What if she falls in love with you?' Miranda said. 'What then?'

'Nicole knows the rules.'

'How often do you see her?' Miranda didn't really want to know. 'Weekly? Monthly?'

'When it's convenient.'

She could feel her lip curling and her insides tightening as if an invisible hand was gripping her intestines. 'So, how often is it convenient? Once a week? Twice a month? Every couple of months?'

'I don't keep a tally, if that's what you're asking,' he said. 'It's not an exclusive relationship.'

Miranda couldn't believe he was living his life in such a shallow manner. He was worth far more than a quick phone call to hook up. Didn't he realise how much he was short-changing himself? Didn't he want more for his life? More emotional intimacy? A deeper connection other than the physical? A casual fling every now and again might have been fine while he was young, but what about as he got older? He was thirty-three years old. Did he really want to spend the rest of his life alone? What about the women he dated? Didn't *they* want more? How could they not want more when he embodied everything most women wanted?

'Don't you have any idea of how *attractive* you are to women?' Miranda said.

His dark eyes were unreadable. 'Am I attractive to you?'

She took a hitching breath, not quite able to hold his gaze. 'I—I don't think of you that way. You're like… like a brother to me.'

He brought her chin up so she had to meet his gaze. 'I'm not feeling like a brother right now. And I have a feeling you're not feeling anything like a sister.'

Miranda swallowed. Was she *that* transparent? Could he see how much of a struggle it was to keep her gaze away from the temptation of his mouth? Could he sense how hard it was keeping her commitment to Mark secure when he looked at her like that? With that smouldering gaze burning through every layer of her resolve like a blowtorch on glacial ice? She sent her tongue out to moisten her sandstone-dry lips and saw his gaze hone in on its passage, as if pulled by a magnet.

She watched spellbound as his mouth lowered towards hers as if in slow motion. There was plenty of time for her to draw back, plenty of time to put some distance between them, but somehow she couldn't get the message through to her addled brain.

She gave a breathless, almost soundless sigh as his lips touched hers. A touch down as soft as fairy feet sent a hot wave of need through her entire body until she felt a shudder go through her from head to toe and back again. She made another helpless noise at the back of her throat as she wound her arms up around his neck, pressing closer, pressing to get more of his firm mouth before it got too far away.

His lips came down harder this time, moving over hers in a possessive manner that made her knees weaken and her spine buckle. His tongue stroked the seam of her mouth, commanding she open to him, and with another little gasp she welcomed him inside. He came in search of her tongue, exploring every corner of her mouth with shockingly intimate, breath-taking expertise. She felt the scrape of his stubble against her chin as he shifted position. Felt the potent stirring of his body against her belly. Felt her own blood racing as desire swept through her like a runaway fire.

Miranda had felt desire as a teenager but it had been nothing like this. That had been a trickle. This was a flood. A tidal wave. A tsunami. This was adult desire. A rampant, clawing need that refused to be assuaged with anything but full possession. She could feel the urgent pleas of her body: the restless ache deep in her core, the tingling of her breasts where they were pressed up hard against his chest.

Kissing in a dark lane wasn't enough. No way was it enough. She wanted to put her hands on his flesh—his gloriously adult, male *healthy* flesh—to feel his body moving over hers with passionate intent. To feel him deep inside her where she ached the most.

But suddenly he pulled away from her.

Miranda felt momentarily off-balance without his arms and body to support her. What was she doing, kissing him like some sex-starved desperado? Her whole body was shaking with the rush of pleasure his mouth had evoked—hot sparks of pleasure that reverberated in the lower regions of her body. Pulsing, throbbing sparks of forbidden, traitorous pleasure. How could she have let it happen? *Why* had she let it happen? But, rather than show how undone she was, she took refuge in defensive pride. 'Happy now?' she said. 'Proved your point?'

He stood a couple of feet away, one of his hands pushing back through the thick pelt of his hair. It should have come as some small compensation to her that he looked as shell-shocked as she felt but somehow it didn't.

Had he found kissing her distasteful? Unexciting? Not quite up to standard? A host of insecurities flooded through her, leaving a storm of hot colour pooling in her cheeks.

She hadn't kissed anyone but Mark. He had been her first and her last. Their kisses had been nice. Clumsy at first, but then nice. The sex…well, it had seemed to be okay for Mark, but she had found it hard to get her needs met. They'd both been each other's first lover so his inexperience and her shyness hadn't exactly helped.

Then the chemotherapy had made things especially awkward. She hadn't always cared for the smell of Mark's breath or the fact that he was ill most of the time. It had made her feel guilty, being so missish. After Mark's diagnosis she had shied away from sharing her body with him because in her youthful ignorance she had thought she might catch cancer. She had compensated in other ways, pleasuring him manually when he felt up to it. Her guilt over feeling like that had compounded—solidified—her decision to remain loyal to him.

But such inexperience left her stranded when it came to dealing with a man as experienced as Leandro. He was used to women who played the game. Used to hooking up for the sake of convenience before moving on. He wouldn't want the complication of tangling with a technical virgin. Had he sensed her inexperience? Had she somehow communicated it with her response to his kiss?

Leandro let out a long, slow breath as if recalibrating himself. 'That was probably not such a great idea on my part.'

Miranda pulled at her lip with her teeth. 'Was I that bad?'

His brows drew closer together. 'No, of course not. How could you think that?'

She gave a one-shoulder shrug. 'I've only kissed one person before. I'm out of practice.'

He studied her for a long moment. 'Do you miss it?'

'Miss what?'

'Kissing, touching, sex—being with someone.'

Miranda resumed walking and he fell into step beside her at a polite arm's length distance. 'I don't think about it. I made a promise and as far as I'm concerned that's the end of it.'

It wasn't the end of it, Miranda thought as she got into bed half an hour later with her body still madly craving the touch and heat of his. She put her fingers to her mouth, touching where his warm lips had moved so expertly against hers. Her mouth felt different somehow. Softer, fuller, awakened to needs she had ignored for so long.

Needs she would continue to ignore even if it took every ounce of will power she possessed.

CHAPTER FIVE

LEANDRO SPENT AN hour or two over some accounts and files he'd brought with him but he couldn't concentrate. He closed the laptop and got to his feet. Miranda had gone to bed hours ago and everything that was male in him had wanted to join her. He shouldn't have kissed her. He still didn't know why he had. He had been so determined to keep his distance and then it had just... happened. He had been the one to make the first move. He hadn't been able to stop himself from leaning down to the lure of her beautiful, soft, inviting mouth. The taste of her, so sweet, warm and giving, had shaken him. Rocked him. Unsettled him.

Miranda had seemed upset at his on-off relationship with Nicole. But that didn't mean he had the right to kiss her. She was just being protective in a sisterly sort of way.

Sisterly? There was nothing sisterly about the way Miranda had kissed him back. He had felt every tremble in her body as she'd leaned into him. Her gorgeous mouth had given back as good as he had served. The tangled heat of their tongues had made his body respond like a hormone-driven teenager. Since when did he lose control like that? What was he doing even *thinking* about doing more than kissing her?

Leandro stood at the window of the study and looked out at the neglected garden. The moon illuminated the overgrown shapes of the hedges, giving them a grotesque appearance. He couldn't see Rosie's statue from here but knowing it was there made the weight of his grief feel like an anchor hanging off his heart.

Would it *never* ease? This awful sense of guilt that plagued him day and night?

Would packing up Rosie's room bring closure or would it make things even worse? Handling the toys she had played with, touching the clothes she had worn, packing them off to where? Charity? For some stranger to use or to throw out when they were finished with them?

Leandro couldn't keep her things. Why would he? He would have no use for them and he didn't want to turn into another version of his father, making a shrine that in no way would help to heal the past.

It was time to move on.

He opened the door to Rosie's room and stood there for a moment. For the two years after Rosie's disappearance he had come to her room during the night. *Every* night. He had stood in exactly this spot in the doorway, hoping, praying, he would find her neat little shape in the princess bed. That he would see one of her starfish hands resting on the pillow near her little angel face with its halo of dark hair. That he would hear the soft snuffle of her breathing and see the rise and fall of her chest.

He remembered the last time he had stood here. The night before he had been taken to England to live with his mother. He had stood in this doorway with a tsunami of emotion trapped in his chest.

Something in him had died along with Rosie. He could feel the place where it had been. It was a hollow space inside him where hope used to be.

The moon shone a beam over the empty bed where Flopsy the rabbit had slumped forward from his propped up position against the pillows. Leandro moved across the carpet and gently straightened the toy so he was back between the pink elephant and the teddy bear.

He turned from the bed, his heart all but stopping when he saw a small figure framed in the doorway. He blinked and then realised it was Miranda, dressed in cream-coloured satin pyjamas. 'What are you doing up at this hour?' he said, surprised his voice came out so even when his heart was still thumping like a mad thing.

Even though it was dark, except for the moonlight, he could see the twin streaks of colour over her pale cheeks. 'I couldn't sleep...' she said. 'I came down for a glass of water and I thought I heard something.'

'You weren't frightened?'

She captured her lower lip between her teeth. 'Only a little.'

Leandro could feel his body calculating the distance between their bodies—every organ, every cell registering her presence like radar picking up a signal. He didn't trust himself to be near her. Not since he'd kissed her. *God, he had to stop thinking about that kiss.*

He could see every line of her slim body beneath the close-fitting drape of the satin pyjamas she was wearing. He could smell the freesia scent of her perfume. He could still taste her in his mouth—that alluring sweetness and hint of innocence that made him hard as stone. Her auburn hair was all mussed up, as if she had been tossing and turning in bed. He wanted to slide those silky strands through his fingers and to breathe in their clean, fresh fragrance. Her skin was luminous in the moonlight, her toffee-brown eyes shining like wet paint. He surged with blood when she moistened her mouth with the quick dart of her tongue. Was she remembering their kiss? Reliving it the way he had been doing for the last couple of hours? Feeling the desire licking along her veins as it had along his until he was almost crazy with it?

'Do you want a glass of milk or something?' he said, leading the way out of the room.

She screwed up her mouth like a child refusing to take medicine. 'I'm not much of a milk drinker.'

'Something stronger, then?'

'No, I'll just head back to bed,' she said. 'I'm sorry for disturbing you.'

'You weren't disturbing me.' He let out a short sigh as he closed the door behind him. 'I was just…remembering.'

Her eyes glistened as if she was about to cry. 'It must be so terribly hard for you, being here again.'

Leandro knew he shouldn't touch her. Touching her was dangerous. Touching her made it harder to keep his resolve in place. But even so his hand reached out and gently tucked a flyaway hair back behind the shell of her ear. He heard her draw in a sharp little breath, her mouth parting slightly, her eyes flicking downwards to his mouth. 'Don't tear yourself up about that kiss,' he said.

Her eyes skittered away from his. 'I'm not. I've forgotten all about it.'

He inched up her chin, holding her gaze with his. 'I can't *stop* thinking about it.'

She rolled her lips together. Blinked. Swallowed. Blinked again. 'You shouldn't do that.'

'Why not?'

'Because it's not right.'

He slid his hand along her cheek, cradling her face as his thumb moved over the silky skin of her face. 'It felt pretty right to me.' Which was the problem in a big, fat, inconvenient nutshell. It felt so damn right he wanted to do it again.

And not just kiss her. He wanted her like he had never wanted anyone. He felt it in his body now—the thunder of his blood heading south. The tingle in his thighs made him want to bring her close enough for her body to feel him. To feel the need he had for her. The hunger that would not go away now it had been awakened. Would she pull away or would she lean in like she had when he'd kissed her earlier? Would her body press urgently against his? Would she make those breathless little gasps of approval as his mouth showed her what it was like to kiss a full-blooded man?

She swept her tongue over her lips in a nervous manner. 'Just because something feels right doesn't make it right.'

Leandro moved his hand on her face to brush the pad of his thumb across her lower lip. 'Are you seriously going to spend the rest of your life being celibate?' he said.

A glitter of hauteur shone in her gaze as it held his. 'I find that imminently preferable to hooking up with people for no other reason than to slake animal lust.'

Was it just sisterly, friendly concern or was she jealous? 'Ah, so Nicole is an issue for you, then?'

Her mouth tightened to a flat disapproving line. 'It's no business of mine if you call her and sleep with her. You can call and sleep with anyone you like.'

'But you would hate it if I did.'

She stepped back from him and folded her arms across the front of her body, reminding him of a starchy schoolmistress from his childhood. 'Don't you want more out of life than that?' she said.

'Don't you?'

She pursed her lips. 'We're not talking about me.'

'No,' he said. 'Because talking about you makes you feel uncomfortable, doesn't it? You're happier dishing out the advice to everyone else while you turn a blind eye to your own needs.'

'You know nothing about my needs,' she flashed back.

He raised one of his brows. 'Are you sure about

that, Sleeping Beauty?' he said. 'I can still taste those needs in my mouth.'

Her cheeks flamed with colour. 'Why are you doing this?'

He took her by the shoulders gently but firmly. 'You're living a lie, Miranda. You know you are. A big, fat lie. You want more but you're too afraid to grow up and ask for it.'

She pulled away from him with a twist of her body, glaring at him. 'Did Julius put you up to this?'

Leandro frowned. 'Why do you say that?'

'He gave me one of his lectures recently,' she said. 'He said the same thing you said—that Mark would've moved on if the tables were turned. It's kind of telling, how you're suddenly taking an interest in me after ignoring me for all these years.'

'I haven't been ignoring you.' *Far from it*, he thought wryly. His awareness of her had been gradual, admittedly. He had always seen her as his mates' little sister. But over time he had watched her blossom from an awkward teenager into a beautiful and accomplished young woman. He noticed the way her creamy cheeks blushed when she was embarrassed, especially for some reason when he was around. He noticed her body; how it made his feel when she was in the same room as him. He noticed her slightest movement: the shy lick of her lips; the downward cast of her gaze; the nervous swallow; the sinking of her small white teeth into the blood-red pillow of her lower lip.

Leandro came to where she was standing with

her arms folded. 'I'm not ignoring you now,' he said, watching as the dark ink of her pupils flared.

She closed her eyes in a slow blink. 'Don't…'

'Don't what?'

The tip of her tongue sneaked out to moisten her lips. 'You're making this so hard for me…'

'Because you want to know what it feels like to be with a man instead of a boy, don't you?' Leandro said. 'That's why you kissed me the way you did. You didn't kiss like some shy little teenager who didn't know what she was doing. You kissed like a hot-blooded, passionate woman because that's who you really are underneath that prim and proper, twin-set-and-pearls façade you insist on hiding behind.'

Her mouth flattened to a thin line of white. 'You know something?' she said. 'I think I preferred it when you ignored me. I'm going to bed. Good night.'

Leandro muttered a stiff curse as she stalked off down the shadowed corridor until she disappeared from sight.

Miranda got to work on the collection first thing. She sorted the paintings into different sections for proper packing and shipping. She had already consulted her associates on one or two paintings that were outside her range of experience. By lunchtime she had done half the collection but that still left the other half, as well as the antiques.

She hadn't seen or heard from Leandro since late last night. She had gone to bed in a fit of temper over him pushing her to admit her needs. Needs she was perfectly happy ignoring, thank you very much. Or she had been, until he'd come along and stopped *ignoring* her. Grr! Was that why he had kissed her in the lane? Just to prove a point? To show her how it felt to kiss a man?

Well, she knew now. It felt good. It felt amazing. It felt so damn amazing she didn't know how she had managed to keep out of his arms last night. She had come close to throwing herself at him. Terrifyingly, shamelessly close. She had looked at his mouth and imagined it pressed on hers, his tongue doing all those wicked things it had done before, and the way hers had responded so wantonly.

Miranda didn't even know if he was still in the villa or whether he had left to meet Nicole. The thought of him with the other woman was like a stone in the pit of her belly.

Would he tell Nicole of the pain he held inside him? Would he share the agony of his childhood? The terrible loss he had experienced? The guilt and torment he still felt? Would he tell her about the estrangement he had suffered from his father and the distant relationship he had with his mother?

Or would they just have monkey sex without any emotional connection at all?

Miranda decided to get out of the villa for a while before she went mad over-thinking about Leandro's sex life. She bought some things for dinner and stopped for a coffee in a café that overlooked the stunning blue of the ocean. It was another mild day with soap-sud clouds gathering on the horizon. Although the late summer crowds had well and truly gone, she was surprised to see only a couple of people swimming in the sea, for the water temperature at this time of year was warmer than in many parts of England in high summer.

Miranda wondered exactly where along the shore Rosie had gone missing. The villa was only a few blocks back from the seafront. She didn't know whether she should ask Leandro to show her. Would it be too painful for him to revisit that tragic spot?

As she walked back to the villa Miranda passed a mother with a baby strapped in a pouch against her chest with a little boy of about two in a pushchair. The baby was sound asleep with its little downy head cradled against its mother's chest. The little toddler was holding a brightly coloured toy and smiled at Miranda as she navigated her way past on the narrow footpath.

Miranda resisted the urge to turn and look back at the little family. When she'd been in her teens, seeing mums with kids hadn't been an issue. Even in the weeks and months after Mark had died she had put the thought out of her mind.

But now every time she saw a mother with a baby she felt a pang, like a nagging toothache.

She would never have a baby of her own.

Somehow that had seemed like a romantic sacrifice when she'd been sixteen, sitting at Mark's bedside with his life draining away in front of her eyes. Now at twenty-three she felt as if the promise was a prison sentence—one without any possibility of parole. How was she going to feel at thirty-three? Forty-three? Fifty?

Miranda pushed the thought to the back wall of her

mind. There were other things she had to concentrate on just now. Like how to get Leandro's father's collection safely shipped to London and the villa packed up ready for sale.

The villa was quiet when Miranda came in. She put her shopping away and then went up the stairs, but instead of going to her room as she had intended she found herself turning to Rosie's instead.

She opened the door and stood there for a moment. The toys were as they had been last night. The bed was still neatly made, all Rosie's things still on the dressing table.

Leandro had intimated he wanted the room to be packed up. Should Miranda do it to save him the pain? *Could* she do it?

Miranda wandered over to the cherry-wood wardrobe and, opening it, looked at the array of neat little hangers with toddler clothes. She ran her fingers along the different fabrics, wondering how any parent could ever navigate the loss of a child. Was there any way of dealing with such overwhelming grief? No wonder Leandro's father had left Rosie's things as they were. Packing them away was so final. So permanent.

Miranda closed the wardrobe with a sigh.

Leandro could smell something delicious as soon as he came into the villa. It was such a homely smell it took him aback for a moment. It had been a long time since he had felt as if this place was anything like a home. But with the sound of dishes clattering in the kitchen and Miranda moving about he got a sense of what the villa could one day be again with the right family. He imagined children coming in from the garden, as he and Rosie had done, their faces shining with exertion and sunshine. He could picture the evening meal with the family gathered around the kitchen table or in the dining room, everyone relating how their day had gone, the parents looking fondly at their children.

His parents hadn't been one-hundred percent happy with each other but they had loved him and Rosie.

Life had seemed so normal and then suddenly it wasn't.

Leandro walked into the kitchen to see Miranda popping something in the oven. She was wearing a cute candy-striped apron around her waist and her hair was tied up in a knot on top of her head. Her cheeks were flushed from the oven but they went a shade darker when she saw him standing there.

She swiped a strand of hair back from her face. 'Dinner won't be long.'

'You didn't have to cook,' he said. 'We could've eaten out or got takeaway.'

'I like cooking.' She rinsed her hands under the tap and dried them on a tea towel. 'So how was your date with Nicole? I presume that's where you've been? Did it all go according to plan?'

'We had a drink.'

Miranda's neat brows lifted. 'Just a drink?'

He held her gaze for a long beat, watching as a host of emotions flitted across her face. 'Yes. Just a drink.'

'You must be losing your touch.'

'Maybe.'

She began to fuss over a salad she was making on the counter. 'I've packed up about half of your father's paintings. I've still got some research to do on the others. I'm waiting to hear back from one of my colleagues. I should have it more or less done by the end of next week, maybe even earlier. I've got the shipping people on standby but I'll need you to authorise the insurance.'

Leandro felt something in his chest slip at the thought of her leaving earlier than he had planned. Had he pushed her too far? Made her feel uncomfortable? All he had wanted to do was make her see how she was throwing her life away... Well, maybe that wasn't all he wanted to do. He couldn't get the memory of their kiss out of his head. He kept reliving it. Kept feeling the sensual energy of it in his body. Every time he looked at her mouth he felt a spark fire in his groin. Did she feel it too? Was that why she was talking so quickly and keeping her eyes well away from his? 'Do you want me to change your flight back home?'

She caught her lip with her teeth, her gaze still avoiding his as she fiddled with the salad she was preparing. 'Do you want me to leave early?'

'No, but what do you want?'

She reached for an avocado and pressed it to see if it was ripe. 'I thought I'd stay on. Help you with the clean-up and stuff.'

'You don't have to.'

'I know, but I'd like to.'

'Why?'

She still actively avoided his gaze. 'I'm enjoying being out of London and not just because of the weather. I can actually walk down the street here without anyone bothering me.'

'Always a bonus, I guess.'

Her cheeks went a faint shade of pink as she reached for some cherry tomatoes. 'Will you be seeing Nicole again before she leaves?'

Leandro couldn't help teasing her. 'For a drink, you mean?'

'For…whatever.'

'No.'

Her brow puckered as she looked at him. 'Why not?'

Leandro hadn't intended to resume his on-off relationship with Nicole in any case but he found it amusing to see Miranda struggle with the notion of him having a sex life. Was she just being a prude or was she actually jealous? Was she envisaging having a fling with him? Maybe she thought she could get away with it while she was away from home. Was that why she kept looking at him with that hungry look in her eyes? Was she rethinking her commitment to her dead boyfriend? Was she finally accepting it was time to move on and live life in the present instead of in the past? Could her fuss over Leandro's love life be a sign she was finally ready to take that first step?

The thought of exploring the spark between them was tempting.

More than tempting.

How long could he ignore the chemistry that swirled in the air when he was in the same room as her? But having a fling with her? How would he explain it to her brothers? It was a line he had sworn he would never cross. Not that he had ever discussed it with Julius or Jake. He hadn't even thought of Miranda that way. He wasn't sure when things had changed—when *he* had changed—but he had started to notice her quiet beauty. The way she moved. The way she spoke. The care and concern she expressed to those she loved. He had held back, kept his distance, not wanting to compromise his relationship with her brothers, or indeed with her.

And yet now he had kissed her. Touched her. Wanted her. How could he simply ignore the attraction he felt for her? Did he want to keep on ignoring it?

Could he ignore it?

Leandro gave a nonchalant shrug. 'It's time to move on.'

Her frown of disapproval deepened. 'So she's past her use-by date?'

'It's how it works these days.'

'I know, but it sounds pretty clinical if you ask me,' Miranda said. 'What if she was secretly hoping for more?'

He reached across for a piece of carrot. 'I make a point of never offering it in the first place.'

'But what if you change your mind?'

He gave her a pointed look. 'Like you might, do you mean?'

Her eyes fell away from his as she put the last touches to the salad. 'I'm not going to change my mind.'

'You sure about that, *ma belle*?'

Her small, neat chin came up. 'Yes.'

CHAPTER SIX

MIRANDA HAD BEEN asleep for a couple of hours when she woke with a sudden start. Had she heard something? She lay there for a moment, wondering if she had been dreaming that plaintive cry. Her sleep had been somewhat restless. Her visit to Rosie's room earlier that day, as well as seeing the mother with her baby and toddler, had made Miranda's slumbering mind busy with nonsensical narratives. Had she imagined that pitiless cry? Was the villa haunted by Rosie's ghost?

Miranda threw off the covers and padded to the door, listening with one ear for any further sound. Her heart was beating like a tattoo, the hairs on the back of her neck lifting as the old house creaked and groaned and resettled into the silence of the night.

It was impossible to go back to sleep. Even though in broad daylight she would swear she didn't believe in anything paranormal, it was a tough call in the middle of the night with shadows and sounds she couldn't account for. She pulled on a wrap, tied it about her waist and went out to the corridor. A shaft of pallid moonlight divided the passage. A branch of a tree scratched at the window nearest her, making her skeleton tingle inside the cage of her skin.

She tiptoed along the corridor but stopped when she got outside Leandro's room. There was a thin band of light shining underneath the door, not bright enough to be the centre light, but more like that of a lamp. There was no sound from inside the room. No sound of a computer keyboard being tapped or the pages of a book being turned.

Just a thick cloak of silence.

'Did you want something?' Leandro said from behind her.

Miranda swung around with her heart hammering so loud she could hear it like a roaring in her ears. 'Oh! I—I thought you were…someone else… I heard something. A cry. Did you hear it?'

'It's a cat.'

'A c-cat?'

'Yes, outside in the garden,' he said. 'There are a few strays around. I think my father must've been feeding them.'

Miranda rubbed her upper arms with her crossed-over hands. *A cat.* Of course it was a cat. How had she got herself so worked up? She didn't even believe in ghosts and yet…and yet she had been so sure that cry had been a small child crying out. 'Oh, right; well, then…'

Leandro looked at her keenly. 'Are you okay?'

She forced a brief tight smile. 'Of course.'

'Sure?'

Miranda licked her dry lips. 'I'd better get back to bed. Goodnight.'

He stalled her by placing a warm hand on her arm. She looked up into his shadowed face and felt her heart do another jerky somersault. She could smell the clean male scent of him, the wood and citrus blend and his own body heat that made her senses spin in dazed circles. His hair was ruffled, as if he had recently ploughed his fingers through it. It made her fingers ache to do the same, to feel those thick, silky strands against her fingertips.

His gaze was trained on her mouth. She felt the searing burn of it as if he had leaned down and pressed his sculptured lips to hers. Every nerve in her body was standing at attention, primed in anticipatory excitement.

'I thought you might be coming to tell me you've changed your mind,' he said.

She gave an involuntary swallow. 'A-about what?'

His eyes gleamed in the darkness, the moon catching the light of desire that blazed there as surely as it did in hers. 'About what you've been thinking from the moment I ran into you at that café in London.'

Miranda pulled a shutter down in her brain as she forced herself to hold his gaze. How could he possibly know what images her wayward mind kept conjuring up? How could he possibly sense the turmoil going on in her body? How could he know of the rampaging fire scorching through her veins at being this close to him? Or of the deep pulsating ache that was spreading through her thighs and pressing down between her legs? 'I'm not thinking...*that*.'

His mouth took on a sardonic slant. 'You're a terrible liar.'

Miranda forgot to breathe as he upped her chin, stroking his thumb against the swell of her lower lip until her senses were reeling. The temptation of his tantalising touch, his alluring proximity and the needs she was desperately trying to control were like a tug of war inside her body. Every organ shifted and strained against the magnetic pull of his flesh but it was too much. It was too powerful to resist. She felt her resolve collapsing like a humpy in a hurricane.

She didn't know who had closed that tiny space between their bodies but suddenly she was in his arms and his mouth was on hers in a passionate collision. The scrape of his stubble against her face made something slip sideways in her stomach. His deep, husky groan of pleasure as their tongues met and mated made her skin lift in delight.

Miranda couldn't control her response to his kiss. It suddenly didn't matter that she was supposed to be keeping her distance. Nothing mattered except tasting the warm, minty perfection of his mouth. Nothing mattered but feeling alive in his arms, feeling wanted, needed and desired. It was like a floodgate had opened up inside her. Her arms wound around his neck, her body pressed up close to the hot, hard heat of his as his lips moved with mind-blowing power on hers. She could feel the swell of his erection against her body, the exciting prospect of his potency triggering the release of intimate moisture within the secret cave of womanhood.

His tongue tangled with hers, teasing and cajoling it into seductive play with his. His arms were wrapped around her tightly, holding her as if he never wanted to let her go. Her flesh sang with the feel of him so aroused against her. It shocked her to realise how much she wanted him, how quickly it happened and how consuming it was to have the pulse of desire racing through her, skittling every sensible or rational objection out of the way.

Her mind was not in control now. Her body was on autopilot—hungry for the satiation of need. She hadn't thought herself capable of such intense passion. Of such wanton abandon that she would be breathlessly locked in Leandro's arms in a darkened corridor with her throat releasing little gasps and groans of encouragement as his mouth worked its breath-snatching magic on hers. How could one kiss do this to her? How could he have such sensual power over her?

His hands glided down her body, settling on her hips to keep her close to the throb of his arousal. All she could think was of how different he felt.

How *adult* he felt.

She could feel the swollen ridge of him against her belly, a spine-melting reminder of all that was different between them and how much she wanted to experience those differences. The intention of his body was clear—he wanted her. Her body was sending the same message back.

Miranda sent her fingers through the thickness of

his hair while her mouth stayed fused to his. One of his hands moved from her hip to settle in the small of her back, bringing her even closer to the thickened heat and throbbing pulse of his body. His blood pounded against her belly, ramping up her need until she was trembling with it. Had she ever felt such a thrill of the flesh? She had never been so aware of her body and how it reacted to the promise of fulfilment. It was like discovering a part of herself she hadn't known existed. A secret, passionate part that wanted, craved, needed. Hungered.

His mouth moved from hers to blaze a trail of fire down the sensitive skin of her neck, the sexy rasp of his stubble making her insides turn over. His tongue found the scaffold of her collarbone, dipping in and out of the shallow dish it created on her flesh. The grazing sensation of his tongue against her smooth skin made her knees loosen until she wondered if she would melt into a pool at his feet. Never had she felt such tremors course through her body. Such shudders and quakes of need that made everything inside her shake loose from its foundations.

'I want you,' Leandro said, his lips moving against her skin like a teasing brushstroke. 'But you've probably guessed that by now.'

Miranda shivered as his mouth came back up to just behind her ear. Every nerve danced as the tip of his tongue created sensual havoc. Where was her will-power? Where was her resolve? It was swamped, enveloped by a need that was clawing at her as his lips skated over her tingling flesh. How could she say no when every cell in her body was pleading for his possession?

Was this why she had hidden behind her commitment to Mark, because of the way Leandro made her feel? The way he had *always* made her feel? She had always been aware of him. Of his quiet strength. Of his heart-stopping attractiveness. Of his arrant maleness that made her female flesh shiver every time he came close.

How was she supposed to resist this assault on her senses? How was she to resist this urgent, primal call of her flesh?

'We shouldn't be doing this...' Her voice came out as a whispery thread that was barely audible. *I shouldn't be doing this.*

Leandro nudged her mouth with his lips, not touching down this time but close enough for their breaths to mingle. 'But you want to,' he said. 'I can feel it in your body. You're trembling with it.'

Miranda tried to still the tumult in her flesh but it was like trying to keep a paper boat steady in a hot tub. How could she deny it? How could she ignore the urgings of her flesh? Her whole body vibrated with clawing need. It moved through her body like a roaring tide. She could feel the pulse of lust low in her core—the hollow ache of need refused to be ignored. Her gaze went to his mouth, her belly doing a flip-turn as she thought of those warm, firm lips on her breasts, on her inner thighs. 'I made a promise...'

He pulled back to look at her. 'When you were a *kid*,

Miranda,' he said. 'You're a woman now. You can't ignore those needs. They're normal and healthy.'

Miranda had ignored those needs for so long but it hadn't really been all that hard to do so. She had never felt she was sacrificing anything. But now Leandro had stirred those needs into life, awakened them from a deep slumber. Sent them into a dizzying frenzy. How could she pretend they weren't clamouring inside her body? How could she deny the primal urges of her body when his presence evoked such a storm within her flesh? A storm she could feel rumbling through her from where his hands were holding her. Burning through her skin. Searing her so she would never be able to forget his touch. Her body would always remember. Her lips would always recall the weight and pressure of his. If she were never kissed by anyone again it would be Leandro's kiss she would remember, not Mark's. It would be Leandro's touch her body would recall and ache and hunger to feel again.

Would it be so wrong to indulge her senses just this once? He wasn't offering her a relationship. He had made it clear he didn't want the happy-ever-after. But then, she couldn't—*wouldn't*—give it to him if he wanted it.

But for this brief moment in time they could connect in a way they had never connected before.

Miranda closed the small distance between their bodies, a shockwave of awareness jolting through her at the erotic contact. She watched as desire flared in his gaze, burning with an incendiary heat that was as powerful as the backdraught of a fire. She slid her hands up the flat plane of his chest, feeling the deep thud of his heart under her palm. She knew he wouldn't take this a step further until she had verbalised her consent. But she didn't want to say the words. She didn't want to own the earthy needs of her body. That would be admitting she was at the mercy of her flesh. That she was weak, frail, human.

Leandro held her gaze with the force field of his. 'Tell me you want me.'

Miranda drew his head back down, her mouth hovering within a breath of his. 'Kiss me.'

'Say it, Miranda,' he commanded.

She stepped up on tiptoe so her lips touched his, trying to distract him, to disarm him. 'Why are we talking when we could be doing other stuff?'

He gripped her by the upper arms in a firm but gentle hold. 'I'm not doing the other stuff until I know it's what you want. That we're clear on where this is going.'

Miranda looked into his implacable gaze. Desire burned in his eyes; she could feel it scorching her through her skin where his hands were cupped around her flesh. 'It doesn't have to go anywhere,' she said. 'It can just be for now.'

His ever-present frown deepened a fraction. 'And you'd be okay with that?'

She would have to be okay. How could she say she wanted more when for all these years she had told everyone she didn't? She had taught herself not to want more. She had blocked all thoughts of a fairy-tale romance, of being married, of one day having a baby, of raising a family with the man she loved, because the man she had loved had died.

But this was a chance to live a little. To break free of the restraints she had set around herself. It didn't have to go anywhere. It didn't have to last. It *couldn't* last.

It was for the moment.

Miranda traced her fingertip over the dark stubble surrounding his mouth, her insides quivering as she felt the graze of his flesh against the pad of her finger. 'Neither of us wants anything permanent,' she said. 'This would be just something that…happened.'

'So you only want it to happen here?' he said. 'While we're in France?'

A French fling. A secret affair. A chance to play while no one was looking. No one need know. Her brothers, her parents, Mark's parents—even Jaz—didn't need to know. It would be over before it began. There wouldn't be time for things to get complicated. No one was making any promises. No one was falling in love. This would change the dynamic of their relationship, certainly, but as long as they were both clear on the boundaries then why not indulge their attraction for each other?

'That would be best, don't you think?' she said.

Leandro searched her gaze for a long moment. 'You don't want your brothers to know about us?'

Miranda bit down on her lip. 'Not just them…'

'Mark's family?'

She let out a breath. 'Look, if you're having second thoughts—'

'I'm not, but I'm wondering if you are,' he said. 'If not now, then later.'

Miranda saw the concern in his dark-as-night gaze. What was he worried about? That she would get all clingy and suddenly want more than he was prepared to give? She knew the rules. He had made them perfectly clear. She was okay with it. Totally okay. More than okay. 'I'm a big girl, Leandro. I can take responsibility for my decisions and actions.'

He brushed a strand of hair back off her face, his expression cast in serious lines. 'I want you to know I didn't ask you here to have an affair with me. The thought didn't cross my mind.'

Miranda raised one of her brows. 'Not even once?'

His mouth took on a rueful angle. 'Well, maybe once or twice.' His arms came around her to draw her close. 'I've always kept my distance because I didn't want to compromise my relationship with your family. It gets messy when things don't work out. Look at Jake and Jasmine.'

Miranda traced his mouth with her fingertip again. 'Did Jake ever tell you what happened that night?'

'No,' he said, kissing the tip of her finger. 'What's Jasmine's version of events?'

'She refuses to discuss it,' Miranda said, suppressing a shiver as Leandro's tongue curled around her finger as he drew it into his mouth. The sucking motion of his mouth made her inner core pull tight with lust.

'Someone needs to lock them in a room together until they thrash it out,' he said as he began to scorch a pathway of kisses up her neck. She shuddered as his tongue outlined the cartilage of her ear, longing coursing through her body in sweeping waves. 'Speaking of being locked in a room together...'

He gathered her up in his arms and carried her inside his room. The lamp was already on, giving the room a muted glow. He set her on her feet but not before sliding her down the length of his body, leaving her in no doubt of his need. The feel of his erection against her made her desire for him escalate to a level she had never experienced before. A restless ache pulsed deep in her body, a hollow sensation that yearned to be filled. Her breasts became sensitive where they were pressed against the hard plane of his chest. She could feel the tight buds of her nipples abraded by the lace cups of her bra. She wanted to feel his hands on her naked flesh, his mouth, his lips and his masterful tongue.

Miranda sucked in a breath as he slid his hands up under her top, the warmth of his palms against her skin sending her senses reeling. His hand came to the sensitive underside of her breast, stilling there as if to give her time to prepare for a more intimate touch. She moved against him, silently urging him to touch her.

'You're so beautiful,' he said.

Miranda had always felt a little on the small side, especially since her mother was so well-endowed. But Leandro's touch made her feel as if she was the most gorgeously proportioned woman he had ever touched.

He brought his mouth down to her right breast in a gentle caress that made her spine tingle from top to bottom. He circled her tight nipple with his tongue before he swept it over the underside of her breast where every nerve fizzed and leapt in response.

He came back to take her nipple in his mouth, drawing on her with just the right amount of suction. A frisson of excitement shot down between her legs, pooling in the warm, moist heart of her body. She had never felt desire like it. Her body had developed cravings and capabilities she'd had no idea it possessed. Never had she felt such intense ripples of delight go through her flesh.

He switched his attention to her other breast, leaving no part of it unexplored by his lips and tongue. The electric sensations ricocheted through her body, making her utter little gasping cries as he came back to cover her mouth.

His kiss was purposeful, passionate, consuming. His tongue came in search of hers, stroking, caressing and conquering, delighting her senses, stirring her passion to an even higher level.

Miranda threaded her fingers through his hair, stroking the back of his neck, going lower to his shoulders and back. She brought her hands around to the front of his shirt, undoing his buttons with more haste than efficiency. He shrugged himself out of it before helping her with her pyjama top. She watched as his eyes feasted on her naked form but, instead of feeling shy and inadequate, she felt feminine and beautiful.

He brought his mouth down to each of her breasts, subjecting them to another passionate exploration that made her insides shudder with longing. She made breathless little sounds of approval, her lower body on fire as it sought the intimate invasion of his.

Her hands glided down his chest, exploring the sculpted perfection of his toned body. She came to the waistband of his jeans, shyly skating her hand over the potent bulge below. He reached down and unfastened his jeans so her hand could go lower. Miranda took up the invitation with new-found boldness, delighting in the feel of his tautly stretched skin, thrilled by the way his body responded to her with every glide and stroke of her fingers. Moisture oozed from him as her thumb moved over the head of his penis, that most primal signal of the readiness to mate. She could feel her own moisture gathering between her legs, the deep, low ache of need throbbing with relentless urgency.

He gently eased her out of her pyjama bottoms, sliding them down her thighs with reverent care. She snatched in a hitching breath when his fingertip traced the seam of her body. His touch was so light, so careful, yet it stirred every nerve in her body into a riotous happy dance.

'I don't want to rush you,' he said.

Rush me! Rush me! Miranda silently pleaded. 'You're not… It's just…been a while.'

Leandro meshed his gaze with hers. 'I want to make it good for you. Tell me what you like.'

Anything you do will be just fine, Miranda thought. Even the way he looked at her was enough to send her senses into the stratosphere. 'I'm not very good at this…'

His brows came together. 'You *have* had sex, haven't you?'

She moved her gaze out of reach of his. 'Yes, of course…'

He gently inched up her chin so her eyes came back to his. 'But?'

Miranda moistened her lips, suddenly feeling shy and hopelessly inadequate again. What a pariah he would think her. So inexperienced she didn't know what worked for her and what didn't. How could she tell him she hadn't had an orgasm other than on her own? That she had found sex a bit one-sided? He would think her a prude, an unsophisticated Victorian throwback. She bet the women he dated—the Nicoles— would know exactly what worked for them and what didn't. They would be totally comfortable with their bodies and its needs. They would know what to say and what to do. They wouldn't be feeling gauche and stupid and useless because they had never had satisfying sex with a partner.

'Miranda?' Leandro prompted softly, his dark eyes holding hers.

Miranda drew her lower lip into her mouth, pressing down on it with her top one. 'It wasn't always good for me with Mark,' she said at last. 'It wasn't his fault. We were both inexperienced. I should've said something earlier. But then he got sick and I just let him do what he needed.'

Leandro's frown was a solid bar across his eyes. 'Did you ever come with him?'

She could feel her cheeks heating up like a radiator. 'No…'

He cupped the side of her face in one of his broad but gentle hands, his thumb moving back and forth in a slow, measured way. 'So you're practically a virgin,' he said.

Miranda lowered her gaze. 'I know you probably think that's ridiculous…that *I'm* ridiculous.'

He continued to stroke her hot cheek, his gaze soft as it held hers. 'I don't think that at all,' he said. 'It's not always easy for young women to get their needs met. Men can be insensitive and ignorant and selfish. That's why communication is so important.'

Miranda looked into the warmth of his coal-black gaze and wondered how she was going to keep her heart secure. He was so considerate, so understanding and so deeply insightful. Hadn't she always sensed he was a cut above other men? Why was he wasting himself on shallow relationships when he had so much to offer? He was 'life partner' material. The sort of man who would stand by his partner through thick and thin. He would be dependable, loyal and trustworthy. He would put his partner's needs before his own. Like he was doing now. He was taking the time to understand her. Treating her with the utmost respect and consideration.

She put her hand against his jaw, her skin tingling at the contact of his stubble. 'Make love to me,' she said in a soft whisper.

He leaned down to kiss her in a lingering exchange that made her body tremble in anticipation. His hands moved over her with tenderness but with the undercurrent of passion. Excitement coursed through her from head to toe, her breathing becoming faster, more urgent, as he stoked the fire of her desire. Sensations flooded her being, showers of them, cascades of them, great, spilling fountains of them that made her feel she had been sleepwalking through life until now.

He kissed his way from her mouth to her belly button, dipping his tongue into its tiny cave before going lower. She forgot to breathe when he came to her folds. His tongue moved down the seam of her body, tracing her without separating her. Fireworks erupted under her skin at the feel of his warm breath skating over her.

He gently separated her with his fingers, waiting for her to take a steadying breath before he put his mouth to her. A host of insecurities rushed through her brain. *Was she fresh enough? Was she waxed enough? Did she look normal? Was he comparing her to his other lovers?*

Leandro placed his hand on her belly in a stabilising manner. 'Relax for me, *cara*,' he said. 'Stop fretting. You're beautiful. Perfect.'

How could he read her mind as well as her body? Miranda wondered. But then she stopped thinking altogether as he put his mouth to her again. His tongue tasted and tantalised her, stroking and caressing her into spine-loosening delight. The tension inside her body built to a breaking point. It was like climbing a mountain only to be suspended at the edge of the precipice. Hovering there. Wavering. Teetering at that one tight, breath-robbing point, every cell in her body straining, pulling and contracting until finally she was pitched into the unknown. She felt like she was exploding into a thousand tiny fragments, like a party balloon full of glitter. Waves of pleasure washed over her, through her, tossing and tumbling her until she was spinning in a whirlpool of physical rapture.

Leandro came back over her to press a tender kiss to the side of her mouth. 'Good?'

Miranda could smell her own female scent on him. Such raw intimacy shocked her and yet somehow it felt right. She looked at him in a combination of wonder and residual shyness. 'You know it was.'

He kissed her on the lips, on the chin, on each of her eyelids and then back on her mouth. 'It'll get better when you feel more comfortable with me,' he said.

You'd better not get too comfortable, a little voice piped up inside her head.

Miranda ignored it as she moved underneath the delicious weight of his body, her senses stirring all over again at the thought of him possessing her fully. She reached down to caress him, stroking his turgid length with increasing confidence, watching as he showed his pleasure at her touch on his features and in the way he gave deep, growly groans in his throat.

He pulled back from her with a sucked-in breath. 'I'd better put on a condom.'

Miranda waited while he got one out of his wallet where it was sitting on the bedside chest-of-drawers. He sheathed himself before coming back over her, making sure she was comfortable with his weight by angling his body over hers. She stroked her hands down his back from the tops of his shoulders to the base of his spine, drawing him closer to the deep ache in her core.

He couldn't have been gentler as he entered her but

even so her breath caught at the sensation of him filling her. 'Am I hurting you?' he said, holding still.

She released a long, slow breath to help herself relax. 'No…'

'Sure?'

She smiled and stroked his lean, tanned jaw as she looked into his concerned gaze. 'You worry too much.'

He brushed her hair back from her forehead in a tender action. 'You're so tiny I feel like I'm going to break you.'

Something hot and liquid spilled and flowed in Miranda's belly. Could there be a man more in tune with a woman's sense of vulnerability? 'I'm tougher than I look,' she said, reaching up to kiss him on the lips.

He deepened the kiss as he moved within her, going in stages so she could have time to adjust to his length and width. He began to move in slow, rhythmic strokes, the gentle friction tantalising her senses, driving up her need until she was making soft little noises of encouragement in case he took it upon himself to stop. Miranda felt she would *die* if he stopped. The craving of her body rose to fever pitch. She felt it clawing at her, frantically trying to attain assuagement. She was almost there…poised to go over the edge but frustratingly unable to let go.

Leandro reached between their bodies, used his fingers to coax her and suddenly she was there, falling, falling, falling. Coming apart in a bigger and more intense way than before. Her body contracted around his, each spasm of her orgasm taking her to new even more exciting heights of pleasure.

She felt the exact moment he let go. He gave a low, deep groan and surged, his breath coming out in a hot gust against the side of her neck as he shuddered and emptied.

Miranda held him close, her hands moving over his muscled back and shoulders, massaging him, stroking and caressing him in that rare moment of male vulnerability.

She didn't know what to say so said nothing. Her senses were so dazed by the power of their physical connection it was impossible to articulate how she felt. She wondered why she didn't feel ashamed. She had broken her promise to Mark but how could she regret something so…so *magical* as Leandro's love-making? He had shown her what her body was capable of feeling. He had opened up a world of pleasure she hadn't known existed. Not like that. Not so powerfully consuming it had made her disconnect from her mind. Her body had taken over. Her primitive nature had driven her. Controlled her. Surprised her. Shocked her.

Leandro shifted his weight to his elbows to look at her. 'Hey.'

'Hey.' Her voice came out husky, whisper-soft.

He stroked his fingertip in a circle over her chin, his look rueful. 'I've given you beard rash.'

Miranda's breath caught on something. 'Just as well we're not around anyone we know,' she said lightly. 'Jaz would spot it in a heartbeat. I'd never hear the end of it.'

A frown created two pleats over his dark, serious eyes. 'You think she'd disapprove?'

Miranda recalled her conversation with her friend at

Jaz's bridal boutique. 'No,' she said. 'She thinks you've been interested in me for a while.'

Something flickered over his face like a wind rippling across sand. He moved away from her to dispose of the condom. It was a long moment before he met her gaze. 'I don't want you to think this is more than it is.'

She did her best to ignore the little jab of disappointment his words evoked. 'I know what this is, Leandro.'

He moved his tongue around the inside of his cheek as if he was rehearsing something before he said it. 'It's not that I don't care about you. I do. You're an incredibly special person to me. As are all of your family. But this is as far as it goes.'

Miranda got off the bed, dragging the sheet with her to cover her nakedness. 'Do we really need to have this conversation?' she said. 'We both know the rules. No one's going to suddenly move the goal posts.'

His expression was as inscrutable as that of one of the marble statues downstairs. 'You deserve more,' he said. 'You're young. Beautiful. Talented. You'd make someone a wonderful wife and mother.'

'I don't want those things any more,' she said. 'That dream was taken away. I don't want it with anyone else.' Even as she said the words Miranda wondered why they didn't sound as convincing as they once had. She had made that heartfelt promise just moments before Mark had died. *There will be no one else for me. Ever. I will always be yours.*

Mark's parents had been there with her at his bedside in ICU. The heart-wrenching emotion of saying goodbye, of watching as someone she loved took their

last breaths, had made Miranda all the more determined to stay true to her promise. But now, as an adult,
she wondered more and more if she had truly loved
Mark enough to sign away her life. Or had his illness
given her a purpose—a mission to follow that gave her
life meaning, direction and significance?

She didn't know who she was without that mission.
That purpose. It was too frightening to live without it.
It had defined her, shaped her and motivated her for
the last seven years.

Leandro made a sound of derision that scraped at
her raw nerves. 'You're a fool to throw your life away
for a selfish teenager who should've known better than
to play with your emotions like that. For God's sake,
Miranda, he didn't even have the decency to satisfy
you in bed and yet you persist with this nonsense he
was the love of your life.'

Miranda didn't want to hear Leandro vocalise what
she was too frightened to think, to confront—to deal
with. She drew in a scalding breath as she turned for
the door. 'I don't have to listen to this. I know what I
felt—*feel.*'

'That's right,' Leandro said. 'Run away. That's what
you do when things cut a little close to the bone.'

She swung back to glare at him. 'Isn't that what
you do, Leandro? You haven't been back here since
you were a child. Your father died without you saying
a proper goodbye to him. Doesn't that tell you something?'

His jaw clamped so tightly two spots of white appeared either side of his mouth. 'I wasn't welcome here. My father made that perfectly clear.'

Miranda dropped her shoulders on a frustrated sigh. How could he be so blind about his father? Couldn't he see what was right in front of his eyes? He was surrounded by everything his father had treasured the most: rooms and rooms full of wonderful, priceless pieces, paintings worth millions of pounds. Not to mention Rosie's things—her clothes and toys, the life-like statue in the garden—all left to Leandro's care. 'And yet he left you *everything*,' she said. 'Everything he valued he left to you. He could have donated it all to charity as you're threatening to do but he didn't. He left it all to you because you meant something to him. You were his only son. I don't believe he would've left you a thing if he didn't love you. He *did* love you. He just didn't know how to show it. Maybe his grief over Rosie got in the way.'

Leandro's throat rose and fell. He turned away to plough his fingers through his hair, the silence so acute she heard the scrape of his fingers against his scalp.

It seemed a decade before he spoke. 'I'd like to be alone.'

Miranda's heart gave a painful spasm at the rawness of his tone. What had made her speak so out of turn? She knew nothing of the heartbreak he had been through. She didn't know his father. She had never met him. She had no idea of how Leandro's relationship with him had operated. She was an armchair survivor. Leandro had every right to be furious with her. What right did she have to criticise his decision to stay away from his childhood home? He had suffered cruelly for his part in his sister's disappearance. A part he wasn't even responsible for, given he had been so young. 'I'm sorry,' she said. 'I should never have said what I said. It was insensitive and…'

'Please.' His voice was curt. 'Just leave.'

Miranda went over to him, undaunted by his terse tone. She didn't want to be dismissed. Pushed away. Rejected. She didn't want their wonderful physical connection to be overshadowed by an argument that should never have happened. What they had shared was too important. Too special to be tainted by a misunderstanding. She placed a gentle hand on his arm, looking up at his tautly set features. 'Please don't push me away,' she said. 'Not now. Not after what we shared.'

He looked at her for a beat or two before he placed his hand over hers where it was resting on his arm. He gave her hand a light squeeze, the line of his mouth rueful. 'You're right,' he said on the back end of a sigh. 'I should've come back before now.'

Miranda put her arms around him and held him close. 'You're back now,' she said, resting her cheek against his chest. 'That's all that matters.'

Leandro held her against him. 'It was hard…seeing him like that,' he said. 'Every time he came to London I had to prepare myself for spending time with him. No matter what time we agreed on meeting, he'd always been a couple of drinks down before I got there. Over the last couple of years it got progressively worse. He would sometimes be so drunk he would start crying and talking incoherently. Other times he would be angry and abusive. All I could think was it was my fault. That *I* had done that to him.'

Miranda looked up at him with tears in her eyes. 'It wasn't your fault.'

His look was grim. 'He never wanted me to come back here after the divorce. He made it clear he couldn't handle having a child around.'

'Maybe he was worried he wouldn't be able to look after you properly,' Miranda said. 'Maybe he just didn't know how to be a parent without having your mum around. Lots of divorced dads are like that, especially back then, when dads weren't so hands-on as they are now.'

'I let things slide as the years went on,' he said. 'Even as an adult it was easier to stay away than to come back and relive the nightmare. But I should've come back before now. I should've allowed my father to die with some measure of peace.'

Miranda hugged him close again. 'I'm not sure there's much peace to be had when you've lost a child. But at least you're doing what he wanted you to do—taking care of everything he left behind.'

He brushed one of his hands down the back of her head, his gaze meshing with hers. 'Don't go back to your room,' he said. 'Stay here with me.'

Miranda wondered if he was allowing her the dignity of not being dismissed now they had made love or whether he truly wanted her to spend the night with him. She didn't know what his arrangement was with other women but she hoped this invitation to sleep the

whole night with him was a unique offer. 'Are you
sure?' she said.

He lowered his mouth to within reach of hers. 'You
don't take up much space. I bet I won't even notice
you there.'

'Then I'll have to make sure you do,' Miranda said
softly as his mouth came down and sealed hers.

CHAPTER SEVEN

LEANDRO HADN'T PLANNED to spend the night with Miranda but, just like when he had run into her in London, it had come out of his mouth as if his brain had no say in it at all. *So much for the rules*, he thought as he watched her sleeping. He never spent the full night with anyone. It wasn't just because he was too restless a sleeper. He didn't want to get too connected, too comfortable with having someone beside him when he woke up. He didn't allow himself to think of long, lazy mornings in bed. Not just making love but talking, dreaming, planning. Hoping.

She looked so beautiful his heart squeezed. Had he done the wrong thing in engaging in an affair with her? He had been so adamantly determined to keep his distance as he had always done in the past. But being alone with her changed everything. That first touch… that first heart-stopping kiss…had made him realise how deep and powerful their connection was. Hadn't he always sensed that connection? Wasn't that why he had respectfully kept clear of her? He hadn't wanted to start something he couldn't finish.

But now it *had* started.

He didn't want to think about how it was going to finish, but finish it must, as all his relationships did.

Her inexperience hardly put them on an equal footing. But he wanted her to realise how crazy it was to put a pause button on her life. He hated seeing her waste her potential because of a silly little schoolgirl promise that had been well meant but totally misguided. She was young—only twenty-three years old. At thirty-three, Leandro felt ancient in comparison. She was far too young to be living like a nun. Her whole life was ahead of her. She had experienced tragedy, yes, but it didn't mean she couldn't find happiness again—if in fact she had actually been happy with Mark Redbank.

The more Leandro reflected on that teenage relationship, the more he suspected how imbalanced it had been. Miranda was a sucker for romance. She had always been the type of girl who cried at soppy movies, or even at commercials with puppies or kittens in them. She had a big heart and gave it away all too easily. He didn't believe she had been truly in love with Mark. At sixteen who knew what they wanted or even who they were? She had wanted to feel special to someone and Mark had offered her that chance. Mark's parents had welcomed her into the bosom of their family and it had made her feel normal.

Normal was important to someone like Miranda. She didn't enjoy the notoriety of her father and mother and the baggage that came with it. Mark's illness had cemented her commitment to him but Leandro truly believed their relationship would not have lasted if Mark had survived.

But was sleeping with her himself going to convince her she was wasting her life?

He had crossed a boundary he couldn't uncross. Their relationship would never be the same. They could never go back to being platonic friends. The intimacy they had shared would always be between them. Would other people see it? Did it matter if they did? Her brothers might have something to say about it but only because they were protective of her. They might even be quite glad he had encouraged her to live a little.

He hadn't coerced her into sleeping with him. They were both consenting adults. He had given her plenty of opportunity to pull back. But he was glad she hadn't. Making love with her was different somehow. It wasn't just her lack of experience, although he'd be lying if he said it hadn't delighted him. It had given their union a certain quality he hadn't experienced with any other partner. Their love-making had had an almost sacred element to it. Or maybe it was because he had opened up a part of himself he had never opened before. He had never shared the pain of his childhood with anyone before. He had never shared his loss. He had never shared his guilt. He had never felt more exposed as a man, yet Miranda's gentle compassion had reached deep inside him like a soothing balm on a raw and seeping wound.

Miranda stirred in her sleep and he watched as the dark fans of her lashes flickered against her cheek. She slowly opened her eyes and blinked at him owlishly. 'What time is it?'

He brushed her mussed-up hair off her face. 'Three-thirty or so.'

She stroked one of her hands down his bare chest, making every cell in his body stand to attention. 'Couldn't you sleep?' she asked with a little frown of concern.

That was another thing that set her apart from his previous partners, Leandro thought. She genuinely cared about him. Worried about him. Put her needs and interests aside to concentrate on his. He smoothed her frown away with the blunt end of his thumb. 'I got a couple of hours.'

She lowered her gaze from his and tugged at her lower lip with her teeth. 'Is my being in your bed disturbing you?'

Leandro cupped her face, bringing her gaze back up to his. 'Only in a good way.'

Her cheeks developed a pink tinge. 'I could go back to my room if you'd like…'

He ran an idle fingertip from behind her ear to her chin, watching as she gave a little shiver, as if his touch had sent a current through her flesh. It thrilled him to think his touch did the same things hers did to him. That their bodies were so finely tuned to each other that the mere brush of a fingertip could evoke such a response. 'That would be a shame,' he said.

She licked her lips with a quick dart of her tongue, her toffee-brown eyes luminous. 'Why?'

'Because I wouldn't be able to do this,' he said, lowering his mouth to hers.

Her arms went around his neck as she gave herself

up to his kiss, her soft little sigh making his blood pound all the harder. He deepened the kiss with a stroke of his tongue against her lips and she opened on another sigh and nestled closer, her lower body searching for his. He put his hand on her naked bottom, drawing her to his straining erection. The feel of her skin on his skin made him want to break all of his rules. The condom rule in particular. But he never had unprotected sex. That was one line he never crossed. He pulled back to get one from his wallet, mentally making a note to replenish his supply.

Miranda looked at him with her clear brown gaze. 'Do you ever make love without a condom?'

'Never.'

'What about for oral sex?'

The thought of her gorgeous mouth surrounding him made him rock-hard. But he would never pressure her to do it. 'Always,' he said.

She rolled her lips together for a moment. 'Do you want me to…?'

'Not unless you want to,' he said. 'It's not for everyone.'

'But I'd like to,' she said, reaching for him, her soft little hand sending shivers up and down his spine. 'You pleasured me that way. I want to learn how to do it properly.'

'Did you do it with—?'

'No,' she said quickly, her gaze moving out of reach of his. 'I only ever used my hand.'

Leandro inched up her chin again. 'You don't need to feel bad about that. You should only ever do what you're comfortable with. No one should force or pressure you into doing something that doesn't feel right.'

She stroked her hand down the length of his shaft. 'I want to do it to you.'

His heart rate soared. His blood quickened. His skin peppered with anticipatory goose bumps. 'You don't have to.'

'I want to,' she said, sliding down his body, her warm breath teasing him as she positioned herself.

He drew in a sharp breath as she sent her tongue down him from the tip to the base. Her warm breath puffed over him as she came back up to circle her tongue around the head, her lips closing over him and then drawing on him. Even with a condom the sensations were electrifying, the sight of her so stimulating he had to fight hard for control. He tried to ease away to give her the chance to take a break but she hummed against him and held on, her mouth taking him over the edge into mind-blowing bliss.

He disposed of the condom once he could move again. His body was so satiated he felt like someone had undone every knob of his spine. Waves of lassitude swept through him, making him realise how long it had been since he had truly relaxed.

His sexual relationships had been pleasurable in a clinical, rather perfunctory way. He always made sure his partners got what they needed but sometimes he felt as if he was just going through the motions: drink, dinner, sex. It had become as simple and impersonal as that. He didn't linger over deep and meaningful conversations. He didn't spend the whole night with anyone.

He didn't allow himself to get that close. Close enough to want more. Close enough to need more.

But looking at Miranda beside him made him realise how much he was missing. His life was full of work and activity and yet…and yet deep down he felt something was missing. He had thought financial security would be enough. He had thought career success would satisfy him. But somehow it just made the empty space inside him seem bigger.

There was a canyon of dissatisfaction inside him. It echoed with the loneliness he felt, especially during the long hours of the night. He knew what would bridge it but he dared not risk it. He couldn't be part of a long-term relationship because he couldn't allow himself to risk letting someone down the way he had let Rosie and his parents down. How could he ever envisage a life with someone? A life with children was out of the question. How could he ever trust himself to keep them safe? He would always live with the gut-churning fear he might not be able to protect them. He had been responsible for so much heartache.

He couldn't bear to inflict more on anyone else.

Miranda lifted her fingertip to his face, tracing the line of his frown. 'Did I disappoint you?'

Leandro captured her hand and pressed his mouth to it. 'Why would you think that?'

'You went so still and quiet and you were frowning… I thought I must've done something wrong…'

He stroked his fingertip down the length of creamy cheek. 'You blew me away, literally and figuratively.'

Her eyes brightened and a smile tilted up the corners of her mouth. 'I did?'

He pressed her back down on the bed, hooking one of her legs over his. 'And now it's my turn to do the same to you.'

Miranda woke to bright sunlight pouring through the windows of Leandro's bedroom. She turned her head to the pillow beside her but, apart from the indentation of where his head had been, the space was empty. She sat up and brushed her sleep- and sex-tousled hair out of her face. When she swung her legs over the bed she felt a faint twinge of discomfort. Her inner muscles had experienced quite a workout last night. Leandro's love-making had been passionate and breathtakingly exciting and her body was still humming with aftershocks of pleasure.

It occurred to her it might not be so easy to put her fling with Leandro to one side when she returned to England. Would she blush every time she saw him, knowing he had pleasured every single inch of her body? That he alone knew exactly what made her cry out with ecstasy? That he alone knew what she looked like totally naked?

Would *he* look at her differently? Would he treat her differently? Would others notice? How on earth would she keep it a secret from Jaz? Or would Jaz guess as soon as she saw her?

Miranda went back to her own room to shower and dress. When she came downstairs she found Leandro in the study working on his laptop. He was so deep in concentration he didn't notice her at first. But then he looked up and his heavy frown was replaced with a brief smile. 'Sleep okay?' he said.

'Yes, but clearly you didn't.'

He stood and rubbed the back of his neck with one of his hands. 'I had some accounts to go through. It's a big job I'm working on for Jake. I need to get it sorted as soon as possible.'

Miranda slipped her arms around his waist and nestled against his tall, lean frame. 'You work too hard.'

He rested his chin on the top of her head as he drew her closer. 'How are you feeling?'

'Fine.'

He eased back to search her gaze with the intensely dark probe of his. 'Not sore?'

Miranda felt her cheeks heat up. 'A little.'

He stroked her cheek with a gentle fingertip, his expression rueful. 'I'm sorry.'

She pressed closer to link her arms around his neck, her pelvis flush against the hardness of his. 'I'm not.' She stepped up on tiptoe to brush her lips against his. 'You were wonderful.'

He looked down at her with that persistent frown between his brows. 'You don't regret getting involved like this?'

'Do you?'

He let out a long breath. 'I'm worried it will change our relationship,' he said. 'In a negative way, I mean.'

'We've always been friends, Leandro,' Miranda said. 'That's not likely to change just because we took it to a new level for a week or two.'

He continued to look at her in a contemplative manner. 'Do you think you'll date someone else when you get back?'

Miranda frowned. 'Why would I do that?'

'Because now you've broken the drought, so to speak.'

She slipped out of his hold and folded her arms across her middle, throwing him a hardened glance. 'So, I suppose you'll call Nicole once we're done?'

His eyes took on a flinty edge. 'I'm not sure why that should be such a sticking point for you.'

Miranda let out a whooshing breath. 'How can you settle for someone who just uses you to scratch an itch? How can you use her? Don't you want more than that?'

'Don't you?'

'I *hate* how you do that,' she said. 'You always shift the focus onto me because you're not comfortable talking about what it is you really want. You think you don't deserve to be happy because of what happened to your sister. It's. Not. Your. Fault. You didn't do anything wrong. Sacrificing your life won't change the past.'

His top lip curled. 'Will you listen to yourself? How about we play a little game of "it's hypothetical"? If I were to ask you to commit to a long-term relationship with me, would you do it?'

Miranda stared at him for a dumbstruck moment. 'I don't— I'm not— You're not—'

He gave a bark of cynical laughter. 'The answer is no, isn't it? You're too invested in living the role of the martyr. I bet you won't even tell your best friend what you got up to with me.'

Jaz will probably guess as soon as she sees me, Miranda thought. 'But you would never ask me to commit to you… Would you?'

'No.'

A sharp pain jabbed her under the ribs. Did he have to be so blunt? So adamant? 'Wow,' she said with a hint of scorn. 'You really know how to boost a girl's self-esteem.'

He swung away to stand with his back to her as he looked out of the window. He drew in a deep breath and let it out in a halted stream. 'I knew this would be a mistake. I have this amazing ability to ruin every relationship I enter into.'

Miranda couldn't bear to see him so tortured with such guilt and self-blame. Her heart ached for him. He was so torn up with regret and self-recrimination. He was so alone in his suffering, yet she wanted to stand by him, to help him work his way through it to a place of peace. She stepped up to him and stroked her hand down the tightly clenched muscles of his back. He flinched as if her touch had sent an electric shock through him. 'You haven't ruined our relationship,' she said softly.

He put an arm around her and drew her close to the side of his body, leaning down to press a soft-as-air kiss to the top of her head. 'I'm sorry, *ma petite*,' he said. 'None of this is your fault. It's me. It's this wretched, bloody house. It's all the stuff I can't fix.'

Miranda looked up at him with compassion. 'Have you told Julius and Jake about your sister yet?'

'I emailed them a couple of days ago.'

'Did that help? Explaining it to them?'

'A bit, I guess,' he said. 'They were good about it. Supportive.'

A little silence passed.

'What about us?' she said. 'Did you tell them we were…?'

'No,' he said. 'Have you?'

Miranda shook her head. 'It's not that I'm ashamed or anything… I just don't feel comfortable discussing my sex life with my older brothers.'

'Fair enough.'

She waited another beat or two before asking, 'Will you take me to the place where Rosie went missing?'

His frown carved a deep trench in his forehead. 'Why?'

'Because it might help you get some closure.'

He turned his gaze back to the view outside the window but his arm was still around her. She felt it tighten momentarily, as if he had come to a decision inside his head. 'Yes…'

Leandro could feel his heart banging against his chest wall like a church bell struck by a madman. A cold sweat was icing down between his shoulder blades and his stomach was pitching as he walked to the place where Rosie and he had been sitting. The beach wasn't crowded like that fateful day in summer but the memories came flooding back. He could hear the sound of children playing—the sound of splashing and happy shrieking—the sound of the water lapping against the shore and the cracking sound of the beach stones shifting under people's feet.

Miranda slipped her arm through his, moving close to his body. 'Here?' she said.

'Here.' Leandro waited for the closure she'd spoken of but all he felt was the ache. The ache of loss, the noose of guilt that choked him so he could barely breathe. He could see his mother's face. The horror. The fear. The dread. He could see the ice-creams dropping from her hands to the sun-warmed stones on the shore. Funny how he always remembered that moment in such incredible detail, as if a camera lens inside his head had zoomed in at close range. One of the cones had landed upside down, the other had landed sideways, and the scoop of chocolate ice-cream had slid down the surface of a dark blue stone.

He could still see it melting there.

He could hear the shouts and cries. He could feel the confusion and the panic. It roared in his ears like he was hearing everything through a distorting vacuum. He could hear the shrieking sirens. He could see the flashes as police cars and an ambulance came screaming down the esplanade.

If only the ocean could talk. If only it could tell what it had witnessed all those years ago. What secrets were hidden below that deep blue vault?

'Are you okay?' Miranda's soft voice brought him back to the present.

Leandro put his arm around her shoulders and

brought her close to his side as they stood looking at the vastness of the ocean. 'My father used to come down here every day,' he said after a moment or two of silence. 'He would walk the length of the beach calling out for her. Every morning and every afternoon and every night. Sometimes I would go with him when I wasn't at school. I don't know if he kept doing it after Mum and I left. Probably.'

She slipped her arm around his waist and leaned her head against his upper arm, as she couldn't quite reach his shoulder. She didn't say anything but he felt her emotional support. It was a new feeling for him, having someone close enough to understand the heart-break of his past.

'I left a part of myself here that day and I can't get it back,' he said after another little silence.

Miranda turned to look up at him with tears shining in her eyes. 'You will get it back. You just have to stop blaming yourself.'

Easier said than done, Leandro thought as they walked back the way they had come.

CHAPTER EIGHT

A COUPLE OF days later, Miranda had finished packing up the last of the paintings ready for the shipping people to collect when she got a phone call from Jaz. Miranda gave her a quick rundown on Leandro's tragic background.

'Gosh, that's so sad,' Jaz said. 'I thought he was a bit distant because of his dad being a drunk. I didn't realise there was more to it than that.'

'Yes, I did too, but I think it's good he's finally talking about it,' Miranda said. 'He even took me to the place on the beach where his sister went missing. I was hoping it would give him some closure but I know he still blames himself. Maybe he always will.'

'Understandable, really,' Jaz said. 'So how are you two getting along?'

Miranda was glad she wasn't using the video-call option on her phone. 'Fine. I've sent off the paintings. Now we're sorting through his father's antiques. Some of them are amazing. His dad might have had a drinking problem but he sure knew how to track down a treasure or two.'

'Has Leandro made a move on you yet?'

Miranda thought of the moves Leandro had made on her last night and that morning. Achingly tender moves, on account of her soreness. It had made it harder to keep her emotions in check. He was so thoughtful and caring; how could she not begin to imagine them having a life together? 'You have a one-track mind,' she said. 'Did you get the dress done?'

'Yep. I'm working on a design for Holly as we speak,' Jaz said. 'Now, tell me all about it.'

Miranda frowned. 'All about what?'

'What you and Leandro have been getting up to apart from sorting out dusty old antiques and paintings.'

'We're not getting up to anything.'

'Hey, this is me—your best friend—you're talking to,' Jaz said. 'We've known each other since we were eight years old. You would've at least hugged him. You wouldn't be able to help yourself after he told you about his little sister. Am I right, Miss "Compassion and Tears at the Drop of a Hat" Ravensdale?'

'Anyone would do the same,' Miranda said. 'It doesn't mean I'm sleeping with him.'

'Aha!' Jaz said. 'Methinks more than a hug. A kiss, perhaps?'

Miranda knew it would be pointless denying it. Jaz was too astute to be fobbed off. 'We kissed and…stuff.'

'Stuff?'

'It's not serious,' she said. 'It's just a thing.'

'A thing?'

'A fling…sort of, but I hate that word, as it sounds so shallow.'

'Seriously?' Jaz said. 'You're *sleeping* with Leandro?'

Miranda frowned at the incredulity in her friend's tone. 'Isn't that what you thought I was doing?'

'You're actually doing the deed with Leandro Allegretti?' Jaz said. 'Oh. My. God. I think I'm going to pass out with shock.'

'It's just sex,' Miranda said. 'It's not as if we're dating or anything.'

'But what about Mark?' Jaz said. 'I thought you said there was never going to be another—'

'I'm not breaking my promise to Mark,' she said. 'Not really.'

'Listen, I never thought much of your promise in the first place,' Jaz said. 'Mark was nice and all, and it was awful that he died, but Leandro? *Seriously?* He's ten years older than you.'

'So?' Miranda shot back. 'Jake was ten years older than you when you had that silly little crush on him when you were sixteen.'

There was a tight little silence.

Miranda knew she shouldn't have thrown Jaz's crush on her brother in her face. She knew how much it upset Jaz to have been so madly infatuated with Jake back then. Even though Jaz had never told her what had actually happened in her brother's bedroom that night, it had obviously been something she wanted to forget. 'I'm sorry,' she said. 'That was mean of me.'

'Are you in love with him?' Jaz said.

'No.'

'Sure?'

The thing was, Miranda *wasn't* sure. She had always cared about Leandro. He was part of the family, a constant in her childhood, someone she had always respected and admired. She had loved him like a brother. Now her feelings for him were different. More mature. More adult.

But *in* love?

Or was it because of the amazing sex? She had read somewhere that good sex was deeply bonding. The more orgasms you had with a lover, the more you bonded with them. She wouldn't be the first woman to mistake physical compatibility for love.

'We're friends as well as lovers,' Miranda said.

'What's going to happen when he breaks it off?' Jaz said. 'Will you still be friends?'

'Of course,' Miranda said. 'Why wouldn't we be?'

'What if you want more?'

Miranda had already starting day-dreaming them as a couple—as a permanent couple. Becoming engaged. Getting married. Going through life as a team, building a future together. Having children and raising them in a household with love and security—all the things he had missed out on.

But then there was her promise to Mark to consider. She would have to tell Mark's parents she was ready to move on with her life. She would have to stop feeling guilty for being alive when Mark was not. She would have to confront the fact that maybe she hadn't loved Mark the way she had thought. That they hadn't been soul mates but just two teenagers who had dated. 'I don't want more.'

'What if Leandro does?' Jaz asked.

'He doesn't,' she said. 'He's not the commitment type.'

'That could change.'

'It won't,' she said. 'He only ever dates a woman for a month or two.'

'So you're his Miss October.'

Miranda didn't care for her friend's blunt summation of the situation. But that was Jaz. She didn't sugar-coat anything—she doused it in bitter aloes. 'Stop worrying about me,' Miranda said. 'I know what I'm doing. But I'd appreciate it if you didn't let it slip to my brothers, okay?'

'Fine,' Jaz said. 'I only ever speak to one of your brothers, in any case. But are you going to tell Mark's parents?'

Miranda bit down on her lip as she thought about that poignant ICU bedside scene seven years ago. Her promise to Mark had comforted his parents. They still got comfort from having her call on them, spending time with them on Mark's birthday and the anniversary of his death. How could she tell them she was falling in love with someone else? It would shatter them all over again. It would be better to let this short phase in her life come and go without comment. She couldn't bear to hurt them when they had been so loving and kind towards her. They needed her. She saw the way their faces lit up every time she called in. She lifted their spirits. She gave them a break from the depressing emptiness of their life without their son. 'Why would I tell them?' Miranda said.

'What if someone sees you with Leandro?' Jaz said. 'He's been photographed in the press before. He's one of London's most eligible bachelors. You and him being linked would be big news, especially right now, with your dad's stuff doing the rounds. Everyone wants to know what the scandalous Ravensdales are up to.'

Miranda groaned. 'Did you have to remind me?'

'Sorry, but you guys are seriously hot property just now,' Jaz said. 'Even I'm being targeted on account of being an adjunct to the family.'

'Really?'

'Yeah. I'm thinking I might meet up with this Kat chick,' Jaz said. 'She sounds kind of cool.'

'Why do you think that?' Miranda said, feeling a sharp sting of betrayal deep in her gut.

'I like her ballsy attitude,' Jaz said. 'She's not going to be told what to do no matter how much money your family's hot-shot lawyer, Flynn Carlyon, waves under her nose.'

Miranda couldn't bear the thought of Jaz kicking goals for the opposition. Jaz was an honorary family member. She was the sister she had always longed for. Ever since Jaz's mother had dropped her off for an access visit at Ravensdene and never returned, Miranda and Jaz had been a solid team. When the mean girls had bullied Miranda at boarding school, Jaz had stepped up and dealt with them. Jaz had been there for her when Mark had got sick and had been there for her when he died. Jaz had been everything and more that a blood sister would be. The prospect of her becoming friendly with Miranda's father's love child was unthinkable. Unpalatable. Unbearable. 'Well, I *don't* want to meet her,' she said. 'I can't think of anything worse.'

'I can,' Jaz said. 'Leandro lost his little sister and here you are pushing away what you've always wanted. It doesn't make sense. The least you could do is make the first move. Be the bigger person and all that.'

Miranda frowned. 'I don't need a sister. Why would I? I have you.'

'But we're not blood sisters,' Jaz said. 'You shouldn't turn your back on blood. Only crazy people do that.'

Miranda knew there was a wealth of hurt in Jaz's words. Jaz put on a brash don't-mess-with-me front but deep down she was still that little bewildered eight-year-old girl who had been dropped off at the big mansion in Buckinghamshire and had watched as her mother drove away from her down the long driveway into a future that didn't include her. Miranda had heard Jaz cry herself to sleep for weeks. It had been years before Jaz had told her some of the things her mother had subjected her to: being left in the care of strangers while her mother had turned tricks to feed her drug habit; being punished for things no child should ever be punished for. Jaz had suffered horrendous neglect because her mother had been too busy, or too manic, or off her face with drugs, to care about her welfare.

But Miranda didn't want to meet the result of her father's infidelity to her mother. If she met Katherine Winwood she would be betraying her mother. Elisabetta was devastated by Richard's behaviour. How could she not be when at the time of his affair with Kat's mother he had been reconciling with her?

Miranda had spent most of her life trying to please her mother, living up to the unreachable standards of her beautiful, talented and extroverted mother. This was one way to get the relationship with her mother she had yearned for. If she met with her father's love child it would undo everything she had worked so hard to achieve.

Besides, Kat Winwood hadn't expressed any desire to meet her half-siblings. She was apparently doing her level best to avoid all contact with the Ravensdales.

Long may it continue, Miranda thought.

Leandro had just finished talking on the phone to an estate agent when Miranda came into the study. 'I think I've got a buyer for the villa,' he said, putting his phone down on the desk. 'Hey, what's wrong?'

She came and perched on the edge of the walnut desk, kicking one of her slim ankles back and forth, her mouth pushed forward in a pout. 'Jaz thinks I should meet Katherine Winwood. She thinks I should make the first move.'

He took her nearest hand and stroked the back of it with his thumb. 'I think that would be a really good thing to do,' he said.

'But what about Mum?' she said, frowning. 'She'll think I'm betraying her if I become best buddies with her husband's love child. God, this is such a mess. Why can't I have normal parents?'

'Your mother will have to deal with it,' Leandro said. 'None of this is Kat's fault, remember.'

Miranda let out a long breath. 'I know, but I hate how Dad wants everything to be smoothed over as if he didn't do anything wrong. He doesn't just want his cake and eat it too, he wants to decorate it and hand out pieces to everyone as well.'

'People do wrong stuff all the time,' Leandro said. 'There comes a time when you have to forgive them for it and move on. For everyone's sake.'

She brought her gaze back to his. 'Is that what you're doing? Forgiving yourself as well as your father?'

Am I? Leandro thought. Was it time to accept some things were outside his control and always had been? He hadn't been able to protect his sister. He hadn't been able to save his parents' marriage. He hadn't been able to protect his father from self-destructing. He hadn't come home in time to say goodbye to his father, but he was here now, surrounded by the things his father had treasured. Being here in the place where his father had spent so many lonely years had given Leandro a greater sense of who his father was. Vittorio Allegretti hadn't planned to live alone. He hadn't planned to drink himself into an early grave. He had once been a young man full of enthusiasm for life, and then life had thrown him things that had made him stumble and fall and he simply hadn't been able to get back up again. 'Maybe a little,' Leandro said.

A little silence passed.

Miranda looked down at their joined hands. 'I hope

you don't mind, but I kind of told Jaz we're seeing each other…'

Leandro frowned. 'Kind of?'

She met his gaze, her cheeks a faint shade of pink. 'It's impossible to keep anything a secret from Jaz. She knows me too well. She put two and two together and… well… I confessed we're having a thing.'

Is that what we're having? he thought. *A thing?* Why did it feel much more than that? It didn't feel like any other relationship he'd had in the past. It felt closer. More meaningful. More intimate. He felt like a different person when he was with her. He felt like a whole person, not someone who had compartmentalised himself into tidy little boxes that didn't intersect.

Why did it make him feel empty inside at the thought of bringing their 'thing' to an end?

'I don't like calling it a fling,' Miranda continued. 'And given what my father did I absolutely loathe the word affair. It sounds so…so tawdry.'

Leandro didn't like the words either. He didn't like using the word 'affair' or 'fling' to describe what he was experiencing with Miranda. As far as he was concerned, there was nothing tawdry or illicit about his involvement with her. He had always had a relationship with her—a friendship that was distant but polite. He had always cared about her because she was a sweet girl who was a part of the family he adored. Even her parents—for all their foibles—were very dear to him. Miranda's brothers were his best mates. He didn't want his involvement with her to jeopardise the long-standing mateship he valued so much.

But defining what he had with her now was complicated. The more time he spent with her, the more he wanted. Her gentle and compassionate nature was soothing to be around. But she deserved to have all the things girls her age wanted. He couldn't commit to that sort of relationship. It wouldn't be fair to her to allow her to think he could. He had been honest with her. Allowing their involvement to go on when they returned to England would be offering her false hope. Postponing the inevitable. It would make it harder to let go if he held on too long.

Once her family found out they were seeing each other, there would be pressure from them to take things to the next level. There would be pressure from the public because everyone loved a celebrity romance. The press had already taken an avid interest in Julius's engagement to Holly. What would they do with the news of Leandro and Miranda's involvement?

'Miranda…' He gave her hand a gentle squeeze. 'I know I've said this before, but you do realise we can't continue this when we go back home, don't you?'

She didn't quite meet his gaze. 'Are you worried what Julius and Jake will say?'

Leandro raised her chin so her eyes met his. 'It's not about what your brothers think. It's about me. About what I can and can't give.'

'But you'd make a wonderful partner,' she said with an earnest expression. 'I know you would. You're so caring and kind and considerate. How can you think you wouldn't be happy in a long-term relationship?'

'But you don't want a long-term relationship,' he said, watching her closely.

Her eyes went back to his chin as if that was the most fascinating part of his anatomy. 'I wasn't talking about me per se… It's just I think you'd be a great person for someone to spend the rest of their life with. To have a family with and stuff.'

He let out a heavy sigh. 'It's not what I want.'

She pressed her lips together for a beat or two of silence. 'I suppose you think I've fallen madly in love with you.'

'Have you?'

Her eyes still didn't quite make the full distance to his. 'That would be rather fickle of me, given this time last week I was in love with Mark.'

Leandro brushed her cheek with his fingertip. 'You're twenty-three—still a baby. You'll fall in love with dozens of men before you settle down.' The thought of her with someone else made his chest ache. What if they didn't treat her right? She was an incredibly sensitive person. She could so easily be taken advantage of. She was always over-adapting to accommodate other people's needs and expectations. Even the fact that she'd settled for his 'thing' with her was evidence of how easily she could be exploited.

Not that he was exploiting her…or was he? He had been as honest as he could be. He hadn't given her any promises he couldn't keep. She had accepted the terms and yet… How could he know for sure what she had invested in their relationship? She acted like a woman in love, but then anyone looking in from the outside would think he was madly in love with her. Being physically intimate with someone blurred the boundaries. Was it lust or love that motivated her to be with him?

How could he tell the difference?

His own feelings he left in the file inside his head labelled 'Do Not Open'. It served no purpose to think about the feelings he had for Miranda. He would have to let her go. He couldn't hold her to him indefinitely. Over the years he had taught himself not to think of the things he wanted—the things most people wanted. He had almost convinced himself he was happy living the single-and-loving-it life. Almost.

Miranda slipped off the desk and smoothed her hands down her jeans. 'I should leave you to get on with your work…'

Leandro captured her hand and brought her close to his body, watching as her pupils flared as his head came down. 'Work can wait,' he said and pressed his mouth to hers.

Desire rose hot and strong in him as her mouth flowered open beneath his. He stroked his tongue against hers, a shudder of pleasure rocketing through him when her tongue came back at him in shy little darts and dives. He spread his hands through her hair, cupping her head so he could deepen the kiss, savouring the sweet, hot passion of her.

Her small dainty frame was pressed tightly against him, her mouth clamped to his as her fingers stroked through his hair. Her touch sent hot wires of need through his body. The slightest movement of her fingers made the blood surge in his veins.

He wondered if he would ever forget her touch. He wondered if he would ever forget her taste. Or the way she felt in his arms, like she belonged there and nowhere else. He wondered how he would be able to make love to someone else without making comparisons. Right now he couldn't envisage ever making love to anyone else. How could someone else's touch make his flesh tingle all over? How could someone else's kiss stoke a fire so consuming inside him he felt it in every cell of his body?

'Make love to me here,' Miranda said, whisper-soft, against his mouth.

Leandro didn't need a second invitation. He was fighting for control as it was. Every office fantasy he had ever had was coming to life in his arms. Miranda was working her way down his body, her hands shaping him through the fabric of his jeans, then unzipping him and going in search of him. The smooth, cool grasp of her fingers around his swollen heat made him stifle an animalistic groan. She read his body like a secret code-breaker, stroking him, caressing him, taking him to the brink, before pulling back so he could snatch in another breath. 'Let's even this up a bit,' he said and started on her clothes.

She gave a soft little gasp as he uncovered her breasts. He brought his mouth to each tightly budded nipple, rolling his tongue around each one. He drew on each nipple with careful suction, delighting in the way she responded with breathless sounds of delight. He moved to the underside of her breast where he knew she was most sensitive. He trailed his tongue over the creamy perfection of her flesh, his groin hard with want as he felt her shudder with reaction.

Miranda wriggled her jeans down to her ankles but he didn't give her time to step out of them. Leandro didn't step out of his either. He eased her back against the desk, deftly sourcing a condom before he entered her with a deep, primal groan of satisfaction. Her tight little body gripped him, milking him with every thrusting movement he made within her. He had to force himself to slow down in case he hurt her or went off early. But she was with him all the way, urging him on with panting cries. He worked a hand between their hard-pressed bodies to give her the extra stimulation she needed. It didn't take much. She was so wet and swollen he barely stroked her before she came hard around him, making it impossible for him to hold on any longer.

He shuddered, quaked, emptied. Then he held still while the afterglow passed through him like the gentle suck and hiss of a wave.

Miranda's legs were still wrapped around him as she propped herself on her elbows to look at him, her features flushed pink with pleasure, a playful smile curving her lips. 'Should I have told you first I was a desk virgin?'

He pressed a kiss to the exposed skin of her belly, letting his stubble lightly graze her flesh. 'I would never have guessed.'

She shivered as he went lower. 'I haven't done it outdoors either.'

Leandro thought of the timeframe on their relationship with a jarring sense of panic. There wasn't time to do all the things he wanted to do with her. In a matter of days they would go back to being friends. There would be no making love under the stars. No making love on a remote beach or in a private pool. No making love on a picnic rug under a shady tree in a secluded spot. He hadn't done those things with anyone else for years. Some of those things he had never done. How had he let his life get so boring and mundane?

The sound of his phone ringing where it was lying on the desk confirmed how much he had hemmed himself in with work. It rang day and night. He had forty emails to sort through, ten text messages to respond to and fifteen calls to make before he missed the time zone differences.

Miranda reached for his phone to hand it to him and then blushed as she glanced at the screen. 'It's Jake,' she said in a shocked whisper, as if her brother could hear without the phone even being answered.

Leandro took the phone off her, turned it to silent and put it back on the desk. 'I'll call him later.'

She slipped off the desk and pulled up her jeans. Her teeth were savaging her bottom lip, her eyes avoiding all contact with his as she went in search of her top and bra.

He pulled up his own jeans before he took her by the hand and drew her close. 'There's no need to feel ashamed of what we're doing.'

Miranda glanced at him briefly before lowering her gaze to his chin. 'I'm not... It's just that... I don't know...' She slipped out of his hold and ran a hand through her hair like a wide-toothed comb. 'What if he finds out?'

'He won't unless you tell him.'

She gave him a worried glance. 'But what if Jaz tells him?'

Leandro gave her a wry look. 'Jaz talking to Jake? You seriously think that's going to happen any time soon?'

She chewed at her lip again, hugging her arms around her body. 'Will you tell him or Julius?'

That was the other file inside Leandro's head—the 'Too Hard' file. The conversation with her brothers about his thing with Miranda wasn't something he was looking forward to. It would have to happen at some point. He couldn't hope to keep it a secret for ever and nor would he want to in case they heard about it later via someone else. He suspected Jake and Julius would guess as soon as they saw him and Miranda together at a Ravensdale gathering.

Like at Julius and Holly's wedding next month. He couldn't get out of going as he was one of the groomsmen, along with Jake, who was best man. Miranda was one of the bridesmaids. Maybe he would have to decline all future invitations. But then that would only increase speculation. 'They'll have to know eventually,' he said. 'I've kept enough secrets from them as it is.'

Her brow was still puckered with a frown. 'I know, but…'

Leandro rubbed his hands up and down her upper arms in a soothing motion. 'But you're worried what they'll think? You don't need to be. I reckon they'll be happy you're finally moving on with your life.'

The trouble was she would be moving on with her life with *someone else*, he thought with another sharp dart of pain in his gut. He would have to stand to one side as she walked up the aisle to some other guy. He would have to pretend it didn't matter because it *shouldn't* matter.

Miranda lifted her toffee-brown gaze to his. 'But what about you?' she said. 'Will you move on with yours?'

Leandro gave her a crooked smile. 'I already have. You've helped me with that.'

'I have?'

'Sure you have,' he said. 'You've helped me understand my father a little better.'

She touched a gentle hand to his face. 'I'm sure he loved you. How could he not?'

Leandro captured her hand and pressed a kiss to the middle of her palm. 'I'd better call your brother back. You want to hang around and say hi to him?'

Her eyes widened in alarm as she started to back away. 'Not right now… I—I think I'll have to take a bath.'

'Leave some hot water for me, okay?'

She nodded and scampered out of the room.

Leandro let out a breath and pressed the call button on his phone. 'Jake, sorry I was busy with something when you called.'

'So, what's this about you doing my little sister?' Jake said.

Leandro felt a chill tighten his skin. 'Where'd you hear that?'

'Joke, man,' Jake laughed.

'Right…'

'You okay?'

'Sure,' Leandro said. 'Been busy sorting out my father's stuff. Now, about this Braystone account—'

'So have you introduced Miranda to any hot French or Italian guys over there?' Jake said.

'No,' he said, trying not to clench his jaw. 'Not yet.'

'Not that it'd work,' Jake said. 'But it's worth a try.'

'I'm sure when she's ready to date again she will,' Leandro said. 'You can't force people into doing stuff until they're ready emotionally. You and Julius shouldn't be giving her such a hard time about it. It's probably why she's been pushing back for all this time. Give her the space to recognise what she needs and stop lecturing her. She's not a fool.'

'Whoa there, buddy,' Jake said. 'No need to take my head off.'

'I'm just saying you need to back off a little, okay?'

'Okey dokey,' Jake said. 'Point taken. Now, about this Braystone account. It's a humdinger of a puzzle, isn't it?'

Leandro mentally gave a deep sigh of relief. *Work.* Now that was something he was comfortable talking about.

CHAPTER NINE

THERE WERE ONLY two days left before Miranda was to fly back to London. How had the last few days gone so quickly? It seemed like yesterday when she had arrived and walked into the villa with Leandro to all the dusts and secrets inside. Now the villa was all but empty apart from the kitchen, the bedroom they'd been sharing and Rosie's room. He hadn't done anything about that yet and Miranda didn't want to push him. She knew he would do it when he was ready. He had a couple more days here after she left before he flew on to Geneva for a meeting over the big account he was working on for Jake.

Miranda looked at the date on the flight itinerary on her phone with a sinking feeling. Forty-eight hours and it would all be over. She and Leandro would go back to being friends. Platonic friends. They would no longer touch. No longer kiss. No longer make love. They would move on with their lives as if nothing had happened. She would have to interact with him at Julius and Holly's wedding, maybe even dance with him and pretend they were as they had been before—distant friends. How was she going to do it? Wouldn't everyone see the chemistry they activated in each other? She didn't think she would be able to hide her emotions or her response to his presence. She had no control over how he made her feel. He had only to look at her and she felt her body tremble with need.

He wasn't in love with her. She was almost sure of it. He certainly acted like it but he had never said the words. Every kiss, every caress, every time he made love to her, she wanted to believe he was doing it out of love instead of lust. But if he loved her why hadn't he changed his mind about the time frame of their involvement? He hadn't even mentioned it since the evening in his office. Had it been her imagination or had he been distancing himself since that night? She knew he was worried about the account he was working on. There were lawyers involved and a court hearing scheduled. Every spare minute when he wasn't sorting out his father's stuff he worked on his laptop with a deep frown etched on his forehead. She had tried to give him the space he needed to work in peace, even though it had been more than tempting to interrupt him and have him make love to her the way he had before.

But at night when he finally came to bed he would reach for her. His arms would go around her; his mouth, hands and deliciously male body would pleasure her until she was tingling from head to foot. She would sometimes wake and see him lying on his side looking at her, one of his hands idly stroking her arm or the back of her hand.

How could that just be lust?

The date blurred in front of Miranda's vision. How could she leave without telling him how she felt? But how could she tell him when he had warned her from the start about moving the goal posts? She was supposed to be an adult about this. Do what everyone else her age did—have flings and 'things' with no strings. She wasn't supposed to fall in love. Not with Leandro. He had always been so honest with her. He hadn't made any promises or misled her in any way. She knew what she had been signing up for and yet she had broken the first rule.

The love she felt for him felt completely different from what she had felt for Mark. More adult. More mature. She loved him with her body and her mind. She couldn't separate the two, which was part of the problem. She couldn't separate her desire for him from her love of him. They were so deeply, inextricably entwined, like two parts of a whole.

Something about that date on her phone calendar began to niggle at the back of her mind.... She was as regular as clockwork. She should have had her period two days ago. She couldn't be pregnant...could she? But they had used protection. Condoms were fairly reliable, weren't they? She wasn't on the pill because she hadn't needed to be.

Surely it was too early to be panicking? Periods could be disrupted by stress and travel—not that hers had ever been disrupted before. They were annoyingly, persistently regular. She could set her watch by when the tell-tale cramps would start.

Miranda put a hand on her abdomen. Could it be

possible? Could Leandro and her have made a tiny baby? The thought of having her very own baby made the membrane around her heart tighten. How could she have thought she could go through life without experiencing motherhood? Of course she wanted a baby. She wanted to be a mother more than anything. She wanted to be a wife, but not just anyone's wife. She wanted to be Leandro's wife. How could she live the rest of her life without him beside her? He was everything to her. He had shown her what she was capable of feeling as a woman. He had unlocked her frozen heart. He had awakened the needs she had suppressed. He was The One. The Only One. How could she not have realised that before now? But maybe a part of her had always been a little bit in love with him.

Would the prospect of having a baby change his mind about them having a future together?

Miranda gnawed at her lip. It would be best to make sure she was actually pregnant first. She would have to slip out and get a test kit and take it from there. There was no point in mentioning it until she was absolutely sure. Her mind ran with a spinning loop of worry. How would he take it if the test was positive? She couldn't imagine how she was going to find the courage to tell him. *'Hey, guess what? We made a baby.'* Like that was going to go down well. How would she explain it to her family? Or Mark's family?

Leandro was tied up with the gardening team who were sorting out the garden in preparation for selling the villa. Miranda told him she was going to do some shopping for dinner, which was fortunately partially true. She was the world's worst liar and didn't want to raise his suspicions. Luckily he was preoccupied with the gardeners, as he simply kissed her on the forehead before turning back to speak to the head gardener.

Inside the pharmacy there were two young mothers. One was buying nappies; the other was looking at nursing aids. Their babies were under six months old. Miranda couldn't stop staring at them sleeping in their prams. In a few months' time she would have one just like them. Would it be a girl or a boy? Would he or she look like her or Leandro or a combination of them both? One of the babies opened its mouth and gave a wide yawn, its little starfish hands opening and closing against the soft blue bunny blanket it was snuggly wrapped in.

Miranda felt a groundswell of emotion sweep through her. How had she managed to convince herself she didn't want to be a mother? She wanted to be just like these young mothers—shopping with their babies, doing all the things mothers do. Taking care of their little family, loving them, nurturing them, watching them grow and mature. Taking the good with the bad, the triumphs with the tragedies, because that was what made a full and authentic life.

Miranda came home with three testing kits and quickly took them upstairs to the bathroom off her suite. Not that she had slept another night in her suite. She had spent every night with Leandro in his. Could that mean he wanted her to be in his life more permanently? Hope lifted in her chest but then it deflated like a pricked balloon. She was in his room because the furniture had been packed up in hers. It was a convenience thing, not an emotional one.

Her heart was in her throat as she waited for the test to work. She blinked when the results came through. *Negative?* How could it possibly be negative? She snatched up the packaging and reread the instructions. Maybe she hadn't followed the directions. No. She'd done exactly what she was supposed to do. Maybe it was too early to tell. She was only a couple of days past her period time. Maybe she didn't have strong enough hormonal activity yet.

But she *felt* pregnant.

Or was it the hope of it she was feeling? The hope of a new life growing inside her—a life that would bond her and Leandro together for ever. A little baby boy or girl like those she had seen in the pharmacy. The little baby who would be the first child of the family she had always wanted.

Miranda did another test and another one. Each one came up negative. The disappointment was worse each time. She held up the first test for another look and her heart stopped like it had been struck with a thick plank when she saw Leandro reflected in the mirror in front of her.

'What are you doing up here?' he said. 'You know you can use my bathroom.'

She turned to face him, hiding the test stick behind her back. 'Erm...nothing...'

His eyes went to the pile of packaging on the marble top near the basin to the right of her. Miranda's heart felt like it was going to pound its way out of her chest.

She could feel it hammering against her breastbone as Leandro stepped into the bathroom. It wasn't a tiny bathroom by any means but now it felt like a shoebox. She watched in scalp-tingling dread as he picked up one of the packages.

He turned and looked at her with a deep frown. 'What's going on?'

Miranda licked her tinder-dry lips. 'I thought I was pregnant, but I'm not, so you don't have to panic. I did a test. Three times. There were all negative.' Tears were close. She could feel them building up behind her eyes. Stinging, burning. Threatening to spill over.

'Pregnant?' His voice sounded hoarse.

'Yes, but it's all good,' she said, swallowing a knotty lump of emotion. 'You don't have to change your brand of condoms. They've done the job.'

His frown was so tight his brows were joined over the bridge of his nose. 'Why didn't you tell me earlier?'

'I only just realised I was late,' Miranda said. 'I'm never late. I wanted to make sure before I told you. I didn't see the point in telling you if there was nothing to worry about. And there's nothing to worry about, so you don't have to worry.'

He put the package down and raked a hand through his hair with a hand that wasn't steady. His face was a strange colour. Not his usual olive tan but blanched, ashen. 'So...you weren't going to tell me unless it was positive?'

'No.'

He studied her for a moment. 'Are you relieved it was negative?'

'I...' Miranda couldn't do it. She couldn't tell another white lie. It was time to face up to what she had been avoiding for the last twelve days—for the last seven years. 'I'm bitterly disappointed,' she said. 'I want a baby. I want to be a mother. I want to have a family. I can't pretend I don't. I *ache* when I see mothers and babies. I ache so deep inside it takes my breath away. I can't do this any more, Leandro. I know you don't want what I want. I know you can't bear the thought of having a child in case you can't keep them safe. But I want to take that risk. I want to live my life and take all the risks it dishes up because locking myself away hasn't made me happy. It hasn't brought Mark back and it hasn't helped his parents move on. I'm ready to move on.' She took a deep breath and added, 'I want to move on with you.'

A flicker of pain passed over his face. 'I can't. I told you before. I can't.'

Miranda's heart sank. 'Are you saying you don't love me?'

His jaw worked for a moment. 'I'm saying I can't give you what you want.'

Miranda fought back tears. 'You love me. I know you do. I see it every time you look at me. I feel it every time you touch me. We belong together. You know we do.'

He turned to grip the edges of the marble counter, his back turned towards her as if he couldn't bear to look at her. Self-doubt suddenly assailed her. Could she be wrong? Could she have got it horribly wrong? Maybe he didn't love her. Maybe all this had been for him was a 'thing'. Maybe she was just another one of his casual flings that didn't mean anything.

'Leandro?'

He pushed himself away from the counter and turned to look at her, his expression taut, his posture stiff as if every muscle was being drawn back inside his body. 'It was wrong of me to get involved with you like this. I'm not the right person for you. I'm not the right person for anybody.'

'That's not true,' Miranda said. 'You're letting the past dictate your future. That's what I was doing. For the last seven years I've been living in the past. Clinging to the past because I was too frightened of loving someone and losing them. I can't live like that any more. I'm not afraid to love. I love you. I think I probably always have loved you. Maybe not quite as intensely as I do now, but the first time you touched me it changed something. It changed me. You changed me.'

'You're in love with the idea of love,' Leandro said. 'You always have been. That's why you latched onto Mark the way you did. You're doing it now to me. You like to be needed. You like to fix things for people. You couldn't fix things for Mark so you gave him the rest of your life. You can't fix me, Miranda. You can't make me into something I'm not. And I sure as hell don't want you to give me the rest of your life so I can ruin it like I've ruined everyone else's.'

Miranda took a painful breath. 'What if that test had been positive?' she said. 'What would you have done then?'

He looked at her with his mouth tightly set. 'I would have respected your decision either way.'

But he would have hated it, she thought. He would have hated her for putting him through it for she could never have made the decision to terminate. Not when she wanted a baby more than anything. Why had it taken her this long to see the lie she had been living? Or had she lived like that because everyone had kept telling her what she should do for so long, she had dug her heels in without stopping to reflect on what she was actually giving up? But if Leandro couldn't give her what she wanted then there was no point in pretending and hoping he would some day change his mind.

She was done with pretending.

She had to be true to herself, to her dreams and hopes. She loved Leandro, but if he couldn't love her back then she would accept it, even though it would break her heart.

But life was full of heart-breaking moments.

It was what life was all about: you lived, you learned, you hurt, you healed, you hurt and healed all over again.

'I know you warned me about changing the rules,' Miranda said. 'But I couldn't control my feelings. Not the way you seem to be able to do. I want to be with you. I can't imagine being with anyone else. I know we only have two days left, in any case, but it would be wrong of me—wrong *for* me—to stay another minute knowing you can't love me the way I want and need to be loved.'

Nothing showed in his expression to suggest that

he was even remotely upset by her announcement. She could have been one of the gardeners outside telling him she had finished for the day. 'If you feel you must leave now, then fine,' he said. 'I'll bring your flight forward.'

Do you need any further confirmation than that? Miranda thought. He couldn't wait to get rid of her. Why wasn't he reaching for her and saying, *don't be silly, ma petite, let's talk about this*? Why wasn't he holding her close and resting his chin on the top of her head the way he so often did that made her feel so treasured and so safe? Why wasn't he saying he had made a mistake and that *of course* he loved her? How he had *always* loved her and wanted the same things she wanted. Why was he standing there as if she was a virtual stranger instead of the lover he had been so intimately tender and passionate with only hours earlier?

Because he doesn't love you.

'If you don't mind, I'll make my own way to the airport,' Miranda said. 'I hate goodbyes.'

'Fine,' he said and pulled out his phone. 'I'll order a cab.'

Miranda didn't waste time unpacking her bag when she got home to her flat. She went to her wardrobe and pulled out the drawer that contained Mark's football jersey. She unwrapped it from the tissue paper she kept it in and held it up to her face but all she could smell was the lavender sachet she had put in the drawer beside it. She gently folded the jersey and put it in a cardboard carrier bag.

Mark's parents greeted her warmly when she arrived at their house a short time later. She hugged them back and then handed them the carrier bag. 'I've been holding onto this for too long,' she said. 'It belongs here with you.'

Mark's mother, Susanne, opened the bag and promptly burst into tears as she took out Mark's jersey and pressed it to her chest. Mark's father, James, put a comforting arm around his wife's shoulders while he fought back his own tears.

'I'm not sure if I've helped or hindered your grieving of Mark,' Miranda said. 'But I think it's time I moved on with my life.'

Susanne enveloped Miranda in a warm motherly hug. 'You helped,' she said. 'I don't know what we would've done without you, especially in the early days. But you're right. It's time to move on. For all of us.'

James stepped forward for his hug. 'You've been marvellous,' he said. 'I'm not sure Mark would've been as loyal if things had been different. Susanne and I are looking into fostering kids in crisis. We're ready now to be parents again, even if it's only in temporary bursts.'

Miranda smiled through her tears. 'Wow, that's amazing. You'll be fantastic at fostering. You're wonderful parents. Mark was so lucky to have you. *I've* been lucky to have you.'

'You'll still have us,' Susanne said, hugging Miranda again. 'You'll always have us. We'll always be here for you.'

Miranda waved to them as she left, wondering if she would ever see them again, but then decided she would.

They would always have a special place in her life, just as Mark would.

Leandro couldn't put it off any longer. He had to pack up Rosie's room. Everything else had been seen to: the paintings had gone; the antiques were sold—apart from a few things he couldn't bear to part with. His father's walnut desk and the brass carriage clock that sat on the bookshelves nearby and gave that soothing tick-tock of time passing steadily by. The villa was an empty shell now everything had been taken away. The floors and corridors echoed as he walked along them. The rooms were like cold caves.

All except for Rosie's room.

He opened the door and the memories hit him like a tidal wave…not of Rosie so much, but of Miranda standing in there with him. Of her standing with him, supporting him, understanding him. Loving him.

His eyes went to Flopsy. The silly rabbit had fallen over again. Leandro walked over and picked the toy up but, instead of putting it back against the pillows, he hugged it against his chest where a knot of tightly bound emotion was unravelling.

He had let Miranda leave.

How could he have done that when she was the only one he wanted to be with? She was the only one who understood his grief. The only one who understood how hard it was to move on from the past.

But at least she'd had the courage to do so.

He had baulked at it.

Seeing those pregnancy tests on the bathroom counter had thrown him. It had thrown him back to the past where he hadn't been careful enough, not diligent enough, to protect his little sister.

But Miranda was right. It was time to move on. He hadn't done anything deliberately. He had been a child—a small, innocent child.

He finally understood why his father had left him his most treasured possessions. His dad hadn't been able to move on from the past but he had known Leandro would have the courage to do so.

He had the courage now. He had it in spades.

He was an adult now and he wanted the things most adults wanted. He wanted to love and be loved. He wanted to have a family. He wanted to build a future with someone who had the same values as he did.

Miranda was that person.

He loved her. He loved her with a love big enough to overcome the past. He loved her with a love that could withstand whatever life dished up. How could he have let her leave? Why had it taken him this long to see what was right before his eyes? Or had he known, always known, but shied away from it? Hadn't he felt it the first time they kissed? The way her mouth met his, the way her arms looped around his neck, the way her body pressed into his, the way she responded to him with such passion and generosity.

He had been a fool to let her go. He had hurt her and the very last thing he wanted to do was that. Her pregnancy scare had thrown him. Terrified him. Shocked him into an emotional stasis. He had locked down. He hadn't been able to process the enormity of his feelings. All the hopes and dreams he had been suppressing for all those years had hit him in the face when he'd seen that pregnancy test. It had been like a carrot being dangled in front of his nose: *this is what you could have if only you had the courage to take it.*

Speaking of carrots… Leandro smiled at the floppy-eared rabbit in his hands. 'I think I've just found the perfect home for you.'

Miranda was on her way out to her car to meet Jaz at the boutique when she saw a dark blue BMW pull up. Her heart gave a little leap when she saw a tall figure unfold from behind the wheel. Leandro was carrying something in a bag but she couldn't see what it was. She wondered if she had left something behind at the villa, as she had packed in rather a hurry. She didn't allow herself to think he was here for any other reason. Her hopes had been elevated before and look how that had turned out.

She opened the door before he pressed the buzzer. 'Hi. I thought you were going to Geneva?'

He smiled at her. An actual smile! Not a quarter-one. Not a half-one, but a full one. It totally transformed his face. It took years off him, made him look even more heart-stoppingly gorgeous than ever. 'I postponed the meeting,' he said. 'Is now a good time to talk?'

Miranda hoped Jaz wouldn't mind her being a few minutes late. Even if he was just returning a stray pair of knickers it would be worth it to see him smile again. 'Sure,' she said. 'Come in.'

He stooped as he came inside and her belly gave a card-shuffling movement as she caught the citrus notes of his aftershave. She had to restrain herself from reaching out and touching him to make sure she wasn't imagining him there. *Why* was he here? He'd said he wanted to talk but that might be about how to keep the news of their 'thing' a secret from her family, especially with Julius' and Holly's wedding coming up. She didn't dare hope for anything more.

Miranda glanced at the bag in his hand. 'Did I leave something behind?'

He handed it to her. 'I want you to have this.'

Miranda opened the bag to find Flopsy the rabbit inside. She took him out and held him close to her thrumming chest. 'Why?'

'Because I want our first baby to have him,' Leandro said.

She blinked and then frowned, not sure she'd heard him correctly. 'But we're not pregnant. I told you, the tests were all negative. You don't have to worry. It was my mistake. I worked myself up into a panic over nothing.'

He stepped closer and held her by the upper arms, a gentle, protective touch that made her flesh shiver in delight. His dark brown eyes were meltingly warm, moist with banked-up emotion. 'I want you to marry me,' he said. 'I want you to have my babies. As many as you want. I love you. I don't think it's possible to love someone more than I love you.'

Miranda's heart was so full of love, joy and relief, she thought it would burst. Could this really be happening? Was he really proposing to her? '*Really?*' she said. 'Did you really just ask me to marry you?'

'Yes, really.'

'What made you change your mind?'

'When you left I kept telling myself it was for the best,' he said. 'I convinced myself it was better that way. I was annoyed with myself for crossing a boundary I'd always told myself I'd never cross. But when I finally worked up the courage to pack up Rosie's room it made me realise what I was forfeiting. I think that's why I was so shocked at seeing that pregnancy test. It was like being slammed over the head with the truth. The truth of what I really wanted all this time but wasn't game to admit. I *want* to risk loving you and our children. I can't promise to keep you and them safe, but I will do everything in my power to do so. No one can offer more than that.'

Miranda threw her arms around his neck, Flopsy getting caught up in the hug. 'I love you,' she said. 'I want to spend the rest of my life with you. I can't imagine being with anyone else.'

Leandro kissed her tenderly before holding her slightly aloft so he could look down at her. 'You know what's ironic about this? That night I returned Jake's call, I lectured him about hassling you all the time about moving on with your life. I told him all you needed was some space to sort it out for yourself. But then I realised that's what I needed. When you left I could finally see what I was throwing away. I didn't want to end up like my father, living alone and desperately lonely, with only liquor for comfort. He knew I would eventually get past the grief and guilt. That's why he left me what he loved most. He knew I would reclaim my life. I want to be with you while I do it, *ma petite*. No one else but you.'

Miranda wrapped her arms around his waist. 'I wonder what my brothers are going to say.'

'I think they'll be pleased,' Leandro said. 'In fact, I'm wondering if Jake's already guessed.'

She looked up him with a twinkling smile. 'You think?'

'I got a bit terse with him when he asked if I'd introduced you to any hot French or Italian guys.'

'Ah, yes, jealousy is always a clue.' Miranda gave a little laugh. 'Or so Jaz says. She'll be so thrilled for us. She's been itching to make me a wedding dress since we were kids. Now it's going to happen for real.'

Leandro brushed an imaginary hair away from her forehead. 'You will be the most beautiful bride. I can't wait to see you walk down the aisle towards me.'

'How long before we get married?'

'I'd do it tomorrow, but I think we shouldn't steal Julius's and Holly's thunder.'

Miranda loved how thoughtful he was. It was one of the reasons she loved him so much. 'I can wait a few months if you can.'

'It'll be worth the wait,' he said. 'We have the rest of our lives to be together.'

Miranda touched the side of his face with her hand, looking deep into his tender gaze. 'I don't care what life throws at us. I can handle it, especially if I've got you by my side. Which is kind of where you've always been, now that I think about it.'

Leandro smiled as he held her close, his head coming down to rest on top of her head. 'It's where I plan to stay.'

* * * * *

ENGAGED TO
HER RAVENSDALE
ENEMY

To Monique Scott. You left an indelible mark
on our family, enriching our lives in so many
fabulous ways. You are the daughter I never had.
You are the most amazing young woman,
a gorgeous mother, and a wonderful friend.
Love always. xxxx

CHAPTER ONE

IT WASN'T GIVING back the engagement ring Jasmine Connolly was most worried about. She had two more sitting in her jewellery box in her flat in Mayfair above her bridal-wear shop. It was the feeling of being rejected. *Again.* What was wrong with her? Why wasn't she good enough? She hadn't been good enough for her mother. Why did the people she cared about always leave her?

But that wasn't all that had her stomach knotting in panic. It was attending the winter wedding expo next weekend in the Cotswolds as a singleton. How could she front up *sans* fiancé? She might as well turn up at the plush hotel she'd booked months and months ago with 'loser' written on her forehead. She had so looked forward to that expo. After a lot of arm-twisting she had secured a slot in the fashion parade. It was her first catwalk show and it had the potential to lead to bigger and more important ones.

But it wasn't just about designing wedding gowns. She loved everything to do with weddings. The commitment to have someone love you for the rest of your life, not just while it was convenient or while it suited them. Love was supposed to be for ever. Every time she designed a gown she stitched her own hopes into it. What if she never got to wear one of her own gowns? What sort of cruel irony would that be?

She glanced at her empty ring finger where it was gripping the steering wheel. She wished she'd thought to shove on one of her spares just so she didn't have to explain to everyone that she was—to quote Myles—'taking a break'.

It didn't matter how he termed it, it all meant the same thing as far as Jaz was concerned. She was dumped. Jilted. Cast off. Single.

Forget about three times a bridesmaid, she thought sourly. What did it mean if you were three times a dumped fiancée?

It meant you sucked at relationships. Really sucked.

Jaz parked the car in her usual spot at Ravensdene, the family pile of the theatre-royalty family where she had grown up as the gardener's daughter and surrogate sister to Miranda Ravensdale and her older twin brothers, Julius and Jake.

Miranda had just got herself engaged. Damn. It.

Jaz was thrilled for her best mate. Of course she was. Miranda and Leandro Allegretti were perfect for each other. No one deserved a happy ending more than those two.

But why couldn't she have hers?

Jaz put her head down against the steering wheel and banged it three times. *Argh!*

There was a sound of a car growling as it came up

the long driveway. Jaz straightened and quickly got out of her car and watched as the Italian sports car ate up the gravel with its spinning tyres, spitting out what it didn't want in spraying arcs of flying stones. It felt like a fistful of those stones were clenched between her back molars as the car came to a dusty standstill next to hers.

Jacques, otherwise known as Jake, Ravensdale unfolded his tall, athletic frame from behind the wheel with animal grace. Jaz knew it was Jake and not his identical twin brother Julius because she had always been able to tell them apart. Not everyone could, but she could. She felt the difference in her body. Her body got all tingly and feverish, restless and antsy, whenever Jake was around. It was as if her body picked up a signal from his and it completely scrambled her motherboard.

His black hair was sexily tousled and wind-blown. Another reason to hate him, because she knew if she had just driven with the top down in that chilly October breeze her hair would have looked like a tangled fishing net. He was dressed casually because everything about Jake was casual, including his relationships—if you could call hook-ups and one-night stands relationships.

His dark-blue gaze was hidden behind designer aviator lenses but she could see a deep frown grooved into his forehead. At least it was a change from his stock-standard mocking smile. 'What the hell are you doing here?' he said.

Jaz felt another millimetre go down on her molars.

'Nice to see you too, Jake,' she said with a sugar-sweet smile. 'How's things? Had that personality transplant yet?'

He took off his sunglasses and continued to frown at her. 'You're supposed to be in London.'

Jaz gave him a wide-eyed, innocent look. 'Am I?'

'I checked with Miranda,' he said, clicking shut the driver's door with his foot. 'She said you were going to a party with Tim at his parents' house.'

'It's Myles,' she said. 'Tim was my...erm...other one.'

The corner of his mouth lifted. 'Number one or number two?'

It was extremely annoying how he made her ex-fiancés sound like bodily waste products, Jaz thought. Not that she didn't think of them that way too these days, but still. 'Number two,' she said. 'Lincoln was my first.'

Jake turned to pop open the boot of the car with his remote device. 'So where's lover-boy Myles?' he said. 'Is he planning on joining you?'

Jaz knew she shouldn't be looking at the way Jake's dark-blue denim jeans clung to his taut behind as he bent forward to get his overnight bag but what was a girl to do? He was built like an Olympic athlete. Lean and tanned with muscles in all the right places and in places where her exes didn't have them and never would. He was fantasy fodder. Ever since her hormones had been old enough to take notice, that was exactly what they had done. Which was damned inconvenient, since she absolutely, unreservedly loathed him. 'No...erm...he's staying in town to do some work,' she said. 'After the party, I mean.'

Jake turned back to look at her with a glinting smile. 'You've broken up.'

Jaz hated it that he didn't pose it as a question but as if it were a given. *Another Jasmine Connolly engagement bites the dust.* Not that she was going to admit it to him of all people. 'Don't be ridiculous,' she said. 'What on earth makes you think that? Just because I chose to spend the weekend down here while I work on Holly's dress instead of partying in town doesn't mean I'm—'

'Where's that flashy rock you've been brandishing about?'

Jaz used her left hand to flick her hair back over her shoulder in what she hoped was a casual manner. 'It's in London. I don't like wearing it when I'm working.' Which at least wasn't a complete lie. The ring was in London, safely in Myles' family jewellery vault. It miffed her Myles hadn't let her keep it. Not even for a few days till she got used to the idea of 'taking a break'. So what if it was a family heirloom? He had plenty of money. He could buy any number of rings. But no, he had to have it back, which meant she was walking around with a naked ring finger because she'd been too upset, angry and hurt to grab one of her other rings on her way out of the flat.

How galling if Jake were the first person to find out she had jinxed another relationship. How could she bear it? He wouldn't be sympathetic and consoling. He would roll about the floor laughing, saying, *I told you so.*

Jake hooked his finger through the loop on the collar of his Italian leather jacket and slung it over his shoulder. 'You'd better make yourself scarce if you're not in the mood for a party. I have guests arriving in an hour.'

Jaz's stomach dropped like a lift with snapped cables. 'Guests?'

His shoes crunched over the gravel as he strode towards the grand old Elizabethan mansion's entrance. 'Yep, the ones that eat and drink and don't sleep.'

She followed him into the house feeling like a teacup Chihuahua trying to keep up with an alpha wolf. 'What the hell? How many guests? Are they all female?'

He flashed her a white-toothed smile. 'You know me so well.'

Jaz could feel herself lighting up with lava-hot heat. Most of it burned in her cheeks at the thought of having to listen to him rocking on with a harem of his Hollywood wannabes. Unlike his identical twin brother Julius and his younger sister Miranda, who did everything they could to distance themselves from their parents' fame, Jake cashed in on it. Big-time. He was shameless in how he exploited it for all it was worth—which wasn't much, in Jaz's opinion. She had been the victim of his exploitative tactics when she'd been sixteen on the night of one of his parents' legendary New Year's Eve parties. He had led her on to believe he was serious about…

But she never thought about that night in his bedroom. *Never.*

'You can't have a party,' Jaz said as she followed him into the house. 'Mrs Eggleston's away. She's visiting her sister in Bath.'

'Which is why I've chosen this weekend,' he said. 'Don't worry. I've organised the catering.'

Jaz folded her arms and glowered at him. 'And I bet I know what's on the menu.' *Him.* Being licked and ego-stroked by a bevy of bimbo airheads who drank champagne like it was water and ate nothing in case they put on an ounce. She only hoped they were all of age.

'You want to join us?'

Jaz jerked her chin back against her neck and made a scoffing noise. 'Are you out of your mind? I couldn't think of anything worse than watching a bunch of wannabe starlets get taken in by your particular version of charm. I'd rather chew razor blades.'

He shrugged one of his broad shoulders as if he didn't care either way. 'No skin off my nose.'

Jaz thought she would like to scratch every bit of skin off that arrogant nose. She hadn't been alone with him in years. There had always been other members of his family around whenever they'd come to Ravensdene. Why hadn't Eggles told her he would be here? Mrs Eggleston, the long-time housekeeper, knew how much Jaz hated Jake.

Everyone knew it. The feud between them had gone on for seven years. The air crackled with static electricity when they were in the same room even if there were crowds of other people around. The antagonism she felt towards Jake had grown exponentially every year. He had a habit of looking at her a certain way, as if he was thinking back to that night in his room when she had made the biggest fool of herself. His dark-blue eyes would take on a mocking gleam as if he could remember every inch of her body where it had been lying waiting for him in his bed in nothing but her underwear.

She gave a mental cringe. Yes, her underwear. What had she been thinking? Why had she fallen for it? Why hadn't she realised he'd been playing her for a fool? The humiliation he had subjected her to, the shame, the embarrassment of being hauled out of his bed in front of his… *Grrhh!* She would *not* think about it.

She. Would. Not.

Jaz's father wasn't even here to referee. He was away on a cruise of the Greek Islands with his new wife. Her father didn't belong to Jaz any more—not that he ever had. His work had always been more important than her. How could a garden, even one as big as the one at Ravensdene, be more important than his only child? But no, now he belonged to Angela.

Going back to London was out of the question. Jaz wasn't ready to announce the pause on her engagement. Not yet. Not until she knew for sure it was over. Not even to Miranda. Not while there was a slither of hope. All she had to do was make Myles see what he was missing out on. She was his soul mate. Of course she was. Everybody said so. Well, maybe not everybody, but she didn't need everyone's approval. Not even his parents' approval, which was a good thing, considering they didn't like her. But then, they were horrid toffee-nosed snobs and she didn't like them either.

Jaz did everything for Myles. She cooked, she cleaned, she organised his social calendar. She turned her timetable upside down and inside out so she could be available for him. She even had sex with him when she didn't feel like it. Which was more often than not, for some strange reason. Was that why Myles wanted a break? Because she wasn't sexually assertive enough? Not raunchy enough? She could do raunchy. She could wear dress-up costumes and play games. She would hate it but if it won him back she would do it. Other men found her attractive. Sure they did.

She was fighting off men all the time. She wasn't vain but she knew she had the package: the looks, the figure, the face and the hair. And she was whip-smart. She had her own bridal design company and she was not quite twenty-four.

Sure, she'd had a bit of help from Jake's parents, Richard and Elisabetta Ravensdale, in setting up. In fact, if it hadn't been for them, she wouldn't have had the brilliant education she'd had. They had stepped in when her mother had left her at Ravensdene on an access visit when she was eight and had never returned.

Not that it bothered Jaz that her mother hadn't come back for her. Not really. She was mightily relieved she hadn't had to go back to that cramped and mouldy, rat-infested flat in Brixton where the neighbours fought harder than the feral cats living near the garbage collection point. It was the principle of the thing that was the issue. Being left like a package on a doorstep wasn't exactly how one expected to be treated as a young child. But still, living at the Elizabethan mansion Ravensdene in Buckinghamshire had been much preferable. It was like being at a country spa resort with acres of verdant fields, dark, shady woods and a river meandering through the property like a silver ribbon.

This was home and the Ravensdales were family.

Well, apart from Jake, of course.

Jake tossed the bag on his bed and let out a filthy curse. What the hell was Jasmine Connolly doing here? He had made sure the place was empty for the weekend. He had a plan and Jasmine wasn't part of it. He did everything he could to avoid her. But when he couldn't he did everything he could to annoy her. He got a kick out of seeing her clench her teeth and flash those grey-blue eyes at him like tongues of flame. She was a pain in the backside but he wasn't going to let her dictate what he could and couldn't do. This was his family home, not hers. She might have benefited from being raised with his kid sister Miranda but she was still the gardener's daughter.

Jaz had been intent on marrying up since she'd been a kid. At sixteen she'd had her sights on him. *On him!* What a joke. He was ten years older than her; marriage hadn't been on his radar then and it wasn't on it now. It wasn't even in his vocabulary.

Jaz did nothing but think about marriage. Her whole life revolved around it. She was a good designer, he had to give her that, but it surely wasn't healthy to be so obsessed with the idea of marriage? Forty per cent of marriages ended in divorce—his parents' being a case in point. After his father's love-child scandal broke a month ago, it had looked like they were going to have a second one. The couple had remarried after their first divorce, and if another was on the way he only hoped it wouldn't be as acrimonious and publicly cringe-worthy as their last.

His phone beeped with an incoming message and he swore again when he checked his screen. Twenty-seven text messages and fourteen missed calls from Emma Madden. He had blocked her number but she must have borrowed someone else's phone. He knew if he checked his spam folder there would be just as many emails with photos of the girl's assets. Didn't that silly little teenager go to school? Where were her parents? Why weren't they monitoring her phone and online activity?

He was sick to the back teeth with teenaged girls with crushes. Jasmine had started it with her outrageous little stunt seven years ago. He'd had the last word on that. But this was a new era and Emma Madden wasn't the least put off by his efforts to shake her off. He'd tried being patient. He'd tried being polite. What was he supposed to do? The fifteen-year-old was like a leech, clinging on for all she was worth. He was being stalked. By a teenager! Sending him presents at work. Turning up at his favourite haunts, at the gym, at a business lunch, which was damned embarrassing. He'd had his work cut out trying to get his client to believe he wasn't doing a teenager. He might be a playboy but he had some standards and keeping away from underage girls was one of them.

Jake turned his phone to silent and tossed it next to his bag on the bed. He walked over to the window to look at the fields surrounding the country estate. Autumn was one of his favourite times at Ravensdene. The leaves on the deciduous trees in the garden were in their final stages of turning and the air was sharp and fresh with the promise of winter around the corner. As soon as his guests arrived he would light the fire in the sitting room, put on some music, pour the champagne, party on and post heaps of photos on social media so Emma Madden got the message.

Finally.

CHAPTER TWO

THE CARS STARTED arriving just as Jaz got comfortable in the smaller sitting room where she had set up her workstation. She had to hand-sew the French lace on Julius's fiancée Holly's dress, which would take hours. But she was happiest when she was working on one of her designs. She outsourced some of the basic cutting and sewing of fabric but when it came to the details she did it all by hand. It gave her designs that signature Jasmine Connolly touch. Every stitch or every crystal, pearl or bead she sewed on to a gown made her feel proud of what she had achieved. As a child she had sat on the floor in this very sitting room surrounded by butcher's paper or tissue wrap and Miranda as a willing, if not long-suffering, model. Jaz had dreamed of success. Success that would transport her far away from her status as the unwanted daughter of a barmaid who turned tricks to feed her drug and alcohol habit.

The sound of car doors slamming, giggling women and high heels tottering on gravel made Jaz's teeth grind together like tectonic plates. At this rate she was going to be down to her gums. But no way was she going back to town until the weekend was over. Jake could party all he liked. She was not being told what to do. Besides, she knew it would annoy him to have her here. He might have acted all cool and casual about it but she knew him well enough to know he would be spitting chips about it privately.

Jaz put down her sewing and carefully covered it with the satin wrapping sheet she had brought with her. This she had to see. What sort of women had he got to come? He had a thing for busty blondes. Such a cliché but that was Jake. He was shallow. He lived life in the fast lane and didn't stay in one place long enough to put down roots. He surrounded himself with showgirls and starlets who used him as much as he used them.

It was nauseating.

Jake was standing in the great hall surrounded by ten or so young women—all blonde—who were dressed in skimpy cocktail wear and vertiginous heels. Jaz leaned against the doorjamb with her arms folded, watching as each girl kissed him in greeting. One even ruffled his hair and another rubbed her breasts—which Jaz could tell were fake—against his upper arm.

He caught Jaz's eye and his mouth slanted in a mocking smile. 'Ah, here's the fun police. Ladies, this is the gardener's daughter, Jasmine.'

Jaz gave him an 'I'll get you for that later' look before she addressed the young women. 'Do your parents know where you all are?' she said.

Jake's brows shot together in a brooding scowl. 'Knock it off, Jasmine.'

Jaz smiled at him with saccharine sweetness. 'Just checking you haven't sneaked in a minor or two.'

Twin streaks of dull colour rode high along his aristocratic cheekbones and his mouth flattened until it was a bloodless line of white. A frisson of excitement coursed through her to have riled him enough to show a crack in his 'too cool for school' façade. Jaz was the only person who could do that to him. He sailed through life with that easy smile and that 'anything goes' attitude but pitted against her he rippled with latent anger. She wondered how far she could push him. Would he touch her? He hadn't come anywhere near her for seven years. When the family got together for Christmas or birthdays, or whatever, he never greeted her. He never hugged or kissed her on the cheek as he did to Miranda or his mother. He avoided Jaz like she was carrying some deadly disease, which was fine by her. She didn't want to touch him either.

But, instead of responding, Jake moved past her as if she was invisible and directed the women to the formal sitting room. 'In here, ladies,' he said. 'The party's about to begin.'

Jaz wanted to puke as the women followed him as though he were the Pied Piper. Couldn't they see how they were being used to feed his ego? He would ply them with expensive champagne or mix them exotic cocktails and tell them amusing anecdotes about his famous parents and their Hollywood and London theatre friends. Those he wouldn't bother sleeping with he would toss out by two or three in the morning. The one—or two or three, according to the tabloids—he slept with would be sent home once the deed was done. They would never get a follow-up call from him. It was a rare woman who got two nights with Jake Ravensdale. Jaz couldn't remember the last one.

The doorbell sounded behind her. She let out a weary sigh and turned to open it.

'I'll get that,' Jake said, striding back into the great hall from the sitting room.

Jaz stood to one side and curled her lip at him. 'Ten women not enough for you, Jake?'

He gave her a dismissive look and opened the door. But the smile of greeting dropped from his face as if he had been slapped. 'Emma…' His throat moved up and down. 'What? Why? How did you find me?' The words came spilling out in a way Jaz had never seen before. He looked agitated. *Seriously* agitated.

'I had to see you,' the girl said with big, lost waif, shimmering eyes and a trembling bottom lip. 'I just *had* to.'

And she was indeed a girl, Jaz noted. Not yet out of her teens. At that awkward age when one foot was in girlhood and the other in adulthood, a precarious position, and one when lots of silly mistakes that could last a lifetime could be made. Jaz knew it all too well. Hadn't she tried to straddle that great big divide, with devastating consequences?

'How'd you get here?' Jake's voice had switched from shocked to curt.

'I caught a cab.'

His brows locked together. 'All the way from London?'

'No,' Emma said. 'From the station in the village.'

Poor little kid, Jaz thought. She remembered looking at Jake exactly like that, as if he was some demigod and she'd been sent to this earth solely to worship him. It was cruel to watch knowing all the thoughts that were going through that young head. Teenage love could be so intense, so consuming and incredibly irrational. The poor kid was in the throes of a heady infatuation, travelling all this way in the hope of a little bit of attention from a man who clearly didn't want to give her the time of day. Jake was here partying with a bunch of women and Emma thought she could be one of them. What a little innocent.

Jaz couldn't stand by and watch history repeat itself. What if Emma was so upset she did something she would always regret, like *she* had done? There had to be a way to let the kid down in such a way that would ease the hurt of rejection. But brandishing a bunch of party girls in Emma's face was not the way to do it.

'Why don't you come in and I'll—?' Jaz began.

'Stay out of it, Jasmine,' Jake snapped. 'I'll deal with this.' He turned back to the girl. 'You have to leave. Now. I'll call you a cab but you have to go home. Understand?'

Emma's eyes watered some more. 'But I can't go home. My mother thinks I'm staying with a friend. I'll get in heaps of trouble. I'll be grounded for the rest of my life.'

'And so you damn well should be,' Jake growled.

'Maybe I could help,' Jaz said and held out her hand to the girl. 'I'm Jaz. I'm Jake's fiancée.'

There was a stunned silence.

Jake went statue-still beside Jaz. Emma looked at her with a blank stare. But then her cheeks pooled with crimson colour. 'Oh… I—I didn't realise,' she stammered. 'I thought Jake was still single otherwise I would never have—'

'It's fine, sweetie,' Jaz said. 'I totally understand and I'm not the least bit offended. We've been keeping our relationship a secret, haven't we, darling?' She gave Jake a bright smile while surreptitiously jabbing him in the ribs.

He opened and closed his mouth like a fish that had suddenly found itself flapping on the carpet instead of swimming safely in its fishbowl. But then he seemed to come back into himself and stretched his lips into one of his charming smiles. 'Yeah,' he said. 'That's right. A secret. I only just asked her a couple of minutes ago. That's why we're…er…celebrating.'

'Are you coming, Jakey?' A clearly tipsy blonde came tottering out into the hall carrying a bottle of champagne in one hand and a glass in the other.

Jaz took Emma by the arm and led her away to the kitchen, jerking her head towards Jake in a non-verbal signal to get control of his guest. 'That's one of the bridesmaids,' she said. 'Can't handle her drink. I'm seriously thinking of dumping her for someone else. I don't want her to spoil the wedding photos. Can you imagine?'

Emma chewed at her bottom lip. 'I guess it kind of makes sense...'

'What does?'

'You and Jake.'

Jaz pulled out a kitchen stool and patted it. 'Here,' she said. 'Have a seat while I make you a hot chocolate—or would you prefer tea or coffee?'

'Um...hot chocolate would be lovely.'

Jaz got the feeling Emma had been about to ask for coffee in order to appear more sophisticated. It reminded her of all the times when she'd drunk vile-tasting cocktails in order to fit in. She made the frothiest hot chocolate she could and handed it to the young girl. 'Here you go.'

Emma cupped her hands around the mug like a child. 'Are you sure you're not angry at me turning up like this? I had no idea Jake was serious about anyone. There's been nothing in the press or anything.'

'No, of course not,' Jaz said. 'You weren't to know.' *I didn't know myself until five minutes ago.* 'We haven't officially announced it yet. We wanted to have some time to ourselves before the media circus begins.' And it would once the news got out. Whoopee doo! If this didn't get Myles' attention, nothing would.

'You're the gardener's daughter,' Emma said. 'I read about you in one of the magazines at the hairdresser's. There was an article about Jake's father's love-child Katherine Winwood and there were pictures of you. You've known Jake all your life.'

'Yes, since I was eight,' Jaz said. 'I've been in love with him since I was sixteen.' *It didn't hurt to tell her one more little white lie, did it?* It was all in a good cause. 'How old are you?'

'Fifteen and a half,' Emma said.

'Tough age.'

Emma's big brown eyes lowered to study the contents of her mug. 'I met Jake at a function a couple of months ago,' she said. 'It was at my stepfather's restaurant. He sometimes lets me work for him as a waitress. Jake was the only person who was nice to me that night. He even gave me a tip.'

'Understandable you'd fancy yourself in love with him,' Jaz said. 'He breaks hearts just by breathing.'

Emma's mouth lifted at the corners in a vestige of a smile. 'I should hate you but I don't. You're too nice. Kind of natural and normal, you know? But then, I guess I would hate you if I didn't think you were perfect for him.'

Jaz smiled over clenched teeth. 'How about we give your mum a call and let her know where you are? Then I'll drive you to the station and wait with you until you get on the train, okay? Have you got a mobile?'

Silly question. What teenager didn't? It was probably a better model than hers.

When Jaz got back from sending Emma on her way home, Jake was in the main sitting room clearing away the detritus of his short-lived party. Apparently he had sent his guests on their merry way as well. 'Need some help with that?' she said.

He sent her a black look. 'I think you've done more than enough for one night.'

'I thought it was a stroke of genius, actually,' Jaz said, calmly inspecting her nails.

'Engaged?' he said. '*Us?* Don't make me laugh.'

He didn't look anywhere near laughing, Jaz thought. His jaw was locked like a stiff hinge. His mouth was flat. His eyes were blazing with fury. 'What else was I supposed to do?' she said. 'That poor kid was so love-struck nothing short of an engagement would've convinced her to leave.'

'I had it under control,' he said through tight lips.

Jaz rolled her eyes. 'How? By having a big bimbo bash? Like that was ever going to work. You're going about this all wrong, Jake—or should I call you Jakey?'

His eyes flashed another round of sparks at her. 'That silly little kid has been stalking me for weeks. She gate-crashed an important business lunch last week. I lost a valuable client because of her.'

'She's young and fancies herself in love,' Jaz said. 'You were probably the first man to ever speak to her as if she was a real person instead of a geeky kid. But throwing a wild party with heaps of women isn't going to convince her you're not interested in her. The only way was to convince her you're off the market. Permanently.'

He snatched up a half-empty bottle of champagne and stabbed the neck of it in her direction. 'You're the last woman on this planet I would ever ask to marry me.'

Jaz smiled. 'I know. Isn't it ironic?'

His jaw audibly ground together. 'What's your fiancé going to say about this?'

Here's the payoff. She would have to tell Jake about the break-up. But it would be worth it if it achieved the desired end. 'Myles and I are having a little break for a month,' she said.

'You conniving little cow,' he said. 'You're using me to make him jealous.'

'We're using each other,' Jaz corrected. 'It's a win-win. We'll only have to pretend for a week or two. Once the hue and cry is over we can go back to being frenemies.'

His frown was so deep it closed the gap between his eyes. 'You're thinking of making an...*an announcement*?'

Jaz held up her phone. 'Already done. Twitter is running hot with it. Any minute now I expect your family to start calling.' As if on cue, both of their phones starting ringing.

'Don't answer that.' He quickly muted his phone. 'We need to think this through. We need a plan.'

Jaz switched her phone to silent but not before she saw Myles' number come up. Good. All going swimmingly so far. 'We can let your family in on the secret if you think they'll play ball.'

'It's too risky.' Jake scraped a hand through his hair. 'If anyone lets slip we're not the real deal, it could blow up in our faces. You know what the press are like. Do you think Emma bought it? Really?'

'Yes, but she'll know something's up if you don't follow through.'

He frowned again. 'Follow through how? You're not expecting me to marry you, are you?'

Jaz gave him a look that would have withered a plastic flower. 'I'm marrying Myles, remember?'

'If he takes you back after this.'

She heightened her chin. 'He will.'

One side of his mouth lifted in a cynical arc. 'What's Miranda going to say? You think she'll accept you're in love with me?'

Miranda was going to be a hard sell, but Jaz knew she didn't like Myles, so perhaps it would work. For a time. 'I don't like lying to Miranda, but she's never been…'

'You should've thought of that when you cooked up this stupid farce,' Jake said. 'No. We'll run with it.'

'What did you tell your party girls?' Jaz said. 'I hope I didn't make things too awkward for you.' Ha ha. She *loved* making things awkward for him. The more awkward, the better. What a hoot it was to see him squirm under the shackles of a commitment.

'I'm not in the habit of explaining myself to anyone,' he said. 'But no doubt they'll hear the news like everyone else.'

Jaz glanced at her bare ring finger. Who would take their engagement seriously unless she had evidence? 'I haven't got a ring.'

His dark eyes gleamed with malice. 'No spares hanging around at home?'

She sent him a beady look. 'Do you really want me to wear some other man's ring?'

His mouth flattened again. 'Right. I'll get you a ring.'

'No fake diamonds,' she said. 'I want the real thing. The sort of clients I attract can tell the difference, you know.'

'This is what this is all about, isn't it?' he said. 'You don't want your clients to think you can't hold a man long enough to get him to marry you.'

Jaz could feel her anger building like a catastrophic storm inside her. This wasn't about what her clients thought. It was about what *she* felt. No one in their right mind wanted to be rejected. Abandoned. To be told they weren't loved in the way she desperately dreamed of being loved. Not after she had invested so much in her relationship with Myles.

What did Jake know of investing in a relationship? He moved from one woman to the next without a thought of staying long enough to get to know someone beyond what they liked to do in bed. Only Jake could make her this angry—angry enough to throw something. It infuriated her that he alone could reduce her to such a state. 'I can hold a man,' she said. 'I can hold him just fine. Myles has cold feet, that's all. It's perfectly normal for the groom to get a little stressed before the big day.'

'If he loved you he wouldn't ask for a break,' Jake said. 'He wouldn't risk you finding someone else.'

That thought had occurred to Jaz but she didn't want to think about it. She was good at not thinking about things she didn't want to think about. 'Listen to you,' she said with a scornful snort. 'Jake Ravensdale, playboy extraordinaire, talking like a world expert on love.'

'Where did you take Emma?'

'I put her on the train once I'd talked to her mother and made sure everything was cool,' Jaz said. 'I didn't want her to get into trouble or do anything she might regret.' *Like I did.* She pushed the thought aside. She wouldn't think about the rest of that night after she had left Jake's bedroom.

Jake picked up a glass, filled it with champagne and knocked it back in one gulp. He shook his head like a dog coming out of water and then poured another glass. With his features cast in such serious lines, he looked more like his twin Julius than ever.

'We need a photo,' Jaz said. 'Hand me a glass.'

He looked at her as if she had just asked him to poke a knitting needle in his eye. 'A photo?' he said. 'What for?'

She helped herself to a glass of champagne and came to stand beside him but he backed away as if she was carrying dynamite. Or knitting needles. 'Get away from me,' he said.

'We have to do this, Jake,' she said. 'Who's going to believe it if we don't do an engagement photo?'

'You don't have a ring,' he said. 'Yet.' The way he said 'yet' made it sound as though he considered the task on the same level as having root canal therapy.

'Doesn't matter,' Jaz said. 'Just a shot with us with a glass of champers and grinning like Cheshire cats will be enough.'

'You're a sadist,' he said, shooting her a hooded

look as she came to stand beside him with her camera phone poised. 'You know that, don't you? A totally sick sadist.'

It was impossible for Jaz not to notice how hard and warm his arm was against hers as she leaned in to get the shot. Impossible not to think of those strongly muscled arms gathering her even closer. Was he as aware of her as she was of him? Was that why he was standing so still? He hadn't been this close to her in years. When family photographs had been taken—even though strictly speaking she wasn't family—she had always been up the other end of the shot close to Miranda or one of Jake's parents. She had never stood right next to Jake. Not so close she could practically feel the blood pumping through his veins. She checked the photo and groaned. 'Oh, come on,' she said. 'Surely you can do better than that. You look like someone's got a broomstick up your—'

'Okay, we'll try again.' He put an arm around her shoulders and leaned his head against hers. She could feel the strands of his tousled hair tickling her skin. Her senses were going haywire when his stubbly jaw grazed her face. He smelt amazing—lime and lemongrass with a hint of ginger or some other spice. 'Go on,' he said. 'Take the goddamn shot.'

'Oh…right,' Jaz said and clicked the button. She checked the photo but this time it looked like she was the one being tortured. Plus it was blurred. 'Not my best angle.' She deleted it and held up the phone. 'One more take. Say cheese.'

'That's enough,' he said, stepping away from her

once she'd taken the shot. 'You have to promise me you'll delete that when this is all over, okay?'

Jaz criss-crossed her chest with her hand. 'Cross my heart and hope to die.'

He grunted as if her demise was something he was dearly praying for.

She sent the tweet and then quickly sent a text to Miranda:

I know you never liked Myles. You approve of fiancé # 4?

Miranda's text came back within seconds.

OMG! Definitely!!! Congrats. Always knew you were hot for each other. J Will call later xxxxx

'Who are you texting?' Jake asked.

'Miranda,' Jaz said, putting her phone down. 'She's thrilled for us. We'll finally be sisters. Yay.'

He muttered a curse and prowled around the room like a shark in a fishbowl. 'Julius is never going to fall for this. Not for a moment.'

'He'll have to if you want Emma to go away,' Jaz said. 'If you don't play along I'll tell her the truth.'

He threw her a filthy look. 'You're enjoying this, aren't you?'

She smiled a victor's smile. 'What's that saying about revenge is a dish best eaten cold?'

He glowered at her. 'Isn't it a little childish to be harking on about that night all these years later? I did you a favour back then. I could've done you that night but how would that have worked out? Ever thought about that? No. You want to paint me as the big, bad guy who made you feel a little embarrassed about that schoolgirl crush. But, believe me, I could have done a whole lot worse.'

Jaz stepped out of his way as he stormed past her to leave the room. *You did do a whole lot worse*, she wanted to throw after him. But instead she clamped her lips together and turned back to look at the discarded bottles and glasses.

Typical. Jake had a habit of leaving his mess for other people to clean up.

step. He could count on half a hand how many times he'd been caught off guard but seeing that kid there was right up there. If anyone had seen her—anyone being the press, that was—he would have been toast. He didn't want to be cruel to the girl but how else could he get rid of her? Jasmine's solution seemed to have worked. So far. But how long would he have to stay 'engaged'?

Then there was his family to deal with. He could probably pull off the lie with his parents and Miranda but not his twin. Julius knew him too well. Julius knew how much he hated the thought of being confined in a relationship. Jake was more like his father in that way. His father wasn't good at marriage. Richard and Elisabetta fought as passionately as they made up. It was a war zone one minute and a love fest the next. As a child Jake had found it deeply unsettling—not that he'd ever showed it. His role in the family was the court jester. It was his way of coping with the turbulent emotions that flew around like missiles. He'd never known what he was coming home to.

Then eventually it had happened. The divorce had been bitter and public and the intrusion of the press terrifying to a child of eight. He and Julius had been packed off to boarding school but, while Julius had relished the routine, structure and discipline, Jake had not. Julius had excelled academically while Jake had scraped through, not because he wasn't intellectually capable but because in an immature and mostly subconscious way he hadn't wanted his parents to think their divorce had had a positive effect on him.

But he had more than made up for it in his business analysis company. He was successful and wealthy and had the sort of life most people envied. The fly-in, fly-out nature of his work suited his personality. He didn't hang around long. He just got in there, sorted out the problems and left. Which was how he liked to conduct his relationships.

Being tied to Jasmine, even if it was only a game of charades, was nothing less than torture. He had spent the last seven years avoiding her. Distancing himself from all physical contact. He had even failed to show up for some family functions in an effort to avoid the tension of being in the same room as her. He'd had plenty of lectures from Julius and Miranda about fixing things with Jasmine but why should *he* apologise? He hadn't done anything wrong. He had done the opposite. He had solved the problem, not made it worse. It was her that was still in a snit over something she should have got over years ago.

She had been a cute little kid but once she'd hit her teens she'd changed into a flirty little vamp. It had driven him nuts. She had followed him around like a loyal puppy, trying to sneak time with him, touching him 'by accident' and batting those impossibly long eyelashes at him. He had gone along with it for a while, flirting back in a playful manner, but in the end that had backfired, as she'd seemed to think he was serious about her. He wasn't serious about anyone. But on the night of his parents New Year's Eve party, when she'd been sixteen and he twenty-six, he had drawn the line. He'd activated a plan to give her the message loud and clear: He was a player, not the soppy, romantic happy-ever-after beau she imagined him to be.

That night she had dressed in a revealing outfit that was far too old for her and had worn make-up far too heavy. To Jake she had looked like a kid who had rummaged around in her mother's wardrobe. In the dark. He had gone along with her flirtation all evening, agreeing to meet with her in his room just after midnight. But instead of turning up alone as she'd expected he'd brought a couple of girls with him, intending to shock Jasmine into thinking he was expecting an orgy. It had certainly done the trick. She had left him alone ever since. He couldn't remember the last time she had spoken to him other than to make some cutting remark and the only time she looked at him was to spear him with a death-adder glare. Which had suited him just fine.

Until now.

Now he had to work out a way of hanging around with her without wanting to… Well, he didn't want to admit to what he wanted to do with her. But he was only human and a full-blooded male, after all. She was the stuff of male fantasies. He would never admit it to anyone but over the years he'd enjoyed a few fantasies of her in his morning shower. She was sultry and sulky, yet she had a razor-sharp wit and intelligence to match. She had done well for herself, building her business up from scratch, although he thought she was heading for a burnout by trying to do everything herself. Not that she would ever ask his advice. She was too proud. She would rather go bankrupt than admit she might have made a mistake.

Jake dragged a hand down his face. This was going to be the longest week or two of his life. What did Jasmine expect of him? How far did she want this act to go? She surely wouldn't want to sleep with him if she was still hankering after her ex? Not that she showed any sign of being attracted to him, although she did have a habit of looking at his mouth now and again. But everyone knew how much she hated him. Not that a bit of hate got in the way of good sex.

Sheesh. He had to stop thinking about sex and Jasmine in the same sentence. He had never seen her as a sister, even though she had been brought up as one at Ravensdene. Or at least not since she'd hit her teens. She'd grown from being a gangly, awkward teenager into an unusual but no less stunning beauty. Her features were not what one could describe as classically beautiful, but there was some indefinable element to the prominence of her brows and the ice-blue and storm-grey of her eyes that made her unforgettable. She had a model-slim figure and lustrous, wavy honey-brown hair that fell midway down her back. Her skin was creamy and smooth and looked fabulous with or without make-up, although she used make-up superbly these days.

Her mouth… How could he describe it? It was perfect. Simply perfect. He had never seen a more beautiful mouth. The lower lip was full and shapely, the top one a perfect arc above it. The vermillion borders of her lips were so neatly aligned it was as if a mas-

ter had drawn them. She had a way of slightly elevat-
ing her chin, giving her a haughty air that belied her
humble beginnings. Her nose, too, had the look of an
aristocrat about it with its ski-slope contour. When she
smiled—which she rarely did when he was around—
it lit up the room. He had seen grown men buckle at
the knees at that smile.

Jake's phone vibrated where he'd left it on the bedside table. He glanced at the screen and saw it was
Julius. His twin had called six times now. *Better get
it over with*, he thought, and answered.

'Is this some kind of prank?' Julius said without
preamble.

'No, it's—'

'Jaz and you?' Julius cut him off. 'Come on, man.
You hate her guts. You can't stand being in the same
room as her. What happened?'

'It was time to bury the hatchet,' Jake said.

'You think I came down in the last shower?' Julius
said. 'I know wedding fever has hit with Holly and
me, and now Miranda and Leandro, but you and Jaz?
I don't buy it for a New York picosecond. What's she
got on you? Is she holding a AK-47 to your head?'

Jake let out a rough-edged sigh. He could lie to
anyone else but not his identical twin. All that time in
the womb had given them a connection beyond what
normal siblings felt. They even felt each other's pain.
When Julius had had his appendix out when he was
fifteen Jake had felt like someone was ripping his guts
out. 'I've been having a little problem with a girl,' he
said. 'A teenager.'

'I'm not sure I want to hear this.'

'It's not what you think,' Jake said and explained the situation before adding, 'Jasmine intercepted Emma at the door and told her we were engaged.'

'How did this girl Emma take it?'

'Surprisingly well,' Jake said.

'What about Jaz's fiancé?'

'I have no idea,' Jake said. 'He's either relieved she's off his hands or he's going to turn up at my place and shoot out my kneecaps.'

'Always a possibility.'

'Don't remind me.'

There was a beat of silence.

'You're not going to sleep with her, are you?' Julius said.

'God, no,' Jake said. 'I wouldn't touch her with a barge pole.'

'Yes, well, I suggest you keep your barge pole zipped in your pants,' Julius said dryly. 'What actually happened with you guys that night at the party? I know she came to your room but you've never said what went on other than you didn't touch her.'

'I didn't do anything except send her on her way,' Jake said. 'You know what she was like, always following me about, giving me sheep's eyes. I taught her a lesson by offering her a foursome but she declined.'

'A novel approach.'

'It worked.'

'Maybe, but don't you think her anger is a little out of proportion?' Julius said.

'That's just Jasmine,' Jake said. 'She's always had a rotten temper.'

'I don't know… I sometimes wonder if something else happened that night.'

'Like what?'

'She'd been drinking and was obviously upset after leaving your room,' Julius said. 'Not a good combination in a teenage girl.'

Jake hung up a short time later once they'd switched topics but he couldn't get rid of the seed of unease Julius had planted in his mind. Had something happened that night after Jasmine had left his room? Was that why she had been so protective of young Emma, making sure she got home safely with an adult at the other end to meet her? The rest of that night was a bit of blur for him. Most of his parents' parties ended up that way. Even some of his parties were a little full-on too. There was always a lot of alcohol, loud music blaring and people coming and going. He had been feeling too pleased with himself for solving the Jasmine problem to give much thought to where she'd gone after leaving his room. At twenty-six what he had done had seemed the perfect solution. The only solution.

Now, at thirty-three, he wasn't quite so sure.

Jaz was making herself a nightcap in the kitchen when Jake strolled in. 'Finding it hard to sleep without a playgirl bunny or three in your bed to keep you warm?'

'What happened after you left my room that night?'

Jaz lowered her gaze to her chocolate drink rather

than meet his piercing blue eyes. The chocolate swirled as she stirred it with the teaspoon, creating a whirlpool not unlike the one she could feel in the pit of her stomach. She never thought about that night. That night had happened to another person. It had happened to a foolish, gauche kid who'd had too much to drink and had been too emotionally unstable to know what she was doing or what she was getting into.

'Jasmine. Answer me.'

Jaz lifted her gaze to his and frowned. 'Why do you always call me Jasmine instead of Jaz? You're the only one in your family who insists on doing that. Why?'

'It's your name.'

'So? Yours is Jacques but you don't like being called that,' Jaz pointed out. 'Maybe I'll start to.'

'Julius knows.'

Her heart gave a little stumble. 'Knows what?'

'About us,' he said. 'About this not being real.'

Jaz took a moment to get her head sorted. She'd thought he meant Julius knew about *that night*… But how could he? He would have said something if he did. He was the sort of man who would have got her to press charges. He wouldn't have stood by and let someone get away with it. 'Oh…right; well, I guess he's your twin and all.'

'He won't tell anyone apart from Holly.'

'Good,' Jaz said. 'The less people who know, the better.'

Jake pulled out a kitchen stool and sat opposite her at the island bench. 'You want to make me one of those?'

She lifted her chin. 'Make it yourself.'

A slow smile came to his mouth. 'I guess I'd better in case you put cyanide in it.'

Jaz forced her gaze away from the tempting curve of his mouth. It wasn't fair that one man had so much darn sex appeal. It came off him in waves. She felt it brush against her skin, making her body tingle at the thought of him touching her for real. Ever since his arm had brushed against hers, ever since he'd slung his arm around her shoulders and leaned in against her, she had longed for him to do it again. It was like every nerve under her skin was sitting bolt upright and wide awake, waiting with bated breath for him to touch her again.

She was aware of him in other parts of her body. The secret parts. Her breasts and inner core tingled from the moment he'd stepped into the same room. It was like he could turn a switch in her body simply by being present. She watched covertly as he moved about the kitchen, fetching a cup and the tin of chocolate powder and stirring it into the milk before he turned to put it in the microwave.

She couldn't tear her eyes away from his back and shoulders. He was wearing a cotton T-shirt that showcased every sculpted muscle on his frame. How would it feel to slide her hands down his tautly muscled back? To slip one of her hands past the waistband of his jeans and cup his trim buttocks, or what was on the other side of his testosterone-rich groin?

Jaz gave herself a mental shake. She was on a mission to win back Myles. Getting involved with Jake was out of the question. Not that he would ever want *her*. He loathed her just as much as she loathed him. But men could separate their emotions from sex. She of all people knew that. Maybe he would want to make the most of their situation—a little fling to pass the time until he could get back to his simpering starlets and Hollywood hopefuls. Her mind started to drift… What would it feel like to have Jake make love to her? To have his hands stroke every inch of her flesh, to have his mouth plunder hers?

Jake turned from the microwave. 'Is something wrong?'

Jaz blinked to reset her vision. 'That was weird. I thought I saw you actually lift a finger in the kitchen. I must be hallucinating.'

He laughed and pulled out one of the stools opposite hers at the kitchen bench. 'I can find my way around a kitchen when I need to.'

Jaz's top lip lifted in a cynical arc. 'Like when no slavishly devoted woman is there to cater to your every whim?'

His eyes held hers in a penetrating lock. She felt the power of it go through her like a current of electricity. 'How much did you have to drink that night?' he asked.

She pushed her untouched chocolate away and slipped off the stool. 'Clean up your mess when you're done in here. Eggles won't be back till Sunday night.'

Jaz almost got to the door, but then Jake's hand came out of nowhere and turned her to face him. His warm, strong fingers curling around her arm sent a shockwave through her body, making her feel as if someone inside her stomach had shuffled a deck of cards. Quickly. Vegas-quick. She moistened her lips with her tongue as she brought her gaze to his dark-blue one. His ink-black lashes were at half-mast, giving him a sexily hooded look. She looked at his mouth and felt that shuffle in her heart valves this time. She could look at his twin's mouth any time without this crazy reaction. What was it about Jake's mouth that turned her into a quivering mess of female hormones? Was it because, try as she might, she couldn't stop thinking about how it would feel pressed to hers? 'I don't remember giving you permission to touch me,' she said.

Instead of releasing her he slid his fingers down to the bones of her wrist and encircled it like a pair of gentle handcuffs. 'Talk to me,' he said in a deep, gravel-rough voice that made the entire length of her spine soften like candle wax in a steam room.

Jaz tested his hold but all it did was take him with her to the doorframe, which was just an inch or so behind her. She pressed her back against it for stability because right then her legs weren't doing such a great job of holding her upright. He was now so close she could see the individual pinpricks of stubble along his jaw and around his nose and mouth. She could feel their breath intermingling. His muscle-packed thighs were within a hair's breadth of hers, his booted feet toe-to-toe with her bare ones. 'Wh-what are you doing?' she said in a voice she barely recognised as her own.

His eyes went to her mouth, lingering there for endless, heart-stopping seconds. 'Ever wondered what would happen if we kissed?'

Like just about every day for the last seven years. 'You'd get your face slapped, that's what.'

A smile hitched up one side of his mouth. 'Yeah, that's what I thought.'

Jaz felt like her heart rate was trying to get into the *Guinness Book of Records.* She could smell those lime and lemongrass notes of his aftershave and something else that was one part musk and three parts male. 'But you're not going to do it, right?'

He moved around her mouth like a metal detector just above the ground where something valuable was hidden. He didn't touch down but he might as well have because she felt the tingling in her lips as if he was transmitting raw sexual energy from his body to hers. 'You think about it, don't you? About us getting down to business.'

Oh, dear God in heaven, where is my willpower? Jaz thought as her senses went haywire. She had never wanted to be kissed more in her life than right then. She had never wanted to feel a man's arms go around her and pull her into his hard body. Desire moved through her like a prowling, hungry beast looking for satiation. She felt it in her blood, the tick of arousal. She felt it in her breasts, the prickly sensation of them shifting against the lace of her bra as if they couldn't wait for him to get his hands or mouth on them. She felt it in her core, the pulse and contraction of her

inner muscles in anticipatory excitement. 'No, I don't.
I never think about it.'

He gave a soft chuckle as he stepped back from
her. 'No, nor do I.'

Jaz stood in numb silence as he went back to the
island bench to pick up his hot chocolate. She watched
as he lifted the mug to his lips and took a sip. He put
the mug down and cocked a brow at her. 'Something
wrong?'

She pushed herself away from the doorframe, tuck-
ing her hair back over one shoulder with a hand that
wasn't as steady as she would have liked. 'We haven't
discussed the rules about our engagement.'

'Rules?'

Jaz gave him a look. 'Yes, rules. Not your favourite word, is it?'

His eyes glinted. 'Far as I'm concerned, they're
only there to be broken.'

She steeled her spine. 'Not this time.'

'Is that a dare?'

Jaz could feel every cell in her body being pulled
and tugged by the animal attraction he evoked in her.
She couldn't understand why someone she hated so
much could have such a monumental effect on her. She
wanted to throw herself at him, tear at his clothes and
crawl all over his body. She wanted to lock her mouth
on his and tangle her tongue with his in an erotic salsa.
She wanted him *inside* her body. She could feel the
hollow vault of her womanhood pulsating with need.
She could even feel the dew of her intimate moisture
gathering. She wanted him like a drug she knew she

shouldn't have. He was contraband. Dangerous. 'Is the thought of being celibate for a week or two really that difficult for you?'

He gave a lip shrug. 'Never done it before, so I wouldn't know.'

Jaz mentally rolled her eyes. 'Do you have shares in a condom manufacturer or something?'

His dark eyes gleamed with amusement. 'Now there's an idea.'

She picked up her mug of chocolate, not to drink, but to give her hands something to do in case they took it upon themselves to touch him. 'I find your shallow approach to relationships deeply offensive. It's like you only see women as objects you can use to satisfy a bodily need. You don't see them as real people who have feelings.'

'I have the greatest respect for women. That's why I'm always honest with them about what I want from them.'

Jaz eyeballed him. 'I think it's because you're scared of commitment. You can't handle the thought of someone leaving you so you don't let yourself bond with them in the first place.'

He gave a mocking laugh. 'You got a printout of that psychology degree you bought online?'

'That's another thing you do,' Jaz said. 'You joke your way through life because being serious about stuff terrifies you.'

His mouth was smiling but his eyes were not. They had become as hard as flint. 'Ever wondered why your three fiancés have dumped you before you could march them up the aisle?'

Jaz ground her teeth together until her jaw ached. 'Myles hasn't dumped me. We're on a break. It's not the same as being…breaking up.'

'You're a ballbreaker. You don't want a man. You want a puppet. Someone you can wind around your little finger to do what you want when you want. No man worth his testosterone will stand for that.'

Jaz could feel her anger straining at the leash of her control like a feral dog tied up with a piece of cotton. Her fingers around the mug of chocolate twitched. How she would love to spray it over Jake's arrogant face. 'You enjoy humiliating me, don't you? It gives you such a big, fat hard-on, doesn't it?'

His jaw worked as if her words had hit a raw nerve. 'While we're playing Ten Things I Hate About You, here's another one for my list. You need to get over yourself. You've held onto this ridiculous grudge for far too long.'

Jaz saw the hot chocolate fly through the air before she fully registered she'd thrown it. It splashed over the front of his T-shirt like brown paint thrown at a wall.

Jake barely moved a muscle. He was as still as a statue on a plinth. Too still.

The silence was breathing, heaving with menace.

But then he calmly reached over the back of his head, hauled the T-shirt off, bunched it up into a rough ball and handed it to her. 'Wash it.'

Jaz swallowed as she looked at the T-shirt. She had

lost control. A thing she had sworn she would never do. Crazy people like her mother lost control. They shouted and screamed and threw things. Not her. She never let anyone do that to her. A tight knot of self-disgust began to choke her. Tears welled up behind her eyes, escaping from a place she had thought she had locked and bolted for good. Tears she hadn't cried since that night when she had finally made it back to her bedroom with shame clinging to her like filth. No amount of showering had removed it. If she thought about that night she would feel it clogging every pore of her skin like engine grease. She took the T-shirt from him with an unsteady hand. 'I'm sorry…'

'Forget about it.'

I only wish I could, Jaz thought. But when she finally worked up the courage to look up he had already turned on his heel and gone.

CHAPTER FOUR

JAKE WAS VAINLY trying to sleep when he heard the sound of the plumbing going in the other wing of the house where Jasmine's room was situated next to Miranda's. He lay there for a while, listening as the pipes pumped water. Had Jasmine left on a tap? He glanced at the bedside clock. It was late to be having a shower, although he had to admit for him a cold one wouldn't have gone astray. He rarely lost his temper. He preferred to laugh his way out of trouble but something about Jasmine's mood had got to him tonight. He was sick of dragging their history around like a dead carcass. It was time to put it behind them. He didn't want Julius and Holly's or Miranda and Leandro's wedding ruined by a ridiculous feud that had gone on way too long.

He shoved off the bed covers and reached for a bathrobe. He seemed to remember Jasmine had a tendency for long showers but he still thought he'd better check to make sure nothing was amiss. He made his way to the bathroom closest to her room and rapped his knuckles on the door. 'You okay in there?' he said.

No answer. He tapped again, louder this time, and called out but the water continued. He tried the door but it was locked. He frowned. Why did she think she had to lock the door? They were alone in the house. Didn't she trust him? The thought sat uncomfortably on him. He might be casual about sex but not *that* casual. He always ensured he had consent first.

Not that he was going to sleep with Jasmine. That would be crazy. Crazy but tempting. Way too tempting, if he was honest with himself. He had spent many an erotic daydream with her body pinned under his or over his, or with her mouth on him, sucking him until he blew like a bomb. She had that effect on men. She didn't do it on purpose; her natural sensuality made men fall over like ninepins. Her beauty, her regal manner, her haughty 'I'm too good for the likes of you' air made men go weak at the knees, himself included. Just thinking about her naked body under that spray of water in the shower was enough to make him rock-hard.

He waited outside her door until the water finally stopped. 'Jasmine?'

It was a while before she opened the door. She was wearing a bathrobe and her hair was wrapped turban-like with a towel. Her skin was rosy from the hot water and completely make-up free, giving her a youthful appearance that took him back a decade. 'What?' She frowned at him irritably. 'Is something wrong with your bathroom?'

He frowned when he saw her red-rimmed eyes and pink nose. 'Have you been crying?'

Her hand clutching the front of her bathrobe clenched a little tighter but her tone was full of derision. 'Why would I be crying? Oh, yes, I remember now. My fiancé wanted a month's break. Pardon me for being a little upset.'

Jake felt a stab of remorse for not having factored in her feelings. He had such an easy come, easy go attitude to his relationships he sometimes forgot other people invested much more emotionally. But did she really love the guy or was she in love with the idea of love and marriage? Three engagements in three years. That must be some sort of record, surely? Had she been in love each time? 'You want to talk about it?'

Her eyes narrowed in scorn. 'What—with *you*?'

'Why not?'

She pushed past him and he got a whiff of honeysuckle body wash. 'I'm going to bed. Good night.'

'Jasmine, wait,' Jake said, capturing her arm on the way past. His fingers sank into the soft velour of her bathrobe as he turned her to face him. He could feel the slenderness of her arm in spite of the pillowy softness of the thick fabric, reminding him of how feminine she was. A hot coil of lust burned in his groin, winding tighter and tighter. 'I might've been a little rough on you downstairs earlier.'

Her brows lifted and she pulled out of his light hold. 'Might've been?'

He let out a whooshing breath. 'Okay, I *was* rough on you. I didn't think about how you'd be feeling about the break-up.'

'It's not a break-up. It's a *break*.'

Jake wasn't following the semantics. 'You don't think it's permanent?'

Her chin came up. 'No. Myles just needs a bit of space.'

He frowned. 'But what about us? Don't you think he's going to get a little pissed you found someone else so soon?'

She looked at him as if he were wearing a dunce's cap. 'Yes, but that's the whole point. Sometimes people don't know what they've got until it's gone.'

'Has he called you since the news of our—' Jake couldn't help grimacing over the word '—engagement was announced?'

'Heaps of times but I'm not answering,' Jaz said. 'I'm letting him stew for a bit.'

'Do you think he believes it's true?'

'Why wouldn't he? Everyone else bought it. Apart from Julius, of course.'

'I'm surprised Miranda fell for it, to tell you the truth,' Jake said.

Jaz frowned. 'Why do you say that? Have you spoken to her?'

'She sent me a congratulatory text but I haven't spoken to her. I've been dodging her calls. But you're her closest friend. She'll suss something's amiss once she sees us together.'

Her lips compressed for a moment. 'I don't think it will be a problem. Anyway, she's busy with her own engagement and wedding plans.'

Jake studied her for a beat. 'Are you in love with this Myles guy?'

Her brow wrinkled. 'What sort of question is that? Of course I am.'

'Were you in love with Tim and Linton?'

'*Lincoln*,' she said with a scowl. 'Yes, I was.'

'You're pretty free and easy with your affection, aren't you?'

Jaz gave him a gelid look. 'That's rich coming from the man who changes partners faster than tyres are changed in a Formula One pit lane.'

Jake couldn't help smiling. 'You flatter me. I'm fast but not that fast.'

'Have you heard from Emma?'

'No.'

'So my plan is working.'

'So far.' He didn't like to admit it but there was no denying it. From being bombarded with texts, emails and calls there had been zilch from Emma since Jasmine had delivered her bombshell announcement. Another thing he didn't like to acknowledge was how he'd had nothing but congratulations from all his friends and colleagues. Even his parents had stopped slinging insults at each other via the press long enough to congratulate him. He had even had an email from a client he'd thought he'd lost, promising not just his business but that of several high-profile contacts.

This little charade was turning out to be much more of a win-win than Jake had expected.

'What we need is to be seen out in public,' Jaz said. 'That will make it even more believable.'

'In public?'

'Yes, like on a date or dinner or something.'

'You reckon we could get through a whole meal together without you throwing something at me?'

Her gaze moved out of reach of his. 'I'll do my best.'

Jaz woke the next morning to a call from Miranda. 'I know it's early but I can't get Jake on his phone to congratulate him,' Miranda said. 'I figured he'd be in bed with you. Can you hand me to him? That is, if it's not inconvenient?' The way she said 'inconvenient' was playful and teasing.

Jaz swallowed back a gulp. 'Erm…he's having a shower right now. I'll get him to call you, okay?'

'Okay,' Miranda said. 'So how's it going? Does it seem real? I mean, for all this time you've been at each other's throats. Is it good to be making love instead of war?'

Jaz got out of bed but on her way to the window caught sight of her reflection in the mirror. How could she lie to her best friend? Lying by text was one thing. Lying in conversation was another. It didn't seem right. Not when they had been friends for so long. 'Miranda, listen, things aren't quite what they seem… I'm not really engaged to Jake. We're pretending.'

'*Pretending?*' Miranda sounded bitterly disappointed. 'But why?'

'I'm trying to win Myles back,' Jaz said. 'He wanted to take a break and I thought I'd try and make him jealous.'

'But why did Jake agree to it?' Miranda said.

'I didn't give him a choice.' Jaz explained the situation about Emma briefly.

'Gosh,' Miranda said. 'I was so excited for you. Now I feel like someone's punched me in the belly.'

'I'm sorry for lying but—'

'Are you sure about Myles?' Miranda said. 'I mean, *absolutely* sure he's the one?'

'Of course I'm sure. Why else would I be going to so much trouble to win him back?'

'Pride?'

Jaz pressed her lips together. 'It's not a matter of pride. It's a matter of love.'

'But you fall in and out of love all the time,' Miranda said. 'How do you know he's the right one for you when you could just as easily fall in love with someone else tomorrow?'

'I'm not going to fall in love with anyone else,' Jaz said. 'How can I when I'm in love with Myles?'

'What do you love about him?'

'We've had this conversation before and I—'

'Let's have it again,' Miranda said. 'Refresh my memory. List three things you love about him.'

'He's…'

'See?' Miranda said. 'You're hesitating!'

'Look, I know you don't like him, so it wouldn't matter what I said about him; you'd find some reason to discount it.'

'It's not that he's not nice and polite, handsome and well-educated and all that,' Miranda said. 'But I worry you only like him because you can control him. You've got a strong personality, Jaz. You need someone who'll stand up to you. Someone who'll be your equal, not your puppet.'

Jaz swung back from the window and paced the carpet. 'I don't like controlling men. I hate them. I always have and I always will. I could never fall in love with someone like that.'

'We'll see.'

She frowned. 'What do you mean, "we'll see"? I hope you're not thinking what I think you're thinking because it's not going to happen. No way.'

'Come on, Jaz,' Miranda said. 'You've had a thing for Jake since you were sixteen.'

'I was a kid back then!' Jaz said. 'It was just a stupid crush. I got over it, okay?'

'If you got over it then why have you avoided him like the black plague ever since?'

Jaz was close to Miranda but not close enough to tell her what had happened that night after she'd left Jake's room. She wasn't close enough to anyone to tell them that. Sharing that shame with someone else wouldn't make it go away. The only way she could make it go away was not to think about it. If she told anyone about it they would look at her differently. They might judge her. Blame her. She didn't want to take the risk. Her tough-girl façade was exactly that—a façade.

Underneath all the bravado she was still that terrified sixteen-year-old who had got herself sexually assaulted by a drunken guest at the party. It hadn't been rape but it had come scarily close to it. The irony was the person who did it had been so drunk they hadn't remembered a thing about it the following morning. The only way Jaz could deal with it was to pretend it hadn't happened. There was no other way. 'Look, I'm not avoiding Jake now, so you should be happy,' she said. 'Who knows? We might even end up friends after this charade is over.'

'I certainly hope so because I don't want Julius and Holly's wedding, or mine and Leandro's, spoilt by you two looking daggers at each other,' Miranda said. 'It's bad enough with Mum and Dad carrying on World War Three.'

'That reminds me. Have you met Kat Winwood yet?' Jaz asked.

'No.' Miranda gave a sigh. 'She won't have anything to do with any of us. I guess if I were in her shoes I might feel the same. What Dad did to her mother was pretty unforgiveable.'

'Yes, well, paying someone to have an abortion isn't exactly how to win friends and influence people, I'll grant you that,' Jaz said.

'What about you?' Miranda said. 'You mentioned a couple of weeks back you were thinking about meeting her. Any luck?'

'Nope,' Jaz said. 'I might not be a Ravensdale but I'm considered close enough to your family to be on the black list as well.'

'Maybe Flynn can get her to change her mind,' Miranda said, referring to the family lawyer, Flynn Carlyon, who had been a year ahead of Jake and Julius at school. 'If anyone can do it he can. He's unlikely to give up until he gets what he wants.'

'But I thought the whole idea was to get her to go away,' Jaz said. 'Wasn't that what Flynn was supposed to do? Pay her to keep from speaking to the press?'

'Yes, but she wouldn't take a penny off him. She hasn't said a word to the media anyway and it's been over a month,' Miranda said. 'Dad's agent called him last night about putting on a party to celebrate his sixty years in showbiz in January. Dad wants Kat there. He says he won't go ahead with it unless she comes.'

'Sixty years?' Jaz said. 'Gosh. What age did he start?'

'Five. He had a walk-on part in some musical way back. Hasn't he shown you the photos?'

'Nope,' Jaz said. 'I must've missed that bragging session.'

'Ha ha,' Miranda said. 'But what are we going to do about Kat? She has to come to Dad's party otherwise he'll be devastated.'

'Well, at least Flynn will have a few weeks to change her mind.'

'I can't work her out,' Miranda said. 'She's a struggling actor who's only had bit parts till now. You'd think she'd be jumping at the chance to cash in on her biological father's fame.'

'Maybe she needs time to get her head around who her father is,' Jaz said. 'It must've come as a huge shock finding out like that just before her mother died.'

'Yes, I guess so.' Miranda sighed again and then added, 'Are you sure you know what you're doing,

Jaz—I mean with Jake? I can't help worrying this could backfire.'

'I know exactly what I'm doing,' Jaz said. 'I'm using Jake and he's using me.'

There was a telling little silence.

'You're not going to sleep with him, are you?' Miranda said.

Jaz laughed. 'I know he's your brother and all that but there are some women on this planet who can actually resist him, you know.'

And I had better keep on doing it.

Jake was coming back in from a morning run around the property when he saw Jaz coming down the stairs, presumably for breakfast. She was wearing light-grey yoga pants and a baby-girl pink slouch top that revealed the cap of a creamy shoulder and the thin black strap of her bra. Her slender feet were bare apart from liquorice-black toenail polish and her hair was in a messy knot on the top of her head that somehow managed to look casual and elegant at the same time. She wasn't wearing a skerrick of make-up but if anything it made her look all the more breath-snatchingly beautiful. But then, since when had her stunning grey-blue eyes with their thick, spider-leg long lashes and prominent eyebrows needed any enhancement?

He caught a whiff of her bergamot-and-geranium essential oil as she came to stand on the last step, making her almost eye-to-eye with him. The urge to touch her lissom young body was overpowering. He had to curl his hands into fists to prevent himself from running a hand down the creamy silk of her cheek or tracing that gorgeous mouth with his finger.

Her eyes met his and a punch of lust slammed him in the groin. The fire and ice in that stormy sea of grey and blue had a potent impact on him. It happened every time their eyes collided. It was like a bolt of electricity zapping him, making everything that was male in him stand to attention. 'I told Miranda the truth about us,' she said with a touch of defiance.

Jake decided to wind her up a bit. 'That we have the hots for each other and are about to indulge in a passionate fling that's been seven years in the making?'

She folded her arms like a schoolmistress who was dealing with a particularly cheeky pupil, but he noticed her cheeks had gone a faint shade of pink. 'No,' she said as tartly as if she had just bitten into a lemon. 'I told her we aren't engaged and we still hate each other.'

He picked up a stray strand of hair that had escaped her makeshift knot and tucked it safely back behind the neat shell of her ear. He felt her give a tiny shiver as his fingers brushed the skin behind her ear and her mouth opened and closed as if she was trying to disguise her little involuntary gasp. 'You don't hate me, sweetheart. You *want* me.'

The twin pools of colour in her cheeks darkened another shade and her eyes flashed with livid blue-tipped flames. 'Do you get charged extra on flights for carrying your ego on board?'

Jake smiled crookedly as he trailed his fingertip from the crimson tide on her cheekbone to the neat hinge of her jaw. 'I see it every time you look at me. I feel it when I'm near you. You feel it too, don't you?'

The point of her tongue sneaked out over her lips in a darting movement. 'All I feel when I'm near you is the uncontrollable urge to scratch my nails down your face.'

He unpeeled one of her hands from where it was tucked in around her middle and laid it flat against his jaw. 'Go on,' he said, challenging her with his gaze. 'I won't stop you.'

Her hand was like cool silk against his skin. A shiver scooted down his spine as he felt the slight scrape of her nails against his morning stubble but then, instead of scoring his face, she began to stroke it. The sound of her soft skin moving over his raspy jaw had an unmistakably erotic element to it. Her touch sent a rocket blast through his pelvis and he put a hand at the base of her spine to draw her closer to his restless, urgent heat. The contact of her body so intimately against his was like fireworks exploding. His mouth came down in search of hers but he didn't have to go far as she met him more than halfway. Her soft lips were parted in anticipation, her vanilla-milkshake breath mingling with his for a spine-tingling microsecond before her mouth fused with his.

She gave a low moan of approval as he moved his mouth against hers, seeking her moist warmth with the stroke and glide of his tongue. She melted against him, her arms winding around his neck, her fingers delving through his hair, holding his head in place as if she was terrified he would pull back from her.

Jake had no intention of pulling back. He was enjoying the taste of her too much, the heat and unbridled passion that blossomed with every stroke and flicker of his tongue against hers. She pressed herself against him, her supple body fitting along his harder contours as if she had been fashioned just for him. He cupped her neat behind, holding her against the throbbing urgency of his arousal as his mouth fed hungrily off the sweet and drugging temptation of hers.

He lifted his mouth only far enough to change position but she grabbed at him, clamping her lips to his, her tongue darting into his mouth to mate wantonly with his. His blood pounded with excitement. His heart rate sped. His thighs fizzed with the need to take charge, to possess the hot, tight, wet vault of her body until this clawing, desperate need was finally satisfied.

Hadn't he always known she would be dynamite in his arms? Hadn't he always wanted to do this? Even that night when she'd been too young to know what she was doing. He had ached and burned to possess her then and he ached and burned now. One kiss wasn't going to be enough. It wasn't enough to satisfy the raging lust rippling through his body. He wanted to feel her convulsing around him as he took her to heaven and back. He knew they would be good together. He had always known it on some level. He felt it whenever their eyes met—the electric jolt of awareness that triggered something primitive in him.

Nothing would please him more than to see her gasping out his name as she came. Nothing would give him more pleasure than to have her admit she wanted him as much as he wanted her. To prove to her it wasn't her 'taking a break' fiancé she was hankering after but *him* she wanted. The man she had wanted since she was a teenager. The man she said she hated but lusted after like a forbidden drug. *That* was what he saw in her eyes—the desire she didn't want to feel but was there, simmering and smouldering with latent heat.

Jake slipped a hand under her loose top in search of the tempting globe of her breast. She hummed her pleasure against his lips as he moved her bra aside to make skin-on-skin contact. For years he had wanted to touch her like this—to feel her soft, creamy skin against his palm and hear her throatily express her need. He passed his thumb over her tightly budded nipple and then circled it before he bent his head and took it into his mouth. She gave another primal moan as he suckled on her breast, using the gentle scrape of his teeth and the sweep and salve of his tongue to tantalise her.

He slipped a hand down between their hard-pressed bodies, cupping her mound, his own body so worked up he wondered if he was going to jump the gun for the first time since he'd been a clumsy teenager.

But suddenly Jaz pulled back, pushing against his chest with the heels of her hands. 'Stop,' she said in a breathless-sounding voice. 'Please…stop.'

Jake held his hands up to show he was cool with her calling a halt. 'Your call, sweetheart.'

She pressed her lips together as she straightened

her top, her hands fumbling and uncoordinated. 'You had no right to do that,' she said, shooting him a hard look.

He gave a lazy smile. 'Well, look who's talking. I wonder what lover boy would say if he'd been a fly on the wall just now? His devoted little "having a break" fiancée getting all hot and bothered with just a friendly kiss.'

Her eyes went to hairpin-thin slits. 'There was nothing friendly about it. You don't even like me. You just wanted to prove a point.'

'What point would that be?'

She tossed her head in an uppity manner as she turned to go back upstairs. 'I'm not having this conversation. You had no right to touch me and that's the end of it. Don't do it again.'

Jake waited until she was almost to the top of the stairs before he said, 'What about when we're out in public? Am I allowed to touch you then?'

A circle of ice rimmed her flattened mouth as she turned to glare at him. 'Only if it's absolutely necessary.'

He smiled a devilish smile. 'I'll look forward to it.'

CHAPTER FIVE

JAZ STORMED INTO her room and shut the door. She would have slammed it except she had already shown Jake how much he had rattled her. She didn't want to give his over-blown ego any more of a boost. She was furious with him for kissing her. How dared he take such liberties? A little voice reminded her that she hadn't exactly resisted but, on the contrary, had given him every indication she was enjoying every pulse-racing second of it.

Which she had been. Damn it.

His kiss had made her face what she didn't want to face. What she hadn't wanted to face for seven years. She wanted him. It was like it was programmed into her genes or something. He triggered something in her that no other man ever had. Her body sizzled when he was around. His touch created an earthquake of longing. How could a kiss make her feel so…so alive? It was crazy. Madness. Lunacy.

It was just like him to make a big joke about everything. This was nothing but a game to him. He enjoyed baiting her. Goading her. *Tempting* her. Why had she allowed him to get that close to her? She should have stepped back while she'd had the chance. Or maybe she hadn't had the chance because her body had other ideas. Wicked ideas that involved him touching her and pleasuring her in a way she had never quite felt before. Why had *his* touch made her flesh tingle and quake with delight? Why had *his* kiss made her heart race and her pulse thrum with longing?

It was just a kiss. It wasn't as if she hadn't been kissed before. She'd had plenty of kisses. Heaps. Dozens. Maybe hundreds… Well, maybe things had been a bit light on that just lately. She couldn't quite recall the last time Myles had kissed her. Not properly. Not passionately, as if he couldn't get enough of her taste and touch. Over the last few weeks their kisses had turned into a rather perfunctory peck on the cheek at hello and goodbye. And as to touching her breasts, well, Myles wasn't good at breasts. He didn't seem to understand she didn't like being pinched or squeezed, like he was someone checking a piece of fruit for ripeness.

Jaz let out a frustrated breath. Why did Jake have to be the expert on kissing her and handling her breasts? It wasn't fair. She didn't want him to have such sensual power over her. He could turn her on by just looking at her with that glinting dark gaze.

Of course it would be *so* much worse now. Now he had actually kissed her and touched her breasts and her lady land. God, she'd almost come on the spot when he'd cupped her down there. How could one man's touch have such an effect on her? She didn't even like him. She loathed him. He was her arch-enemy. He wasn't just a thorn in her side. He was the whole damn rose bush. Unpruned. He was everything she avoided in a partner.

But he sure could kiss. Jaz had to give him that. His lips had done things to hers no man had ever done before. His tongue had lit a blazing fire in her core and it hadn't gone out. The hot coals were smouldering there even now. Her body felt restless. Feverish. Hungry. Starving for more of his electrifying caresses. What would it feel like to have him deep inside her? Moving in her body in that hectic rush for release?

Sex had always been a complicated issue for her. She put it down to the fact her first experience of it had been so twisted and tangled up with shame. She had taken a drink from a young man at the party, more to get back at Jake for rejecting her. She had flirted with the man, hoping Jake would see that not all men found her repulsive. But she hadn't factored in the amount of alcohol she had already consumed or her overwrought emotional state. She couldn't quite remember how she had ended up in one of the downstairs bathrooms with the man, sweaty and smelling of wine as he tore at her clothes and groped and slobbered all over her until she'd finally got away. All she could remember was the shame—the sickening shame of not being in control.

Now whenever she had sex that same shame lurked at the back of her mind. Although she enjoyed some aspects of making love—the touching and being needed—she hadn't always been able to relax enough to orgasm. Not that any of her partners had seemed to notice. She might not be a proper Ravensdale but she sure could act when she needed to. Pretending to orgasm every time hadn't been her intention. But once had turned into twice and then it had been far easier than explaining.

How could she explain her behaviour that night? The rational part of her knew the man at the party had some responsibility to acquire proper consent before he touched her, but how did she know if she'd given it or not? It would be his word against hers, that was, if he'd actually remembered. She'd seen him the next morning as the overnight guests were leaving but he had looked right through her as if he had never seen her before. Had she agreed to kiss him in the bathroom or had he come in on her and seized the opportunity to assault her? She didn't know and it was the not knowing that was the most shameful thing for her.

Jaz wasn't into victim blaming but when it came to herself she struggled to forgive herself for allowing something like that to happen. She had buried her shame behind a 'don't mess with me' façade and a sharp tongue but deep inside she was still that shocked and terrified girl.

And she had a scary feeling if she spent too much time alone with Jake Ravensdale he would begin to see it.

Jaz was doing some work on Holly's dress in her room and when her phone rang she picked it up without thinking. 'Jasmine Connolly.'

'Jaz. Finally you answered,' Myles said. 'Why on earth haven't you returned my calls?'

'Oh, hi, Myles,' she said breezily. 'How are you?'

He released a whooshing breath. 'How do you think I am? I turn my back for a moment and my fiancée is suddenly engaged to someone else.'

Jaz smiled as she put her needle and thread down. It was working. It was actually working. Myles was insanely jealous. She had never heard him speak so possessively before. 'You were the one who suggested we take a break.'

'Yes, but dating other people is not the same as getting engaged to them. We'd only been apart twenty-four hours and you hooked up with him. No one falls in love that quickly. No one, and especially not Jake bloody Ravensdale.'

Jaz hadn't really taken in that bit. The bit where Myles had said they were free to date other people. She'd thought he was just having some breathing space. Her 'engagement' to Jake wouldn't have the same power if Myles was seeing someone else. What if he fell in love? What if *he* got engaged to someone else? 'Are you seeing other people?'

There was a short silence.

'I had a drink with an old friend but I haven't got myself bloody engaged to them,' he said in a sulky tone.

Jaz twirled a tendril of her hair around her finger as she walked about the room with the phone pressed to her ear. How cool was this, hearing Myles sound all wounded and affronted by her moving on so quickly?

Didn't that prove he still loved her? The irony was he'd been the first to say those three magical little words. But he hadn't said it for weeks. Months, even. But a couple more weeks of having Jake Ravensdale brandished in his face would do the trick. Myles would soon be begging her to take him back. 'I have to go,' she said. 'Jake is taking me out to dinner.'

'I give it a week,' Myles said. 'Two at the most. He won't stick around any longer than that. You mark my words.'

Two is all I need. The winter wedding expo in the Cotswolds was the coming weekend. It was her stepping stone to the big time. She hoped to expand her business and what better way than to attend with a heart-stopping, handsome fiancé in tow? There was no way she wanted to go alone. She would look tragic if she went without a fiancé. She couldn't bear to be considered a fraud, making 'happy ever after' dresses but failing to find love herself. But if she took Jake Ravensdale as her fiancé —the poster boy for pick-ups—it would give her serious street cred. Besides, it would be the perfect payback to him for humiliating her. It would be unmitigated torture for commitment-phobe Jake to be dragged around a ballroom full of wedding finery.

She smiled a secret smile. Yes, staying 'engaged' to Jake suited her just fine.

Jake was scrolling through his emails in the library— thankfully none were from Emma Madden—when Jaz came sashaying in, bringing with her the scent of flowers and temptation. His body sprang to attention when she approached the desk where he was sitting. She had changed out of her yoga pants and top and was now wearing skin-tight jeans, knee-length leather boots and a baby-blue cashmere sweater with a patterned scarf artfully gathered around her slim neck. Her honey-brown hair was loose about her shoulders and her beautiful mouth was glistening with lip-gloss, drawing his gaze like a magnet. He could still taste her. Could still feel the way her tongue had danced with his in sensual heat. He saw her gaze drift to his mouth as if she were recalling that erotic interlude. 'Forgiven me yet?' he said.

She tossed her hair back over her shoulders in a haughty manner, giving him an ice-cool glare. 'For?'

'You know exactly what for.'

She shifted her gaze, picked a pen off the desk and turned it over in her slender hands as if it was something of enormous interest to her. 'I was wondering what you're up to next weekend.'

He leaned back in the leather chair and balanced one ankle over his thigh. 'My calendar is pretty heavily booked. What did you have in mind?'

Her grey-blue eyes came back to his. 'I have a function I need to attend in Gloucester. I was hoping you'd come with me—you know, to keep up appearances.'

'What sort of function?'

'Just a drinks thing.'

Jake steepled his fingers against his nose and mouth. The little minx was up to something but he would play along. He might even get another kiss or two out of her. 'Sure, why not?'

She put the pen down. 'I'm going to head back to London now.'

He felt a swooping sensation of disappointment in his gut. It would be deadly boring staying here without her to spar with. They hadn't had any time together without anyone else around for years. He hadn't realised how much he was enjoying it until the prospect of it ending now loomed. But there would be other opportunities as long as this charade continued. And he was going to make the most of them. 'You're not staying till morning?'

'No, I have stuff to do at the boutique first thing and I don't want to get caught up in traffic.'

Jake suspected she was wary of spending any more time with him in case she betrayed her desire for him. He wasn't being overly smug about it. He could see it as plain as day. It mirrored his raging lust for her. Not that he was going to act on it but it sure was a heap of fun making her think he was. 'Are you going to see Myles?'

Her gaze slipped out of reach of his. 'Not yet. We agreed on a month's break.'

'A lot can happen in a month.'

Her lips tightened as if she was trying to remove the sensation of his on them. 'I know what I'm doing.'

'Do you?'

Her eyes clashed with his. 'I know you think relationships are a complete waste of time but commitment is important to me.'

'He's not the right man for you,' Jake said.

Her hands went to her slim hips in a combative

pose. 'And I suppose you think you're an expert on who exactly would be?'

He pushed back his chair to come around to her side of the desk. She took half a step backwards but the antique globe was in the way. Her eyes drifted to his mouth and her darting tongue took a layer of lip-gloss off her lips. 'If Myles was the right man for you he'd be down here right now with his hands at my throat.'

Her eyes glittered with enmity. 'Not all men resort to Neanderthal tactics to claim a partner.'

He took a fistful of her silky hair and gently anchored her. 'If I was in love with you I would do whatever it took to get you back.'

Her eyelids went to half-mast as her gaze zeroed in on his mouth for a moment. 'Men like you don't know the meaning of the word love. Lust is the only currency you deal in.'

Jake glided his hand down from her hair to cup her cheek, his thumb moving over the creamy perfection of her skin like the slow arm of a metronome. He watched as her pupils enlarged like widening pools of black ink, her mouth parting, her soft, milky breath coming out in a soundless gasp. 'There's nothing wrong with a bit of lust. It's the litmus test of a good relationship.'

'You don't have relationships,' she said, still looking at his mouth. 'You have encounters that don't last longer than it takes to change a light bulb.'

He gave a slanted smile. 'Who needs a light bulb when we've got this sort of electricity going on?'

She pursed her lips. 'Don't even think about it.'

He brushed his thumb across her bunched up lips. 'I think about it all the time. How it would feel to have you scraping your nails down my back as I make you come.'

She gave a tiny shudder. Blinked. Swallowed. 'I'd much rather scrape them down your arrogant face.'

Jake smiled. 'Liar. You're thinking about it now, aren't you? You're thinking about how hot I make you feel. How turned on. I bet if I slipped my fingers into you now you'd be dripping wet for me.'

Twin pools of pink flagged her cheekbones. 'It's not going to happen, Jake,' she said through tight lips. 'I'm engaged to another man.'

'Maybe you'll feel different once you're wearing my ring. I'll pick you up at lunchtime tomorrow at the boutique. Be ready at two p.m.'

Her eyes flashed with venom. 'I have an appointment with a client.'

'Cancel it.'

She looked as if she was going to argue the point but then she blew out a hiss of a breath and stormed out of the room, slamming the door behind her for good measure.

Barely a minute later he heard her car start with a roar and then the scream of her tyres as she flew down the driveway.

He smiled and turned back to his laptop. *Yep. A heap of fun.*

CHAPTER SIX

JAZ HAD JUST finished with a customer who had purchased one of her hand-embroidered veils for her daughter when Jake came into the boutique. The woman smiled up at him as he politely held the door open for her. 'Thank you,' she said. 'I hear congratulations are in order. You've got yourself a keeper there.' She nodded towards Jaz. 'She'll make a gorgeous bride. When's the big day?'

Jake smiled one of his laidback smiles. 'We haven't set a date yet, have we, sweetheart?'

'No, not yet,' Jaz said.

'I can't wait to see the ring,' the woman said. 'I bet you'll give her a big one.'

Jake's dark-blue eyes glinted as they glanced at Jaz. 'You bet I will.'

Jaz felt a tremor go through her private parts at his innuendo. Did the man have no shame? She was trying to act as cool and professional as she could and one look at her from those glittering midnight-blue eyes and she felt like she was going to melt into a sizzling pool at his feet. She wouldn't have mentioned anything about their 'engagement' to the customer but it seemed there wasn't a person in the whole of London who hadn't heard fast-living playboy Jake Ravensdale was getting himself hitched.

The woman left with a little wave, and the door with its tinkling bell closed. Jake came towards the counter where Jaz had barricaded herself. 'So this is your stamping ground,' he said, glancing around at the dresses hanging on the free-standing rack. 'How much of a profit are you turning over?'

She gave him a flinty look. 'I don't need you to pull apart my business.'

His one-shoulder shrug was nonchalant. 'Just asking.'

'You're not just asking,' Jaz said. 'You're looking for an opportunity to tell me I'm rubbish at running my business, just like you keep pointing out how rubbish I am at running my personal life.'

'You have to admit three engagements—four, if you count ours—is a lot of bad decisions.'

She gripped the edge of the counter. 'And I suppose you've never made a bad decision in the whole of your charmed life, have you?'

'I've made a few.'

'Such as?'

He looked at her for a long moment, his customary smile fading and a slight frown taking its place. 'It was crass of me to bring those girls to my room that night. There were other ways I could've handled the situation.'

Jaz refused to be taken in by an admission of regret seven years too late. 'Did you sleep with them?'

'No.'

There was a pregnant pause.

'Where did you go after that?' he said. 'I didn't see you for the rest of the night.'

Jaz looked down at the glass-topped counter where all the garters were arranged. 'I went back to my room.'

He reached across the counter to take one of her hands in his. 'Look at me, Jasmine.'

She slowly brought her gaze up to his, affecting the expression of a bored teenager preparing for a stern lecture from a parent. 'What?'

His eyes moved between each of hers as if he was searching for something hidden behind the cool screen of her gaze. She could feel the warm press of his hand against hers, his long, strong, masculine fingers entwining with hers, making her insides slip and shift. She could smell the sharp citrus of his aftershave. She could see the dark shadow of his regrowth peppered along his jaw. She could see every fine line on his mouth, the way his lips were set in a serious line— such a change from his usual teasing slant. He began to move the pad of his thumb in a stroking fashion over the back of her hand, the movements drugging her senses.

'It wasn't that I wasn't attracted to you,' he said. 'I just didn't want to make things awkward with you being such a part of the family. That and the fact you were too young to know what you were doing.'

Jaz pulled her hand away. 'Then why lead me on as if you were serious about me? That was just plain cruel.'

He let out a deep sigh. 'Yeah, I guess it was.'

She studied his features for a moment, wondering if this too was an act. How could she believe he was sorry for how he'd made her think he was falling in love with her? He had been so charming towards her, telling her how beautiful she was and how he couldn't wait to get her alone. She had fallen for every lie, waiting in his room, undressing down to her underwear for him in her haste to do anything she could to please him. She had been too emotionally immature to realise he had been winding her up. She had been too enamoured with him to see his charm offensive for what it was. He had pulled her strings like a puppet master. Hating him was dead easy when he wasn't sorry for how he'd treated her. For the last seven years she had stoked that hatred with every look or cynical lip curl he aimed her way. But if this apology were genuine she would have to let her anger and hatred go.

That was scary.

Her anger was a barrier. A big, fat barricade around her heart because falling in love with Jake would be nothing less than an exercise in self-annihilation. She only fell in love with men she knew for certain would love her back. Her ex-fiancés were alike in that they had each been comfortable with commitment. They'd wanted the same things she wanted...or so they had said.

Jake glanced at his watch. 'We'd better get a move

on. I made an appointment with the jeweller for two-fifteen. Have you got an assistant to hold the fort for you till you get back?'

'No, my last girl was rude to the clients,' Jaz said. 'I had to let her go. I haven't got around to replacing her. I'll just put a "back in ten minutes" sign on the door.'

He frowned. 'You mean you run this show all by yourself?'

She picked up her purse and jacket from underneath the counter. 'I outsource some of the cutting and sewing but I do most of everything else because that's what my customers expect.'

'But none of the top designers do all the hack work,' Jake said as they walked out of the boutique into the chilly autumn air. 'You'll burn yourself out trying to do everything yourself.'

'Yes, well, I'm not quite pulling in the same profit as some of those houses,' Jaz said. 'But watch this space. I have a career plan.'

'What about a business plan? I could have a look at your company structure and—'

'No thanks,' Jaz said and closed and locked the boutique door.

'If you're worried about my fee, I could do mate's rates.'

She gave him a sideways look. 'I can afford you, Jake. I just choose not to use your…erm…services.'

He shrugged one of his broad shoulders. 'Your loss.'

The jeweller was a private designer who had a studio above an interior design shop. Jaz was acutely conscious of Jake's arm at her elbow as he led her into the viewing area. After brief introductions were made a variety of designs was brought forward for her to peruse. But there was one ring that was a stand out. It was a mosaic collection of diamonds in an art deco design that was both simple yet elegant. She slipped it on her finger and was pleased to find it was a perfect fit. 'This one,' she said, holding it up to see the way the light bounced off the diamonds.

'Good choice,' the designer said. 'It suits your hand.'

Jaz didn't see the price. It wasn't the sort of jeweller where price tags were on show. But she didn't care if it was expensive or not. Jake could afford it. She did wonder, however, if he would want her to give it back when their 'engagement' was over.

Jake took her hand as they left the studio. 'Fancy a quick coffee?'

Jaz would have said no except she hadn't had lunch and her stomach was gurgling like a drain. 'Sure, why not?'

He took her to a café a couple of blocks from her boutique but they had barely sat down before someone from a neighbouring table took a photo of them with a camera phone. Then a murmur went around the café and other people started aiming their phones at them. Jaz tried to keep her smile natural but her jaw was aching from the effort. Jake seemed to take it all in his stride, however.

One customer came over with a napkin and a pen. 'Can I have your autograph, Jake?'

Jake slashed his signature across the napkin and handed back the pen with an easy smile. 'There you go.'

'Is it true you and Miss Connolly are engaged?' the customer asked.

Jaz held up her ring hand. 'Yes. We just picked up the ring.'

More cameras went off and the Twitter whistle sounded so often it was as if a flock of small birds had been let loose in the café.

'Nice work,' Jake said when the fuss had finally died down a little.

'You were the one who suggested a coffee,' Jaz said, shooting him a look from beneath her lashes.

'I heard your stomach rumbling at the jeweller's. Don't you make time for lunch?'

She stirred her latte with a teaspoon rather than lose herself in his sapphire-blue gaze. 'I've got a lot on just now.'

He reached across the table and took her left hand in his, running his fingertip over the crest of the mosaic ring. 'You can keep it after this is over.'

Jaz brought her gaze back to his. 'You don't want to recycle it for when you eventually settle down?'

He released her hand and sat back as he gave a light laugh. 'Can you see me doing the school run?'

'You don't ever want kids?'

'Nope,' he said, reaching for the sugar and tipping two teaspoons in. 'I don't want the responsibility. If I'm going to screw anyone's life up, it'll be my own. *That* I can live with.'

'Why do you think you'd screw up your children's lives?' Jaz said.

He stirred his coffee before he answered. 'I'm too much like my father.'

'I don't think you're anything like your father,' she said. 'Maybe in looks but not in temperament. Your father is weak. Sorry if I'm speaking out of turn but he is. The way he handled his affair with Kat Winwood's mother is proof of it. I can't see you paying someone to have an abortion if you got a girl pregnant.'

He shifted his lips from side to side. 'I wouldn't offer to marry her, though.'

'Maybe not, but you'd support her and your child,' Jaz said. 'And you'd be involved in your child's life.'

He gave her one of his slow smiles that did so much damage to her resolve to keep him at a distance. 'I didn't realise you had such a high opinion of me.'

She pursed her lips. 'Don't get too excited. I still think you'd make a terrible husband.'

'In general or for you?'

Jaz looked at him for a beat or two of silence. She had a sudden vision of him at the end of the aisle waiting for her with that twinkling smile on his handsome face. Of his tall and toned body dressed in a sharply tailored suit instead of the casual clothes he preferred. Of his dark-blue eyes focused on her, as if she were the only woman he ever wanted to gaze at, with complete love and adoration.

She blinked and refocused. 'Good Lord, not for me,' she said with a laugh. 'We'd be at each other's throats before we left the church.'

Something moved at the back of his gaze as it held hers, a flicker like a faulty light bulb. But then he picked up his coffee cup and drained it before putting it down on the table with a decisive clunk. 'Ready?'

Jake walked Jaz back to the boutique holding her hand for the sake of appearances. Or so he told himself. The truth was he loved the feel of her small, neat hand encased in his. He couldn't stop himself from thinking about those soft, clever little fingers on other parts of his body. Stroking him, teasing him with her touch. Why shouldn't he make the most of their situation? He had a business deal to secure and being engaged to Jasmine Connolly was going to win him some serious brownie points with his conservative client Bruce Parnell. It wasn't as if it was for ever. A week or two and it would be over. Life would go back to normal.

'I have a work function on Wednesday night,' he said when Jaz had unlocked the door of the boutique. 'Dinner with a client. Would you like to come?'

She looked at him with a slight frown. 'Why?'

He tugged a tendril of her hair in a teasing manner. 'Because we're madly in love and we can't bear to be apart for a second.'

Her frown deepened and a flash of irritation arced in her gaze. 'What's the dress code?'

'Lounge suit and cocktail.'

'I'll have to check my calendar.'

Jake put his hand beneath her chin and tipped up her face so her eyes couldn't escape his. 'I'm giving you the weekend for the wedding expo. The least you could do is give me one week night.'

Her cheeks swarmed with sheepish colour. 'How did you know it was a wedding expo?'

He gave her a teasing grin. 'I knew there had to be a catch. Why else would you want me for a whole weekend?'

Her mouth took on that disapproving schoolmarm, pursed look that made him want to kiss it back into pliable softness. 'I don't want *you*, Jake. You'll only be there for show.'

He bent down and pressed a brief kiss to her mouth. 'I'll pick you up from here at seven.'

Jaz was still doing her hair when the doorbell sounded on Wednesday evening. She had run late with a client who had taken hours to choose a design for a gown. She gave her hair one last blast with the dryer and shook her head to let the waves fall loosely about her shoulders. She smoothed her hands down her hips, turning to one side to check her appearance in the full-length mirror. The black cocktail dress had double shoestring straps that criss-crossed over her shoulders, the silky fabric skimming her figure in all the right places. She was wearing her highest heels because she hadn't been able to wear them when going out with Myles, as he was only an inch taller than her. A quick spray of perfume and a smear of lip-gloss and she was ready.

Why she was going to so much trouble for Jake was not something she wanted to examine too closely. But when she opened the door and she saw the way his eyes ran over her appreciatively she was pleased she had chosen to go with the wow factor.

But then, so had he. He was dressed in a beautifully tailored suit that made his shoulders seem all the broader and, while he wasn't wearing a tie, the white open-necked shirt combined with the dark blue of his suit intensified the navy-blue of his eyes.

Jaz opened the door a little wider. 'I'll just get my wrap.'

Jake stepped into her flat and closed the door. She turned to face him as she draped her wrap over her shoulders, a little shiver coursing over her flesh as she saw the way his gaze went to her mouth as if pulled there by a powerful magnet.

The air quickened the way it always did when they were alone.

'Is something wrong?' she said.

He closed the small distance between their bodies so that they were almost touching. 'I have something for you,' he said, reaching into the inside pocket of his jacket.

Jaz swallowed as he took out a narrow velvet jewellery case the same colour as his eyes. She took it from him and opened it with fingers that were suddenly as useless as a glove without a hand. Jake took it from her and deftly opened it to reveal a stunning diamond pendant on a white-gold chain that was as fine as a gossamer thread.

Jaz glanced up at him but his face was unreadable. She looked back at the diamond. She had jew-

ellery. Lots of it. Most of it she had bought herself
because jewellery was so personal, a bit like perfume
and make-up. She hadn't had a partner yet who had
ever got her taste in jewellery right. But this was…
perfect. She would have chosen it herself if she could
have afforded it. She knew it was expensive. Hid-
eously so. Why had Jake spent so much money on her
when he didn't even like her? 'I'll give it back once
we're done,' she said. 'And the ring.'

'I chose it specifically for you,' he said, taking it
out of the box. 'Turn around. Move your hair out of
the way.'

Jaz did as he commanded and tried not to shudder
in pleasure as his long strong fingers moved against
the sensitive skin on the back of her neck as he secured the pendant in place. She could feel the tall,
hard frame of his body against her shoulder blades, his
strongly muscled thighs against her trembling ones.
She knew if she leaned back even half an inch she
could come into contact with the hot, hard heat of
him. She felt his hands come down on the tops of her
shoulders, his fingers giving her a light squeeze as he
turned her to face him. She looked into the midnight
blue of his inscrutable gaze and wondered if her teenage crush was dead and buried after all. It felt like it
was coming to life under the warm press of his hands
on her body.

He trailed a lazy fingertip from beneath her ear to
her mouth, circling it without touching it. But it felt
like he had. Her lips buzzed, fizzed and ached for the
pressure of his. 'You look beautiful.'

'Amazing what a flashy bit of jewellery can do.'

He frowned as if her flippant comment annoyed him. 'You don't suit flashy jewellery and I wouldn't insult you by insisting on you wearing it.'

'All the same, I don't expect you to spend so much money on me. I don't feel comfortable about it, given our relationship.'

His eyes went to her mouth for a moment before meshing with hers. 'Why do you hate me so much?'

Jaz couldn't hold his gaze and looked at the open neck of his shirt instead. But that just made it worse because she could see the long, strong, tanned column of his throat and smell the light but intoxicating lemony scent of his aftershave. She didn't know if it was the diamond olive branch he had offered her, his physical closeness or both that made her decide to tell him the truth about that night. Or maybe it was because she was tired of the negative emotion weighing her down. 'That night after I left your room... I... Something happened...'

Jaz felt rather than saw his frown. She was still looking at his neck but she noticed the way he had swallowed thickly. 'What?' he said.

'I accepted a drink off one of the guests. I'm not sure who it was. One of the casual seasonal theatre staff, I think. I hadn't seen him before or since. I was upset after leaving you. I didn't care if I got drunk. But then... I, well, you've probably heard it dozens of times before. Girls who get drunk and then end up regretting what happened next.'

'What happened next?' Jake's voice sounded raw,

as if something had been scraped across his vocal chords.

Jaz still couldn't meet his gaze. She couldn't bear to see his judgement, his criticism of her reckless behaviour. 'I had a non-consensual encounter. Or at least I think it was non-consensual.'

'You were...*raped*?'

She looked at him then. 'No, but it was close to it. Somehow I managed to fight him off, but I was too ashamed to tell anyone what happened. I didn't even tell Miranda. I haven't told anyone before now.'

Jake's expression was full of outrage, shock and horror. 'The man should've been charged. Do you think you'd recognise him if you saw him again? We could arrange a police line-up. We could check the guest list of that night. Track down everyone who attended...'

Jaz pulled out from under his hold and crossed her arms over her body. 'No. I don't want to even think about that night. I don't even know if I gave the guy the okay to mess around. I was the one who started flirting with him in the first place. But then things got a little hazy. It would be his word against mine and you know what the defence lawyers would make of that. I was too drunk to know what I was doing.'

'But he might've spiked your drink or something,' Jake said. 'He committed a crime. A crime for which he should be punished.'

'That only happens in the movies,' Jaz said. 'I've moved on. It would make things so much harder for me if I had to revisit that night in a courtroom.'

His frown made a road map of lines on his forehead. 'I can see why you hate me so much. I'm as guilty as that lowlife.'

'No,' she said. 'That's not true.'

'Isn't it?'

Jaz bit her lip. 'I know it looks like I've blamed you all this time but that's just the projection of negative emotion. I guess I used you as a punching bag because I felt so ashamed.'

Jake came over to her and took her hands from where they were wrapped around her body, holding them gently in his. 'You have no need to be ashamed, Jaz. You were just a kid. I was the adult and I acted appallingly. I shouldn't have given you any encouragement. Leading you on like that only to throw those girls in your face was wrong. I should've been straight with you right from the get-go.'

Jaz gave him a wobbly smile. 'You just called me Jaz. You haven't done that in years.'

His hands gave hers a gentle squeeze. 'We'd better get a move on. My client isn't the most patient of men. That is if you're still okay with going? I can always tell him you had something on and go by myself.'

'I'm fine,' she said. And she was surprised to find it was true. Having Jake of all people being so understanding, caring and protective made something hard and tight inside her chest loosen like a knotted rope suddenly being released.

He gently grazed her cheek with the backs of his knuckles. 'Thank you for telling me.'

'I'd rather you didn't tell anyone else,' Jaz said. 'I don't want people to look at me differently.'

'Not even Miranda?'

She pulled at her lip with her teeth. 'Miranda would be hurt if I told her now. She'd blame herself for not watching out for me. You know what a little mother hen she is.'

Jake's frown was back. 'But surely—?'

'No,' Jaz said, sending him a determined look. 'Don't make me regret telling you. Promise me you won't betray my trust.'

He let out a frustrated sigh. 'I promise. But I swear to God, if I find out who hurt you I'll tear him apart with my bare hands.'

CHAPTER SEVEN

LATER, IN THE car going back to Jaz's place, Jake wondered how on earth he'd swung the deal with his client. His mind hadn't been on the game the whole way through dinner. All he'd been able to think about was what Jaz had told him about that wretched night after she had left his room. He was so churned up with a toxic cocktail of anger, guilt and an unnerving desire for revenge that he'd given his client, Bruce Parnell, the impression he was a distracted, lovesick fool rather than a savvy businessman. But that didn't seem to matter because at the end of the dinner his client had signed on the dotted line and wished Jake and Jaz all the best for their future.

Their future.

What *was* their future?

Jake was so used to bickering with her that he wasn't sure how he was going to navigate being friends with her instead. While it had been pistols and pissy looks at dawn, he'd been able to keep his distance. But now she'd shared her painful secret with him he couldn't carry on as if nothing had changed.

Everything had changed. The whole dynamic of their relationship was different. He wanted to protect her. To fix it for her. To give her back her innocence so she didn't have to carry around the shame she felt. A shame she had no need to feel because the jerk who had assaulted her was the one who should be ashamed.

But Jake too felt shame. Deep, gut-clawing shame. Shame that he hadn't handled her infatuation with him more sensitively. His actions had propelled her into danger—danger that could have been avoided if he had been a little more understanding. He could see now why Jaz had stepped in with the engagement charade when Emma Madden had turned up at the door. She had been sensitive to the girl's need for dignity, offering her a safe way home with someone at the other end to make sure she was all right.

What had *he* done? He had sent Jaz from his room in an acute state of public humiliation only to fall into the hands of some creep who'd plied her with drink and drugs and God knew what else. Had that been her first experience of sex—being groped and man-handled by a drunken idiot? He couldn't remember if she'd had a boyfriend back then. Miranda had been going out with Mark Redbank from a young age but Jaz had never seemed all that interested in boys. Not until she'd developed that crush on him.

He couldn't bear the thought of her being touched in such a despicable way. Was that why she only ever dated men she could control? None of her ex-fiancés were what one would even loosely consider as alpha men. Was that deliberate or unconscious on her part?

Jake glanced at her sitting quietly in the passenger seat beside him. She was looking out at the rain-lashed street, her hands absently fiddling with the clasp on her evening bag. 'You okay?' he said.

She turned her head to look at him, a vacant smile on her face. 'Sorry. I think I used up all my scintillating conversation at dinner.'

'You did a great job,' Jake said. 'Bruce Parnell was quite taken with you. He was being cagey about signing up with me but you had him at hello.'

'Did you know he fell in love with his late wife the very first time they met? And they married three months later and never spent more than two nights apart for the whole of their marriage? He would fly back by private jet if he had to just to be with her.'

He glanced at her again between gear changes. 'He told you all that?'

'And he's still grieving her loss even though it's been ten years. It reminded me of Miranda after Mark died.'

'Luckily Leandro got her to change her mind,' Jake said. 'I was sure she was going to end up a spinster living with a hundred cats.'

Jaz gave a tinkling laugh. 'I was worried too, but they're perfect for each other. I've known it for ages. It was the way Leandro looked at her. He got this really soft look in his eyes.'

Jake grunted. 'Another one bites the dust.'

'What have you got against marriage? It doesn't always end badly. Look at Mr Parnell.'

'That sort of marriage is the exception,' Jake said.

'Look at my parents. They're heading for another show-stopping divorce as far as I can tell. It was bad enough the first time.'

'Clearly Julius doesn't hold the same view as you,' she said. 'And yet he went through the same experience of your parents' divorce.'

'It was different for Julius,' Jake said. 'He found solace in studying and working hard. I found it hard to adjust to boarding school. I pushed against the boundaries. Rubbed the teachers up the wrong way. Wasted their time and my own.'

'But you've done so well for yourself. Aren't you happy with your achievements?'

Was he happy? Up until a few days ago he had been perfectly happy. But now there was a niggling doubt chewing at the edge of his conscience. He moved around so much it was hard to know where was home. He had a base in London but most of the time he lived out of hotel rooms. He never cooked at home. He ate out. He didn't spend the night with anyone because he hated morning-after scenes. He didn't do reruns. One night was enough to scratch the itch. But how long could he keep on moving? The fast lane was a lonely place at times. Not that he was going to admit that to Jaz—or to anyone, when it came to that.

But this recent drama with Emma Madden had got him thinking. Everyone saw him as shallow and self-serving. He hadn't given a toss for anyone's opinion before now but now it sat uncomfortably on him like an ill-fitting jacket. What if people thought he was like the man who had groped Jaz? That he was taking advantage of young women who were a little star-struck. It had never concerned him before. He had always enjoyed exploiting his parents' fame. He had used it to open doors in business and in pleasure. But how long could he go on doing it? He was turning into a cliché. The busty blondes he attracted only wanted him because he was good looking and had famous parents. They didn't know him as a person.

Jake pulled up outside Jaz's flat above her boutique. 'How long have you been living above the shop?' he asked as he walked her to the door.

She gave him a wary look. 'Is this another "how to run your business" lecture?'

'It's a nice place but pretty small. And the whole living and working in the same place can be a drag after a while.'

'Yes, well, I was planning to move in with Myles but he put the brakes on that,' she said, scowling. 'His parents don't like me. They think I'm too pushy and controlling. I think that's the main reason he wanted a break.'

What's not to like? What parents wouldn't be proud to have her as their daughter-in-law? She was smart and funny, and sweet when she let her guard down. His parents were delighted with their 'engagement'. He hadn't figured out yet how he was going to tell them when it was over. They would probably never speak to him again. 'Do you really want to take Myles back?'

Her chin came up. 'Of course.'

'What if he doesn't want to come back?'

She averted her gaze. 'I deal with that *if* it happens.'

Jake looked at her for a long beat. 'You're not in love with him.'

Her eyes flashed back to his. 'And you know this how?'

'Because you're more concerned about what other people think of you than what he does. That's what this thing between us is all about. You're trying to save face, not your relationship.'

She flattened her lips so much they disappeared inside her mouth. 'I know what I'm doing. I know Myles better than anyone.'

'If you know him so well why haven't you told him about that night?'

She flinched as if he had struck her. But then she pulled herself upright as if her spinal column were filling with concrete. 'Thank you for dinner,' she said. 'Good night.'

'Jaz, wait—'

But the only response he got was the door being slammed in his face.

Jaz was at the boutique the next morning when Miranda came in carrying coffee and muffins. 'I thought I'd drop in to start the ball rolling on my wed—' Miranda said, but stopped short when her gaze went to Jaz's ring hand. 'Oh, my God. Did Jake buy that for you?'

'Yes, but it's just for show.'

Miranda snatched up Jaz's hand and turned it every which way to see how the light danced off the diamonds. 'Wow. I didn't realise he had such good taste in rings *and* in women.'

Jaz gave her a speaking look. 'You do realise none of this is for real?'

Miranda's eyes twinkled. 'So you both say, but I was just at Jake's office and he's like a bear with a sore paw. Did you guys have a tiff?'

'That's nothing out of the normal,' Jaz said, taking her coffee out of the cardboard holder.

Miranda cocked her head like an inquisitive bird. 'What's wrong?'

'Nothing. We just argued…about stuff.'

'All couples argue,' Miranda said. 'It's normal and healthy.'

'We're *not* a couple,' Jaz said. 'We're an act.'

Miranda frowned. 'You're not seriously still thinking of going back to Myles?'

Jaz pushed back from her work table. 'That's the plan.'

'It's a dumb plan,' Miranda said. 'A stupid plan that's totally wrong for you and for Myles. Can't you see that? You're not in love with him. You're in love with Jake.'

Jaz laughed. 'No, I'm not. I'm not that much of a fool.'

'I think he's in love with you.'

Jaz frowned. 'What makes you think that?'

'He bought you that ring for one thing,' Miranda said. 'Look at it. It's the most beautiful ring I've ever seen—apart from my own, of course.'

'It's just a prop.'

'A jolly expensive one.' Miranda leaned over the counter and lifted the scarf Jaz had tied around her neck. 'Aha! I knew it. More diamonds. That brother of mine has got it *so* bad.'

'It's a goodwill gesture,' Jaz said. 'I helped him nail an important business deal last night.'

Miranda stood back with a grin. 'Has he sent you flowers?'

Just then the bell at the back of the door pinged and in came a deliveryman with an armful of long-stemmed snow-white roses tied with a black satin ribbon. 'Delivery for Miss Jasmine Connolly.'

'I'll take that as a yes,' Miranda said once the deliveryman had left.

'They might be from Myles,' Jaz said. Not that Myles had ever bought flowers in the past. He thought they were a waste of money—ironic, given he had more money than most people ever dreamed of having.

'Read the card.'

Jaz gave her a brooding look as she unpinned the velum envelope from the arrangement. She took out the card and read the message: *I'm sorry. Jake.*

'They're from Jake, aren't they?' Miranda said.

'Yes, but—'

Miranda snatched the card out of Jaz's hand. 'Oh, how sweet! He's saying sorry. Gosh, only a man in love does that.'

'Or a man in the wrong.'

Miranda's smooth brow furrowed in a frown. 'What did he do?'

Jaz shifted her lips from side to side. Why was everything suddenly so darn complicated? 'Haven't you got heaps of dusty old paintings to restore?' she said.

Miranda chewed at her lower lip. 'Is it about that night? I know that's always been a sore point between you two. Is that what he was apologising for?'

Jaz let out a long breath. 'In a way.'

'But he didn't do anything. He didn't sleep with you. He's always flatly denied it. He would never have done anything like that. He thought you were just a kid.' Miranda swallowed. 'He didn't sleep with you… did he?'

'No, but someone else tried to,' Jaz said.

Miranda's eyes went wide in horror. 'What do you mean?'

'I stupidly flirted with this guy at the party after I left Jake's room,' Jaz explained. 'I only did it as a payback to Jake. I don't know how it happened but I suddenly found myself fighting off this drunken guy in one of the downstairs bathrooms. I thought he was going to rape me. I was so shocked and frightened but somehow I managed to get away.'

Miranda's hands were clasped against her mouth in shock. 'Oh, my God! That's awful! Why didn't you tell me?'

'I wanted to tell you,' Jaz said. 'Many times. But I just couldn't bring myself to do it. You were dealing with Mark's cancer and I didn't want to add to your misery. I felt so ashamed and dirty.'

'Oh, you poor darling,' Miranda said, flinging her arms around Jaz and hugging her. 'I wish I'd known so I could have done something to help you. I feel like I've let you down.'

'You didn't,' Jaz said. 'You've always been there for me.'

Miranda pulled back to look at her. 'So that's why you only ever dated vanilla men, isn't it?'

She scrunched up her nose. 'What do you mean?'

'You know exactly what I mean,' Miranda said. 'Bland men. Men you can control. You've never gone for the alpha type.'

Jaz gave a little lip shrug. 'Maybe…'

Miranda was still looking at her thoughtfully. 'So Jake was the first person you've ever told?'

Jaz nodded. 'Weird, huh?'

'Not so weird,' Miranda said. 'You respect him. You always have. That's why he annoys you so much. He sees the you no one else sees.'

Jaz fingered the velvet-soft petals of the roses once Miranda had left. Why had Jake sent her white roses? They were a symbol of purity, virtue and innocence. Was that how he saw her?

Miranda was full of romantic notions because she was madly in love herself. Of course she would like to think her brother was in love with her best friend. But Jake wasn't the type to fall in love. He was too much of a free agent.

Not that Jaz had any right to be thinking along those lines. She was on a mission to win back Myles. Myles was the man she planned to settle down with. Not a man like Jake who would pull against the re-

straints of commitment like a wild stallion on a leading rein.

Myles was safe and predictable.

Jake was danger personified.

But that didn't mean she couldn't flirt with danger
just a wee bit longer.

Jake had never been so fed up with work. He couldn't
get his mind to focus on the spreadsheets he was supposed to be analysing. All he wanted to do was go to
Jaz's boutique and see if she was still speaking to him.
She hadn't called or texted since they had parted last
night. The absence of communication would have delighted him a week ago. Now it was like a dragging
ache inside his chest. She was a stubborn little thing.
She would get on her high horse and not come down
even if it collapsed beneath her. That was why she was
still hung up on Myles. She wasn't in love with her
ex. It was her pride that had taken a hit. She hadn't
even told the guy the most devastating thing that had
happened to her.

Jake couldn't think about that night without feeling sick. He blamed himself. He had brought that on
her by being so insensitive. Why hadn't he gone and
checked on her later? He could at least have made an
effort to see she was okay. But no, he had partied on
as if nothing was wrong, leaving her open to exploita-
tion at the hands of some lowlife creep who had tried
to take advantage of her in the worst way imaginable.

Jake's phone buzzed with an incoming message.
He picked it up to read it:

Thanks for the roses. Jaz.

He smiled and texted back:

Free for dinner tonight?

Her message came back:

Busy.

He frowned, his gut tensing when he thought of whom she might be busy with. Was it Myles? Was she meeting her ex to try and convince him to come back to her? He waited a minute or two before texting back:

We still on for the w/end?

She texted back.

If u r free?

Jake grimaced as he thought of wandering around a wedding expo all weekend but he figured a man had to do what a man had to do.
He texted back.

I'm all yours.

CHAPTER EIGHT

JAZ WAS READY and waiting for Jake to come to her flat on Friday after work to pick her up. They had only communicated via text messages since yesterday. He had called a couple of times but she hadn't answered or returned the calls. Not that he had left a voice mail message. She hadn't realised how much she had been looking forward to hearing his voice until she checked her voice mail and found it annoyingly silent. Myles, on the other hand, had left several messages asking to meet with her to talk. They were each a variation on his earlier call where he'd told her Jake would never stick around long enough to cast a shadow.

The funny thing was Jake had cast a very long shadow. It was cast all over her life. She could barely recall a time when he hadn't been in it. Ever since she was eight years old she had been a part of his life and he of hers. Even once their charade was over he would still be a part of her life. There would be no avoiding him, not with Julius and Holly's wedding coming up, not to mention Miranda and Leandro's a few months after. Jaz was going to be a bridesmaid at both. There would be other family gatherings to navigate: Christmas, Easter and birthdays. His mother Elisabetta was turning sixty next month in late November and there was no way either Jake or Jaz could ever do a no-show without causing hurt and the sort of drama everyone could do without.

The doorbell sounded and her heart gave a little flutter. Jake was fifteen minutes early. Did that mean he was looking forward to the weekend? Looking forward to being with her? She opened the door to find Myles standing there with a sheepish look on his face.

'Myles…' Jaz faltered. 'Erm… I'm kind of busy right now.'

'I have to talk to you,' he said. 'It's important you hear it from me before you hear it from someone else.'

'Hear what?'

'I'm seeing someone else. It's…serious.'

Jaz blinked. 'How serious?'

'I know it seems sudden but I've known her for ages. We were childhood friends. Do you remember me telling you about Sally Coombes?'

'Yes, but—'

'I wasn't unfaithful to you, if that's what you're thinking,' Myles said. 'Not while we were officially together.'

Jaz hadn't been thinking it, which was kind of weird, as she knew she probably should have been. All she could think was that she had to get rid of Myles before Jake got here, as she didn't want Jake to end their 'engagement' before she attended the wedding expo. She couldn't bear to go to it alone.

Everyone would be taking photos and posting messages about her being so unlucky in love. Not a good look for a wedding designer. What would that do to her credibility? To her pride? People would find out eventually. She couldn't hope to keep Jake acting as her fiancé indefinitely. But one weekend—maybe another couple of weeks—was surely not too much to ask? 'But you've been calling and leaving all those messages,' she said. 'Why didn't you say something then?'

'I wanted to tell you in person,' Myles said. 'I'm sorry if I've hurt you, Jaz. But I've had my doubts about us for a while now. I guess that's why I instigated the break. It was only when I caught up with Sally I realised why I was baulking. As soon as we started talking, I realised she was the one. We dated when we were younger. She was my first girlfriend and I was her first boyfriend. It's like it's meant to be. I hope you can understand and find it in yourself to forgive me for messing you around.'

'I don't know what to say...' Jaz said. 'Congratulations?'

Myles looked a little pained. 'I want you to be happy. I really do. You're a great girl. I care about you. That's why I'm so concerned about your involvement with Jake Ravensdale. I don't want him to break your heart.'

Jaz stretched her lips into a rictus smile. 'I'm a big girl. I can handle Jake.'

Myles looked doubtful. 'Sally and I aren't making a formal announcement for a week or two. We thought it would be more appropriate to wait for a bit. I just wanted you to be one of the first to know.'

'Thanks for dropping by,' Jaz said. 'I appreciate it. Now, I'm sure you have heaps to do. I won't keep you. Say hi to Sally for me. Tell her if she wants a good deal on a wedding dress I'm the person she needs to see.'

'No hard feelings?' Myles said.

'No hard feelings,' Jaz said, and was surprised and more than a little shocked to find it was true.

Myles had not long disappeared around the corner when Jake's sports car prowled to the kerb. Jaz watched as he unfolded himself from behind the wheel with athletic grace. He was wearing dark-blue jeans and a round-neck white T-shirt with a charcoal-grey cashmere sweater over the top. His hair was still damp from a recent shower as she could see the deep grooves where either his fingers or a wide-toothed comb had been. His jaw was freshly shaven and as he came up to where she was standing on the doorstep she could smell the clean, sharp citrus tang of his aftershave.

Funny, but she hadn't even noticed what Myles had been wearing, the scent of his aftershave or even if he had been wearing any.

'Am I late?' Jake asked with the hint of a frown between his brows.

'No,' Jaz said. 'Perfect timing.'

He leaned down to press a light-as-air kiss to her mouth. 'That's for the neighbours.' Then he put his arms around her and pulled her close. 'And this one's for me.'

Jaz closed her eyes as his lips met hers in a drugging kiss that made her toes curl in her shoes. His tongue mated with hers in a sexy tangle that mimicked the driving need rushing through her body, and his, if the hard ridge of his erection was any indication.

Her hands went around his waist and her pelvis jammed against the temptation of his, her heart skipping all over the place as he made a deep, growly sound of male pleasure as she gave herself up to the kiss. His hands pressed against her bottom to pull her closer, his touch so intimate, so possessive, she could feel her body preparing itself for him. The ache of need pulsed between her legs, her thighs tingling with nerves activated by the anticipation of pleasure.

Only the fact they were on a busy public street was enough to break the spell as a car went past tooting its horn.

Jake released her with a teasing smile. 'Nice to know you've missed me.'

Jaz gave a dismissive shrug. 'You're a good kisser. But then, you've had plenty of practice.'

'Ah, but there are kisses and there are kisses. And yours, baby girl, are right up there.'

Don't fall for his charm. Don't fall for him, she thought as she followed him to the car.

The drive to Gloucester took just over two hours but the time passed easily with Jake's superb driving and easy conversation. He told her about Bruce Parnell, who was so impressed with Jake's choice of fiancée he had recommended several other big-name clients. 'It's the sort of windfall I'd been hanging out for,' he said. 'Word travels fast in the corporate sector.'

'What are you going to say to him when we're no longer a couple?'

He didn't answer for a moment and when he flashed her a quick smile she noticed it didn't quite make the distance to his eyes. 'I'll think of something.'

It was only as Jaz entered the hotel where the wedding expo was being held that she remembered she had only booked one room. It would look suspicious if she asked for another room or even a twin. She and Jake were supposed to be engaged. Everyone would automatically assume they would share a suite. People had already taken out their camera phones and taken snapshots as they came in. She would look a fool if she asked for separate rooms. What woman in her right mind would pass on the chance to spend the night with Jake Ravensdale? Herself included.

Hadn't she always wanted him? It had been there ever since she'd been old enough to understand sexual attraction. It had gone from a teenage crush to a full-blown adult attraction. It simmered in the air when they were together. How long could she ignore it or pretend it wasn't there? Hadn't she already betrayed herself by responding so enthusiastically to his kiss? Had her overlooking of the hotel reservation been her subconscious telling her what she didn't want to face?

As if Jake sensed her dilemma he leaned down close to her ear and whispered, 'I'll sleep on the sofa.'

Jaz was so distracted by the sensation of his warm breath tickling the sensitive skin around her ear she didn't hear the attendant call her to the counter. Jake put a gentle hand at her back and pressed her forward. She painted a smile on her face and said, 'I have a booking for Connolly.'

'Welcome, Miss Connolly,' the attendant said. 'We have your king deluxe suite all ready for you.'

King deluxe. At least there would be enough room in the bed to put a bank of pillows up as a barricade, Jaz thought as she took the swipe key.

The hotel was going to town on the wedding theme. The suite, on the thirteenth floor, was decked out like a honeymoon suite. French champagne was sitting chilled and frosted in a silver ice bucket with a white satin ribbon tied in a big bow around it. There were two crystal champagne flutes and a cheese-and-fruit plate with chocolate-dipped strawberries on the table. The bed was covered in fresh rose petals and there were heart-shaped chocolates placed on the pillows.

'Hmm,' Jake said, rubbing thoughtfully at his chin. 'No sofa.'

Something in Jaz's belly slipped like a Bentley on black ice. There were two gorgeous wing chairs in the bay window, and a plush velvet-covered love seat, but no sofa. 'Right; well, then, we'll have to use pillows,' she said.

'Pillows?'

'As a barricade.'

He gave a soft laugh. 'Your virtue is safe, sweetheart. I won't touch you.'

Jaz rolled her lips together. Shifted her weight from foot to foot. Knotted her hands in front of her body where they were clutching her tote bag straps. Of course she didn't want to sleep with him. He was her enemy. She didn't even like him... Well, maybe a little. More like a lot. Why the heck didn't he want to sleep with her? She hadn't cracked any mirrors lately. She might not be his usual type but she was female and breathing, wasn't she? Why was he being so fussy all of a sudden? He'd kissed her and she'd felt his re-action to her. He wanted her. She knew it as surely as she knew he was standing there. 'What?' she said. 'You don't find me attractive?'

He frowned. 'Listen, a kiss or two or three is fine, but doing the deed? Not going to happen. Not us.'

'Why not us?'

'You're not my type.'

Jaz bristled. 'I was your type when you kissed me outside my flat. Half of flipping Mayfair was wit-ness to it.'

His frown carved a little deeper. 'You're not seri-ous about taking this to that extreme, are you? This is supposed to be an act. When actors do a love scene they don't actually have sex, you know.'

She moved to the other side of the room to stand in front of the window, folding her arms across her body. 'Fine. I get the message. I'd better tape up all the mirrors. The last thing I need is another seven years of bad luck.'

Jake came up behind her, placed his hands on the tops of her shoulders and gently turned her to face him. He searched her face for endless seconds. 'What about Myles?'

Jaz pressed her lips together and lowered her gaze. 'He's engaged to someone else.'

'God, that was quick.'

'He's known her since childhood. I'm happy for him. I really am. It's just I can't bear the thought of everyone knowing I've been dumped,' she said. 'Especially this weekend.'

His fingers massaged her shoulders. 'What's so important about this weekend?'

Jaz rolled her eyes. 'Duh! Look around you, Jake. This is a winter wedding expo. One of my designs is in the fashion parade tomorrow. Next year I want ten. This is my chance to expand my business. To network and get my name out there.'

'But your personal life should have nothing to do with your talent as a designer.'

'Yes, but you told me on the way down how Mr Parnell looks at you differently now you're—' she put her fingers up in air-quotation marks '—"engaged". It's the same for me. I design wedding gowns for everyone else but I'm totally rubbish at relationships. What sort of advertising for my brand is that?'

He drew in a breath and dropped his hands from her shoulders, using one hand to push through his hair. 'So…what do you want me to do?'

'Just play along a little longer,' she said. 'I know it's probably killing you but please can you do this one thing for me? Just pretend to be my fiancé until… well, a few more days.'

His brow was furrowed as deep as a trench. 'How many days?'

Jaz blew out an exasperated breath. 'Is it such torture to be tied to me for a week or two? *Is* it? Am I so hideous you can't bear the thought of people thinking you've sunk so low as to do it with—?'

Jake's hands came back to hold her by the upper arms. 'Stop it. Stop berating yourself like that.'

She looked into his midnight-blue gaze, trying to control her spiralling emotions that were like a twisted knot inside her stomach. 'Do you know what it's like to be the one no one wants?' she said. 'No, of course you don't, because everyone wants you. Even my mother didn't want me. She made that perfectly clear by dumping me on my dad. Not that he wanted me either.'

'Your dad loves you,' Jake said.

Jaz gave him a jaded look. 'Then why did he let me move into the big house instead of staying with him at the gardener's cottage? He was relieved when your parents offered to take me in and pay for my education. He didn't know what to do with an eight-year-old kid. I was an inconvenience he couldn't wait to pass off.'

Jake's expression was clenched so tightly in a frown his eyebrows met over his eyes. 'Did he actually say that to you?'

'He didn't need to,' she said on an expelled breath. 'I'm the one no one wants. It should be tattooed across my forehead—*Unwanted*.'

Jake's hands tightened on her arms. 'That's not true. I want you. I've wanted you for years.'

Jaz moistened her tombstone-dry lips. 'You do? You're not just saying that to make me feel better?'

He brought her close against his body. 'Do you think I could fake that?'

She felt the thickened ridge of him swelling against her body. 'Oh…'

'I've always kept my distance because I don't want the same things you want,' he said. 'I'm not interested in marriage—it's not my gig at all. But a fling is something else. I don't even do those normally. My longest relationship was four days when I was nineteen.'

She pulled at her lower lip with her teeth. 'So you'd agree to a fling with me? Just for a week or two?'

He brushed his thumb over her savaged lip. 'As long as you're absolutely clear on the terms. I'm not going to be that guy waiting at the altar of a church aisle for the bride to show up. I'm the guy working his way through the bridesmaids.'

'I happen to be one of the bridesmaids,' Jaz said. 'At two weddings.'

He gave her a sinful smile as his mouth came down to hers. 'Perfect.'

It was a smouldering kiss with an erotic promise that made Jaz's body quake and shudder with want. Every time his tongue touched hers a dart of lust speared her between the legs. Her body wanted him with a desperation she had never felt with such intensity before. It moved through her flesh in tingling waves, making her aware of her erogenous zones as if it was the first time they had been activated. Her breasts were pressed up against his chest, her nipples already puckered from the friction of his hard body. Her hands fisted in his sweater, holding him in case he changed his mind and pulled back.

His mouth continued its passionate exploration of hers, his tongue making love with hers until she was making whimpering sounds of encouragement and delight.

His light stubble grazed her face as he changed position, his hands splaying through her hair as he held her in an achingly tender embrace. He lifted his mouth off hers, resting his forehead against hers. 'Let's not rush this,' he said.

'I thought you lived in the fast lane?' Jaz said, tracing his top lip with her fingertip.

His expression was gravely serious as he caught her hand and held it in the warmth of his against his chest. 'You deserve more than a quick tumble, Jaz. Way more.'

She looked into the sapphire density of his gaze and felt a fracture form in the carapace around her heart like a fissure running through a glacier. 'Are you worried about what happened in the past? Then don't be. I'm fine with sex. I've had it heaps of times.'

'But do you enjoy it?'

'Of course I do,' she said then added when he gave her a probing look, 'Well, mostly.'

He threaded his fingers through her hair like a parent finger-combing a child's hair. 'Are you sure you want to go through with this? It's fine if you've changed your mind. No man's ever died from having an erection, you know.'

Jaz couldn't help smiling. 'Perhaps not, but I think I might if you don't finish what you started.'

He brought his mouth back down to hers, giving her a lingering kiss that was hot, sexy, sweet and tender at the same time. His hands gently moved over her, skimming her breasts at first before coming back to explore them in exquisite detail. He peeled away her top but left her bra in place, allowing her time to get used to being naked with him. He kissed his way down the slope of her breast, drawing on her nipple through the lace of her bra, which added a whole new dimension of feeling. Then, when he had removed his sweater and shirt, he unhooked her bra and gently cradled her breasts in his hands.

Jaz wasn't generously endowed but the way he held her made her feel as if she could be on a high street billboard advertising lingerie. His thumbs brushed over each of her nipples and the sensitive area surrounding them. He lowered his mouth to her puckered flesh and subjected her to the most delicious assault on her senses. The nerves beneath her skin went into a frenzy of excitement, her blood thrumming with the escalation of her desire.

She ran her hands over his muscled chest, delighting in the lean, hard contours of his body. He hadn't followed the trend of being completely hairless. The masculine roughness of his light chest hair tickled her fingers and then her satin-smooth breasts as he drew her closer. It made her feel more feminine than she had ever felt before.

His hands settled on her hips, holding her against his erection, letting her get the feel of him; not rushing her, not pressuring her. Just holding her. But Jaz's body had urgent needs it wanted assuaged and she moved against him in a silent plea for satiation. She had rarely taken the initiative with a partner before. But with Jake she wanted to express her desire for him, to let him know her body ached to be joined to his.

Jaz went for the waistband of his jeans, unsnapping the metal stud and then sliding down his zip. He sucked in air but let her take control. She traced her fingertips over the tented fabric of his underwear, her belly doing a cartwheel when she thought of how potent he was, of how gorgeously turned on he was for her, yet controlling it to make her feel safe. She peeled back his underwear, stroking him skin to skin, flicking her gaze up to his to see how he was reacting to her touch. 'You like that?'

'This is getting a little one sided,' he said, pushing her hand away. 'Ladies come first according to my rules.'

'I think I like your rules,' Jaz said as he carried her to the bed as if she weighed no more than one of the feather pillows.

He placed her down amongst the scented rose petals and then, shucking off his jeans but leaving his underwear in place, he joined her. He helped her out of her trousers but left her knickers on. Not that they hid much from his view. Had that been another sub-conscious thing on her part, to wear her sexiest underwear?

He traced the seam of her body through the gossamer-sheer lace. 'Do you have any idea of how long I've wanted to do this?'

Jaz shivered as his touch triggered her most secret nerves into a leaping dance of expectation. 'Me too,' she said but it was more a gasp of sound as he brought his mouth to her and pressed a kiss to her abdomen just above the line of her knickers.

He slowly peeled the lace down to reveal her womanhood. For once she didn't feel that twinge of shame at being naked and exposed in front of a man. It was like he was worshiping her body, treating it with the utmost respect with every stroke and glide of his hands.

He put his mouth to her, separating her folds so he could pleasure the most sensitive part of all. She had never been entirely comfortable with being pleasured this way. Occasionally she had been tipsy enough to get through it. But this time she didn't need the buffer of alcohol. Nor did she need to pretend. The sensations took her by surprise, every nerve pulling tight before exploding in a cascade of sparks that rippled through her body in pulsating waves.

When it was over she let out a breath of pure bliss. 'Wow. I think that might've measured on the Richter scale.'

He stroked a hand down the flank of her thigh in a smooth-as-silk caress. 'Want to try for a ten?'

Jaz reached for him, surrounding his taut thickness with her fingers. 'I'd like to see you have some fun first, in the interests of being fair and all.'

He smiled a glinting smile. 'I can't argue with that.'

He reached across her to where he'd left his wallet when he'd removed his jeans and took out a condom, dealing with the business of applying it before he came back to her. He moved over her so she was settled in the cradle of his thighs, one of his legs hitched over her hip so she wasn't taking his whole weight. 'Not too heavy for you?' he said. 'Or would you like to go on top?'

Jaz welcomed the press of his body against hers, the sexy tangle of their limbs sending a frisson of anticipation through her female flesh. 'No, I like it like this. I don't like feeling like I'm riding a horse.'

He gave a deep chuckle. 'I wouldn't throw you off.'

No, but you'll cast me off when you're ready to move on. Jaz pushed the thought aside and ran her hands up his body from his pelvis to his chest and back again. This was for now. A fling she'd wanted since she was a teenager. This was her chance to have what she had always wanted from him: his sole attention, his searing touch, his mind-blowing caresses, and his gorgeously hot body. She knew and understood the rules. There were no promises being made. There was no hope of 'happy ever after'. It was a mutual lust fest to settle the ache of longing that had started so long ago and had never been sated. It was a way—she rationalised it—to rewrite that night seven years ago. This was what she had wanted from

Jake way back then—not to be pawed over by some drunk but to be treated with respect, to be pleasured as well as give it. This was the healing she needed to move on with her life, to reclaim her self-respect and her sexual confidence. 'I want you,' she said. 'I don't think I've ever wanted to have sex more than right now.'

He brushed a wayward strand of hair off her face, his dark gaze lustrous with desire. 'I'm pretty turned on myself.'

She stroked him again, watching as his breathing rate increased with every glide of her hand. 'So I can tell.'

He moved her hand so he could access her body, taking his time to caress her until she was swollen and wet. Her need for him was a consuming ache that intensified with every movement of his fingers. She writhed beneath him, restless to feel the ultimate fulfilment, wanting him to possess her so they both experienced the rapture of physical union.

Finally he entered her, but only a short distance, holding back, allowing her to get used to him. His tenderness made her feel strangely emotional. She couldn't imagine him being so tender with his other lovers. She knew it didn't necessarily mean he was falling in love with her. She wasn't that naïve. But it made her feel special all the same. Wasn't this how her teenaged self had imagined it would be? Jake being so tender and thoughtful as he made beautiful, magical love to her?

He thrust a little deeper, his low, deep groan of

pleasure making her skin come up in a spray of goose bumps. He began to move, setting a slow rhythm that sent her senses reeling with delight. Each movement of his body within hers caused a delicious friction that triggered all her nerve endings, making them tingle with feeling. She lifted her hips to meet each downward thrust, aching for the release that was just out of reach. Her body was searching for it, every muscle contracting, straining, swelling and quivering with the need to fly free.

He slipped his hand down between their rocking bodies, giving her that little bit of extra coaxing that sent her flying into blessed oblivion. Her body shook with the power of it as each ripple turned into an earthquake. It was like her body had split into thousands of tiny pieces, each one spinning off into the stratosphere. She lost all sense of thought. Her mind had switched off and allowed her body free rein.

He didn't take his own pleasure until hers was over. She held him to her as his whole body tensed before he finally let go, but he did so without any increase in pace, without sound. Had he done that for her sake? Held back? Restrained his response so she hadn't felt overwhelmed or threatened? He hadn't rushed to the end. He hadn't breathed heavily or gripped her too hard, as if he had forgotten she was there.

He didn't roll away but continued to hold her as if he was reluctant to break the intimate union of their bodies.

Or was she deluding herself?

Had he been disappointed? Had she not measured

up to his other lovers? She was hardly in the same league. She might have had multiple partners but still nowhere near the number he'd had. Compared to him, she was practically a novice.

One of his hands glided up and down the length of her forearm in a soft caress that made her skin tingle as if champagne bubbles were moving through her blood. 'You were amazing,' he said.

Jaz couldn't ignore the doubts that were winding their way through her mind like a rampant vine. Hadn't she been exciting enough for him? Hadn't her body delighted his the way his had delighted hers? Was that why his response had been so toned down? Maybe he hadn't toned it down. Maybe she hadn't quite 'done it' for him. The chemistry he had talked about hadn't delivered on its promise.

It was *her* fault. Of course it was. Wasn't that why she had been engaged three times and summarily dumped?

She was rubbish at sex.

Jaz eased out of his embrace, reached for one of the hotel bathrobes and slipped it on, tying the waist ties securely. 'You don't have to lie to me, Jake,' she said. 'I know I'm not crash-hot in bed. There's no point pretending I am.'

He frowned as if she was speaking Swahili instead of English. 'Why on earth do you think that?'

She folded her arms, shooting him a flinty look. 'It's probably my fault for talking you into it. If you didn't want to do it then you should've said.'

He swung his legs over the edge of the bed and

came over to stand in front of her. He was still completely naked while Jaz was wrapped as tightly as an Egyptian mummy. He put one of his hands on her shoulder and used the other to edge up her chin so her eyes meshed with his. 'You didn't talk me into anything, Jaz,' he said. 'I just didn't want you to feel uncomfortable. Not our first time together.'

She rolled her lips together before releasing a little puff of air. 'Oh…'

He gently brushed back her hair, his eyes searching hers for a moment or two. 'Was that night at the party your first experience of kissing and touching?' he finally asked.

Jaz chewed one corner of her mouth. 'I wanted it to be you. That was my stupid teenage fantasy—that you would be the first person to make love to me.'

He gave her a pained look, his eyes dark and sombre with regret. 'I'm sorry.'

She twisted her lips in self-deprecating manner. 'I guess that's why sex has always been a bit awkward for me. I never felt comfortable unless I was in a committed relationship. But even then I often felt I wasn't up to the mark.'

'You have no need to feel inadequate,' he said. 'No need at all.'

She rested her hands on the wall of his naked chest, her lower body gravitating towards his arousal as if of its own volition. 'You said "our first time together". Does that mean there's going to be a second or a third?'

He put a hand in the small of her back and drew

her flush against him, his eyes kindling with sensual promise. 'Start counting,' he said and lowered his mouth to hers.

CHAPTER NINE

JAKE HAD NEVER made love with such care and concern for a partner. Not that he'd been unduly rough or selfish with any of his past lovers, but being with Jaz made him realise what he had been missing in his other encounters. The level of intimacy was different, more focused, more concentrated. The slow burn of desire intensified and prolonged the pleasure. Each stroke of her soft hands made his blood pound until he could feel it in every cell of his body. Her lips flowered open beneath his, her tongue tangling with his in an erotic duel that sent a current of electricity through his pelvis. He held her to his hardness, delighting in the feel of her lithe body moulded against his.

He slipped a hand through the V-neck of her bathrobe to cup her small but perfect breasts; her skin was as smooth as satin, her nipples pert with arousal. He lowered his mouth to her right breast, teasing her areola with his tongue, skating over her tightly budded nipple, before drawing it into his mouth as she gave a breathless moan of approval. He moved to her left breast, taking his time to explore and caress it with the same attention to detail.

He worked his way up from her breasts to linger over the delicate framework of her collarbone, dipping his tongue into the shallow dish below her neck. Her skin was perfumed with grace notes of honeysuckle and lilac with a base note of vanilla. He spread his fingers through her hair, cradling her head as he kissed her deeply. Her soft little sounds of longing made his heart race and his blood run at fever pitch. Her tongue danced with his in flicks, darts and sweeps that made him draw her even closer to his body.

He eased her bathrobe off her shoulders, letting it fall in a puddle at her feet. He slid his hands down her body to grasp her by the hips, letting her feel the fullness of his erection against her mound. She moved against him, silently urging him on. He left her only long enough to get another condom, quickly applying it before he led her back to the bed. She held her arms out to him as he joined her on the mattress, wrapping them around his neck as he brought his mouth back down to hers.

When he entered her tight, wet heat he felt every ripple of her body welcoming him, massaging him, thrilling him. He began to move in slow thrusts, each one going deeper than the first, letting her catch his rhythm. She whimpered against his mouth, soft little cries of need that made the hairs on his scalp tingle. He continued to rock against her, with her, each movement of their bodies building to a crescendo. He could feel the build-up of tension in her body, the way she strained, gasped and urged him on by gripping his shoulders, as if anchoring herself.

He reached down to touch her intimately, stroking her slick wetness, feeling her swell and bud under his touch, the musky scent of her arousal intermingled with his, intoxicating his senses like the shot of an illicit drug. Her orgasm was so powerful he could feel it contracting against his length, triggering his own release until he was flying as high and free as she.

This time he didn't hold back. He couldn't. He gave a deep groan and pumped and spilled. The rush of pleasure swept through him, spinning him away from everything but what was happening in his body.

Jake had never been big on pillow talk or cuddling in the afterglow. He'd never been good at closeness and contact once the deed had been done.

But with Jaz it was different.

He felt different.

He wasn't sure why. Maybe it was because she wasn't just another girl he had picked up hardly long enough to catch her name. She was someone he knew. Had known for years. She was someone who mattered to him. She was a part of his life—always had been and probably always would be.

He felt protective of her, especially knowing his role in what had happened to her. He wanted her to feel safe and respected. To be an equal partner in sex, not a vessel to be used and cast aside.

But isn't that what you usually do? Use them and lose them?

The thought came from the back of his conscience like a lone heckler pushing through a crowd.

He used women, yes, but they used him back. They knew the rules and played by them. If he thought a woman wasn't going to stick to the programme, he wouldn't allow things to progress past a drink and a flirty chat. He was a dab hand at picking the picket-fence-and-puppies type. But the women that pursued him were mostly out for a good time, not a long time, which suited him perfectly.

He didn't want the responsibility of a relationship. He found the notion of a committed relationship suffocating. Having to answer to someone, having to take care of their emotional needs, being blamed when things didn't work out, seemed to him to nothing short of torture. He didn't need that sort of drama. He had seen enough during his childhood. Watching his parents fight and tear each other down only to make up as if nothing was wrong had deeply unsettled him. He never knew what was real, what was dependable and what wasn't. Life with his parents had been so unpredictable and tempestuous he had decided the only way he could tolerate a connection with someone would be to keep it focused solely on the physical. Emotion had no place in his flings with women.

But for some reason it felt right to hold Jaz in his arms: to idly stroke his fingers up and down her silky skin, her slender back, her neat bottom, her slim thighs. He liked the feel of her lying up against him, her legs still entangled with his. He liked the soft waft of her breath tickling the skin against his neck where her head was buried against him.

He liked the thought that she trusted him enough to share her body with him without fear or shame.

Or maybe it was a pathetic attempt on his part to right the wrongs of the past. To absolve himself from the yoke of guilt about what had happened to her.

As if that's ever going to happen.

Jaz lifted her head out from against his neck and shoulder to look at him. 'Thank you,' she said softly.

Jake tucked a strand of her hair back behind her ear. 'For what? Giving you a ten on the Richter scale?'

'It was a twelve,' she said with a crooked little smile, then added, 'But no. For being so…considerate.'

He picked up one of her hands and kissed the ends of her fingers. 'I'm not sure anyone I know would ever describe me as considerate.'

'You like people to think you're selfish and shallow but deep down I know you're not. You're actually really sensitive. The rest is all an act. A ruse. A defence mechanism.'

He released her hand as he moved away to get off the bed. He shrugged on the other fluffy bathrobe, watching as her teeth started pulling at her lower lip as if she sensed what was coming. *Good*, he thought. *Because I'm not going to pull any punches.* There was no way he was going to play at happy families. No way. Sure, the sex was good. Better than good, when it came to that. But that was all it was: sex. If she was starting to envisage him dressed in a tux standing at the end of the aisle then she had better think again.

Freaking hell. Next she would be talking about kids and kindergarten bookings.

'Here's what a selfish bastard I am, Jasmine,' he said. 'If you don't stop doing that doe-eyed thing to me, I'm going to head back to London and leave you to face that bunch of wedding-obsessed wackos downstairs all on your own.'

She sat up and pulled the sheet up, hugging her knees close to her chest, her misty eyes entreating. 'Please don't leave... This weekend is important to me. I have everything riding on it. I don't want anything to go wrong.'

He wanted to leave. Bolting when things got serious was his way of dealing with things. But there was young Emma Madden to consider. If Jaz took it upon herself to let that particular cat out of the bag as payback if he left then he could say goodbye to his business deal. Bruce Parnell would withdraw from the contract for sure. That sort of mud had a habit of sticking and making a hell of a mess while it did. Jake's reputation would be shot. He wouldn't be seen in the public eye as just a fun-loving playboy. He would be seen as a lecherous cradle snatcher with all its ghastly connotations.

'I signed up for two weeks.' He held up two fingers for emphasis. 'That's all. After that, we go our separate ways. Those are the rules.'

'Fine,' she said. 'Two weeks is all I want from you.'

He sent her a narrow look. 'Is it?'

Her expression was cool and composed but he noticed how her teeth kept pulling at her lip. 'I'm not falling in love with you, Jake. I was merely making an observation about your character. Your prickliness proves my point. You don't like people seeing your softer, more sensitive side.'

What softer side? She had romantic goggles on. A couple of good orgasms and she was seeing him as some sort of white knight. 'Don't confuse good physical chemistry with anything else, okay? I'm not interested in anything else. And nor should you be until you've sorted out why you keep attracting the sort of guys who won't stick around long enough to put a ring on your finger and keep it there.'

She gave him a pert look. 'Maybe you could tell me what I'm doing wrong, since you're the big relationships expert.'

Jake watched as she took her sweet ass time getting off the bed to slip on a bathrobe. She didn't bother doing up the waist ties but left the sides hanging open, leaving her beautiful body partially on show. For some reason it was more titillating than if she had been standing there stark naked. His blood headed south until he was painfully erect.

Everything about her turned him on. The way she moved like a sleek and graceful cat. The way she tossed her hair back behind her shoulders like some haughty aristocrat. The way she looked at him with artic eyes while her body radiated such sensual heat. It was good to see her act more confident sexually but he couldn't help feeling she was driving home a point. But he was beyond fighting her over it. He wanted her and he only had two weeks to make the most of it. 'What time do you have to be downstairs?' he asked.

She pushed back her left sleeve to check the watch on her slender wrist. It was one his parents had bought for her for her twenty-first birthday. Another reminder of how entwined with his life she was and always would be. 'An hour,' she said. 'I have to check my dress is properly steamed and pressed for the fashion parade tomorrow.'

He held out his hand. 'Have a shower with me.'

She looked at his hand. Returned her gaze to his with a little flicker of defiance in hers. 'Won't you be quicker on your own?'

'Yeah, but it won't be half as much fun.'

CHAPTER TEN

JAZ'S BODY WAS still tingling when she went downstairs with Jake for the welcome-to-the-expo drinks party. He kept giving her smouldering glances as they mingled amongst the other designers and expo staff. She wondered if people knew what they had been up to in the shower only minutes earlier. She had hardly had time to get her hair dry and put on some make-up after he had pleasured every inch of her body.

Of course people knew. He was Jake Ravensdale. What he didn't know about sex wasn't worth knowing. Wasn't her thrumming body proof of that? He only had to look at her with that dark-as-midnight gaze and her inner core would leap in excitement. She saw the effect he had on every woman in the room. Hers wasn't the only pulse racing, the only breath catching in her throat, the only mind conjuring up what she would like to do with him when she got him alone.

Congratulations came thick and fast from the people Jaz knew, as well as many she didn't. It made her feel a little less conflicted about continuing the charade. It was only for two weeks. Two weeks to enjoy the sensual magnificence of a man she had hated for years.

Just shows how easy it is to separate emotion from sex.

One of the models came over with a glass of champagne in one hand. 'Hi, Jake, remember me? We met at a company party last year.'

Jake gave one of his charming smiles. 'Sure I do. How are you?'

The young woman gave a little pout. 'I was fine until I heard you got yourself engaged. No one saw *that* coming.'

Jaz was getting a little tired of being ignored like she was a piece of furniture. 'Hi,' she said holding out her hand to the model. 'I'm Jake's fiancée, Jasmine Connolly. And you are…?'

'Saskiaa with two "a"s,' the girl said with a smile that lasted only as long as her handshake. 'When's the big day?'

'December,' Jaz said. 'Boxing Day, actually.' Why shouldn't she make Jake squirm a bit while she had the chance? 'We're hoping for a white wedding in every sense of the word.'

Jake waited until the model had moved on before he leaned down close to Jaz's ear. 'Boxing Day?'

Jaz looked up at him with a winsome smile. 'I quite fancy the idea of a Christmas wedding. The family will already be gathered so it would be awfully convenient for everyone, don't you think?'

He smiled but it got only as far as his mouth, and that was probably only for the benefit of others who were looking at them. 'Don't overplay it,' he said in an undertone only she could hear.

Jaz kept her smile in place. 'You didn't remember that girl, did you?'

A frown pulled at his brow. 'Why's that an issue for you?'

'It's not,' she said. 'I don't expect you even ask their name before you sleep with them.'

'I ask their permission, which is far more important in my opinion.'

Jaz held his look for as long as she dared. 'I know it comes as naturally to you as breathing, but I would greatly appreciate it if you wouldn't flirt with any of the women, in particular the models. Half of them look as if they should still be in school.'

His mouth curved upward in a sardonic smile. 'My parents would be enormously proud of you. You're doing a perfect jealous fiancée impersonation.'

She snatched a glass of champagne off a passing waiter for something to do with her hands. 'Don't screw this up for me, Jake,' she said through tight lips in case anyone nearby could lip-read. 'I need to secure the booking for next year's expo. Once that's in the bag, you can go back to your "single and loving it" life.'

He trailed a lazy fingertip down her arm from the top of her bare shoulder to her wrist. 'Just wait until I get you alone.'

Jaz shivered as his eyes challenged hers in a sexy duel. His touch was like a match to her tinderbox senses. Every nerve was screaming for more. 'Now who's overplaying it?'

He slipped a hand to the nape of her neck and drew her closer, bending down to press a lingering kiss on her lips. Even though Jaz's eyes were closed in bliss she could see the bright flashes of cameras going off around them. After a moment he eased back and winked at her devilishly. 'Did I tell you how gorgeous you look tonight?'

Jaz knew he was probably only saying it for the benefit of others but a part of her wanted to believe it was true. She placed a hand on the lapel of his suit jacket, smoothing away an imaginary fleck of lint. 'You've scrubbed up pretty well yourself,' she said. 'Even without a tie.'

He screwed up his face. 'I hate the things. They always feel like they're choking me.'

Typical Jake. Hating anything that confined or restrained him. 'I suppose that's why you got all those detentions for breaking the uniform code at that posh school you went to?'

He grinned. 'I still hold the record for the most detentions in one term. Apparently I'm considered a bit of a legend.'

Jaz shook her head at him, following it up with a roll of her eyes. 'Come on.' She looped her arm through his. 'I want to have a look at the displays.'

Oh, joy, Jake thought as Jaz led him to where the wedding finery was displayed in one of the staterooms. The sight of all those meringue-like wedding gowns and voluminous veils was enough to make him break out in hives. Or maybe it was the flowers. There were arrangements of every size and shape: centrepieces, towers of flowers, bouquets, bunches and buttonholes. There were displays of food, wine and French champagne, a honeymoon destination stand and a bespoke jeweller in situ. There were a few men there partnering their fiancées or girlfriends but they were pretty thin on the ground. Jake understood Jaz wanted to secure her signing for next year but he couldn't help feeling she had insisted he accompany her as a punishment.

But that was one of the things he secretly admired in her. She was feisty and stood her ground with him. She was the only woman he knew who didn't simper at him or adapt to suit him. He felt the electric buzz of her will tussling with his every time she locked gazes with him. For years they had done their little stand-off thing. What would they do once they parted company? Would they go back to their old ways or find a new way of relating? With two family weddings coming up, it would be tasteless to be at loggerheads. There was enough of that going around with his parents' carry-on. The dignified thing would be to be mature and civil about it and be friends.

But would he ever be able to look at her as a friend without thinking of how she came apart in his arms? How it felt when he held her close? How her mouth tasted of heat, passion and sweetness mixed in a combustible cocktail that made his senses whirl out of control? Would he ever be able to stand beside her and not want to pull her into his arms?

He'd slept with a lot of women but none of them had had that effect on him. He barely gave his lovers another thought once he moved on to the next. Was it because Jaz was someone who had always been on the periphery of his life? Sometimes even at the centre, at the very heart, of his family?

Had that familiarity added something to their lovemaking?

It wasn't just physical sex with her. There were feelings there…feelings he couldn't describe. He cared about her. But then everyone in his family cared about her.

Every time he looked at her he felt the stirring in his groin. He couldn't look at her mouth without thinking of how it felt fused to his own. How her tongue felt as it played with his, how her body felt as she pushed herself, as if she wanted to crawl into his skin and never leave. Even now with her arm looped through his he could feel the brush of her beautiful body against his side. He couldn't wait to get her back to their suite and get her naked.

They walked past a photographer's stand but then Jaz suddenly swivelled and, pulling Jake by the hand, led him back to where the photographer had set up a romantic set with love-hearts, red roses and a velvet-covered sofa in the shape of a pair of lips. 'Can you take our picture?' she asked the photographer.

'Sure,' the photographer said. 'Just sit together on the sofa there for a sec while I frame the shot.'

Jake looked down at Jaz sitting snuggled up by his side as if butter wouldn't melt in her hot little mouth.

'I'm keeping a score,' he said in an undertone. 'Just thought I'd put that out there.'

She gave him a sly smile. 'So am I.'

Jaz thought she might have overdone it with the champagne, or maybe it was being with Jake all evening. Being with him made her tipsy, giddy with excitement. He never left her side; his arm was either around her waist or he held hands with her as she worked the room. It was a torturously slow form of foreplay. Every look, every touch, every brush of his body against hers was a prelude to what was to come. She could see the intention in his dark-blue gaze. It was blatantly, spine-tinglingly sexual. It made every inch of her flesh shiver behind the shield of her clothes, every cell of her body contracting in feverish anticipation.

'Time for bed?' Jake said, his fingers warm and firm around hers.

Jaz felt something in her belly slip sideways. When he touched her like that she couldn't stop thinking of where else he was going to touch her when he got her alone. Her entire body tingled in anticipation. Even the hairs on the nape of her neck shivered at the roots. 'I wonder if we'll win the "most loved-up couple" photo competition?' she said. 'Or the all-expenses-paid wedding and honeymoon package? That would be awesome.'

His eyes sent her a teasing warning. 'Don't push it, baby girl.'

She laughed as he led her to the lift. 'I can't remember a time when I've enjoyed myself more. You should have seen your face when that florist threw you that bouquet. You looked like you'd caught a det-onated bomb.'

The lift doors sprang open and Jake pulled her in, barely waiting long enough for the doors to close to bring his mouth down to hers in a scorching kiss. Jaz linked her arms around his neck, pressing as close to him as she could to feel the hardened length of him against her tingling pelvis. He put a hand on one of her thighs and hooked it over his hip, bringing her into closer contact with the heat and potency of him. She could see out of the corner of her eye their reflection in the mirrored walls. It was shockingly arousing to see the way their bodies strained to be together, the flush on both of their faces as desire rode hard and fast in their blood.

Jake put his hand on the stop button and the lift came to a halt. Jaz looked at the erotic intent in his eyes and a wave of lust coursed through her so force-fully she thought she would come on the spot. He nudged her knickers to one side while she unzipped his trousers with fingers that shook with excitement. How he got a condom on so quickly was a testament to how adept he was at sex, she thought. He entered her with a slick, deep thrust that made her head bang against the wall of the elevator. He checked himself at her gasp, asking, 'Are you okay?'

Jaz was almost beyond speech, her breath com-ing out in fractured, pleading bursts. 'Yes…oh, yes… Don't stop. *Please* don't stop.'

He started moving again, each thrust making her wild with need. He put one of his hands on the wall beside her head to anchor himself as he drove into her with a frantic urgency that made the blood spin, sizzle and sing in her veins. He brought his hand down between their joined bodies, his fingers expertly caressing her until her senses exploded. She clung to him as the storm broke in her, through her, over her.

He followed close behind, three or four hard pumps; a couple of deep, primal grunts and it was over.

Jaz wriggled her knickers back in place and smoothed her dress down as the lift continued up to their floor. 'I reckon you must hold some sort of record for getting a condom on,' she said into the silence. 'It's like a sleight of hand thing. Amazing.'

He gave her a glinting look as he zipped his trousers. 'Always pays to be prepared.'

A shiver danced its way down her spine as he escorted her out of the lift to their suite, his hand resting in the small of her back. Once they were inside their suite he closed the door and pulled her to him until she was in the circle of his arms. 'Happy with how tonight went?' he said.

Was he talking about her business or their lovemaking? 'I've got a meeting with the expo organisers next week,' Jaz said. 'It's an exciting opportunity. I'm hoping it will lead to bigger events, maybe even internationally.'

He smoothed a wisp of her hair back off her face. 'Why did you choose to design wedding gear? Why not evening, or fashion in general?'

Jaz slipped out of his hold, feeling a lecture coming on. Of course he would think weddings were a waste of time and money. He was a playboy. A wedding was the last thing on earth that would interest him. But to her they signified everything she had dreamed about as a child. Her parents hadn't married. They hadn't even made a formal commitment to each other. They had just hooked up one night and look how that had turned out. She had been passed between them like a parcel no one wanted until finally her mother had dumped her with her dad without even saying goodbye or 'see you later'.

'Jaz?'

She turned to look at him, her mouth set. 'Do you know what it's like to grow up without a sense of family? To have to *borrow* someone else's family in order to feel normal?'

Jake frowned. 'I'm not sure what that has to do with your choice of career but—'

'It has *everything* to do with it,' Jaz said. 'For as long as I can remember, I wanted to be normal. To have normal parents, not one who's off her face most of the time and the other who hadn't wanted a kid in the first place. I didn't have anything from either of my parents that made me feel a part of a unit. I was a mistake, an accident, an inconvenience.' She folded her arms and continued. 'But when a couple marries, it's different. It's a public declaration of love and commitment and mostly—not always, but mostly—one expressing a desire to have children.'

Jaz looked at him as the silence swelled. Had she said too much? Revealed too much? What did it matter? She was tired of him criticising her choices. 'A wedding dress is something most brides keep for the rest of their lives,' she said. 'It can be passed down from a mother to a daughter. General fashion isn't the same. It's seasonal, transient. Some pieces might be passed on but they don't have the emotional resonance a wedding dress has. That's why I design wedding gowns. Every woman deserves to be a princess for a day. I like being able to make that wish come true.' *Even if I can't make it come true for myself.*

Jake gave a slow nod. 'Sounds reasonable.'

'But you think I'm crazy.'

'I didn't say that.'

Jaz went to the drinks fridge and poured a glass of mineral water, taking a sip before she turned to face him again. He was looking at her with a contemplative look on his face, his brows drawn together, his mouth set in a serious line, his gaze centred on hers. 'I'm sorry if tonight's been absolute torture for you but this weekend's really important to me.'

His mouth tilted in a wry smile. 'You're not one bit sorry. You've enjoyed every minute, watching me squirm down there.'

Jaz smiled back. 'It was rather fun, I have to admit. I can't wait to see what press photos show up. I wonder if they got the one of you with the bouquet. Or maybe I should text it or post it online?'

He closed the distance between them and pulled her down to the bed in a tangle of limbs. 'Cheeky minx,' he said, eyes twinkling with amusement.

Jaz stroked the sexy stubble on his face, her belly fluttering with excitement as his hard body pressed against hers. His hooded gaze went to her mouth, his thumb coming up to brush over her lower lip until it tingled, as if teased by electrodes. 'What are you thinking?'

'You mean you can't tell?' he said with a wicked sparkle in his eyes.

She snatched in a breath as his body moved against her, triggering a tide of want that flooded her body, pooling hotly in her core. 'When you hook up with someone, how many times do you have sex with them in one night?'

A frown creased his forehead. 'Why do you want to know?'

Jaz traced the trench of his frown with her finger. 'Just wondering.'

He caught her hand and pinned it on the bed beside her head, searching her gaze for a pulsing moment. 'Wondering what?'

'If you've done it more with me than with anyone else.'

'And if I have?'

She looked at his mouth. 'Is it...different...? With me, I mean?'

He nudged up her chin with a blunt fingertip, locking his gaze with hers. 'Different in what way?'

Jaz wasn't sure why she was fishing so hard for compliments. He had made it clear how long their fling was going to last. Just because he had made love to her several times tonight didn't mean anything other than he had a high sex drive. He was, after all, a man in his sexual prime. But their love-making was so different from anything she had experienced with other partners. It was more exciting, more satisfying, more addictive, which was a problem because she couldn't afford to get too used to having him. 'I don't know...more intense?'

He slid his hand along the side of her face to splay his fingers through her hair. It was an achingly tender hold that made Jaz's heart squeeze as if someone had crushed it in a vice. Could it be possible he was coming to care for her? *Really* care for her? Was that why their intimacy was so satisfying? Did their physical connection reflect a much deeper one that had been simmering in the background for years?

But she didn't love him.

Not the slavish way she had as a teenager. She was an adult now. Her feelings for him were mature and sensible. She knew his faults and limitations. She didn't whitewash his personality to make him out to be anything he was not. She was too sensible to hanker after a future with him because he wasn't the future type. He was the 'for now' type.

Falling in love with Jake Ravensdale once had been bad enough. To do it twice would be emotional suicide.

'It is different,' Jake said. 'But that doesn't mean I want it to continue longer than we agreed.'

'I'm not asking for an extension,' Jaz said. 'I can't afford to waste my time having a long-term fling with someone who doesn't want the same things I want. I want to get on with my life and find my soul mate. I want to start a family before I'm thirty.'

His frown hadn't quite gone away but now it was deeper than ever. 'You shouldn't rush into your next relationship. Take your time getting to know them. And what's the big rush on having kids? You're only twenty-three. You've got heaps of time.'

'I don't want to miss out on having kids,' Jaz said. 'I know so many women who've left it too late or circumstances have worked against them. I can't imagine not having a family. It's what I've wanted since I was a little girl.'

He moved away from her and got off the bed, scraping a hand through his hair before dropping it back by his side.

Jaz chewed at her lower lip. 'Did I just kill the mood?'

He turned around with a smile that didn't involve his eyes. 'It's been a long day. I'm going to have a shower and hit the sack. Don't wait up.'

When Jake came out of the bathroom after his shower half an hour later, Jaz wasn't in the bed. In fact, she wasn't in the suite. He frowned as he searched the room, even going so far as to check under the bed. Where the hell was she? He glanced at her bag on the luggage rack. She obviously hadn't checked out of the hotel as her things were still here. Although, come to think of it, he wouldn't put it past her to flounce off, leaving him to pack her things. What was she up to? Their conversation earlier had cut a little close to the bone...for him, that was. Why did she have to carry on about marriage and kids all the time? She was a baby herself. Most twenty-three-year-olds were still out partying and having a good time.

But no, Jaz wanted the white picket fence and a bunch of wailing brats. What would happen to her stellar career as a wedding designer then? She would be doing more juggling than a circus act.

And as to finding her soul mate… Did she really believe such a thing existed? There was no such thing as a perfect partner. She was deluding herself with romantic notions of what her life could be like.

Well, he had news for her. It would be just like everyone else's life—boring and predictable.

Jake called her number but it went straight through to voice mail. He paced about the suite, feeling more and more agitated. The weird thing was he spent hours of his life in hotel rooms, mostly alone. He rarely spent the whole night with anyone. It was less complicated when it came to the 'morning after the night before' routine.

But every time he looked at that bed he thought of how it had felt with Jaz, her arms and legs wrapped around him and her hot little mouth clamped to his. He couldn't stop thinking about the lift either. He probably wouldn't be able to get into one ever again without thinking of taking Jaz up against that mirrored wall. His blood pounded at the memory of it. He had been close to doing it without a condom. He still didn't know how he'd got it on in time. He had been as worked up as a teenager on his first 'sure thing' date.

What was it about Jaz that made him so intensely attracted to her? It wasn't like this with his other flings. Once or twice was usually enough before he was ready for more excitement. But with Jaz he was mad with lust. Crazy with it. Buzzing with it. Making love with her eased it for a heartbeat before he was aching for her again. It had to blow out eventually. It *had* to. He wasn't putting down tent pegs just because the sex was good. Just as well they'd agreed on an end date. Two weeks was pushing it. He didn't take that long for holidays because he always got bored. There was no way this was going to continue indefinitely.

No. Freaking. Way.

Jake threw on some clothes and finger-combed his damp hair on his way to the lift. She had to be in the hotel somewhere. He jabbed at the call button. Why the hell was it so slow? Was some other couple holed up in there, doing it? His gut tightened. Surely Jaz wouldn't pick up someone and…? No. He slammed his foot down on the thought like someone stomping on a noxious spider.

The lift was empty.

So was his stomach as he searched the bar for the glimpse of that gorgeous honey-brown head. He went to the restaurant, and then looked through the foyer, but there was no sign of her anywhere. He hadn't re-alised until then what had fuelled his heart-stopping panic. It hit him like a felling blow right in the middle of his chest. He couldn't draw breath for a moment. His throat closed. He could feel his thudding pulse right down to his fingertips.

He had dismissed her. Rejected her. What if she had been upset and gone downstairs to God knew what? What if some unscrupulous guy had intercepted her? Shoved her into a back room and done the un-thinkable?

The stateroom where the displays were set up was closed with a burly security guard posted outside.

The security guard gave Jake the eye as he tried the doorknob. 'Sorry, buddy,' the guard said with a smirk. 'You'll have to wait till morning to try a dress on.'

Jake wanted to punch him.

He retraced his steps; his growing dread mak-ing his skin break out in a clammy sweat until his shirt was sticking to his back like cling-film. Where could she have gone? He couldn't get the image of her trapped in some room—*some locked bathroom*—with an opportunist creep mauling her. He would never be able to live with himself if she got hurt under his watch. She was with him. He was supposed to be her partner. Her 'fiancé'. What sort of fiancé would let her wander off alone to be taken advantage of by some stranger? She was gullible with men. Look at the way she'd got engaged three times. He hadn't liked one of them. They were nice enough men but not one of them was worthy of her.

Jake strode past the restrooms. Could she be in there? Locked inside one of the cubicles with some-one? He did a quick whip round and checked that no one was watching before he pushed open the outer door. 'Jaz? Are you in there?' There was no answer so he went in through to where the cubicles were.

A middle-aged woman turned from the basins with

her eyes blazing in indignation. 'This is the ladies' room!'

'I—I know,' Jake said, quickly back-pedalling with the woman following him like an army sergeant. 'I'm looking for my...er...fiancée.'

The woman blasted him with a look that was as icy as the wind off the North Sea in winter. 'I've met men like you before. Lurking around female toilets to get your sick thrills. I've a good mind to call security.'

Jake looked at her in open-mouthed shock, which didn't seem to help his cause one little bit, because it looked like he'd been sprung doing exactly what the woman accused him of. 'No, no, no,' he said, trying to placate her as she took out her phone. If she took a snapshot of him in the female restrooms and it went viral he could forget about his reputation and his career. Both would be totally screwed. 'My fiancée is this high...' He put his hand up to demonstrate. 'Really pretty with light-brown hair and grey-blue eyes and—'

'Is there a problem?' The security guard from outside the display room spoke from behind Jake.

Jake rolled his eyes. This was turning into such a freaking farce. And meanwhile Jaz was still missing. He turned to face the guard. 'I'm looking for my fiancée. She's not answering her phone. I thought she might be in the ladies' room.'

The security guard's mouth curled up on one side. 'You seem to have a thing for what belongs to the ladies, don't you, buddy?'

Jake clenched his hands in case he was tempted

to use them to knock that sneer off the guard's face. *Time to play the famous card.* 'Look, I'm Jake Ravensdale,' he said. 'I'm—'

'I don't care if you're Jack the bloody Ripper,' the guard said. 'I want you out of here before I call the cops.'

'You can check with Reception,' Jake said. 'Get them to check the bookings. I'm here with Jasmine Connolly, the bridal designer.' *Dear God, had Jaz put him on the booking information?* he thought in panic as the guard took out his intercom device and called the front desk.

The guard spoke to someone at Reception and then put his device back on his belt, his expression now as nice as pie. 'Nice to meet you, Mr Ravensdale,' he said. 'Enjoy your stay. Oh, and by the way…' He put on a big, cheesy grin. 'Congratulations.'

Jake went back to the suite with his whole body coiled as tight as a spring. He pushed open the door to see Jaz getting ready for bed. 'Where the bloody hell have you been?' he said. 'I've been scouring the hotel from top to bottom for the last hour looking for you.'

'I went down to check on my dress before the room was locked.'

'Did you not think to leave a note or a send me a text?'

A spark of defiance shone in her grey-blue gaze as it collided with his. 'I assumed you were finished with me for the evening. You told me not to wait up.'

Jake smothered a filthy curse under his breath. 'Do you have any idea of how damned worried I was?'

She looked at him blankly. 'Why would you be worried?'

He pushed his hand back through his hair. 'I was worried, that's all.'

She came over to him to lay a hand on his arm. Her soft fingers warmed his flesh, making every one of his taut muscles unwind and others south of the border tighten. 'Are you okay?'

Was he okay? No. He felt like he would never be okay again. *Ever.* His head was pounding with the mother of all headaches. His heart rate felt like someone had given him an overdose of adrenalin. Two overdoses. His legs were shaking. His guts had turned to gravy. 'I'm fine.' Even to his own ears he knew he sounded unnecessarily curt.

'You don't sound it,' Jaz said, frowning at him in concern. 'Are you unwell? Have you caught food poisoning or something? You look so pale and sweaty and—'

'I almost got myself arrested.'

Her eyes rounded. 'What on earth for?'

'Long story.'

'Tell me what happened, Jake,' she said. 'I need to know, since we're here at this expo together, because it could reflect badly on me.'

Should he tell her it all or just a cut-down version? 'I panicked when you weren't in the suite. I didn't know where you'd gone.'

She began to stroke his arm, her eyes as clear, still

and lustrous as a mountain tarn as she looked into his. 'Were you worried I wasn't coming back?'

His hands came down on her shoulders in a grip that was unapologetically possessive. 'I was out of my mind with worry,' he said. 'I tried to check the display room but the security guard gave me a hard time. And then he found me coming out of the ladies' toilets—'

Her brow puckered. 'Why'd you go in there?'

Jake swallowed. 'I was worried someone might have cornered you in there and…' He couldn't even say what he'd thought. It was too sickening to be vocalised.

Her eyes softened. 'Oh, you big goose,' she said. 'I'm a big girl now. I can fend for myself, but thanks anyway.'

He brought her closer so her hips were against his, watching the way her tongue came out to moisten her lips; it made every one of those muscles in his groin go rock-hard. 'I swear to God I've aged a decade in the last hour.'

'Doesn't feel like it to me.'

He pressed her even closer. 'I want you.'

A little light danced like a sprite in her gaze. 'Again?'

He walked her backwards toward the bed, thigh to thigh, hip to hip, need to need. 'How much sleep do you need?' he said as he nibbled at her mouth, their breaths intermingling.

'Seven hours—five in an emergency—otherwise I get ratty.'

Jake helped her out of her clothes with more haste than finesse. 'I can handle ratty.'

She gave a tinkling laugh. 'Don't say I didn't warn you.'

He put his mouth on her naked breast, drawing her tight nipple into his mouth. It was music to his ears to hear her breathless moan of pleasure. It made his blood pump all the more frantically. He pushed her gently down on the bed, shoving pillows, petals and clothes out of the way as he came down beside her. He wanted to go slow but his earlier panic did something to his self-control. He needed to be inside her. He needed to be fused with her, to have her writhing and shuddering as he took her to paradise. He needed to quell this feverish madness racing in his blood. Her body gripped him like a fist as he surged into her velvet heat. The ripples of her inner core massaged him inexorably closer to a mind-blowing lift-off. He held on only long enough to make sure she was with him all the way. When she came around him he gave a part-growl, part-groan as he lost himself to physical bliss…

CHAPTER ELEVEN

JAZ WAS TRYING not to show how nervous she was the next morning but Jake must have sensed it because he kept looking at her with a watchful gaze. She picked at the breakfast he had had delivered to their suite but barely any made it to her mouth.

'At least have a glass of juice,' he said, pushing a glass of freshly squeezed orange juice towards her.

'I think I'm going to be sick.'

He took her hand from across the table and gave it an encouraging squeeze. 'Sweetheart, you're going to knock them for six down there.'

She bit down on her lip, panic and nerves clawing at her insides like razor blades whirled in a blender. 'Who am I fooling? I'm just a gardener's daughter from the wrong side of the tracks. What am I doing here pretending I'm a high street designer?'

'Imposter syndrome,' Jake said, leisurely pouring a cup of brewed coffee. 'That's what all this fuss is about. You don't believe in yourself. You think you've fluked it, that someone is going to come up behind you and tap you on the shoulder and tell you to get the hell out of here because you're not up to standard.'

That was exactly what Jaz was thinking. She had been thinking it most of her life. Being abandoned by her mother had always made her feel as if she wasn't good enough. She tried so hard to be the best she could be so people wouldn't leave her. But invariably they eventually did. Three times she had got engaged and each time it had ended. Her fiancés had ended it, not her. She was ashamed to admit she might well have married each and every one of them if they hadn't pulled the plug first. She was so terrified of failing, she over-controlled everything: her work, her relationships, her life. Her business was breaking even…just. But she'd had a lot of help. If it hadn't been for Jake's parents, she might never have got to where she was.

How long could she go on doing everything herself? She was constantly juggling. Sometimes she felt like a circus clown on stilts with twenty plates in the air. She couldn't remember the last time she'd taken a holiday. She took her work everywhere. She had Holly's dress with her in case there was a spare minute to work on the embroidery. She hadn't had a chance to draw a single sketch for Miranda. How long could she go on like that? Something had to give. She was going to get an ulcer at this rate. Maybe she already had one.

'You're right,' she said on a sigh. 'Every time I get myself to a certain place, I make myself sick worrying it's going to be ripped out from under me.'

'That's perfectly understandable given what happened with your mother.'

Jaz lowered her gaze as she smoothed out a tiny crease in the tablecloth. 'For years I waited for her to come back. I used to watch from the window whenever a car came up the drive. I would get all excited thinking she was coming back, that she had got herself sorted out and was coming back to take me to the new life she'd always promised me. But it never happened. I haven't heard from her since. I don't even know if she's still alive.'

Jake covered her hand with the warm solidness of his. 'You've made your own new life all by yourself. You didn't need her to come back and screw it up.'

'Not *all* by myself,' Jaz said. 'I'm not sure where I'd be if it hadn't been for your parents.' She waited a beat before adding, 'Do you think you could have a look over my books some time? I'm happy to pay you.'

'Sure, but you don't have to pay me.'

'I insist,' Jaz said. 'Your family has helped me enough. I don't want to be seen as a charity case.'

Jake lightly buttered some toast and handed it to her. 'One mouthful. It'll help to settle your stomach.'

Jaz took the toast and bit, chewed and swallowed but it felt like she was swallowing a cotton ball. 'Do you have it?'

'Have what?'

'Imposter syndrome?'

He smiled crookedly, as if the thought was highly amusing. 'No.'

'I suppose it was a silly question,' she conceded. 'Mr Confidence in all situations and with all people.'

A shadow passed over his features like a hand moving across a beam of light. 'There have been times when I've doubted myself.'

'Like when?'

'At boarding school, especially in my senior year,' he said, frowning slightly as he stirred his coffee. 'I played the class clown card so often I lost sight of who I really was. It wasn't until I left school and went to university that I finally found my feet and became my own person instead of being Julius's badly behaved twin brother.'

Jaz had always seen Jake as a supremely confident person. He seemed to waltz through life with nary a care of what others thought of him. She was the total opposite. Her desperate desire to fit in had made her compromise herself more times than she cared to admit. Weren't her three engagements proof of that? She had wanted to be normal. To belong to someone. To be wanted. 'I guess it must be hard, being an identical twin and all,' she said. 'Everyone is always making comparisons between you and Julius.'

There was a small silence.

'Yeah. We look the same but we're not the same,' Jake said. 'Julius is much more grounded and focused than I am.'

'I don't know about that,' Jaz said. 'You seem pretty grounded to me. You know what you want and go for it without letting anyone get in your way.'

He was frowning again as if a thought was wandering around in his head and he wasn't quite sure where to park it. 'But I don't stick at stuff,' he finally said. 'Not for the long haul.'

'But you're happy living your life that way, aren't you?'

After another moment of silence he gave her an absent smile. 'Yeah, it works for me. Now, have a bit more toast. It'd be embarrassing if you were to faint just when it's your chance to shine.'

Jaz did a last-minute check with the model for the gown she had prepared for the show. It was the first time any of her work would be worn by a professional model on a catwalk. The advertising she had done in the past had been still shots with models from an agency and a photographer who was a friend of a friend.

But this was different. This was her dream coming to life in front of her. Hundreds, possibly thousands or even millions, would see her design if the images went global. It would be the start of the expansion of her business she had planned since she had left design college.

Why then did she still feel like a fraud?

Because she was a fraud.

A fake.

Not because she didn't know how to design and sew a beautiful wedding gown. But because she wasn't in a committed relationship and the ring she was wearing on her finger was going to be handed back in two weeks' time. She was like the blank-faced models wearing the wedding gowns. They weren't really brides. They were acting a role.

Like *she* was acting a role.

She was pretending to be engaged to Jake when all she wanted was to be engaged to him for real. How had she not realised it until now? Or had she been shying away from it because it was a truth she hadn't wanted to face?

She was in love with Jake.

Hadn't she always been in love with him? As a child she had looked up to him as a fun older brother. He had been the playful twin, the one she could have a laugh with. Then when her female hormones had switched on she had wanted him as a woman wanted a man. But she hadn't been a woman back then—she had been a child. He had respected that and kept his distance. Wasn't that another reason why she loved him? He hadn't exploited her youthful innocence. Yes, he hadn't handled her crush with the greatest sensitivity, but at least he hadn't taken advantage of her.

Jaz was done with acting. Done with pretending. How could she stretch this out another week or two? Jake wasn't in love with her. Didn't their conversation over breakfast confirm it? He was happy with the way his life was a single man. He would go back to that life as soon as their 'engagement' ended.

Jake said she could keep the ring but why would she do that? It was little more than a consolation prize. A parting gift. Every time she looked at it she would be reminded of what she wanted and couldn't have. It might be enormous fun being with Jake. It might be wonderful to be his lover and feel the thrill of his desire and hers for him.

But what was she *doing*?

She was living a lie. That was what she was doing. Fooling people that she was in a real relationship with real hopes and dreams for the future. What future? Two weeks of fantastic, mind-blowing sex and then what? Jake would pull the plug on their relationship just like her three exes had done. She would be abandoned. Rejected. Left hanging. Alone.

Not this time. Not again.

This time she would take control. Do the right thing by herself and set the boundaries. Two weeks more of this and she would want it to be for ever. Good grief! She wanted it to be for ever now. That was how dangerous their fling had become. One night of amazing sex and she was posting the wedding invitations.

It was ridiculous.

She was ridiculous.

Jake wasn't a 'for ever' type of guy. He wanted her but only for as long as it took to burn out their mutual attraction. How long would it take? He had set the limit at two weeks. Most of his relationships didn't last two days. Why should she think *she* was so special? Sure they knew each other. They had a history of sorts. They would always be in each other's lives in some way or another.

It would be best to end it now.

On *her* terms.

Before things got crazy. Crazier…because what was crazier than falling in love with a man just because you couldn't have him? That was what she had done. It was pathological. She was in love with a man who didn't—*couldn't*—love her.

It was time to rewrite the script of her life. No longer would she fall for the wrong men. No longer would she settle for second best…even though there was no way she would ever describe Jake as second best. He was first best. *The* best. The most fabulous man she had ever known—but he wasn't hers.

He wasn't anyone's.

It would break her heart to end their affair. Weird to think she'd thought her heart had been broken by her three failed engagements; none of them, even all of them put together, had made her feel anywhere near as sad as ending her fling with Jake.

It wasn't just the sex. It was the way he made her feel as a person. He valued her. He understood her. He knew her doubts and insecurities. He had taught her to put the dark shadow of the past behind her. He protected her. He made her feel safe. He had helped her heal. His touch, his kisses, his glorious love-making, had made her fully embrace her femininity.

He had given her the gift of self-acceptance, but with that gift had come realisation. The realisation she could no longer pretend to be something she was not. She had to stop hiding behind social norms in order to feel accepted. If she never found love with a man who loved her equally, unreservedly and for ever, then she would be better off alone. Settling for anything less was settling for second best. It was compromising and self-limiting and would only bring further heartbreak in the end.

But it would be hard to be around Jake as just a friend. She would go back to being the gardener's daughter—the little ring-in who didn't really belong in the big house.

The girl who didn't belong to anyone.

Jake watched from the front row beside Jaz as her design came down the catwalk. She had only just got to her seat in time to see her moment in the spotlight. The dress was amazing. He found his mind picturing her wearing it. It had a hand-sewn beaded bodice and a frothy tulle skirt that was just like a princess's dress. The veil was set back from the model's head and flowed out behind her like a floating cloud.

If anyone had told him a week ago he'd be sitting at a wedding expo oohing and aahing at wedding gowns he would have said they were nuts. The atmosphere was electric. The ballroom was abuzz with expectation. The music was upbeat and stirring, hardly bridal or churchy at all. The applause was thunderous when Jaz's design was announced and continued even after the model had left the catwalk. He clapped as loudly as anyone, probably louder. 'Told you they'd love your work,' he said. 'You'll have orders coming out of your ears after this.'

She looked at him with a tremulous smile. 'You think?'

She still doubted herself. Amazing, he thought. What would it take for her to believe she was as good if not better than any of the other designers here? He tapped her on the end of her retroussé nose. 'Sure of it.'

Jake took her hand while the press did their interviews after the show. He was getting quite used to the role of devoted fiancé. Who said he couldn't act? Maybe some of that Ravensdale talent hadn't skipped a generation after all. Or maybe he was getting used to being part of a couple. There was certainly something to be said about knowing who he was going to sleep with that night—earlier, if he could wangle it. Instead of wondering how the sex would be, he knew for certain it would be fantastic. He had never had a more satisfying lover.

Jaz's body was a constant turn-on as it brushed against his as the crowd jostled them. He drew her closer as a photographer zoomed in on them. Her cheek was against his; the fresh, flowery scent of her made his sinuses tingle. She turned her head and he swooped down and stole a kiss from her soft-as-a-pillow mouth, wishing he could get her alone right here and now.

But instead of continuing the kiss she eased back, giving him a distracted-looking smile. Her hands went back to her lap where she was gripping the programme as if she had plans to shred it.

'You okay?' Jake said.

Her gaze was trained on the next set of models strutting their stuff. 'We need to talk,' she said. 'But not here.'

Here it comes. The talk. The talk where she would say she wanted the whole shebang: the promises of for ever, the kids, the dog and the house. The things he didn't want. Had never wanted. Would never want. Why had he thought she would be any different? He had broken his own rules for what? For a fling that should never have started in the first place.

Might as well get it over with. Once the show was over, he took her by the elbow and led her back to their suite. *Their suite*. How cosy that sounded. Like they were a couple. But they weren't a couple. A couple of idiots, if anything. They had no right to be messing around. *He* had no right. She was a part of his family. By getting involved with her he had jeopardised every single relationship she had with his family. Would everyone treat her differently now they knew she had been his lover? Would they look at her differently? Would he be harangued for the next decade for not doing the right thing by her and leaving her alone?

'I know what you're going to say,' Jake said even before he had closed the door of the suite.

She pressed her lips together for a moment. Turned and put the programme and her bag on the bed, then turned back to him and handed him her engagement ring. 'I think it's best if we end things now,' she said. 'Before we head back to London.'

Jake stared at the ring and then at her. She wanted to end it? *Now?* Before the two weeks were up? That wasn't how 'the talk' usually went. Didn't she want more? Didn't she want them to continue their affair? Wasn't she going to cry, beg and plead with him to fall in love with her and marry her? She looked so composed, so determined, as if she had made up her mind hours ago.

'But I thought you said two weeks?'

'I know but I can't do it any more, Jake,' she said, putting the ring in the top pocket of his jacket and patting it as if for safekeeping. 'It was fun while it lasted but I want to move on with my life.'

'This seems rather…sudden.'

She stepped back and looked up at him with those beautiful storm, sea and mountain-lake eyes. 'Remember when we talked at breakfast?' she said. 'I've been thinking since… I can't pretend to be someone I'm not. It's not right for me or for you. You're not the settling down type and it was wrong of me to shackle you to me in this stupid game of pretend. I should've just accepted Myles's break-up with dignity instead of doing this crazy charade. It will hurt too many people if we let it continue. It has to stop.'

Jake wanted it to stop. Sure he did. But not yet. Not until he was satisfied his attraction to her had burned itself out. It was nowhere near burning out. It had only just started. They'd been lovers two days. *Two freaking days!* That wasn't long enough. He was only just starting to understand her. To know her. How could she want to end it? They were good together. Brilliant. The best. Why end it when they could have two more weeks, maybe even longer, of fantastic sex?

But how *much* longer?

The thought stood up from a sofa in the back of his mind where it had been lounging and stretched. Started walking toward his conscience…

Jake knew she was right. They had to end it some time. It was just he was usually the one to end flings. He was the one in the control seat. It felt a little weird to be on the receiving end of rejection. 'What about Emma Madden?' he said. 'Aren't you worried she might make a comeback when she hears we've broken up?'

'I think Emma is sensible enough to know you're not the right person for her. It will hurt her more if we tell even more lies.'

'What about Bruce Parnell?' *God, how pathetic was he getting? Using his clients as a lever to get her to rethink her decision?*

'Tell him the truth,' she said. 'That you're not in love with me and have no intention of marrying me or anyone.'

The truth always hurt, or so people said. But it didn't look like it hurt Jaz. She didn't seem to be the least bit worried he wasn't in love with her. She hadn't even asked him to declare his feelings, which was just as well, because they were stuffed under the cushions on that sofa in his mind and he wasn't going looking for them any time soon.

'You're right,' he said. 'Best to end it now before my parents start sending out invitations.'

She bit her lip for a moment. 'Will you tell them or will I?'

'I'll tell them I pulled the plug,' Jake said. 'That's what they'll think in any case.'

Her forehead puckered in a frown. 'But I don't want them to be angry with you or anything. I can say I got cold feet.'

'Leave it to me. Do you still want me to have a look over your business?'

'You wouldn't mind?'

'Why would I?' he said with a smile that was harder work than it had any right to be. 'We're friends, aren't we?'

Her smile was a little on the wobbly side but he could see relief in every nuance of her expression. 'Yes. Of course we are.'

It was on the tip of his tongue to ask for one more night but before he could get the words out she had turned and started packing her things. He watched her fold her clothes and pack them neatly into her bag. Every trace of her was being removed from the suite.

'I'm getting a lift back to London with one of the photographers,' she said once she was done. 'I thought it would be easier all round.'

'Is the photographer male?' The question jumped out before Jake could stop it and it had the big, green-eyed monster written all over it.

His question dangled in the silence for a long beat.

'Yes,' she said. 'But I've known him for years.'

Jaz had known *him* for years and look what had happened, Jake thought with a sickening churning in his gut.

She stepped up on tiptoe to kiss his cheek. 'Good-bye, Jake. See you at Julius's wedding.'

Wedding.

Jake clenched his jaw as the door closed on her exit. That word should be damned well banned.

CHAPTER TWELVE

JAZ WAS WORKING on Miranda's dress a few days later when the bell on the back of her shop door tinkled. She looked up and saw Emma Madden coming in, dressed in her school uniform. 'Hi, Emma,' she said, smiling as she put down the bodice she was sewing freshwater pearls on. 'How lovely to see you. How are you?'

Emma savaged her bottom lip with her teeth. 'Is it because of me?'

Jaz frowned. 'Is what because of you?'

'Your break-up with Jake,' she said. 'It's because of me, isn't it? I made such a stupid nuisance of myself and now you've broken up and it's all my fault.'

Jaz came out from behind the work counter and took the young girl's hands in hers. 'Nothing's your fault, sweetie. Jake and I decided we weren't ready to settle down. We've gone back to being friends.'

Emma's big, soulful eyes were misty. 'But you're so perfect for each other. I can't bear the thought of him having anyone else. You bring out the best in him. My stepdad says so too.'

Jaz gave Emma's hands a little squeeze before she

released them. 'It's sweet of you to say so but some things are not meant to be.'

'But aren't you...*devastated*?' Emma asked, scrunching up her face in a frown.

Jaz didn't want to distress the girl unnecessarily. No point telling Emma she cried every night when she got into her cold bed. *On. Her. Own.* No point saying how she couldn't get into a lift without her insides quivering in erotic memory. No point saying how every time she ate a piece of toast or drank orange juice she thought of Jake helping her through her fashion show nerves at the expo. 'I'm fine about it,' she said. 'Really. It's for the best.'

Emma sighed and then started looking at the dresses on display. She touched one reverently. 'Did you really make this from scratch?'

'Yup,' Jaz said. 'What do you think? Not too OTT?'

'No, it's beautiful,' Emma said. 'I would love to be able to design stuff like this.'

'Have you ever done any sewing?'

'I did some cross-stitch at school but I'd love to be able to make my own clothes,' Emma said. 'I sometimes get ideas for stuff... Does that happen to you?'

'All the time,' Jaz said. 'See that dress over there with the hoop skirt? I got the idea from the garden at Ravensdene. There's this gorgeous old weeping birch down there that looks exactly like a ball gown.'

Emma traced the leaf-like pattern of the lace. 'Wow... You're amazing. So talented. So smart and beautiful. So everything.'

So single, Jaz thought with a sharp pang. 'Hey, do

you fancy a part-time job after school or at weekends? I could do with a little help and I can give you some tips on pattern-making and stuff.'

Emma's face brightened as if someone had turned a bright light on inside her. 'Do you mean it? *Really?*'

'Sure,' Jaz said. 'Who wants to work for a fast-food chain when you can work for one of London's up-and-coming bridal designers?'

Take that, Imposter Syndrome.

Three weeks later...

'Jake, can I get you another beer?' Flynn Carlyon asked on his way to the bar at Julius's stag night. 'Hey, you haven't finished that one—you've barely taken a mouthful. You not feeling well or something?'

Jake forced a quick smile. 'No, I'm good.'

He wasn't good. He was sick. Not physically but emotionally. He hadn't eaten a proper meal in days. He couldn't remember the last time he'd had a decent sleep. Well, he could, but remembering the last time he'd made love with Jaz caused him even more emotional distress.

Yes, *emotional* distress.

The dreaded E-word—the word he'd been trying to escape from for the last few weeks. Maybe he'd been trying to escape it for the last seven years. He couldn't stop thinking about Jaz. He couldn't get the taste of her out of his mouth. He couldn't get the feel of her out of his body. It had been nothing short of torture to drop in the business plan for her last week and not touch her. She had seemed a little distracted, but when she told him she'd employed Emma Madden to help in the shop after school he'd put it down to that—Jaz was worried he would have a problem with it. He didn't. He thought it was a stroke of genius, actually. He wished he'd thought of it himself.

Julius came over with a basket of crisps. 'He's off his food, his drink and his game,' he said to Flynn. 'He hasn't looked twice at any of the waitresses, even the blonde one with the big boobs.'

Flynn grinned. 'No kidding?'

'I reckon it's because he's in love with Jaz,' Julius said. 'But he's too stubborn to admit it.'

Jake glowered at his twin. 'Just because you're getting married tomorrow doesn't mean everyone else wants to do the same.'

'Mum's still not speaking to him,' Julius said to Flynn. 'She quite fancied having Jaz as a daughter-in-law.'

'Pity she isn't so keen on having Kat Winwood as a daughter,' Flynn said wryly.

'So, how's all that going with you and Kat?' Jake said, desperate for a subject change. 'You convinced her to come to Dad's Sixty Years in Showbiz party yet?'

'Not so far but I'm working on it,' Flynn said with an enigmatic smile.

'Better get your skates on, mate,' Julius said. 'You've only got a month and a bit. The party's in January.'

'Leave Kat Winwood to me,' Flynn said. 'I know how to handle a feisty Scotswoman.'

'I bet you've handled a few in your time,' Jake said.

'You can talk,' Flynn said with another grin. 'How come you haven't handled anyone since Jaz?'

Good question. Why hadn't he? Because he couldn't bear to wipe out the memory of her touch with someone else. He didn't want anyone else. But Jaz wanted marriage and kids. He had never seen himself as a dad. He had always found it so…terrifying to be responsible for someone else. He was better off alone. Single and loving it, that was his credo.

Jake put his untouched beer bottle down. 'Excuse me,' he said. 'I'm going to have an early night. See you lot in church.'

'You look amazing, Holly,' Jaz said outside the church just before they were to enter for Julius and Holly's wedding. 'Doesn't she, Miranda?'

Miranda was wiping at her eyes with a tissue. 'Capital A amazing. Gosh, I've got to get control of myself. My make-up is running. If I'm like this as a bridesmaid, what I am going to be like as a bride?'

Holly smiled at both of them. She was a radiant bride, no two ways about that. But happiness did that to you, Jaz thought. There could be no happier couple than Julius and Holly… Well, there was Miranda and Leandro, who were also nauseatingly happy. It was downright painful to be surrounded by so many blissfully happy people.

But Jaz was resolved. She wasn't settling for anything but the real deal. Love without limits. That was what she wanted. Love that would last a lifetime.

Love that was authentic and real, not pretend.

As Jaz led the way down the aisle she saw Jake standing next to Julius. It was surreal to see them both dressed in tuxedos looking exactly the same. No one could tell them apart, except for the way Julius was looking at Holly coming behind Miranda. Had a man ever looked at a woman with such love? *Yes*, Jaz thought when she caught a glimpse of Leandro, who was standing next to Jake looking at Miranda as if she was the most adorable girl in the world. Which she was, but that was beside the point. It was so *hard* not to be jealous.

Why couldn't Jake look at her like that?

Jaz caught his eye. He was looking a little green about the gills. Her own stomach lurched. Her heart contracted. Had he hooked up with someone last night after Julius's stag night? Had he had a one-nighter with someone? Several someones? She hadn't heard anything much in the press about him since they had announced they'd ended their 'engagement'. But then she had been far too busy with getting Holly's dress done on time to be reading gossip columns.

Miranda had let slip that Jake had left the stag night early. Did that mean he had hooked up with some-one? One of the barmaids at the wine bar the boys had gone to? Why else would he leave early? He was the party boy who was usually the last man standing. It didn't bear thinking about. It would only make the knot of jealousy tighten even more in the pit of her stomach. She had to put a brave face on. She couldn't let her feelings about Jake interfere with Julius and Holly's big day.

Jaz smiled at Elisabetta and Richard Ravensdale, who were sitting together and giving every appearance of being a solid couple, but that just showed what excellent actors they both were. Elisabetta had dressed the part, as she always did. She would have outshone the bride but Jaz had made sure Holly's dress was a show-stopper. Holly looked like a fairy-tale princess. Which was how it should be, as she'd had a pretty ghastly life up until she'd met Julius, which kind of made Jaz feel hopeful that dreams did come true... at least sometimes.

The service began and Jaz tried not to look at Jake too much. She didn't want people speculating or commenting on her single status. Or worse—pitying her. Would she ever be seen as anything other than the charity case? The gardener's daughter who'd made good only by the wonderful largesse of the Ravensdales?

Even the business plan Jake had drawn up for her was another example of how much she owed them. He wouldn't take a penny for his time. He hadn't stayed for a coffee or anything once he'd talked her through the plan. He hadn't even kissed her on the cheek or touched her in any way.

But looking at him now brought it all back. How much she missed him. How much she loved him. Why couldn't he love her?

Young Emma was right—they were perfect together. Jake made her feel safe. He watched out for her the way she longed for a partner to do. He stood up *to* her and stood up *for* her. How could she settle for anyone else? She would never be happy with anyone else. It wouldn't matter how many times she got engaged, no one would ever replace Jake. Nor would she want them to.

Jake was her soul mate because only with him could she truly be herself.

The vows were exchanged and for the first time in her life Jaz saw Julius blinking away tears. He was always so strong, steady and in charge of his emotions. He was the dependable twin. The one everyone went to when things were dire. Seeing him so happy made her chest feel tight. She wanted that same happiness for herself. She wanted it so badly it took her breath away to see others experiencing it.

Jake was still looking a little worse for wear. What was *wrong* with him? Didn't he have the decency to pull himself together for his brother's wedding? Or maybe it was the actual wedding that was making him look so white and pinched. He hated commitment. It had been bad enough at the wedding expo, although she had to admit he'd put on a good front. Maybe some of that Ravensdale acting talent had turned up in his genes after all. He could certainly do with some of it now. The very least he could do was look happy for his twin brother. He fumbled over handing Julius the wedding rings. He had to search in his pocket three times. But at least he had remembered to bring them.

Jaz decided to have a word with him while they were out with the bride and groom for the signing of the register. If she could put on a brave front, then so could he. He would spoil the wedding photos if he didn't get his act together. She wasn't going to let anyone ruin Julius and Holly's big day. No way.

Jake couldn't take his eyes off Jaz. She looked amazing in her bridesmaid dress. It was robin's-egg blue and the colour made her eyes pop and her creamy skin glow. How he wanted to touch that skin, to feel it against his own. His fingers ached; his whole body ached to pull her into his arms and kiss her, to show her how much he missed her. Missed what they'd had together.

Seeing his identical twin standing at the altar as his bride came towards him made Jake feel like he was seeing another version of himself. It was like seeing what he might have been. What he could *have* if he were a better man. A more settled man—a man who could be relied on; a man who could love, not just physically, but emotionally. A man who could commit to a woman because he could see no future without her by his side. A man who could be mature enough to raise a family and support them and his wife through everything that life threw at them.

That was the sort of man his twin was.

Why wasn't *he* like that?

Or was he like that in the part of his soul he didn't let anyone see? Apart from Jaz, of course. She had seen it. And commented on it.

Jake gave himself a mental shake. No wonder he hated weddings. They made him antsy. Restless.

Frightened.

For once he didn't shove the thought back where it came from. It wasn't going back in any case. It was front and centre in his brain. He *was* frightened. Frightened he wouldn't be good enough. Frightened he would love and not be loved in return. Frightened of feeling so deeply for someone, allowing someone to have control over him, of making himself vulnerable in case they took it upon themselves to leave.

He loved Jaz.

Hadn't he always loved her? Firstly as a surrogate sister and then, when she'd morphed into the gorgeous teenager with those bedroom eyes, he had been knocked sideways. But she had been too young and he hadn't been ready to admit he needed someone the way he needed her.

But he was an adult now. He'd had a taste of what they could be together—a solid team who complemented each other perfectly. She was his equal. He admired her tenacity, her drive, her passion, her talent. She was everything he wanted in a partner.

Wasn't that why he'd been carrying the engagement ring she had given back to him everywhere he went? It was like a talisman. The ring of truth. He loved Jaz and always would.

How could he have thought he could be happy without her? He had been nothing short of morose since they'd ended their fling. He was the physical embodiment of a wet weekend: gloomy, miserable, boring as hell. He had been dragging himself through each day. He hadn't dated. He hadn't even looked at anyone. He couldn't bear the thought of going through the old routine of chatting some woman up only so he could have sex with her. He was tired of no-strings sex. No-strings sex was boring. He wanted emotional sex, the sort of sex that spoke to his soul, the kind of sex that made him feel alive and fulfilled as a man.

He had to talk to Jaz. He had to get her alone. How long was this wretched service going to take? Oh, they were going to sign the wedding register. Great. He might be able to nudge Jaz to one side so he could tell her the words he had told no one before.

Jaz wasted no time in sidling up to Jake when Julius and Holly were occupied with signing the register. 'What is *wrong* with you?' she said in an undertone.

'I have to talk to you,' he said, pulling at his bow tie as if it were choking him.

She rolled her eyes. 'Look, I know this is torture for you, but can you just allow your brother his big day without drawing attention to yourself? It's just a bow tie, for pity's sake.'

He took her by the hand, his eyes looking suspiciously moist. Did he have an allergy? There were certainly a lot of flowers about. But then the service had been pretty emotional. Maybe it was a twin thing. If Julius cried, Jake would too, although she had never seen it before.

'I love you,' he said.

Jaz's eyelashes flickered at him in shock. *'What?'*

His midnight-blue eyes looked so amazingly soft she had to remind herself it was actually Jake looking at her, not Julius looking at Holly. 'Not just as a friend,' he said. 'And not just as a lover, but as a life partner. Marry me, Jaz. Please?'

Jaz's heart bumped against her breastbone. 'You can't ask me to marry you in the middle of your brother's wedding!'

He grinned. 'I just did. What do you say?'

She gazed at him, wondering if wedding fever had got to her so bad she was hallucinating. Was he really telling her he loved her and wanted to marry her? Was he really looking at her as if she was the only woman in the world who could ever make him completely happy? 'You're not doing this as some sort of joke, are you?' she asked, narrowing her eyes in suspicion. It would be just like him to want to have a laugh to counter all the emotion, to tone down all the seriousness, responsibility and formality.

He gripped her by the hands, almost crushing her bridesmaid's bouquet in the process. 'It's no joke,' he said. 'I love you and want to spend the rest of my life proving it to you. The last three weeks have been awful without you. You're all I think about. I'm like a lovesick teenager. I can't get you out of my head. As soon as I saw you walking down the aisle, I realised I couldn't let another day—another minute—go by without telling you how I feel. I want to be with you. Only you. Marry me, my darling girl.'

Jaz was still not sure she could believe what she was hearing. And nor, apparently, could the bridal party as they had stalled in the process of signing the register to watch on with beaming faces. 'But what about kids?' she said.

'I love kids. I'm a big kid myself. Remember how great I was with you and Miranda when you were kids? I reckon I'll be a great dad. How many do you want?'

Jaz remembered all too well. He had been fantastic with her and Miranda, making them laugh until their sides had ached. It was her dream coming to life in front of her eyes. Jake wanted to marry her and he wanted to have babies with her. 'Two at least,' she said.

He pulled her closer, smiling at her with twinkling eyes. 'I should warn you that twins run in my family.'

Jaz smiled back. 'I'll take the risk.'

'So you'll marry me?'

Could a heart burst with happiness? Jaz wondered. It certainly felt like hers was going to. But, even better, it looked like Jake was feeling exactly the same way. 'Yes.'

Jake bent his head to kiss her mouth with such heart-warming tenderness it made Jaz's eyes tear up. When he finally lifted his head, she saw similar moisture in his eyes. 'I was making myself sick with worry you might say no,' he said.

She stroked his jaw with a gentle hand, her heart now feeling so full it was making it hard for her to breathe. 'You're not an easy person to say no to.'

He brushed her cheek with his fingers as if to test she was real and not a figment of his imagination. 'How quickly can you whip up a wedding dress?'

She looked at him in delighted surprise. 'You want to get married sooner rather than later?'

He pressed a kiss to her forehead, each of her eyelids, both of her cheeks and the tip of her nose. 'Yes,' he said. 'As soon as it can be arranged. I don't even mind if it's in church or a garden, on the top of Big Ben or twenty leagues under the sea. I won't be happy until I can officially call you my wife.'

'Ahem.' Julius spoke from behind them. 'We're the ones trying to get married here.'

Jake turned to grin at his brother. 'We should've made it a double wedding.'

Julius smiled from ear to ear. 'Congratulations to both of you. Nothing could have made my and Holly's day more special than this.'

Miranda was dabbing at her eyes as she came rushing over to give Jaz a bone- and bouquet-crushing hug. 'I'm so happy for you. We're finally going to be sisters. Yay!'

Jaz blinked back tears as she saw Leandro looking at Miranda just the way Jake was looking at her—with love that knew no bounds. With love that would last a lifetime.

She turned back to Jake. 'Do you still have that engagement ring?'

Jake reached into his inside jacket pocket, his eyes gleaming. 'I almost gave it to Julius instead of the wedding rings.' He took it out and slipped it on her finger. 'There. That's got to stay there now. No taking it off. Ever. Understood?'

Jaz wrapped her arms around his waist and smiled up at him in blissful joy. 'I'm going to keep it on for ever.'

* * * * *

MILLS & BOON

MODERN

Power and Passion

Prepare to be swept off your feet by sophisticated, sexy and seductive heroes, in some of the world's most glamourous and romantic locations, where power and passion collide.

Julia James

Helena's
**PREGNANCY
SCANDAL**

MILLS & BOON
MODERN

Jennie Lucas

Choosen as the
**SHEIKH'S ROYAL
BRIDE**

MILLS & BOON

Kim Lawrence

A WEDDING
at the
ITALIAN'S DEMAND

MILLS & BOON

Sharon Kendrick

The
**SHEIKH'S
SECRET BABY**

MILLS & BOON
MODERN